'Tell me what you kı

Trembling, Campion
them again to ensure th

'I ... I see shadows,
followed. I tell myself t
imagination. But in truth

Pietro persisted. 'Two ... murders have been committed, *Eccellenza*, and we can have no reason to suppose that there will not be others. It is imperative that you tell me all you know. Who are the Firebirds?'

The two men stared at one another for a long moment, and then Campioni placed his arm about Pietro's shoulder and led him farther off. When at last he spoke, his voice was troubled and uncertain.

'I speak of a cult, *amico*, a secret organisation led by a man known only as the Chimera, or *il Diavolo* – no man knows his true identity. I speak of a satanic cult whose head is here in Venice and whose limbs stretch far onto Terra Firma ... It is said that their power and influence extend beyond the republic, beyond Italy itself. These, then, are the Firebirds. But there is worse, much worse ...'

Arnaud Delalande is a screenwriter and author, whose first novel, *The Underground Notre Dame*, has been translated into several languages. His other novels are *The Church of Satan* and *The Music of the Dead*. He lives in France.

The Dante Trap

ARNAUD DELALANDE

Translated from the French by Frank Wynne

PHOENIX

A PHOENIX PAPERBACK

First published in France as *La Piège de Dante*
by Grasset & Fasquelle, 2006

First published in Great Britain in 2007
by Weidenfeld & Nicolson
This paperback edition published in 2007
by Phoenix,
an imprint of the Orion Books Ltd,
Orion House, 5 Upper St Martin's Lane,
London WC2H 9EA

An Hachette Livre UK company

A CIP catalogue record for this book
is available from the British Library.

Typeset by Input Data Services Ltd, Frome

Printed in Great Britain by Clays Ltd, St Ives plc

The Orion Publishing Group's policy is to use papers that are natural, renewable and recyclable products and made from wood grown in sustainable forests. The logging and manufacturing processes are expected to conform to the environmental regulations of the country of origin.

www.orionbooks.co.uk

To Guillaume, Emmanuelle, Oliver.
To Jean Martin Martinière

And in tribute to Françoise Verny,
godmother and good fairy

THE FIRST CIRCLE

CANTO I

THE DARK FOREST

MAY 1756

Francesco Loredan, prince of the *Serenissima*, 116th doge of Venice, was sitting in the sala del collegio where, in ordinary circumstances, he was wont to receive ambassadors. From time to time, he admired Veronese's vast *Battle of Lepanto*, which graced one of the walls. Sometimes lost in thought, he gazed up at the ornate gilded mouldings of the ceiling or stared, rapt, at *Mars and Venus* or *Venice with Justice and Peace*, only to be brought back to the urgent matter at hand.

Francesco was an old man; his deeply weathered face a stark contrast to the smooth expanse of purple robes which swathed him. A few unruly strands of hair peeked out from the ducal *corne*. His snow-white brows and thick beard gave him the stern appearance of a patriarch, entirely at odds with his temperament in administering the affairs of the republic. Before him on the desk, claws bared, sat a statue of a winged lion, a symbol of power and majesty. The doge was a plump man. He wore a heavy cape trimmed with ermine and a golden clasp about his shoulders, open to reveal a lighter robe which fell to his red silk leggings. He held the *bacheta*, the symbol of his power as a doge, limply. His long, delicate hands, which bore the ring engraved with the Venetian coat of arms and balance, nervously clutched the record of the proceedings of the Council of Ten, delivered together with a letter bearing the official seal of the Consiglio dei Dieci, which had met in an extraordinary session that very morning. The note advised Francesco of a matter which was, to say the least, mysterious. It concluded:

> *A shadow walks abroad, looming over the republic, a treacherous shadow of which this murder is but a portent, one of the myriad manifestations of its power. Venice is in desperate straits, the vilest criminals move through its streets like wolves in a dark forest. The stench of decadence hangs over the city: we can no longer afford to ignore such matters.*

The doge cleared his throat, tapping the missive with his fingers. *And so the terrible thing had come to pass.*

The Carnival of Venice had first been celebrated in the tenth century. Nowadays, the festival was six months long – extending from the first Sunday in October until 15 December, and again from Epiphany until Lent, finally blossoming once more during *la Sensa*, the Ascension.

The whole city was humming with preparations for the coming festivities. The women of Venice thronged the streets, their faces powdered white beneath their carnival masks and flaunting their finery: necklaces and pearls glimmering against folds of satin, wide ruffs and yards of lace; breasts squeezed into tightly laced bustiers. Their flaxen hair was immaculate; some wore it in elegant chignons, some plaited it with jewels, some wore it loose and flowing with studied casualness, and others had it crimped and teased into the most extravagant styles.

Behind their masks they played at being noblewomen: strutting about the city, heads held high, careful to observe the rules of *portamento*, assuming the regal bearing of the aristocracy. With their sumptuous garments and haughty deportment they exuded a sovereign grace for, after all, were they not the most coveted, the most ardently desired, the most beautiful women in all the world during the carnival? Together they comprised a sea of beauty, a rainbow of charming colours; one might wear a translucent dress of white lawn, trimmed at the hem with lace frills and flounces; another had adorned her dress with leg-of-mutton sleeves in Italian taffeta and a girdle of blue ribbons which trailed behind her as she walked. Still another might wear a large silk kerchief knotted about her delicate throat over an *andrienne* or a *pannier*, clutching a parasol. Now and then, they adjusted their *moretta*, the black mask held in place by biting down on a small spur. Or they would smooth the folds of their dresses or snap open a fan with a flick of the wrist. Courtesans of impeccable bloodline mingled with ladies of the night in a confusion of silk and lace. Copies of the *Catalogo di tutte le principale e più onorate cortigiane di Venezia* and a guide to the *Tariffa delle puttane di Venezia*, accompanied by reflections on the technical prowess of these mistresses of the night, surreptitiously began to circulate.

For their part, men of a classical disposition wore the wraith-like white mask known as the *larva*, the tricorne hat, the *bauta*, which covered the body, and the black cape or *tabarro*. Others dressed as characters from folktales, plays or from their own imaginations. While some were dressed as traditional characters: Tracagnin, Harlequin, Pantaloon, the Doctor or Pulcinella, others masqueraded as fiends armed with bladders, Moors riding old nags, Turks puffing on hookahs or disguised themselves as French, German or Spanish officers, to say nothing of the hordes of bakers, chimney-sweeps, flower-sellers, colliers and rag-and-bone men … Charlatans selling the secret of eternal youth, quacks selling love potions, beggars, tramps and penniless peasants who had come from Terra Firma, blind men and cripples flooded the city, and it was impossible to tell whether their infirmities were genuine or contrived. Crowds were beginning to gather outside the cafés and numerous marquees erected for the occasion, whose banners invited passers-by to come and encounter 'Monsters': dwarves, giants and three-headed women.

The moment had come, the moment when dreams come true, when a commoner could imagine himself king of the world and a nobleman the vulgar rogue. A time when roles were reversed, the world turned upside-down and lawlessness and excess were permitted. The gondoliers, in full livery, punted their masters along the canals. The city was festooned with triumphal arches. Here and there, people played *pelota* or *meneghella* while onlookers took bets, tossing a few lire into plates, or coins were hidden at random in sacks of flour where people might try their luck, each hoping to happen on a coin greater than the wager. Food-sellers had laid out thousands of fritters and fried sole on stalls throughout the city. From their tartan, Chioggia fishermen called out to the crowd. A mother slapped her daughter for allowing herself to be held a little too closely by her suitor. Milliners and haberdashers moved through the crowds with trays filled with garments to tempt those on the barges. On the *campi*, oakum marionettes disgorged sweetmeats and dried fruits. A crowd of *frombolatori*, young masked men, scoured the *sextiers*, throwing rotten eggs at the fine ladies in their elegant costumes and old ladies on their balconies before running off in a gale of laughter. From one end of the city to the other, bizarre and curious sights abounded: a swinging dog on a length of rope, men struggling to climb a greasy pole to reach a sausage or a flask of liquor, while others plunged their faces into brackish water trying to catch an eel with their teeth. On the *piazzetta*, a wooden contraption in the shape of a cream cake tempted the hungry; crowds gathered around the rope dancers, impromptu theatrical performances and puppet theatres.

Bazaar astronomers stood on stools, index fingers pointing toward the invisible stars, and held forth about the impending Apocalypse. There was cursing and mirth and hilarity as someone knocked a *gelato* onto the cobbles or dropped a pastry. The air was alive with the simple joy of living.

It was at this moment that the woman known as the Queen of Hearts stepped from the shadows. She stepped from her hiding place beneath the arcades and took a few tentative steps, opening her fan as she walked. Her long eyelashes fluttered behind her mask and her vermillion lips formed an 'O' as she dropped her handkerchief while smoothing a fold in her dress. As she bent to pick it up, she glanced at the agent posted some distance away on the corner of the *piazzetta* to see whether he had noticed the signal. The signal meant: *he is here*.

And indeed he was there, in the midst of the throng, the man whose sworn mission it was to slay the doge of Venice. An ivory horn seemed to burst from either side of the head, the face was that of a bull fitted with a muzzle of alarming proportions. A pair of cunning eyes glinted behind the heavy mask. The armour he wore, however, was genuine: chain-mail and a silver-plate armour, light enough to allow him to move as quickly and easily as his task required. A blood-red cape concealed the twin pistols he would need to carry out his task and he wore metal kneepads over leather boots. The Minotaur: the mythical creature whose thunderous breath seemed to steam forth from its snout.

Ready to devour the children of Venice in the labyrinthine streets of a city at play, the Minotaur was preparing to change the course of history. Carnival had begun.

Some months earlier, on a coal-black night, the silence had been split by the agonised screams of Marcello Torretone in the Teatro San Luca. This was the work of the Shadow. The

Shadow that moved over the city, gliding over the roofs of the *Serenissima*. The Shadow had slipped furtively into the theatre with the last rays of the dying day. Father Caffelli called it *il Diavolo*, the Devil, but Marcello, in his report, had mentioned the name by which the man was known by his acolytes: the Chimera. The priest had done everything in his power to warn Marcello, who realised that something baleful was at work. That night, Marcello walked into a trap. A mysterious stranger had arranged to meet him in the Teatro San Luca, as the crowds were spilling out after his triumphant first-night performance in *L'Impresario di Smirne*. The owners of the theatre, the Vendramins, were the last to leave. As the theatre emptied, the stranger concealed himself in the wings.

Marcello had crumpled the costume he had been wearing and left it behind the curtains. He had reread the sealed letter he had received, marked as of the utmost urgency, in which a man who signed himself simply Virgil, promised him information concerning a threat. A threat to the highest institutions in Venice and to the doge himself. Marcello intended to pay a visit to Emilio Vindicati the following morning: it was imperative that the Council of Ten be advised of the matter without delay. Now, however, he could only curse his imprudence, for he now knew that he would not keep his appointment or see the sun rise.

Someone had stunned him with a blow, beaten him, and attached him to these rough-hewn timbers. Barely conscious, he watched a hooded form moving about and he struggled in vain to see the man's face. His eyes fell on the hammer, the nails, the lance, the crown of thorns – and a curious glass implement which glinted in the stranger's hand. Marcello was petrified.

'Who … who are you?' Marcello's mouth felt dry.

The other man allowed himself a derisive laugh in answer to the question. After that, Marcello could hear nothing but his breath, heavy and deep. The stranger finished tying Marcello to the timbers, which cast upon the empty stage the shadow of the crucifixion.

'You are ... you are *il Diavolo* – the Chimera?'

For a moment, the hooded figure turned towards him and Marcello strove once more to glimpse the man's features through the darkness.

'Then you truly exist? I thought it was merely ...'

The laugh came again. '*Vexilla regis prodeunt inferni*,' murmured the Chimera.

The voice was solemn and terrible. In truth, it seemed to come from beyond the grave.

'W ... what?'

'*Vexilla regis prodeunt inferni*. We shall see to it that you have a fitting end. I shall complete my task and you will be hoisted right here on this stage. Cheer up, my friend. Tonight, you will play your finest role.'

Then the Chimera picked up the hammer and two long, finely honed nails. Marcello's eyes bulged in terror.

'What will you do?'

'*Vexilla regis prodeunt inferni*, Marcello Torretone!' He placed the point of the first nail against Marcello's bound feet. Then, hammer in hand, he threw back his arm.

'NOOOOOOOOO!' Marcello screamed as he had never screamed.

Vexilla regis prodeunt inferni. The banner of the King of Hell is raised.

Ashen-faced, Francesco Loredan moved quickly through the corridors of the Palazzo Ducale. *This man must be apprehended at all costs*.

Francesco was one of the patricians intimately familiar with his magistrates. He had come to power four years earlier, in 1752. From the age of twenty-five young Venetian aristocrats were trained in the service of the republic. Francesco was one of those for whom the doors of the Great Council opened as a matter of birthright. In his time in the corridors of the palace, he had learned from his elders the vicissitudes of government; a knowledge all the more valuable given that the constitution of the republic was essentially oral. It was commonplace for ambassadors to bring their sons with them to initiate into the mysteries of diplomacy. A number of these young noblemen, the *Barbarini*, chosen by the drawing of lots on the feast of Santa Barbara, were permitted to witness the deliberations of the Great Council before they came of age. In this manner, all of the functionaries of the State instructed their sons in the ways of court. The careers of the sons of noble houses were mapped out in advance: the Great Council, the Consiglio dei Pregadi, the Stato di Terra Firma, a posting as an ambassador, the Council of Ten, and rising, eventually, to the rank of procurator or, who knows, perhaps even to doge, the primate of the city of Venice.

This political arrangement had been the foundation of the power and the might of the city on the *Laguna Veneta*, which had developed thanks to the talent of its leaders, even if the calculations of the Venetian nobility sometimes rebounded on the republic. The alliance with Florence against Milan, a pact negotiated in the *pax Lodi* three centuries earlier, had made it possible for the *Serenissima* to work towards the liberation of Italy while preserving its independence. Second only to Constantinople, the most prestigious of all cities, the Republic of Venice began to open embassies in Paris, London, Madrid, and Vienna. The division of sovereignty in the Mediterranean between the Turks and the Catholic flotilla, which marked the waning power of the Levant, had done much to ensure the continuity of Venice. The republic might not have invented political intrigue, but as mistress of the seas, arbiter of cultures, and master of the smoke screen, its contribution might be favourably compared to Machiavelli's *The Prince*, and the Medicis.

Francesco's innate pragmatism and his flair for public concerns, whether commercial, juridical, diplomatic or financial, made him a worthy son of Venice. As he walked quickly toward the sala del collegio clutching the letter, he thought, not for the first time, that the position of doge was an arduous responsibility. From time to time, a palace sentry, his halberd raised, moved discreetly aside to let Francesco pass, only to immediately resume his position. The ten are right, thought Francesco, we must move quickly. Since the twelfth century the power of the doge had strengthened and the people of Venice were determined that the primate of the city should not arrogate power to himself. Even today, as the city expanded, the most noble families were intent on conserving their pre-eminent right to participate in all important decisions and, although Venice eschewed all forms of monarchism, the State was quick to demarcate the supposed power of the people, which was illusory, and the supremacy of those families which had made Venice great.

Like all Venetians, Francesco wished he had been born in the golden age when Venice and its colonies had flourished, when he might have been, if not the sole master, then at least one of the architects of the vast machinery of conquest. Certainly, he took immoderate delight in the title, the attendant power, and the constant ceremonial bustle which surrounded him, but at times he felt himself a prisoner of his ceremonial role, *rex in purpura in urbe captivus*, 'a king in purple, a prisoner in his own city'. When he had first been proclaimed doge in the Basilica di San Marco, he had appeared before the jubilant crowd on the Piazza San Marco before being crowned with the *corno ducale* atop the Scala dei Giganti. But hardly had his nomination been uttered than he was obliged to solemnly vow never to exceed the rights accorded him in the *promissio ducalis*, which, when solemnly read aloud each year, reminded him of the limits of his authority.

Francesco, doge of Venice, member of the Privy Council and repository of the highest secrets of the State by virtue of his office, his authority and his power personified, more than anyone else, the permanence of the Serenissima Repubblica Veneta. It was he who presided over the Great Council, over the Consiglio dei Pregadi, and the Quaranti; he who sat with the six members of his Privy Council to hear petitions and grievances. Each week he visited one of the three hundred magistracies which made up Venice. He verified the nature and amount of all taxation and approved the public statements of accounts, to say nothing of the countless official visits and receptions. In truth, the doge had no private life. It was an arduous role that took such a toll on the health of an old man – for a man could not be made doge before the age of sixty – that it had been thought prudent to add an upholstered velvet rest to the throne in the Great Council. There he might doze when he did not feel inclined to follow the debate.

Francesco slipped into the palace and stepped into the great hall of the Maggior Consiglio, the Great Council, in which hung the portraits of all of his valiant predecessors. In other circumstances, he might have stopped, as he sometimes did, to study the features of the doges of the golden age to see whether he could identify some symbolic filiation. He might have considered Pietro Ziani: judge, councillor, *podestà* of Padua, the richest man in Venice whom the 'new' families, those who had grown rich during Venice's expansion, had forced from public life. Ziani would have sat before Pietro Tiepolo: armourer and merchant, Duke of Crete, *podestà* of Treviso and *baile* in Constantinople who, not content with endorsing the founding of a Senate, had written the statutes of 1242 and had done much to reunite Venice and to re-establish the supremacy of the republic. As he left the room, Francesco passed the black veil that concealed the portrait of Marino Faliero, a doge whose disconcerting destiny it had been to have dreamed of overthrowing the government so that he would be prince and, for his efforts, charged with treason and executed. As for Francesco, he wondered what legacy he would leave, and in what manner his reign as Head of State would be remembered. *There is*, he thought, *every reason to wonder.*

For this April morning, Francesco had much to occupy his mind. He was about to receive Emilio Vindicati, one of the Council of Ten. He had not yet decided how to respond to the singular suggestion Vindicati had made that same morning. Francesco arrived at the sala del collegio where he rested for a few moments, but found he could not sit still for long. Nervously, he walked to the window where a balcony overlooked the dyke in front of the *laguna*; one or two gondolas plied the waters, along with military vessels from the Arsenal, and some barges laden with produce. In the distance he could make out the winged line of San Marco, and the shadow of the campanile rising like daggers into the dawn. Francesco rubbed his eyes and took a deep breath. He looked out over this ballet of ships as they cut across each other's wake, watching the turbulent spray. He sighed once more and reread the letter that had accompanied the report from the Council of Ten:

A shadow walks abroad, looming over the republic, a treacherous shadow of which this murder is but a portent, one of the myriad manifestations of its power. Venice is in desperate straits, the vilest criminals move through its streets like wolves in a dark forest. The stench of decadence hangs over the city: we can no longer afford to ignore such matters.

After a moment, the doge informed one of the palace guards that he was ready to receive Emilio Vindicati.

'Si, illustrissimo mio Signore.'

As he waited Francesco gazed absent-mindedly at the

shimmering reflections on the waters. Venice. Once again you shall have to be saved.

The struggles of the doges against sea and silt to preserve the 'Venus of the waters' had been many; it was a miracle on which Francesco often pondered, for the survival of this city was surely no less than a miracle. Once, it had been the frontier that divided the Byzantine Empire from the Carolingian, but slowly Venice had won its independence. San Marco became the city's patron in AD 828 when two merchants from the Rialto had returned to the city bearing relics of the saint stolen from Alexandria. But it had been the first crusade and the taking of Jerusalem which had signalled the beginning of the city's golden age. As the gateway between civilisations: Byzantine, Slav, Islamic and Oriental, the significance of Venice could not be ignored. Through here came timber and iron from Brescia, Carinthia and Styria, copper and silver from Bohemia and Slovakia, gold from Silesia and Hungary, textiles, linens, silk, cottons and dyes, spices, wines, wheat and sugar. Venice had also begun to develop its own industries: shipbuilding and the manufacture of luxuries such as crystal, glass and salt.

Venice was a port which gave access to great fleets of galleys, some heading east to Constantinople, the Black Sea and Cyprus, others south to Trebizond and Alexandria or to the west, heading for Majorca and Barcelona and farther still to Lisbon, Bruges and London.

Venice, a provincial backwater, was becoming an empire. Colonial bases and trading posts multiplied from Crete to Corinth, Smyrna to Thessalonica and ever farther afield, creating so many colonies ripe for exploitation that people began to dream of building a new Venice, a Venice of the East. People in every corner of these new territories became Venetian citizens. But to govern such vast swathes of territory and to to develop and exploit them required administrative and commercial ties to the republic that weakened the state and many of the poorest lands had to be abandoned.

Venice succeeded in maintaining its supremacy until the sixteenth century. Only then, in the dark days that followed the Battle of Lepanto, struggling against the incursions of the Spanish, who could rely on the papacy for support, did the glory and magnificence of Venice begin to pall. In 1718, as part of the Treaty of Požarevac, Venice lost extensive lands to the Ottoman Empire. And so the City of the Doges adopted a policy of benign neutrality, all the while pouring senseless sums into rebuilding its arsenal. The city's slow decline was masked for a time by the flourishing of the arts as Titian, Veronese and Tintoretto vied with one another to create the apogee of beauty. Canaletto could make the waters of the *laguna* shimmer and the very air of the city seem to shimmer in a gossamer haze. But, as Francesco knew only too well, the city struggled to maintain its position in the eyes of the world. Venice could no longer hide the cracks. Its harshest critics compared the black gondolas moving slowly through the canals to so many languid sarcophagi. The reputation of the city, of the Most Serene Republic, the very credo on which the empire had been built, was threatened. Gambling, corruption, idleness and cupidity had slowly eroded ancient values. All the evidence presented to Francesco in his four years as doge revealed an ongoing decline in shipping. As a port, Venice could no longer compare to Livorno, Ancona or Trieste. Noble Venetian families could not bring themselves to practise 'trade', an occupation they thought too plebeian, worthy only of the English, the French and the Dutch. Still, mercantilism and vested interests held sway. It was only one short step from decadence. *Vindicati is right. The rot has already set in.*

At that moment, the great doors of the sala del collegio opened and Emilio Vindicati appeared. Francesco Loredan turned from the window.

Vindicati had abandoned the livery of his office in favour of a long black coat. He was a man of considerable height but his slender form in his capacious coat made it seem as though his limbs floated. A powdered wig sat atop an oval face and his eyes, steely and piercing, flashed with a glint of mockery which echoed the half-smile which played on his lips. He was thin-lipped; his mouth a single, almost invisible line which looked like a slash drawn in charcoal and when he smiled, it formed a rictus of scorn. The sense of calm, the determination and energy he exuded seemed like the tranquil surface of a lake whose turbid depths masked a warrior, a storm of fury, passion and intransigence – all the qualities, in fact, a man might need to steer the decisions of the Council of Ten. A Florentine by birth, Emilio had grown up in Venice and had been elected head of the Council of Ten after twenty-five years of devoted service to the Maggior Consiglio, where he had made a reputation for himself as an able politician and ruthless orator. There were those who thought his bearing haughty, his politics at times extreme but, like Francesco Loredan himself, Emilio shouldered his responsibilities; he too regretted the passing of the golden age. He was one of the few who believed in the State above all things. And, unlike many of his peers, Emilio intended to do everything in his power to return the republic to its former glory.

As he stepped into the sala del collegio, Vindicati removed his hat and bowed ceremoniously before the doge. His hand lingered on his ebony cane, its handle carved with two griffins intertwined. Francesco Loredan turned back toward the lagoon.

'Emilio, I have studied the deliberations of the Council carefully and read the recommendation you made in your communiqué. You know as well as I how the government of the city functions, how political influence is traded and bought. But I can truly say that it was with horror that I read what you had written. Are we truly as blind as you would have me believe; is the peril to the city as great as you suppose ... or have you perhaps exaggerated the danger to compel us to action?'

Emilio arched an eyebrow and ran his tongue over his

lips. 'Surely you do not question the advice of the Council of Ten?'

'Come, Emilio, we have not come here to discuss our various sensibilities ... You indicated that a brutal murder was perpetrated at the Teatro San Luca last evening.'

Emilio drew himself up to his full height, his hands behind his back still toying with his cane. He sighed, then stepped a little farther into the sala de collegio.

'Indeed, *Serenissimus*, I have spared you the details of this sordid crime. You need only know that it is a crime of a malevolence unprecedented in Venice. Even now, the body is as it was found. I ordered that nothing be touched while awaiting your decision, and that of the Council, on how best to proceed with the investigation, in view of the details which I communicated in my letter ... But such a situation cannot continue for long.'

'Have you informed the Great Council of this horror?'

'Not precisely, *Serenissimus*. And if I may be so bold ... I think that it would be a most unwise course of action.'

The two men fell silent for a moment. The doge moved away from the window and paced the hall. He came to stand before Emilio, the *bacheta* in hand, and said: 'This does not please me. As you well know, I am not permitted to open even personal letters except in the presence of my Privy Council. Ergo, this meeting, too, is in contravention of the constitution. I need not remind you, Emilio, of my reasons for scrupulously respecting such protocol ... And you know that my power to make such a decision is severely limited. You say there are exceptional circumstances that justify a breach of customary protocol, but many would see this as a conspiracy. So tell me, Emilio, do you truly believe that members of the government of Venice could be embroiled in such a business? You must admit that such an accusation would be of the utmost seriousness.'

Emilio did not demur. 'The threat to the security of the republic is no less serious, *Serenissimus*.'

There was a silence, then Francesco raised his hand, frowning.

'Indeed, my friend ... but this threat is but conjecture on your part. The line of reasoning you advance in your letter is, to say the least, shocking, and you have no proof whatever.'

The doge turned, and went to stand beneath Veronese's *Battle of Lepanto*.

'We cannot even contemplate conducting a public investigation; merely to initiate such an inquiry would place us in a most uncomfortable position and might trigger a crisis of government, something we can ill-afford in these difficult times.'

'It is for this reason, *Serenissimus*, that I have advised against calling upon one of our usual informants to find out more about this matter.'

The doge frowned. 'Yes, I can understand that. And so you have decided to employ a criminal to investigate this crime? A fly-by-night who, as we speak, is languishing in a cell in this very palace, awaiting his execution? This seems to me a most curious subterfuge. In the first instance, how can you know that the moment he steps outside these walls, he will not immediately fade into the rabble?'

Emilio smiled. 'You need have no fear of that, *Serenissimus*. The man I have in mind is much too enamoured of his freedom to wrangle or to attempt to outwit me. He knows what awaits him should he renege on his bargain. He is, I grant you, a man who has often made a mockery of the republic and has been the cause of some considerable unrest occasioned, shall we say, by his audacious and rebellious temperament. But we are offering him his freedom and, more importantly, to spare his life. For this he will be eternally indebted to us, and a rogue though he be, he has a keen sense of honour. I know whereof I speak, *Serenissimus*, for he served under my command for four years. He has worked for the Republic before, indeed for the Council itself. He is adept in the ways of leading a criminal investigation, and skilled at mingling with a crowd in order to elicit information. He is quick-witted and peerless in his ability to extricate himself from the most difficult situations.'

'Indeed,' said Francesco. 'Though he clearly has as much facility for getting himself into such situations.'

Emilio's smile was a little contrite. 'That, I grant you. But the very irresponsibility you speak of is also our greatest weapon: no one would ever suspect him of working for us. For my part, I shall ensure he accomplishes his task, believe me.'

The doge pondered a moment. 'Let us say, Emilio ... Say, for a moment, that we proceed as you suggest, with all the risks such an action represents ... Have you spoken of this matter to the prisoner? How can we know he will agree?'

'It is done, *Serenissimus*, and naturally, he has accepted. He waits upon our decision. Believe it or not, he is taking advantage of his incarceration to write his memoirs. Of course the affair of which we speak must on no account feature in such a memoir. Not that I believe his tale is of interest to posterity, but I need not tell you that it would be inopportune if any mention of this enterprise were to appear, thus heaping disgrace upon us, the Council and the government itself.'

'Indeed you need not.' Francesco sat back in an armchair, stroking his beard.

Emilio came closer. '*Illustrissimo mio Signore*, what do we risk? At worst, our criminal escapes, at best he may serve as a most valuable tool in our endeavours. He handles a sword as a man, he has earned the trust of the common horde, and he is possessed of a formidable intelligence that, if placed in the service of a noble cause, may save Venice itself. It is an irony of which he is not unaware, but one in which he delights. In this manner he might earn some form of redemption.

Redemption, as your Serene Highness knows, is a powerful lure.'

The doge considered the matter. He closed his eyes, bringing his cupped fingers to his lips. Then, with a sigh, he opened his eyes and looked at Emilio. 'Very well. Have him brought before me. I have every confidence in your judgement but, as you may imagine, I wish to see and speak to this man myself so that I may form a better opinion as to his character.'

Emilio smiled. He got up slowly and bowed deeply. He raised his eyebrows and smiled as he spoke: 'So be it, *Serenissimus*.'

He had already left the Great Hall when the doge, preoccupied, murmured, 'The very idea … releasing the Black Orchid!' He closed his eyes once more.

He could see armed galleys, cannon-fire over the *laguna*, hooded figures running into the dark streets of the city, the carnival. He could smell the gunpowder and hear the gunfire. He could see *La Serenissima* sinking beneath the waves, lost for ever. The glorious spectacle of his own annihilation inflamed his spirit.

Someone had brought him coffee, which sat beside the sceptre. He gazed into the dregs. And as he did so, Francesco Loredan, prince of the *Serenissima*, the 116th doge of Venice thought: *Let slip the dogs of war …*

CANTO II

THE ANTECHAMBER OF HELL

The cells beneath the roofs of the doge's palace, *i Piombi*, were named after the thick lead slabs that lined its roof and, it was said, made the prison the most secure in all of Italy. One might reach them directly through the Palazzo Ducale, or from the adjoining building, crossing the Bridge of Sighs. These were not the sighs of amorous lovers, but the howling lamentations of the damned being lead to the place of execution. Crossing the *Ponte dei Sospiri*, a man might catch a glimpse of the *laguna* through the ornamental latticed windows, only to be immediately plunged into the narrow labyrinth of corridors winding to *i Piombi*, the cells in which the most terrible criminals were caged.

In one such cell sat a man accused of disturbing the civil peace of *la Serenissima*. Even though he was not the most contemptible of villains, his unscrupulous and immoral behaviour had frequently landed him in these cells; and which, on this occasion, seemed likely to lead him to the gallows. But, despite the fact that the case against him was still being prepared, a recent conversation with Emilio Vindicati had given him hope that he would yet escape from this difficult position unscathed. He wore his hair long, yet every day he shaved and groomed himself as meticulously as if, that very evening, he were expected at a *masquerade*. His eyebrows were arched and perfectly sculpted, a slender nose sat atop the insolent curve of his lips and his eager eyes sparkled with what might be considered the shining beacon of truth, or a glimmer of deceit. His elegant appearance contrasted sharply with the bleak surroundings in which he now found himself. He had been permitted books and, in addition to the straw mattress on which he slept, a writing desk. He had befriended his gaoler, Lorenzo Basadonna, who kept him supplied with quills, ink, and parchment so that he could continue to set down fragments of his memoirs. From time to time, captor and captive enjoyed lively conversations and, in spite of his uncomfortable predicament, the prisoner, for whom to be denied his freedom was the worst privation, was often heard to laugh. On certain days he was allowed to play a hand of cards with a prisoner in another cell, an old friend, whose name was not unknown in Venice, one Giovanni Giacomo Casanova, who had also been accused of crimes against the peace. On other days his valet, Landretto, would come to cheer his master, faithfully bringing piles of books, provisions or news from the city.

When Emilio Vindicati came to free him, the prisoner, as was his wont, was bowed over the parchment, quill in hand, furiously jotting down an account of his curious destiny. A young man of humble birth, he had been born on 12 June 1726 in the *sestiere* of San Marco, the beating heart of the city on the *laguna*. His parents lived near Santa Trinità where they, with Casanova's parents, worked at the Teatro San Samuele, founded half a century before by the Grimani family. His mother, Julia Pagazzi, was an actress, an unpredictable *artiste*; his father Pascuale, a cobbler's son, was a wardrobe master and a strolling player who disappeared when he was still a child. Soon after, his mother left for a theatrical engagement in France. The boy found himself alone. Though he had brothers and sisters, he had little contact with them, and was raised by his elderly grandmother, Elena Pagazzi. It had been in an attempt to emulate Giacomo, his boyhood friend on the campo San Samuele, that he had left Venice to study in Padua. Here he fell into the clutches of Alessandro Bonacin, a family friend, dissolute poet and penniless aristocrat who, under the guise of instructing him in the ways of God, initiated him into the pleasures of the flesh. When he had secured his doctorate, the boy – by now a young man – returned to Venice where he received the clerical tonsure and was ordained a deacon. Everyone expected him to pursue a career in the church – an eminently practical route to social advancement. In one respect, it was a vocation ideally suited to his temperament: he had a deep and abiding need for recognition, the paradoxical but understandable result of the feelings of abandonment which had haunted him since childhood; however, his licentious living quickly earned him a spell in the Forte di Sant' Andrea on the island of La Certosa. This was the first time he and his friend Casanova were to share adjoining cells. On his release, a cardinal attempted, in vain, to guide him back to the path of righteousness, but the young man escaped by enlisting in the army. Later, he would ply the Mediterranean, from Corfu to Constantinople, returning to Venice as a violinist with the Teatro San Samuele orchestra, where his parents had once worked. This was a new 'vocation', to which he was utterly unsuited, but in Giacomo and his *compagnos* from San Samuele, he found friends with whom he could indulge his vices. If his intention was to abandon himself to debauchery, he was in good hands.

And yet, fortune smiled on him. One night, a stone's throw from Santa Trinità, as he was leaving the Palazzo Mandolini where he had been engaged to play the violin at a *masquerade*, he managed, by some miracle, to extricate Senator Ottavio from a delicate predicament, offering him some advice at the gambling table. With astonishing nerve, he declared that it was a talent he owed to the esoteric knowledge that allowed him, by judicious use of numerology, to divine the answer to any question that he – or indeed another – might pose. The credulous senator was instantly taken with the young man, and all but adopted him as a son. He hired a manservant for his protégé, paid his board and lodging, offered him a gondola and a monthly salary of ten *sequini*. From that day, the young man travelled in style, and lived like a lord. Occasionally, he met Giacomo, who had been blessed with similar good fortune. It seemed a fine revenge on his previous life! He performed thrilling feats of prognostication for the benefit of the noble patricians of Venice, and regularly replenished his purse at the gaming tables of the *casini*. He was, it must be said, more than simply the sum of his vices. An admirable rhymester, he could also philosophise tolerably well, recite Aristotle by heart; his erudition, charm, rapier wit and his gift for *le mot juste* and talent as a raconteur able to move an audience to tears or hold them spellbound for hours, made him an agreeable and much sought-after guest. But, in a city teeming with secrets and delights both sacred and profane, innocent and depraved, he could not but succumb to his demons. He would spend whole nights in the *casini*, indulging in every form of dissipation. To his political acquaintances, meanwhile, he had proved a useful informant. So useful, in fact, that one evening Emilio Vindicati – then *capo* of the Quarantia Criminale – sought him out. He was recruited almost by mistake. Though he did not yet know it, a number of his exploits – three successive duels and some feats of prestidigitation designed to humiliate rivals in love and *cavalieri* of his acquaintance – had already persuaded Vindicati to engage him. Restless and enticed by the prospect of adventure, he agreed to join the network of informants to the Council of Ten. In a few short years he became one of their most valuable spies. Thus, he was promoted – who would have thought it? – to the rank of secret agent in the service of the republic.

Since he often wore a *boutonnière* grown from seeds he shipped directly from South America via the good offices of

Senator Ottavio, and because the soubriquet pleased him, he was given the *nom de guerre* that was to make his reputation: the Black Orchid. Exquisite and deadly, it was an apt code name. He was charged with hunting down traitors, enemies of the powerful, and brigands of every hue. Capitalising on his military experience, he quickly completed his apprenticeship and became a master swordsman. Ever his mother's son, he was studied in the arts of acting and of disguise; he was a consummate chameleon. The Black Orchid was considered the linchpin of the service.

His career might well have continued in this fashion had he not made the grievous mistake of seducing his protector's wife, the radiant Anna Santamaria. She had a sylph-like figure, the eyes of a gazelle, a delectable beauty spot by the corner of her mouth, a generous bosom and grace enough to drive a man to folly. Against her will, she had been married to the senator when she was but a girl. The lovers were helplessly drawn to one another. The Black Orchid had had his share of conquests, but never before had he loved so completely that he was willing to risk his life. Anna Santamaria yielded to his amorous advances; once too often. In the whirlwind that followed, he found his career in ruins. On 18 November 1755, the State inquisitors dragged him from his bed and arrested him on trumped-up charges of atheism and conspiring against *la Serenissima*. He was taken to *i Piombi*. A month later, as he was plotting his escape, his gaoler Basadonna moved him to another cell. This forced him to revise his plans, but he was not disheartened and with the help of Casanova, who was in the adjoining cell – *Ciao, compagno!* – the prisoner began to formulate new stratagems. As for Ottavio's wife; the Black Orchid and his mistress had had no word of one another since his arrest. Anna Santamaria was surely still in Venice, unless the senator had had her confined somewhere on Terra Firma. For months the prisoner waited for a letter from her; a letter that never came. For his part, he wrote countless letters to her, but doubted they reached their destination. If, by nature, he was fickle in his affections, now he was truly heartbroken.

This, then, was how his erstwhile benefactor Emilio Vindicati found him when he first came to visit the prisoner in his cell. The man had too much spirit, too much imagination to succumb to the apathy or the madness that ate into the souls of so many of his caged companions. He and Giacomo would hear their anguished howls, their mournful groans borne away on the dark air. Some resorted to choking themselves with their own shackles to hasten their end; others beat their heads so viciously against the cell walls that their faces, when they were led to their execution, were covered with blood. Others would return emaciated from bouts of torture perpetrated by officers of the republic in shadowy rooms which could only be reached by one of the countless secret tunnels in the palace walls. The Black Orchid had been spared such bloody interrogations, at least until now. He had never given up hope. On the contrary, though he was denied his freedom – something almost unendurable for him – now, more than ever, he felt life course through his veins. To be forced to forsake the best years of his youth, the spice of his picaresque adventures and thrilling escapades, this was something which offended his nature. Often, he prowled like a lion in a cage, struggling to maintain his self-control. This was why he had devised his routine: every day he would spend hours grooming himself, adjusting the suit of clothes fashioned to his design that Landretto had brought, contemplating some intractable problem of philosophy, devising some new strategy to beat his fellow prisoner at cards or working on the fresco he had outlined in chalk on one of the walls of his cell.

As he heard the rasp of the key in the lock he set down his quill, smoothed the full sleeves of his shirt, and turned to the door. There stood Basadonna, holding a lantern and smiling. In addition to his unkempt beard he now sported a sty weeping pus in one eye.

'You got a visitor.'

The prisoner looked up and saw that the man in the black frock coat was Emilio Vindicati. He raised an eyebrow and fleetingly brought his hand to his lips, his rings glinting on his fingers. The fingers of an artist.

'Well, well. Emilio Vindicati. It is always an honour to welcome you to my humble palace! I find it heartening to note that your visits are more frequent of late.'

'Leave us.' Emilio addressed the gaoler.

Basadonna growled, something between a grunt and a laugh, and slowly ambled down the corridor. Emilio's expression, stern and emotionless, suddenly brightened. He opened his arms wide. The prisoner stood, and the men embraced warmly.

'My friend, my friend,' said Emilio. 'The doge has sent for you, as I hoped he would. Mind that you are civil to him, scoundrel, and tell him what he wishes to hear.'

'You have saved me, Emilio. Don't think I do not know it, nor shall I forget it. If the price for my life is to undertake the mission we spoke of, I shall see it through to the bitter end. After all, though it is an unexpected mission, *La Serenissima* is my home, and the city well deserves what I can do for it.'

'Come, let us not keep the duke waiting.'

Half-smiling, Pietro Luigi Viravolta de Lansalt got to his feet, ran a hand across his chest, smoothing a crease in his shirt, then, with a resolute air, fell into step behind his benefactor. Before leaving the prison, he stopped for a moment before the adjoining cell. Through the slot in the cell door a hand emerged; the middle finger, like his own, bore a signet ring and the ring finger a ruby.

'You are leaving?'

'Perhaps,' said Pietro. 'If I do not return ... take care.'

'Do not worry on my account, I have more than one trick up my sleeve. We shall meet again, *amico*.'

'My blessings go with you.'

'And mine with you, Pietro. When you get out ...' he paused for a moment, '... make me proud.'

Pietro smiled. 'I should hope so, Giacomo.'

He kissed Casanova's hand and followed Emilio Vindicati into the dark corridor.

It had been some time since Pietro had set foot outdoors. It was cold, but the sun on his face, the dazzle in his eyes, was like a benediction. He revelled in the scents of Venice. Emilio had to pause to allow him to contemplate the Bridge of Sighs. Though he had barely stepped out of his prison cell, Pietro already felt a surge of energy; he would have devoured the world itself if given the opportunity. But they could not tarry, the prince of the *Serenissima* was waiting for their arrival in the sala de collegio. Pietro Viravolta was prepared to do whatever was required to win round the doge; certainly the investigation which Vindicati wished him to undertake did not worry him unduly. He took deep breaths striding through the halls of the Palazzo Ducale, which was not simply a gaol, but a symbol of the very structure of everything he admired in the pulsing heart of the *Serenissima*. As he walked, he imagined himself master of his own fate. He imagined stepping through the *porta del frumento*, which opened onto the magnificent interior courtyard, the elegant Renaissance wing, the clock tower and the dungeons – *i pozzi* – with their bronze coping. When the Palazzo Ziani, the old Byzantine palace was consumed by fire, it had been rebuilt to incorporate a flamboyant new facade overlooking the lagoon and a lavish new hall, the Sala del Maggior Consiglio, its windows looking out onto the midday sun. The facade of the new palace, with its intricately patterned damask of pink and white stone and carved Gothic windows overlooking the sea, looked like a cathedral. The openwork crenellations, the marble pinnacles and the graceful columns of the upper gallery all contrived to make this Gothic edifice one of the wonders of the world. Even a second conflagration, in 1577, had not laid it low: Antonio Da Ponte rebuilt the palace exactly as it had been, and the *palazzo* now seems to float, eternally triumphant, upon the waters of the *laguna*. The distant gaiety and laughter of Venice reached Pietro as a rumbling murmur made his heart soar. Whether or not it pleased the doge, Pietro felt himself at one with the city and the indefinable spirit of its people. *Free! Free at last!*

Pietro and Vindicati quickly reached the sala del collegio, and announced themselves to the sentry.

The great double doors opened before them as if by enchantment. In other circumstances, Pietro might well have been impressed. The doors opened to reveal the *Battle of Lepanto* behind the ducal throne, and the painted ceiling depicting *Mars and Neptune* seemed somehow symbolic, like a mystical portal opening onto the corridors of power, the secret history of the republic. At the far end of hall, the prince of the *Serenissima* sat enthroned. Slowly, they walked towards him.

At the doge's invitation, they sat facing him.

Francesco Loredan gazed intently at the prisoner for a long moment then, clearing his throat, he began: 'To recapitulate: you are a numerologist, a liar, a gambler, a womaniser, skilled in fencing, a master of disguise and a double – perhaps a triple – agent. In short, you are a blackguard. Your escapades have not gone unremarked by the several councils of the State; we have long protected you for the considerable services you have rendered to the republic, but I confess, Viravolta, the idea of releasing you so that you may once more roam the streets of Venice bewilders me. You are not unlike your renegade friend, Casanova ...'

Pietro smiled self-consciously then, recovering his wits, said, 'Venice has always smiled upon all manner of chimeras, *Serenissimus*.'

The insolent tone was not lost upon the doge. Emilio glanced at Pietro, entreating him to keep his temper.

'Indeed,' Francesco Loredan continued, 'You are aware of the troubles with which we are beset. The Consiglio dei Dieci have had the most irregular idea that I should entrust to you an investigation. A matter in which, I am given to believe, many reputations are at stake. You remember the Council of Ten, I trust?'

Indeed I do. Pietro nodded silently. It was at the whim of the Consiglio dei Dieci that he had served four years' hard labour. Here was a faction to be feared. From its inception, the Republic of Venice had been governed by a number of assemblies. At first, Venice elected a Committee of Wise Men – excluding members of the clergy – who were to be the quintessence of the nascent state. Later, it had been deemed vital to convene the Maggior Consiglio, the Great Council, who now held sole responsibility for enacting laws and who alone elected officials and those who would serve on the Council of Ten and the Quarantia Criminale. Since the golden age, the Senate had been responsible for matters of diplomacy and foreign policy, the administration of the colonies and waging of wars, while also governing the economy of the republic. The administration was divided into two sections: the 'offices of the palace', comprising six judicial courts, the offices of the exchequer, the military and naval departments, and the ducal chancellery, which was responsible for state archives and notarised protocols; and the offices of the Rialto which, for the most part, made up the fiscal offices.

Within this centralised government the Council of Ten held a key role. It had been born of the fears of a government which had long since lost its popular support. Though Venice was admired throughout the world for its political stability in which, it seemed, were melded aristocracy, monarchy and democracy, in fact, it was rule by fear. Together with the Quarantia Criminale, the *Tenebræ*, as the

Council of Ten was known, was the supreme branch of the police in Venice. Ten ordinary members who served for a term of one year were elected by the Great Council from several noble Venetian families. In addition, the doge himself, his councillors, a public lawyer, the commanders of the three branches of the Quarantia Criminale, and a commission composed of twenty members, participated in administrative affairs. Fearing that some renegade faction might destabilise the government, the Council of Ten, whose very name could make the soul of a man tremble, was chiefly charged with keeping a watchful eye on the disenfranchised. The council was endowed with exceptional powers and gifted with secret funds and a vast network of informants, a network to which Pietro had long belonged.

For a time, this ruthless body attempted to encroach upon the prerogatives of the Senate in matters of diplomacy and finance; only a grave crisis had forced it to render unto Caesar that which was Caesar's. But the Ten were not content with this. The powers of the three inquisitors appointed by the Ten to expose spying and enemy conspiracy were bolstered and the Dark Council continued to usurp many of the judicial powers of the Quarantia Criminale. Even now, a secret police operating under the aegis of the Ten spread terror though the antechambers of the palace, and though their actions often led to gross miscarriages of justice, their formidable powers went unchecked. All deliberations were made *in camera*. They had the power to torture and to absolve, and to gaol or free those who might further their interests – a policy from which Pietro was hoping to benefit. It was poetic justice. In the past, the Ten had made its reputation counteracting a European plot against the Serene Republic led by the Marquis of Bedmar; since that time they had seen conspiracy everywhere. Any member of the council was forbidden, on pain of death or of seizure of his goods and chattels, from revealing even the nature of their deliberations. They hunted down and eliminated those they deemed suspect, secretly organised operations which were conducted by their private militia, encouraged informants and decided whether prisoners should be put to death. The Tenebrae was inured to wading through blood.

The standard-bearer and first officer of the Ten was Emilio Vindicati himself. It was down to the determination of Emilio alone that Pietro owed his life and the slender possibility that, in spite of the excesses which had so often almost been his ruin, he might soon be set free. As a young man, he and his companions had wreaked havoc in the streets of San Samuele, summoning doctors, priests and midwives to false addresses to tend to imaginary patients and they cut the lines of the gondolas of patrician families and watched them float, rudderless, down the *Canal Grande*. As he thought of this, Pietro smiled. If, later, his transgressions had been more serious, he had never plotted against the State, quite the contrary. From the first, Emilio Vindicati had been captivated by Pietro's individuality, a passion that merely grew as he followed the fantastical exploits of his protégé in the guise of the Black Orchid. The two men had unwittingly shared more than one mistress before Pietro finally fell in love with Anna Santamaria. But Emilio believed, not without reason, that the risks Pietro incurred were as nothing to those which currently threatened the republic.

The doge spoke again. 'The Council of Ten has compiled a police report chronicling, in detail, their suspicions. But before I may permit you to read a line of it, I will require some further guarantee of your good conduct. How can I be sure that you will not take advantage of this pardon to flee, or indeed defect to the enemy, if enemy there be?'

Pietro smiled and ran his tongue over his lips. He crossed his legs and placed a hand on one knee. *The moment has come to be persuasive.*

'Your Serene Highness, Messer Vindicati has clearly explained to me that the pardon you speak of will take effect only upon successful completion of the investigation. The charges against me are being prepared, and the stench of the death sentence – ill-deserved, if truth be told – hangs over my head. Do you truly believe that I would seek to flee like a vulgar brigand without attempting to clear my name of the calumnies proclaimed against it? It is hardly fitting for a man such as I to run from city to city pursued by the officers whom, I have little doubt, you would set upon me; moreover, I have no wish to spend the rest of my days ensuring that I am not being followed or about to fall into some trap of your contrivance.'

The doge peered at Pietro, a smile flitting across his face.

'Furthermore, *Serenissimus*,' Pietro continued, 'I realise that my imprisonment results entirely from insolence and the incivility of which I am accused; I grant that I am responsible for my behaviour and I would not wish to pretend that, in some damascene conversion, I have accepted some new article of faith, nor that I have suddenly been redeemed. My enemies say that I am selfish, unpredictable and cynical; it is a sombre portrait indeed! It is true that I have unwittingly been caught up in a number of political imbroglios. But I would remind your Serene Highness that the affair for which I was incarcerated was an affair of the heart, and the suffering I have endured for the love of this woman is greater than any that can be inflicted upon me. It is no secret that Senator Ottavio used every possible wile to have me locked up and that, more than anything, he wishes me dead. It is something I greatly regret. For I cherish my freedom above all else. The word may make you smile, *Serenissimus*, but I too have my code of honour and – if I may – my own code of ethics. I am not a murderer; if I have been called upon to kill, it has been for the glory of the republic, in the service of the State when I worked incognito for the Council, or while defending myself from some assault. Like you, I deplore murder. Had I known that the very services that were asked of me would one day be turned against me, I would have declined to play the roles you have had me play! It is easy to reproach me today for actions for which, yesterday, I would have been commended.'

Francesco Loredan listened on; the interview lasted an hour.

Pietro was aware of the doge's possible reservations and tackled them directly, marshalling all his considerable eloquence. The idea of finding himself thrust once more into the secret affairs of the *Serenissima* greatly appealed to him. The possibility thrilled him, although he knew, better than any man alive, the perils he might have to face. He and Emilio Vindicati shared a taste for the preposterous, an insight into the human soul. Emilio had been right in believing he could trust this 'prisoner', his friend. Pietro was determined by fair means or foul to be free. Not content with offering his life as warranty, Pietro confided to the doge much of what he had overheard while he languished in *i Piombi*. Even in a prison cell – especially in a prison cell – one might hear much that would be of interest to the *Serenissimus*. Upon his honour, his voice heavy with the lilt of sincerity, he offered as surety his personal fortune, riches amassed here and there which he now intended to return to Venice. He impressed upon the doge that the republic was deserving of his service, he who had been so well served by the republic. So convincing, in fact, was he, that finally Emilio Vindicati felt compelled to intervene.

'Very well,' murmured Francesco Loredan, his hand resting on his chin. 'I think …'

He allowed the silence to hang in the air a moment. 'I think I shall consent to this proposal.'

I have done it! Pietro struggled to contain his relief.

'But,' the doge continued, 'I must remind you that everything you read, everything you hear from the Ten is of the utmost secrecy. Should you break this sacred trust, you will pay the ultimate penalty. The mission entrusted to you is confidential. We must find a manner to explain your sudden release without unduly troubling the public. Emilio, I entrust the informing of Senator Ottavio of our decision to you, and keeping him in check. Once he knows the Black Orchid is free, he is likely to cause a scandal we can ill afford. You should also inform the Council of Ten since they alone have your complete trust. But I insist on two further conditions: firstly, my Privy Council must be informed – on this I will not be swayed, Emilio, it protects me from eventual repercussions. Secondly, the chief of the Quarantia Criminale must also be notified. And, the most difficult part, they must all keep silent.'

Emilio nodded. 'Depend upon it, *Serenissimus*.'

Francesco Loredan turned once more to Pietro. 'You, Viravolta, you are free to go. I will personally write you a letter of safe conduct so that you may carry out your investigation. But know this ...' The doge raised his hand above the *corno ducale*.

'The sword of Damocles hangs above you. At the first sign of treachery the lions of Venice will fall upon you and tear you to pieces. And far from preventing them, I will urge them on with all my considerable power.'

Pietro bowed. 'I understand, *illustrissimo mio Signore*.'

Then he smiled and added, 'You shall not regret this.'

Pietro took the steps of the Scala d'Oro four at a time, like a small boy, with Emilio on his heels. He felt exhilarated. As he passed the palace guard he laughingly touched the sharp point of the man's halberd, tugged the sentry's beard, and bowed.

'Free! I'm free, my friend!'

Emilio placed his hand on Pietro's shoulder.

'I shall be indebted to you for the rest of my life,' said Pietro.

'I understand your joy. But remember your freedom depends on several conditions. Know that I shall be keeping a watchful eye on your investigation, and that I am personally accountable for your behaviour to the Ten.'

'Come, Emilio. I have sworn to complete my mission and I shall. You know me, this investigation shall be resolved in less time than it takes to speak of the matter.'

'It will not be as simple as you believe, Pietro, this is a most serious matter, as you shall discover this very evening.'

'This evening? But … Well, I had thought to celebrate my freedom this evening in the company of a coterie of noble friends whom I have not seen for some time; some conversation, a little wine, and perhaps a little tenderness from a Venetian wench. We would be most honoured, of course, if you would join us.'

Pietro stopped. Emilio looked at him sternly, tightening his grip on his shoulder.

'No. This investigation cannot be delayed. There can be no question of you renewing your acquaintances with courtesans – and, in particular, with the woman for whose love you were imprisoned. Pietro … Anna Santamaria is no longer in Venice, she has been sent away.'

'Where is she?'

'Somewhere it is best you do not seek to discover. Do not forget that there are many noblemen who wish you dead – Ottavio chief amongst them.'

Regretfully, Viravolta nodded. 'Fear not. I am not mad. Anna … the Black Widow, as you were wont to call her, though she was neither black nor a widow. Her only crime was to love me …' His eyes shimmered with momentary sadness.

'… and it was also mine. But all of that is in the past, my friend. Now, let the merriment commence.'

Emilio frowned. He opened his black greatcoat and took out a leather file sealed with an iron clasp from which a number of dog-eared sheets of parchment protruded.

'Pietro, I feel I should reiterate my warning. Mark my words, you are about to step into the antechamber of hell, as you shall soon discover. This is the police report on the murder of which I spoke. The victim was Marcello Torretone, an actor in the employ of the Vendramin brothers at the Teatro San Luca. Before going there, you must read the file; afterwards, burn it. Understood?'

'Understood.'

'Excellent,' murmured Emilio Vindicati. 'Remember that I am entirely accountable for your actions, Pietro. I have staked my honour and my reputation on this. It is inconceivable that you should fail. If, however, as I expect, we successfully resolve this matter, much, if not all of the glory will be mine. For the moment, as you know, all is well in the Great Council and in the Senate, but who knows, perhaps even I might wish to change them. After all, Loredan is not immortal ...'

Pietro smiled and Vindicati became visibly less tense.

'Come,' said Emilio, 'I have a surprise waiting.'

In the interior courtyard of the palace, before the *porta del frumento*, stood a young man. Pietro's face lit up when he recognised his valet.

'Landretto!'

'There you are, master. I was beginning to miss you and to grow weary of spending endless hours here, waiting to see you cross the Bridge of Sighs ...'

The two men laughed. Landretto, with his shock of long blond hair, was not yet twenty. He was a slender youth with a charming face in spite of a nose which was a little too long. He had been in Pietro's service for more than five years, and his loyalty had never been in doubt. Pietro had taken the boy out of the gutter, and not in some mere figurative sense. When he had first come upon Landretto, the lad had been robbed and beaten by brigands in a taverna and lay drunk and whimpering on the pavement in a pool of his own blood. Pietro nursed and dressed the lad; it had been Landretto himself who had suggested that he might serve Pietro, to whom he had become both servant and friend. Landretto kept Pietro informed, followed in his master's footsteps as he courted the fair maidens of the city, carried *billets doux* for him and, from time to time, collected some crumb which his master had cast aside. Serving Pietro had numerous advantages – delights, in truth – which meant that Landretto would not have changed his station for all the world.

'Well then, you have abandoned Messer Casanova to his fate?'

Pietro glanced back at the palace and murmured a silent prayer for his friend. Casanova, too, had been condemned to five years for offences against the Holy Office. Another expiatory sacrifice.

'I hope that he will come through it unscathed.'

He turned to his valet, who opened his arms wide to illustrate what delights he had brought with him. And he was truly laden.

'Here is something to bring you to yourself again,' said Landretto.

Pietro stood before a pier-glass contemplating his reflection with satisfaction. He had washed and powdered himself with an extravagance that he had been denied during the months of his incarceration. He tied up his hair and adjusted the wig which Landretto handed to him. He powdered himself again, slipped on his pale Venetian jacket trimmed and adorned with gold. Then a black coat whose long tails fell to his ankles. He checked his cuffs and the ruffled collar and threaded a belt about his waist, snapping the buckle. He drew his sword, letting it whistle through the air, and taking his guard, he examined the finely worked hilt before slipping it into its scabbard with a joyful cry. He holstered two pistols by his side and covered them with the folds of his coat. He slid a long, finely honed dagger into his boot;

then carefully polished the buttons on his sleeves. Landretto turned, spraying his master in a vaporous cloud of perfume. Lastly, Pietro donned a wide-brimmed hat, whistling as he adjusted the brim, then seized his cane carved in the shape of a lion. A winged lion, like the insignia of Venice.

'Master, you have forgotten something,' said Landretto.

Smiling, he handed Pietro a black flower. Pietro smiled back and pinned the flower to his lapel, arranging the petals carefully. He glanced one last time in the mirror. The master of appearance, a man of a thousand faces, a virtuoso in the arts of love and of seduction, and one of the finest duellists in all Italy. The Black Orchid had returned!

Pietro smiled again. 'I am ready.'

CANTO III

LIMBO

Night was falling over Venice. Pietro savoured every instant of this freedom, this homecoming to the city he loved. Though on his way to the Teatro San Luca to investigate a murder of grisly horror, he was feeling particularly alive. He had shivered with delight as he stepped, for the first time in many months, onto the gondola which now sliced through the dark waters heading for San Luca. An hour earlier he had rediscovered the many and varied disguises he had been wont to use on his missions. This evening, he had chosen to add a beauty spot to his powdered face and was wearing an eyepatch beneath his broad-brimmed hat, which gave him the appearance of a buccaneer.

Onward! And as Emilio might say ... let the merriment commence. Standing in the prow of the gondola while Landretto sat in the stern, Pietro felt the cool darkness of the twilight and his soul exulted to be reunited with the splendours he had last savoured almost a year ago. Venice. *His* city. Six *sestieri*, each of which he knew like the back of his hand: San Marco, Castello and Cannaregio on this side of the *Canal Grande*, and Dorsoduro, San Polo and Santa Croce on the other. The *sestieri* comprised seventy-two parishes and Pietro knew each of them intimately. As a boy he had bounded from gondola to gondola, zipped like an arrow across the bridges, eager to lose himself in the delights of these labyrinthine streets. He had played on the *piazzi* of San Samuele and San Luca, by the drinking fountains, in the churchyards, in front of the shops of wine merchants and tailors, apothecaries, greengrocers and timber merchants ... He had run up and down the Mercerie, which linked San Marco to the Rialto, stopping before the dairymaids with their churns, the stalls where butchers, cheesemakers and jewellers laid out their wares. He would pilfer something small and run away, laughing, in a volley of insults ...

He smiled, but slowly the smile faded. These days, Venice had a rather different air. The rapture Pietro felt was now tinged with unease as, still standing in the prow of the gondola, they slipped past decrepit villas, some already foundering, water pouring in from all sides; facades buttressed with makeshift struts. The balconies, the *altane* made for sighs and declarations of love, seemed about to collapse. Venice had always suffered from a climate which was harsher than one might think. In summer, the wells of fresh water often ran dry; in winter the groaning sheet of ice over the *laguna* was transformed into a skating rink. Pietro remembered cheerful moments when, slipping free of Julia's petticoats, he would slide and sprawl across the ice between the doge's palace and the Giudecca, over waves suddenly frozen into a thousand crystal shards carpeted with snowflakes which fell silently from a leaden sky. To him, these were magical memories, but they had taken their toll on the buildings of Venice. Then there were the earthquakes, and the constant fires that had forced the government to establish a special squad lead by an 'official equipped with a hydraulic machine'. More frequent still was the torrential rain which caused a terrifying rise in the water level, the virulently destructive *acqua alta*. The public offices strove to react, to restore and to beautify the city, numbering the buildings, improving public hygiene and sanitation and constantly restoring and rebuilding the *sestieri*. Now the porters with their lanterns who helped pedestrians in the maze of streets in the dark had been joined by the *Signori della notte* – the Lords of the Night – entrusted to safeguard the inhabitants of Venice. A vast project to light the city was in progress, and streetlights had begun to appear all over the city.

Pietro shivered. The temperature plummeted at night and now he felt cold. He turned up the collar of his coat and reopened the dossier which Emilio Vindicati had given him. He ran his gloved hand over the leather wallet for an instant. The matter was, it appeared, deathly grave.

> *Truly, it is an abominable crime, unparalleled in the annals of Venice, but certain details might lead one to suspect that this is not some gratuitous act. Indeed, the manner in which the assassin has disposed the scene may veil some political threat, something which might very well perturb the most noble personages in the republic.*

The victim, Marcello Torretone, was not unknown to Pietro. Marcello was an actor of some renown. The Council's report succinctly encapsulated the details of the victim's life and character. Born in the *sestiere* Santa Croce, his parents, like Pietro's, had worked in the theatre – this common trait could not but bring him closer to the deceased. Marcello had taken to the boards as a boy. His father had died on the steps of the theatre of gangrene from an infected wound. His mother, Arcangela, an invalid at the age of thirty-three, retired to the convent of San Biagio de la Giudecca. At first the young Marcello had played juvenile roles at the Teatro San Moisé, where he attracted the attention of the *capomico*; he left to join the repertory company of the Teatro San Luca two years later. But it was another matter in the dossier that attracted Pietro's attention. Marcello Torretone had had a zealous Catholic upbringing. According to the police report, Marcello's mother had been devout to the point of mania, utterly obsessed with sin, an obsession her son had inherited. According to the report, the boy had grown up with a troubled, complex personality. He too was accustomed to multiple identities. *A comrade of sorts*, thought Pietro.

Sin. This was something that had always fascinated Pietro. He had often been reproached for sins, things which Pietro saw as only as the satisfaction of natural urges. Certainly, he had cuckolded a number of senators and driven Octavio's wife to distraction. At times, perhaps, he had gone too far, but Pietro had only ever followed his heart. But the mirror held up to him was always that of sin – the mark of evil on earth and in the heart of man.

Perhaps it had been because of his upbringing; his mother's obsessive piety and his own rejection by the church, that Marcello Torretone had felt called upon to play the role of a man consumed by fear, by dread. For Pietro, it enabled him to play his favourite part – the secret agent – a role of which he never tired. Playing this role, Pietro had begun to realise, was a logical extension of the roles he had played all his life: in the military, at countless masked balls, at the hunt with noblemen of Venice ... Now, in the blink of an eye, he had moved from being a prisoner in *i piombi* to the role of government agent.

He had had to deploy all of his talent, his charm, and his artifice to be worthy of this role he had fashioned for himself – a role entirely founded on appearances, which proved a poor camouflage for his weaknesses. Mercurial and hungry for recognition, Pietro rushed to meet adversity head on – a foible he not only recognised, but cultivated – as though he were determined to question the founding principles of this society, to challenge its arrogant certainty. Pietro was certain of nothing. In this game he played on a razor's edge, on the brink of the abyss, and his nonchalance fed upon the fever his exploits inspired in others. This freedom came at a price: many bore a furious resentment towards him. What they called his inconstancy, his dissipation, was often no more than a reflection of their own desire to be like him. He was in the service of power, and also a thorn in its side; he rebelled against all forms of authority. Pietro was a free man. This, surely, was why so many feared him.

Pietro knew in his heart that the whiff of scandal which hung about him was both the fruit of his actions and the latent frustration of his critics. To imitate him would have been a simple matter: one would merely have to embrace the uncertainty of complete self-abnegation to the dictates of the heart, something all civilised societies strove to contain. Pietro had never been able to rid himself of this disquiet. When he thought of it, it induced a dizzying fever, which thrilled him and threatened to overwhelm him. And yet God, love, women, all these things stirred his soul, but if he felt himself being drawn too close he withdrew, ever afraid of becoming a mere plaything. It was pride which saved him, and pride which damned him. And this impasse in his heart filled him with a sense of emptiness, of ridiculousness – feelings in which those around him seemed to delight.

And then there had been Anna Santamaria, the Black Widow. The only woman who might have changed him, who might have swept him up in her net. The Black Widow ... It had been Emilio who had first given her the soubriquet. Pietro could no longer quite remember why. Perhaps because her very beauty was so startling it seemed dangerous. A beauty that coursed through a man like venom, though she looked for all the world like an angel come to earth. But also, perhaps, because she was a widow, in a certain sense. Widowed by the love she had never had. She was in mourning for a life which was not hers by right. For her, Pietro knew, he would have renounced his freedom, he would have come to heel. Had he met her in other circumstances; had her family not betrothed her to Ottavio, thrust her into the arms of this man she did not love, she might have borne Pietro's children. He would have used his political connections to secure an honourable profession. Things might have been different. From the moment he first saw her in the house of his protector Senator Ottavio, even as she was introduced to him as his patron's future wife, he had seen his destiny written in her eyes. He had known he would love her. She had known that she could not spurn him. In that instant, their fate was sealed. Together they would rush headlong into disaster. The solemn look which passed between them, their laboured breaths ... A Black Widow and a Black Orchid. She was not a widow, nor he an orchid, and yet they would have made a handsome couple. But now ... it had left Pietro with a bitter taste in his mouth. The alien taste of something unfinished. A taste for revenge ... Anna ... Where might she be? He hoped, truly hoped, that wherever she was, she was not too unhappy. But he dared not risk their lives again ... and he did not care to brood upon his pain. He had promised Emilio that he would not attempt to see her – it had been the *sine qua non* of his release. He tried not to think of her, tried not to wonder if she loved him still. Though he did not try too hard.

Come ... try to forget. Pietro tried to calm himself. After all, he reminded himself, he was a free man and he would live as he had always lived: he would transform this headlong flight into a conviction which would be a fount of energy by which he might grow and be fulfilled. He had his freedom again, yet his heart did not rejoice, for he was both a gambler and philosopher, gifted yet troubled, a hunter in constant pursuit of a glory he scorned. But as he had told the doge, he too had his principles: he was an adventurer in search of love, of passion, he knew the true meaning of justice and, if he had tasted the fruits of darkness, he had learned its snares and its illusions. He knew all too well the line that demarcated great good from great evil, a line he endeavoured not to cross. Perhaps from some last vestige of respect for a God he had forsaken. Perhaps only out of self-respect, for Pietro fervently believed that such was his responsibility as a man, even if he could not always be an 'honest man'. From the moment he had stepped free of his prison he had been consumed by the thought of satisfying insistent urges pent up for too long. But he could not break his word to Emilio, at least not yet. So whatever the feast, it would have to wait.

Ah! We are here.

As the gondola pulled into San Luca, Pietro put away the report filed by the Council of Ten and stepped onto the pier with Landretto close behind. Together they walked carefully through the slippery alleyways towards the *campo* where the Teatro San Luca stood. The theatre had been built in 1622 and, like the theatres of San Moisé, San Cassiono and Sant'Angelo, it had taken its name from the parish. Since they had begun to forsake commerce and trade, many of the city nobles had begun to invest in the theatre. Padua had shown the way, and it had been here that the first theatre repertory had been founded, with actors contracted exclusively to a single theatre and rewarded with a share of profits for their enterprise. From this, the professional theatre had been born. Each was managed by a *capomico* who employed actors contracted to play Harlequin, Pantaloon or Brighella. The opera, which had first flowered in Florence and Mantua, began to blossom in Venice. The Teatro San Luca was owned by the Vendramin brothers, who were among the few theatre owners to directly employ playwrights and actors, since most investors delegated the management to an *impresario*, himself an actor or a minor figure in the nobility. Impresarios were not universally esteemed; actors frequently complained of their shameful lack of culture or their clumsy and continual corruption. This was a pitfall the Vendramin brothers had avoided. Unlike the prestigious Teatri San Giovanni Crisostomo, where opera, tragedy and tragicomedy were played to great acclaim, the Teatro San Luca performed only comedy. Nonetheless, it had become one of the most successful theatres in Venice.

Pietro stood at the foot of the building in front of a facade of pale sandstone, double doors in dark wood flanked by Doric columns. A man holding a lantern awaited them. Pietro handed the man his letter of safe conduct bearing the ducal seal. He ordered Landretto to wait outside. The doors were opened and Pietro entered.

The San Luca theatre was everything it was reputed to be, a little dusty perhaps, but the rows of red velvet seats trimmed with gold gave it an air of distinction and the hall itself was lavishly decorated. Four balconies contained 170 private boxes, decorated with frescoes and baroque paintings. Here and there were allegorical references to Venice: Callipygian Venus, Diana crowned with stars and surrounded by the Virtues. In the distance was the stage, the lights, the polished boards and the great crimson curtains trimmed with gold braid.

There were three people inside. They spoke in hushed voices, but the tone seemed anxious. One of them he recognised as Francesco Vendramin, one of the brothers who owned the theatre; the face of the second man looked familiar to Pietro though he could not quite place it, and the third was a stranger. Pietro removed his hat and walked towards them. As he approached, the three men fell silent and turned towards him. He nodded to them, proffering his letter of safe conduct.

'I am here on a mission for the Council of Ten,' Pietro said by way of introduction.

For a moment Francesco Vendramin looked surprised, but his look quickly hardened into distrust. Perhaps he feared that he was dealing with one of the Council's inquisitors. The second man approached Pietro. He seemed to be about fifty, his features were neither handsome nor ugly and he wore a jacket edged with black pearls over an immaculate doublet and hose.

'Emilio Vindicati informed us that he would send one of his agents. Signore, your name is ... ?'

'My identity need not concern you,' interrupted Pietro. 'My work here is conducted under a seal of strict secrecy and has been approved at the highest level. Your identity, however, concerns me.'

'My name is Carlo Goldoni.'

Pietro smiled. Now he remembered. He had attended a number of Goldoni's plays – he could still remember *Il cavaliere giocondo* and *Le smanie per la villeggiatura*. Indeed, he knew some of the speeches by heart. Ever eager to discuss the arts, Pietro would have liked to converse further with the brilliant playwright who had been crowned the 'King of Comedy', but the third man walking towards him reminded Pietro that time was of the essence. He had a grey beard and wore a dark tunic with a white ruff. He was holding an open knapsack in which Pietro could make out a number of surgical instruments.

'I am Antonio Brozzi, coroner with the Quarantia Criminale.'

It was at that moment that Pietro noticed the smell. The foul stench of blood and putrefaction overwhelmed him and he tried to make out from whence it came. He turned towards the crimson drapes.

'Prepare yourself for what you are about to see, Messer,' said Brozzi. 'I have been waiting upon your arrival. We have much work to do.' He nodded to Vendramin, who whistled to someone in the wings. Pietro saw a shadowy figure hoist the curtains.

Oh, sweet Lord. The scene was revealed to him in all its abject horror.

In the middle of the stage was a man – if this carrion might still be called a man. He hung suspended above a pool of clotting blood that had spurted over half the stage.

The man's feet had been nailed to a post. Tight-lipped, Pietro lifted his black eyepatch for a moment. He gazed up. The corpse was completely naked. A deep gash had lacerated the man's side. Marcello Torretone had been crucified. His arms, spread wide, had been nailed to the cross-beam. As he studied the livid corpse Pietro choked back a cry of revulsion. The body wore a crown of thorns – but there was something else. The eyes had been gouged from their sockets. Marcello's mouth was fixed in a terrible rictus. At his feet glittering shards of glass mingled with blood. Cut into his torso was an inscription although from where he stood, Pietro could not make out what it said. After a moment he climbed onto the stage as the coroner appointed by the Quarantia Criminale mounted the stairs at the other corner of the stage. The two men met at the foot of the body.

'When precisely did he die?' Pietro addressed Goldoni and Vendramin.

'That is something only Sier Brozzi can tell us,' answered Vendramin. 'There was a performance last night ...'

'Ah yes, *The Businessman from Smyrna*,' said Goldoni. 'A comedy in three acts. Marcello, may his soul rest in peace, played Ali, a merchant from the Orient who has come to Venice where he wishes to found an opera company.'

Brozzi put down his open case and began to survey the scene. Pietro drew nearer to the mutilated body upon whose disfigured torso he managed to read:

Io ero nuovo in questo stato,
Quando ci vidi venire un possente
Con Segno di vittoria coronato

I was new to this condition when I beheld
A Mighty One who descended here arrayed
With a crown of victory

The inscription was cut into the flesh and, here and there, one could glimpse the ribs. The inscription, scrawled in tiny letters, continued across the whole torso as though the author of this crime had used the body as a piece of parchment. Brozzi, in turn, slipped on his pince-nez and read the inscription. For a moment he looked like an alchemist on the brink of discovering the secret of the philosopher's stone.

He grunted in disgust and turned to Pietro. 'Does it mean anything to you?'

'No,' Pietro admitted. 'Though the turn of phrase seems familiar.'

'The scene before us is clearly intended to be a biblical allegory.'

'You think the passage comes from the Bible?'

Behind them, Vendramin murmured, 'The performance ended at eleven o'clock. The company would have left at about midnight, at which time I can assure you that the theatre was empty.'

'Empty? Did anyone actually see Marcello leave?'

Goldoni and Vendramin exchanged a glance. 'In truth, no,' said the playwright. 'No one in the company saw him after the performance.'

'Then it would be more accurate to say that you *believed* the theatre was empty,' said Pietro. 'Marcello might have stayed behind after you left, hiding in the wings perhaps?'

As he said this, Pietro stepped around the corpse and into the wings, which were plunged in darkness. Ropes and stays trailed along the floor. There was a basin of water tinged with blood and a rag smeared with crimson. A faint odour of vinegar floated above the stench of death. Resting against the wall was a lance, a theatrical prop. But the sharp metal tip was all too real – it had been used to pierce Marcello's side and, perhaps, to gouge out his eyes. It too was streaked with blood.

'Hiding?' muttered Vendramin, astonished. 'But why would he hide?'

'I have no idea,' said Pietro. 'Perhaps he had an assignation with a woman ... or with someone else?'

Stumbling upon a heap of clothing which had been abandoned in a dark corner behind the curtain, Pietro leaned down and saw a turban, a pair of breeches, and a long-sleeved tunic which looked very much like a Turkish caftan. Marcello's costume in *L'impresario delle Smirne*, perhaps, or a costume for Pantaloon, the bigoted penny-pinching Venetian merchant – a favourite character in Italian comedy. Nearby was a trunk stuffed with costumes for Zanni, Villano or Magnifico, some shimmering and gaudy, others threadbare and austere. Pietro rummaged through the masks and the fineries.

'Was Marcello having an affair? Did he have any enemies that you know of?'

After a moment's hesitation, Goldoni answered. 'Affairs, yes. Enemies, no. You know how actors are. He had a woman here, a woman there but Marcello was not close to anyone. We often saw him in the company of the courtesans who ply the Mercerie after nightfall. I believe Marcello did not truly understand women. He gave the impression that he cared little for them. As to enemies, he had none that I know of. On the contrary, he was much loved ...'

There was a silence as Pietro walked back to the centre of the stage. Brozzi, kneeling, was examining the wounds on Marcello's feet where they had been nailed to the cross. Taking a brush, he cleaned the blood from around the nails, measured the gash in Marcello's side and then turned to rummage in his medical bag. Pietro knelt beside him. Brozzi took out a small translucent flask and, using another brush, gathered the splinters of glass which formed a halo in the shadow of the crucifixion. The two men again exchanged a glance.

'Glass ...'

Pietro picked up a shard or two which he then slipped into a kerchief.

The two men stood up. Brozzi mopped his forehead, staring up at the gaping eye sockets – dark holes ringed with vermillion. Glints of silver were visible in the gouged wounds and a jagged splinter hung from a tattered flap of eyelid.

'I would not be surprised to discover that the eyes were gouged out with a piece of glass. In time he would have died of his wounds. *Santa Maria*, what fiend could have perpetrated such an abomination?'

Pietro pursed his lips. 'Brozzi, I take it the Quarantia Criminale have taken you into their confidence,' he said in a whisper. 'So, tell me … What is the connection between the murder of an actor and the government of the Serene Republic?'

Brozzi coughed and looked at Pietro over his pince-nez. 'The connection?'

With his index finger he pointed to a small object on the stage which Pietro had overlooked. 'There is the connection, Messer.'

Pietro walked over to the object and turned it between his fingers. It was a gold brooch with the letters *L* and *S* entwined and, above the initials, a pair of crossed swords and a rose in mother-of-pearl. Pietro looked at Brozzi enquiringly.

'*L* and *S*,' observed the physician. 'The rose and the crossed swords suggests that it belongs to Luciana Saliestri, a famous courtesan and mistress of Giovanni Campioni who, as you know, is one of the most powerful men in the Senate. There are those who suspect him of, shall we say, being too fond of the populace. Campioni, it is said, has his own ideas for reforming the republic, and has deliberately passed over those whose ideas do not agree with his own. Some say he is an idealist whose ideas are dangerous; others claim that his altruistic ideas are merely a mask for his own lust for power. Campioni has long been an ambassador, representing the interests of the republic in England, in France, and in the Netherlands, where he has befriended philosophers and men of power. There are those who claim he wishes to implement these preposterous foreign theories to style a new government.'

Brozzi slipped his hands into his black cape. 'The relationship between the doge, the State, and the good people of Venice, as you know, has always been a complex one, but one on which the survival of our constitution rests. And it is a delicate balance. Our system of government has always been more advanced than those of other peoples; it is the envy of all Europe. Venice is free but closely guarded. The love the people bear the state is absolute, yet shrewd. It is always difficult to find a balance between such extremes, difficult to always heed the voice of reason when passions can flare at any moment and at times veer towards unexpected violence. It would take little for the edifice to crumble to one side or the other and it is this that terrifies our politicians. They are determined to snuff out any spark; nothing may be allowed to fester which might be injurious to the republic. The spectre of Bedmar still walks abroad. To that, add the fact that Campioni has the allegiance of more than a third of the members of the Maggior Consiglio. It is hardly surprising, then, that the Dark Council imagine that they see in this some conspiracy. Hardly a week goes by when they do not imagine they have uncovered a plot. But there is something of which you have not perhaps been informed ... something which might make you more disposed to give credence to such a conspiracy.'

'What do you mean?'

Brozzi smiled enigmatically and said in a whisper, 'Marcello Torretone was not simply an actor, Messer. He, like you, was the servant of two masters – he was a secret agent for the Council of Ten and the Quarantia Criminale. The Tenebrae referred to him as Harlequin.'

'Ah. I see. It is an important detail, and one which they were careful to omit from their report. Emilio should have informed me.'

He got up. 'Thank you, Sier Brozzi.'

Pietro pursed his lips pensively. Emilio Vindicati must have known this when he entrusted him with this mission. Furthermore, the report he had been given had said nothing of Luciana Saliestri, nor made mention of Senator Giovanni Campioni. Perhaps, rather than risk committing such names to paper, Emilio had allowed him to discover them through Brozzi. A man can never be too careful, especially in matters concerning personages of the highest rank in the republic …

Whatever the case, thought Pietro, *none of this bodes well …*

The murder now appeared to him in a very different light than it had when he had first read the report. Now he understood what sin might mean to Marcello, how a fear of some divine retribution might have influenced his character. His secret life had finally caught up with him. The role of Harlequin, the servant of two masters, took on a new meaning. In his service to the Serene Republic, Marcello would have had to conceal that which he could cry aloud from the stage, but only by proxy, only in the guise of ephemeral roles which offered merely illusory redemption. It was this weakness the Council of Ten had wished to exploit when they recruited Marcello to the ranks of their informants. By joining them, Marcello agreed to act in silence for the public good; but even this represented a loss of face for, after all, he, like Pietro, had merely become one of the countless paltry messengers of the *Serenissima*. Whom had he denounced, whom had he betrayed? Had he killed, did he have another man's blood on his hands? Pietro had a sense of the terrible confusion which Marcello must have felt, caught between the twin faces of Janus in moments of despair. An actor and an agent of the republic; he was caught between Scylla and Charybdis.

Pietro stepped down from the stage. Goldoni was sitting in the theatre, his head in his hands, devastated.

'This, I think, is the last straw,' he said. 'I have long planned to retire to Parma. I think that time has come.'

'Carlo,' said Vendramin. 'It's out of the question – what about carnival? You promised me three more plays and they must go on as planned. The autumn season was a triumph; in large part due to you. We have both finally achieved what we have always dreamed of. There can be no more talk of giving up. If this terrible business is hushed up, as I hope it will be, then there will be no scandal. If we are the only ones who know …'

'Messer Goldoni, there can be no question of your leaving Venice for the moment,' said Pietro. 'For the duration of the investigation you must remain here in the city. As soon as it can be arranged, I shall need to speak to everyone in the company: the librettist, the members of the orchestra, the stage designer, choreographer, and the members of the chorus. In short, everyone who worked in the Teatro San Luca.'

'But … If you do so, then this will be public knowledge …' cried Vendramin. 'It will destroy the theatre.'

'There will need to be some explanation for Marcello's disappearance, but you need have no fear, each shall be told as much as is necessary, no more. The details of this ignoble crime are to be told to no one except on my express authority – though I'll wager you have no wish to do so.'

Vendramin and Goldoni nodded their assent. Pietro turned once more to the crucified cadaver. 'One final question …'

'Yes?' asked Goldoni.

'Marcello was a religious man, I believe?'

'He was,' said Goldoni. 'Few in the theatre render unto the good Lord that which is his by right, but Marcello, despite leading a turbulent and sometimes foolhardy life, went to the church of San Giorgio Maggiore every Sunday.'

Pietro frowned pensively. Would a spy be so assiduous in his spiritual duties? Perhaps, thought Pietro, but what intrigued him was the connection between Marcello's evident religious temperament and the symbolic nature of his murder. It was an idea worth pursuing: a man consumed with the constant thought of his sins, crucified on the very stage where he practised his deception amid the costumes of the various characters he played, his eyes gouged out ... Had Marcello *seen* something which made him a threat? Was there a link between the murder and Marcello's faith – or was Pietro simply imagining a connection where there was none?

Suddenly, he had a thought. 'Who is the priest at San Giorgio Maggiore?'

It was Vendramin who responded this time. 'Father Cosimo Caffelli.'

Caffelli. Well, well ...

'I know the man,' said Pietro.

'He was also Marcello's confessor,' added Goldoni.

'His confessor, you say? Interesting ...'

Pietro stopped and brought his fingers to his lips. Caffelli had crossed his path in the past, and the good father could not help but remember the Black Orchid. After all it had been Caffelli who, at the request of Senator Octavio, had accused Pietro, before the holy inquisition, of atheism, conspiracy and immorality. The priest had played an important role in Pietro's incarceration. This promises to be interesting ...

Pietro smiled. 'Thank you, gentlemen.'

Brozzi called to him and Pietro turned. The coroner was still on the stage. He opened his arms wide and rolled up his sleeves.

'If you could help me take down him now?'

The body of Marcello Torretone was laid out upon a slab in one of the cellars reserved for the use of the Quarantia Criminale. There was no gilded moulding or marble panelling here; just walls of bleak, bare stone. A glacial wind whipped in from the basement window which looked out onto the alley. For a moment, Pietro felt as if he were back in his prison cell. In the centre of the room Brozzi busied himself. Despite his revulsion, Pietro had helped the physician lay the body, stiff with rigor mortis, on the examining table. Brozzi had begun his detailed examination. There was no need for dissection, but it was vital that Brozzi should miss nothing of the exact nature of Marcello's wounds, which alone could tell him what had occurred. Murmuring to himself, Brozzi clipped his pince-nez onto his nose and examined Torretone's hair, the vacant sockets of his eyes, his teeth, his tongue, the wounds to his feet and hands, the gash in his side, and the inscription which had been carved onto his torso. The physician then paced the room, stopping to examine the fingernails, then to study a bruise on the thigh. He had sprayed the room with perfume but it had done little to dissipate the terrible stench. His medical bag lay open by his side; his instruments neatly arranged on a small table covered with a white napkin: scalpels and surgical knives, scissors, magnifying glass, brushes, callipers, surgical spirit, and a variety of strange chemicals. Near at hand stood a basin in which Brozzi rinsed his instruments from time to time, the clank of metal on metal echoing in the stark basement. Pietro had seen a good many dead bodies and yet, as he stood in the middle of this icy chamber lit by the dim glow of a pair of lanterns, he could not help but shiver. The very sight of this withered carcass, the pale flesh traversed by bluish veins, whose very eyes had been ripped out, chilled his soul. And watching Brozzi manhandle the victim like so much butcher's meat was particularly sickening. *To think I had planned to visit the secret garden of some forsaken damsel this evening,* thought Pietro. He had hoped to lose himself between the breasts, thighs, and buttocks of some maiden so that he might forget Anna Santamaria and the long months spent in prison. Instead, Pietro found himself before this lifeless body laid out upon its funereal shroud, trying to learn what he could about the case. Bent over the corpse Brozzi's audible observations were intended as much for himself as for Pietro.

'Lesion to the left flank caused by the tip of a lance found in the wings of the Teatro San Luca. The weapon was recovered at the scene. The wound is deep, puncturing the left side, but missing the heart itself; it would have hastened the victim's death, but not in itself have killed him. The body was composed in order to mimic Christ on the cross; a crown of thorns was pushed down onto the forehead and there are traces of vinegar on the lips.'

Pietro had taken advantage of their journey back to the Quarantia to become better acquainted with this curious man. As physician to the Quarantia Criminale for more than ten years, he too, was sworn to secrecy.

Antonio Brozzi was not of noble birth, he was a mere *cittadino* whose abilities had elevated him to his present rank. He had previously acted as personal physician to a number of senators and members of the Maggior Consiglio. In this way his fame and his reputation had spread. Antonio had been honoured when called upon to serve the republic and his devotion had stood him in good stead, he confided to Pietro, given the morbid nature of his work. His own father had been murdered on a Santa Croce street corner, an incident not unrelated to the young Antonio's later decision to become a coroner.

Pietro mopped his brow, beginning to feel weary. He stifled a yawn and said, 'This is all just theatre – a piece of stagecraft. The open drapes which seem to frame the scene ... I am beginning to think that the mind that conceived this murder is less brutish than it first appears. Or rather, a brutish man concealed by the most elegant manner. There is something in the cruel sophistication of this which is the mark of the true decadent. The crucifixion, the curious, enigmatic poem carved into the torso, everything was chosen for dramatic effect …'

'It is possible,' Brozzi continued his commentary, 'that the victim was forced to drink vinegar from a rag so that he would be forced to endure the same torments which Christ suffered on his path from Calvary until his death. The eyes have been entirely excised. The remains of the right eyeball contains particles of a piece of glass which shattered as it cut the optic nerve. The glass itself is soft and highly polished. It should be possible to trace the glassblower. From the craftsmanship and the translucence it may well be from Murano. The shards are too small to determine anything further.'

'The thing is, Brozzi, Marcello could have been murdered because of his work for the Council of Ten and the Criminale, but why stage the murder in such a curious manner? Why these veiled references, this mocking invitation to step onto the stage as if we too were intended to play a part in this drama conceived and written by a madman? A playwright who has little in common with Sier Goldoni, whom I think I can eliminate as a suspect, together with the Vendramin brothers. But the murderer is a lover of the theatre, of spectacle … of Pantaloon, whose costume I found rolled into a ball not far from the body. Then there is the brooch you found, the one which belongs to Luciana Saliestri. A strange coincidence, don't you think? Too strange, perhaps to be a coincidence, unless perhaps Marcello was her lover. But Luciana was already the lover of Senator Giovanni Campioni. I would be relieved to think this was the banal result of a lover's jealousy, but I cannot believe it. Everything about the murder has been diabolically contrived, Brozzi.'

The physician looked up and said, 'Contrived indeed. Just as a playwright contrives a scene and decides the fate of his characters. I am of the same opinion.'

'Considerable effort and skill were required to carry out

this terrible crime. Upon this deserted stage Marcello would have screamed from the moment the hammer fell, driving the first nail into the cross, until the moment, many hours later, when he finally succumbed. This is no mere *vendetta* which might have been settled more quickly, more cleanly with a sword, a pistol or an harquebus. The idea is too grotesque: the murderer wanted Marcello to suffer, wanted to make him *talk*. This was *torture*. But even if it were, Brozzi, why stage the scene so meticulously? Why not abduct Marcello and kill him elsewhere?'

'Because we were intended to find him, *amico*,' said Brozzi, bending over the body once more.

Pietro clicked his tongue approvingly. 'You have a point. The strange inscription on the torso is further proof that the murderer was attempting to tell us something. This was not *commonplace* torture, if I may use the word, it was a message intended specifically for us – by which I mean for the republic itself. But there is something else that puzzles me ...'

'The eyes?' asked Brozzi, taking his kerchief to wipe his pince-nez. Sweat beaded on his forehead.

Pietro raised his finger and smiled. 'Indeed. The eyes. Why gouge out his eyes? There is nothing like it in the Passion. Perhaps it was a mistake, one false note in this pale imitation of the crucifixion, and yet I fear that nothing here is attributable to chance.

'Well, we have threads enough to follow already: the courtesan, Luciana Silvestri; the senator, Giovanni Campioni, and perhaps Marcello's confessor at San Giorgio; Father Caffelli.'

Pietro sighed, remembering what Emilio had said as they left the doge's palace: Mark my words, you are about to step into the antechamber of hell, as you shall soon discover.

Pietro glanced at Brozzi, who smiled, scratching his beard. He tossed a bloody stylet into the basin with a soft clank. Blood eddied in the water.

'Welcome to limbo, where the cases of the Quarantia Criminale dwell,' he said.

Pietro made his way though the streets of Venice toward the *albergo* where he and Landretto were to stay until Emilio arranged more comfortable lodgings for them. He walked slowly, his eyes fixed on the street, his hands clasped behind his back, still plagued with sombre thoughts. It was late. A chill wind whipped the tails of his greatcoat. As he turned into a side street, lost in thought, he barely noticed the four men. Dressed in dark clothes and carrying lanterns, they might have passed for Lords of the Night had it not been for the unsettling masks they wore. In the half-light they seemed somehow fantastical, like wraiths. By the time Pietro became aware of their presence, he was cornered. Two men barred the way ahead, the others blocked the way back. Beneath their masks he could see their twisted smiles. They set down their lanterns and the alley, for a moment, looked like a stage as the curtain rises, or a splendid hall as an important dignitary arrives. Pietro looked up.

'To what do I owe the pleasure, gentlemen?'

'To your good fortune that we should so kindly relieve you of your purse, Messer,' quipped one of the thieves.

Pietro studied the speaker and the man beside him, then turned to look at the two standing firmly at his back. All were armed, one with a bludgeon, another a dagger, and the others brandished short swords.

Slowly, Pietro smiled. 'And should I choose to decline your generous offer?'

'Then we may choose to cut your throat, Messer.'

'At the very least, you shall lose your one good eye,' said his friend, nodding to the eye patch Pietro was still wearing.

I see.

'Decidedly it is no longer safe to walk abroad in Venice these days.'

'Don't I know it. Come on. Cough up.'

'Gentlemen, I feel I should warn you that were I blind, I could outwit the four of you. Walk away, and I shall not harm you and, believe me, you shall be getting off lightly.'

The men cackled. 'Hear that? On your knees, sir, and hand over your *zecchini*.'

'I feel obliged to reiterate my warning.'

'Reiterate what you like, just hand over your reticule.' The man stepped forward menacingly.

Very well, thought Pietro. *A little exercise will do me no harm.*

He drew himself up to his full height, slowly opened his coat and let it drop to the ground revealing the sword and the pair of pistols at his side. His adversaries hesitated for an instant. Pietro placed a hand on the hilt of his sword. The brigands advanced, closing in on him.

'Very well, for your sakes I shall use only my rapier,' said Pietro. He drew his sword. The blade glinted in the moonlight as the four pseudo *Signori della Notte* fell upon him. It all happened in an instant. There was a flash, and then another, then the sword cleaved the air, slashing the first man who dropped his bludgeon. The second man's dagger traced a graceful arc across the night sky followed by three of his fingers which Pietro had severed. He spun around to face the others. He dropped to one knee as the third man lunged, his sword stabbing the empty air as Pietro slashed the back of the man's knees, felling him. He stood up again suddenly and, still spinning, with a lunge he had perfected, traced upon the brow of the fourth a five-point star which immediately streamed blood. The man's mask fell to the ground. He stared for a moment and then, more out of fear than pain, he reeled and fell in a faint at Pietro's feet.

All four were down; one clutched at his shoulder, howling, another groped for his missing fingers, the third tried to stanch his bleeding calves and the fourth, the ringleader, had left for the more clement skies of oblivion.

Pietro smiled, picked up his coat and, taking the orchid from his buttonhole, approached the man doubled up in pain and clutching his bleeding legs. The man stifled his screams and looked up. Pietro dropped the flower which fluttered to the ground at the man's feet. Then he turned on his heel and walked away.

The man stared, wide-eyed at the flower. It was a signature. It said: The Black Orchid was here.

THE SECOND CIRCLE

CANTO IV

THE LUSTFUL

Luciana Saliestri was not among those gracious ladies called upon to grace the official receptions at which Venice, not content to flex its political might, liked to parade the flower of its youth. That she was thought undesirable was hardly surprising since Luciana, though illustrious, was a courtesan of tumultuous fortune. Luciana prided herself on being a writer of verse and philosophy, and used this facade of respectability to conceal her smouldering sensuality. Her intoxicating charm lay in the fact that she embodied Madonna and whore, scholar and slattern, the dregs of society and the flower of youthful nobility. Thought of as a *puttana*, she was bound by the injunctions of the law; in practice, a benighted indifference and the protection of her powerful lovers meant that she had no fear of judicial wrath. She was, in a way, an institution unto herself: if she sold her body it was to enthral distinguished visitors, to facilitate crucial business dealings or to relieve the quotidian tensions of important political figures. Certainly, the inquisitors persecuted the *puttani*, but they contented themselves with hounding the penniless whores who worked the *campo* San Polo and the gallerias of San Marco and Santa Trinità. For her part, Luciana, a widow from the age of twenty-two after the death of her husband, an enormously wealthy textile merchant famed for his avarice, strolled around the gardens of the doge's palace, taking delight in stoking the fires of her nebulous reputation. She was a charming creature: she had a face of startling loveliness, dark expressive eyes, a beauty spot in the corner of her mouth and a perfect body; her curves accentuated by gowns of moiré silk, flounces and lace. She had been a dancer and her gait alone could entice a passing stranger. To these charms she would add the spice of mystery to inflame a man's imagination: donning a mask or dazzling him with witty, enigmatic conversation; thus, with her wiles, did she fetter the hearts of her admirers. She received guests in her *palazzo* overlooking the Grand Canal which, along with so many things, she had inherited. Marriage had spared her the anonymity of the convent, but it was to widowhood that she owed her freedom. Messer Saliestri's penny-pinching was legendary; it was whispered that he counted time in fractions of a ducat and thought it a rare resource. To this day, Luciana paid tribute to this consummate skinflint. She burned votive candles to his memory as she burned her way through the fortune he had spent a life accruing, as profligate as her husband had been parsimonious. Luciana had found other activities to satisfy her propensities: she gave herself to any man she thought worthy of her. For a time she had toyed with the affections of Marcello, but with Senator Giovanni Campioni she was playing for altogether higher stakes. Clearly, however – unless she were dissembling, something of which she was quite capable – she knew nothing of the events at the Teatro San Luca.

Following Emilio Vindicati's instructions, Pietro had burned the report his mentor had delivered the previous evening. He had spent his morning with Brozzi and Landretto interrogating the personnel of the theatre, establishing alibis. The results of their inquiry were scarcely conclusive; consequently he had resolved to meet with Luciana at her villa on the Grand Canal. The Palazzo Saliestri was one of the jewels of Venice whose incomparable glories the idle stroller, deceived by the dilapidated facade, could barely imagine. If he could but step through the vaulted gateway he would find a dreamlike garden; winding paths weaving between luxuriant flowerbeds and, at the centre, a fountain. Stepping into the garden was akin to stepping into another world; suddenly the drone of the city miraculously faded, giving way to the restful murmur of water.

The *palazzo* itself ranged over two floors and deployed the same contrasts to harmonious effect. The decrepit walls, mottled here and there with damp, the dappled colour adding to its crumbling beauty, gave no hint of the opulent interiors within. As he entered, Pietro was immediately dazzled by the glow of polished wood, the golden hasps and escutcheons, deep divans upholstered in rich velvets and silks, family portraits, pier-glasses reflecting one another in a luminous *mise en abyme*, doors left discreetly ajar to reveal intimate boudoirs and whorls of shimmering drapes framing niches and alcoves ...

To cross the threshold was to be enveloped in an intimate, baroque cocoon, and yet for Pietro, the encounter was a torment. Though she had heard tell of the Black Orchid, Luciana Saliestri could not know the true identity of this man who presented himself as an emissary of the doge. For his part, Pietro, who had heard much prattle and idle gossip concerning the beautiful courtesan, could not but let his mind stray to crimes more delectable than that which he had witnessed at the Teatro San Luca. Luciana's smile, her lips, her delicate throat, her breasts, which with all her wiles and charms, she flaunted for him; all these things would have been torture for him had not the memory of Anna Santamaria soared like a battlement about his heart. But to feign indifference in the face of Luciana Saliestri's redoubled efforts, her impatient sighs, all the specious artlessness which is the very essence of womanliness, required considerable determination. Pietro ached to give this seductress the punishment she so richly deserved, to force her to surrender to him until she pleaded to be permitted to assuage his desires. Instead he was obliged to speak to her of conspiracies and crucifixion. *I do not know if I can endure much longer.*

He sat facing her in an armchair of amethyst velvet, his fingers drumming on the armrests; she lay semi-recumbent on the divan, glancing from time to time through the open windows towards the balcony and the clamour of the Grand Canal. A copy of Plautus' *Miles Gloriosus* lay casually open by her side.

Pietro was not wearing his eyepatch preferring, on this occasion, to sport a scar which ran down his right cheek and a gold hoop through his right ear. He was wearing a jacket of white and gold and matching gloves. He had removed his dark hat and set it down beside him.

He crossed his legs. 'Can you tell me what you were doing on the night before last?'

A smile. She exhaled sharply, blowing from her forehead a lock of blonde hair, that distinctive reddish blonde so favoured by the women of Venice. Long, languid afternoons had to be spent in the sun to create this colour. A woman would sit out on her *altana* wearing a straw hat from which the lining had been removed, her hair stained with rhubarb juice whose acidity, together with the sun's rays, produced this characteristic colour.

'What does a woman such as I do at night, in your opinion?'

His mouth dry, Pietro forced a smile. 'She would be unlikely to attend the premiere of a new Goldoni play at the Teatro San Luca.'

Luciana ran a finger over her cheekbone flushed with rouge, allowing it to trail down to her throat where she idly toyed with a pendant in the form of a dolphin. She smiled again.

'Ah … A veiled reference to Marcello. I see you are admirably informed about my vices. But no … If truth be told, that night I decided not to work. I stayed here alone, reposing myself: once in a while won't hurt.'

'Alone? Really?' Pietro smiled.

'Luciana, tell me about Senator Giovanni Campioni. I hear that, like Marcello, he too is one of your vices ...'

For a moment Luciana Saliestri seemed startled, then she laughed, quickly regaining her composure.

'Manifestly nothing escapes the eye of the republic!'

'Not inasmuch as it concerns its worthy ambassadors. Was our illustrious senator with you that evening, perchance? Might he be prepared to substantiate ... your alibi?'

Luciana Saliestri frowned. 'Why should I have need of an alibi? I fear there is something I do not understand. Perhaps it is time that you explained the precise reason for your visit.'

She folded one of her legs beneath her, allowing her gown to slide up to her knee. Pietro's brief glance caught a hint of lace which merely magnified his frustration. The distraction was entirely deliberate. Pietro fumbled in the pocket of his coat, opened the kerchief and held the golden brooch beneath her nose.

'Do you recognise this?'

She gave a little cry of amazement, seized the brooch, and studied it minutely.

'It is mine, certainly. Giovanni had it crafted by a goldsmith on the Rialto as an especial gift. It is my brooch, there can be no doubt whatever. Look, here is my monogram. I have been searching for it for two days, it must have been stolen. You may well imagine my distress, fearful as I was of angering Giovanni. But where did you find it?'

'Forgive me if I come as a bird of ill omen ... but the brooch was discovered at the scene of a crime. It was found next to the body of Marcello Torretone.'

Luciana fell silent, her great doe eyes widening. It was magnificent. Whether she was a consummate actress or her incredulity was entirely unfeigned, it was some moments before she came to herself again.

'Marcello ... *dead*? How could such a thing be possible?'

'He was murdered.'

'Lord …'

There was another silence. 'But … how was he done to death?'

Pietro pursed his lips. 'I shall spare you the details, Signora, for they are grisly indeed.'

'But who could have done such a thing?'

'That is precisely what I intend to determine, which is why I would ardently hope that I might count on your cooperation.'

Luciana Saliestri stared vacantly into the middle distance. She brought her hand to her heart as she shook her head, her face suddenly a mask of sorrow.

'My God … This is a tragedy. I had been wondering why I had had no word of Marcello. We had planned an assignation last evening …'

She said no more, keenly aware of Pietro's misgivings. She endeavoured to seem more candid. 'You must believe that I had nothing whatever to do with this! The brooch was stolen from me, what more can I say?'

'Do you have any idea who might have purloined it? Marcello himself, perhaps?'

'What a preposterous suggestion. Why would he do such a thing?'

'And Giovanni?'

'Giovanni? Why should he wish to steal a brooch he himself gave to me? Moreover, he could not have done so, I have not seen him for some time.'

Pietro uncrossed his legs and inclined himself towards her. 'To your knowledge, did Marcello have any enemies?'

Luciana smiled abstractedly. 'Yes. He had one such.'

She raised an eyebrow, mysteriously. 'His only enemy was himself.'

Pietro clasped his hands beneath his chin. Could it be that the courtesan was aware of Marcello's double life? He could not tell.

'Marcello was a … complicated … boy. It was one of his most alluring qualities. He was consumed with guilt for his sins, obsessed with evil. I believe … I believe he felt responsible for what befell his poor mother. She is half-crazed now, an invalid. But she was ever so. Crazed about God, you catch my meaning? She was always somewhat disturbed, as indeed was her husband. When she gave up acting, her wits deteriorated. Marcello was born a tortured soul.'

'What more did you know about him?'

Luciana stared once more into Pietro's eyes. 'I have told you much already, have I not? Marcello was a great actor. But he was a man who concealed his sufferings. In lovers … his tastes were particular. Not all were … women.'

Pietro raised an eyebrow. Luciana cleared her throat. 'You will forgive me if I do not dwell unduly upon the subject. I believe the dead deserve a modicum of respect. Let me say simply that I do not believe that Marcello ever felt truly loved. Hence, I, in my humble way, endeavoured to offer him some comfort …'

'I see,' said Pietro. He thought for a moment, then asked, 'Would it be indiscreet of me to enquire as to the names of any other admirers who may have visited you of late, Signora?'

She studied him intently. She was not, he considered, entirely oblivious to his charms. Her cheeks flushed once more. She moistened her lips. 'It's just that … they habitually come to me masked, you understand? There have been three … One is a Frenchman, to judge by his accent. I have never set eyes on the other two, nor do I know anything of them. They come, they possess me, they leave … It might be anyone. It might be *you*.' This last word she whispered, their faces now inches apart.

Pietro averted his gaze, looking up at the ceiling. The interview with Luciana Saliestri continued for some minutes more; Pietro endeavoured to revisit the courtesan's remarks, but to no avail. Had Marcello had lovers she considered less than proper? *Not all were women*, she had said. And Pietro recalled something Goldoni had said at the Teatro San Luca: *Marcello did not truly understand women ... He gave the impression that he cared little for them*. Marcello Torretone, actor, spy for the Ten ... also loved men? It was possible, certainly, only too possible. Ambivalent to the end. Here was something else which had not figured in the report delivered to him by the Council of Ten. Had they been entirely ignorant of his predilections, or had it been simply one more in the armoury of weapons they used to control Marcello? Certainly, Marcello's dissembling was almost heroic. Pietro considered the matter, intrigued and frustrated. After abandoning Luciana Saliestri to her divan, it took some moments for him to collect his thoughts, and as he walked away from the *palazzo*, she gazed down at him from her vantage point on the balcony where she sat pensively toying with her hair. As Pietro stepped back onto the gondola which had brought him, the undeniable charms of the young woman danced still in his mind. Luciana Saliestri was a troubling and enchanting woman. At once sensual, provocative and submissive, in thrall to extravagance, to pleasure, giving of her body to any man free with his *zecchini*, all the while reckoning and tallying the fortune left her by her husband ... How had her brooch come to be next to the body of Marcello in the Teatro San Luca? She claimed to be unaware of who might have stolen it, and, assuming this were true, it could have been Marcello or Giovanni Campioni or any of her legion of suitors. Senator Campioni might well provide the key, but to approach a personage of such stature would require subtlety, and any such interview would necessitate much strategic preamble, which stratagems would have to be discussed with Emilio Vindicati and with the doge himself, something he would attend to later. In the interim the Black Orchid, like a good little soldier, would go about his investigation.

The church of San Giorgio Maggiore, which sits upon the island which bears its name, is separated from San Marco by a narrow inlet of the *laguna*. Work on the chapel began in 1565 under the supervision of Andrea Palladio and was completed by his pupil Vincenzo Scamozzi some forty years later; the master did not live to see his work fulfilled. The island of San Giorgio Maggiore, facing the doge's palace and the *piazzetta*, had long played a significant role in the republic, controlling as it did all maritime access in the city. A church had first been built here in AD 790 and some two centuries later, a Benedictine monastery rose beside it; both were destroyed in the earthquake of 1223 and were not rebuilt until the fifteenth century. It is, together with *Il Redentore* on the *Canale della Giudecca*, the only church entirely conceived by Palladio. Stepping from the *scafo* onto the piazza before the church, Pietro could not but be dazzled by the magnificent facade carved in Istrian stone, embellished with Corinthian columns. Pietro smiled as he gazed up at the monument to the Doge Leonardo Donà on the grand inner portal, erected in appreciation of his aid to the monastery. A new *campanile*, rivalling that on the piazza San Marco, had just been completed, replacing the ruined fifteenth century bell tower. It was here, in the shadow of the basilica, that Father Caffelli, confessor to the late Marcello Torretone, officiated.

Leaving his valet, Pietro crossed the piazza to the great double doors and entered the cold gloom of the chapel. As he stepped between the pews, Pietro mentally prepared himself for the encounter, vowing to himself that he would keep his temper – and a measure of good humour. But Pietro had not forgotten Father Caffelli's role in his incarceration. Had he been free to act, he would readily have given this deceitful, perfidious minister a good thrashing by way of reminding him of his manners. *I fear our meeting may be somewhat strained.*

Pietro found Caffelli before the altar of the *Cappella dei*

Morti contemplating *The Deposition*. Aside from a hooded figure – doubtless a nun come to say the rosary – who now rose and slipped silently from the chapel, San Giorgio was deserted. Caffelli turned as he heard Pietro's footfalls. He placed the bible he had been carrying on the altar, snuffed the two candles, and turned to welcome his guest with a slight frown. Pietro glanced up at *The Deposition* and, for a moment, it seemed to him that the painting depicted himself with Brozzi, the coroner, taking down Marcello's lifeless body from where it hung, exposed for all to see, on the stage of the Teatro San Luca. He quickly dispelled the image and looked again at Caffelli. The latter hesitated a moment and then, recognising Pietro's face despite the gloom and Pietro's finery, stifled an astonished cry. The two men faced one another for a moment or two. The priest brought his hands together before his alb. He was a corpulent, balding man, his heavy, thick-lipped face so bulbous it seemed out of proportion to his body, but it was his pallor that immediately alerted Pietro.

In a flash of inspiration, Cosimo Caffelli allowed the silence to hang in the air for an instant, and then spoke. 'Pietro Viravolta. Well, I never!'

'At your service,' said Pietro.

Silence fell again, then Caffelli continued, 'I had heard you were condemned to cross the Bridge of Sighs to be executed or, at the very least, to receive the flogging you so richly deserve …'

'I humbly regret denying you your pleasure.'

'Surely you have not escaped? No … Undoubtedly you bargained with your soul to extricate yourself from your terrible situation. Pray, tell me, what did you offer the Council of Ten that they should grant this amnesty? I am keen to know. I only hope this clemency is provisional and that you shall spend many years yet in *i Piombi*. My personal sentiments notwithstanding, I am inured to welcoming reprobates; God always extends His hand to those who have strayed from His path. Come then, Viravolta! Are you come to repent yourself?'

Pietro could not suppress a chuckle, one of the cutting laughs he was wont to let slip and which, unsurprisingly, did not please Father Caffelli.

'Not precisely, Father. But enough of this flattery. When troubles come, they come not as single spies, but in battalions. You will be pleased to learn that I am here as an emissary of the Most Serene Republic. Though the messenger may not be to your liking, I am certain you will accord me the respect due my office. In return for my freedom, I have been charged with a mission by the Council of Ten and the doge himself. An especial mission and one which, for the moment, is highly confidential. It is upon this mission that I have come to see you, though I must insist that what passes between us remain secret or you shall certainly fall foul of our valiant inquisitors or, indeed, the Quarantia Criminale, which is not renowned for its sense of humour.'

Pietro fumbled in his pocket and proffered the letter of authorisation which bore the seal of the doge. Caffelli took the letter sceptically and read it carefully, his face inscrutable. Then, with a brusque gesture he thrust it towards Pietro.

'You, a guardian in the defence of the interests of Venice? Astounding. And is Senator Ottavio aware of this travesty? You can certainly count on my ...'

Pietro's half-smile faded. He stepped forward menacingly. 'I do not doubt it,' he interrupted caustically, 'but, as I have said, I am charged with a secret mission. Should you do anything to disclose that fact, you will incur the wrath of the Ten. But enough of this, whether or not you approve their decision, the Black Orchid has returned.' *And do not try my patience, or I shall crucify you myself.*

He frowned. 'I have come to speak to you about one of your flock, Father Caffelli, a certain Marcello Torretone, a celebrated actor with Messer Goldoni's theatrical company.

It so happens that Marcello has been found murdered … crucified on the stage of his own theatre. You were his confessor, I believe.'

'W … what?'

At Pietro's words, Father Caffelli blanched. He ran his hand over his brow and his lower lip quivered. He suddenly seemed shaken, his equanimity crumbled, and for a fraction of a second he reeled. Pietro thought he might collapse, but at the last moment the priest recovered himself. He looked deeply into Pietro's eyes and stammered: 'I see,' his voice was barely a whisper, 'but be careful what you say. You have no idea of the dangers.'

'But we are alone,' said Pietro, surprised at the priest's reaction.

'The enemy is ever-present. Come.'

The shift in Caffelli's demeanour at the mere mention of Marcello's name told Pietro that he had been wise to come and his curiosity was excited. Caffelli took Pietro by the arm and firmly led him to the confessional. The priest stepped inside, gesturing to Pietro that he should take his place in the compartment on the other side of the grille. Pietro slipped into the shadowy compartment, drew back the purple blind, and leaned towards the grille separating him from the priest.

'I confess, Father, it has been some considerable time since my last confession. Though I did once masquerade as the Curate of Naples in order to seduce a fair maiden, and counselled her that she should throw herself into my arms … A delightful memory …'

'That will do, Pietro! You said Marcello was crucified?'

Pietro raised an eyebrow. All the self-possession in Caffelli's voice had faded. 'Yes. Though his murderer also gouged out his eyes.'

'*Santa Maria …*'

'What do you know of this? Come, Father, it is your turn to make your confession. Bear in mind the defence of the republic. Who is this enemy of whom you speak?'

'*Il Diavolo!* Have you not heard of him? The Great Council and the Senate know of him, they tremble at the mere mention of his name. Surely the doge spoke to you of him? The Devil has come to Venice!'

'*Il Diavolo*?' Pietro raised an eyebrow. 'Who is this Devil you speak of?'

'No one knows. I believe ... I believe Marcello was preparing to meet with him in person. He called him by another name ... the Chimera. That's all I can tell you.'

'Marcello arranged to meet the Prince of Darkness at the Teatro San Luca?'

'Ignorant fool. This is no laughing matter. This shadow has slipped among us to sow wickedness and evil, and if he is not Lucifer in the flesh, he has all the cruelty of his namesake, believe me! Surely what you have seen in the theatre is enough to convince you?'

Caffelli made the sign of the cross. Pietro heaved a sigh.

'Tell me. Is this what you and Marcello spoke of when he came to confess?'

Behind the fretwork grille, Caffelli scowled. 'As you well know, if you are bound to secrecy, I am bound by a higher authority still, Pietro, and I am not about to break the sacred seal of the confessional for a brute ruffian, regardless of the mission entrusted to him. I can say only that catastrophe is imminent, of that I am certain.'

If Marcello were a spy for the Council of Ten, thought Pietro, it was unlikely that he would have confided secret matters of State to Caffelli while in the throes of his torturous confession. And yet it seemed that Caffelli did know something of the investigation entrusted to Marcello. Did he perhaps know more than he was prepared to reveal? Probably. Perhaps the priest was somehow implicated in this murder. If he himself was not an informer in the pay of the Ten, he might have proved a valuable fount of information for Marcello. His sudden invocation of the seal of the confessional seemed to Pietro as genuine as it might be fictitious. And there was the question of the precise nature of his relationship with the actor, a matter on which Pietro feared the worst.

'How much did you know about Marcello?'

'What everyone knew. He was an actor with Goldoni's repertory company.'

'No more than that?'

The priest hesitated, then took his head in his hands. 'No.'

Pietro knew instinctively that the man was lying. 'But surely you were his confessor? Father ... what did Marcello tell you? Was he afraid, had someone threatened him?'

'*Santa Madonna* ... Day and night I prayed for some deliverance from this shame. How could it end thus, Lord? Marcello was a boy who deserved to live. He was ...'

'Others have portrayed Marcello as a man haunted by sin. Is this true?'

'Marcello was ... lost. He had renounced his baptism. I was struggling to lead him back to the path.'

Pietro peered at the priest. 'Apostasy? Why should Marcello renounce his faith, Father? Was there something about which he felt ashamed?'

Caffelli nodded, but did not answer. Pietro decided to be more candid.

'Do you think that perhaps his amatory relationships had some bearing upon his decision?'

Caffelli was breathing harder now. Aware that a refusal to reply might be taken for a confession, the priest steeled himself to answer. 'Marcello's romantic entanglements concerned no one but himself, and they have no bearing on your investigation.'

'I am not so persuaded. But if what you say is true, there can be no reason for you to be silent about the company he kept. I know that he had an amorous intrigue with Luciana Saliestri. Was there someone else?'

The priest did not react. Pietro decided to take a different approach.

'Very well, Father. To your knowledge, did Marcello mingle in dangerous circles? Did he have any enemies?'

The priest ran his tongue over his lips; after a second or two he spoke, pronouncing the words as though they burned his lips. 'The Striges,' Caffelli said in a hoarse whisper. 'The Firebirds ...'

'The Firebirds? Explain yourself.'

'The Striges, who are also called the Firebirds. Seek them out ...'

'I do not understand, Father. Are they—'

'No, no! I can tell you no more. Now, go. Leave me!'

Pietro posed another question, and another, but Caffelli sat mute. There was a quiet rustle. Pietro strained to discern the figure of the priest through the grille of the confessional, then closed the curtain and looked out. Caffelli's footsteps echoed in the silent basilica as he fled. He moved quickly, his hand clutching his waist, leaning forward as though in pain.

The Strix, thought Pietro, a mythical creature, part-woman, part-hound, which, like the vampire, fed on human blood. Creatures of darkness, the Striges were associated with demonic forces. But what of *il Diavolo*, this Chimera? What did these things signify? Pietro sat in the confessional for a long moment, turning matters over in his mind. He had the disagreeable sensation that Caffelli had said too much, or not enough. Anyway, he would get no more from the priest now. Pietro growled before opening the curtain and emerging into the shadowy church.

He stepped out onto the piazza of San Giorgio Maggiore where Landretto awaited him. 'So?' enquired the valet.

'Our friend knows many things, indeed, I should not be surprised if he is somehow embroiled in this affair. It is important that we do not lose our grip upon him. He shall yield up what he knows in time; men of the church are weak. But we shall have to proceed with delicacy. One thing is certain: Marcello feared for his life, and it seems that Caffelli fears for his now. Tell me, Landretto, do the names, the Striges or the Firebirds mean anything to you?'

'No. Nothing whatever.'

'I thought as much.'

'Because?'

'Because, according to the good Father Cosimo, the Devil is come to Venice.'

'That is most regrettable. But I have other news.'

'Ah?' said Pietro, smoothing his jacket as he stared out over the *laguna*.

'Brozzi dispatched an envoy with a message for you. He has identified the fragments of glass found in Marcello's eye sockets. They come from the workshop of a man named Spadetti, on Murano, which is hardly surprising since Spadetti is a member of the Guild of Glaziers.'

Pietro glanced at his valet.

'Spadetti ... I know the name. A master glassblower. Excellent work, my friend.'

They walked together towards the gondola. The setting sun hovered on the horizon, bathing the city in an tawny glow.

'We shall set off at daybreak. But tonight, Landretto, my lad ...' Pietro flung his arms wide. He felt weary; the investigation weighed heavily upon him, but he could no longer adjourn the small pleasures he felt were his due. After all, it was not a breach of his vow simply to go in search of a little restorative.

Moreover, he would be acting on the authority of Casanova, whose parting words in the prison echoed in his mind: '... make me proud'. Pietro smiled and turned to his valet.

'This evening, Landretto, I have authorised a pass out. It is time for me to make my comeback, time to assuage certain privations. Crime has made me melancholy and the most beautiful women in all the world await us. *Andiamo, e basta!*'

*

After Pietro's departure, Father Caffelli locked the great portals of San Giorgio Maggiore and sat alone in the gloom. Night crept into the chapel, stealing between the statues and drawing its veil over the cold, dusty ground. In the heart of the nave a few votive candles flickered. Caffelli knelt before the high altar, gazing up at *The Deposition*. All was silent but for his breathing, broken by sobs and a curious gasping. Cosimo Caffelli, his eyes misted with tears, knelt in penitent supplication before his Redeemer. From time to time, he thought he saw the shadows coalesce into some shifting form, heard some whispered voice. 'Shadow theatre', Marcello would have said. The priest dared not close his eyes for when he did, he was pulled down into terrible, tormented dreams. Images suffused in brimstone surged from deep within his soul wreaking untold pain and suffering. *My God, my God, why hast thou forsaken me?* The enemy now knew everything. The Bible lay open before Caffelli at an engraving of the *Temptation of Christ*, depicting Satan bidding Christ to follow him, his face a twisted, mocking grin, his forked tail coiled about his cloven hooves. Swirls of demons hovered about him. But evil did not simply whirl about Cosimo Caffelli; it was *within* him, as it was in every sinner. It had grown worse with time, more terrifying, more impenetrable. Caffelli had strayed from the path of righteousness, he was lost, and soon the unthinkable would be revealed to the world and he would be tarnished by disgrace, damned for all time by Venice and by mankind. *I am a miserable wretch, Lord! I have sinned against you! Why hast thou forsaken me?*

The flickering radiance of the flames cast upon the stone floor of San Giorgio Maggiore the shadow of Cosimo Caffelli as he scourged himself, mortifying his flesh with a birch rod until the blood flowed.

*

Pietro and Landretto followed the *codega* – the lantern bearer – joking from time to time with this rude *bergamasca.* Their evening had begun at *Il Selvaggio* and by now they were somewhat merry; they sang as they walked. Pietro found that toasting the health of the Serene Republic with liquor paid for by the abundance of gold ducats given to him by Emilio Vindicati to cover disbursements incurred during his investigation, was doubly sweet. Occasionally, they encountered a brigade of the black-robed *Signori della Notte*, who sharply enjoined the little troop to quieten their revelries. Pietro immediately proffered his *salvacondotto*, stamped with the seal of the doge himself, and thereafter they were left unmolested. In any case, since his altercation with the brigands outside the Teatro San Luca, Pietro felt ready to take on anyone who dared cross them. Thus did he and Landretto make their stumbling way along the rain-slicked streets. After *Il Selvaggio*, they had tarried awhile in a small *bastione* which sold wine by the goblet and to slake their appetites they had some biscuits, a little raki, some orange-blossom ratafia and *gelati* washed down with malmsey. They made a swift detour to the Caffè Florian near the Procuratie, before repairing to another *albergo* where they enjoyed a feast fit for a king: stewed mutton, slices of grilled *salsiccia*, a whole capon with rice and haricot beans, truffles, a quail or two, ricotta and, to round off the meal, *zaletti con zebibo*: cornmeal and wheat biscotti kneaded with butter, milk and eggs and garnished with candied citron and raisins. Then, intent on renewing old acquaintance, Pietro and his manservant headed to the Ridotto, a celebrated gaming house where one might play baccarat, piquet or dice. Fortune smiled on them and they amassed a tidy pot of winnings, so much indeed that as they left they dispensed ducats freely to the ladies of mystery on the Piazza San Marco, marquises of the twilight, doges of their own republics, who with their charms enticed patrons from the safe shadows of the arcade. Pietro and Landretto danced with them to the music of the fiddlers by the Procuratie; even Pietro, who had not played a *vitula* in many a year, was persuaded to mangle an air by Gabrielli. The moon was high in heaven's vault by the time they were wending their way to one of the many private members' clubs that flourished in Venice.

Pietro was overjoyed to be reunited with Landretto once more, to have his manservant and his drinking companion again. Though one was indentured to the other, the two men were friends and tonight the disparity of their several ranks vanished in their renewed camaraderie. Indeed, Pietro had never forgotten that he too had once been a street urchin, roaming the *Sestiere* San Samuele. Landretto, however, was not Venetian by birth. Born in Parma, Landretto's father, like Pietro's, had died when the boy was but a babe in arms and his mother had swiftly followed her husband. Landretto had long roamed the highways and byways of Italy, erring between beggary and thievery. He had twice been taken in by penniless noblemen, first in Pisa, and again in Genoa. Landretto was a free spirit, and Pietro knew only too well that the lad had more than one trick up his sleeve. Though he seemed merry and open, he harboured a streak of cynicism, a vestige of his turbulent travels. Beneath the surface of a callow, handsome, beardless youth was a young man capable of using his considerable intellect to manipulate events to his advantage. Though he freely confessed to being of ignoble birth, he had no difficulty in having his voice heard by influential, high-born friends and had had a hand in securing his master's freedom. Pietro knew that his manservant had done everything in his power to have his master freed. In time, even Emilio Vindicati found himself browbeaten by the importuning of Pietro's diplomatic and devoted manservant. Pietro suspected that it had been Landretto who had persuaded Emilio to entrust him with a mission in exchange for his liberty.

The private members' club to which the two men were headed was on an annexe of the Contarini *palazzo*, and comprised elegant salons, gaming rooms, a *conservatorio*, even a kitchen; but it also had a number of boudoirs: it was here, at Vindicati's insistence, that Pietro and Landretto had rented, for a paltry six hundred *zecchini*, the apartments of the English ambassador's *capocuoco*. Pietro, who knew the establishment well, commended his mentor on his taste. Upon their arrival, they spent some two hours in the gaming rooms, joined an impassioned discussion on the relative merits of the poems of Ludovico Ariosto, during which Pietro astounded the company by declaiming several choice verses. Many ladies were in attendance, and yet there was not a moment when Pietro's thoughts did not turn to Anna Santamaria; not a moment when he was not troubled by a thousand teeming questions. Where was she? What was she doing? Were her thoughts of him? Did she love him still? Vindicati's formal interdiction that he should make no attempt to contact her weighed heavily on him, but he was mindful too that he did not wish to yield to this suffering which seemed to come in waves, to the bondage which his obsession represented. It had become intolerable. He had to free himself of this attachment, he had to lance the boil, forget his uncertainties. Forget ... What choice had he but to forget this woman and move on? *Oh, Anna, Anna, will you ever forgive me?*

Fight – he could fight for her – but how, and against whom? Let it go.

That evening he drank his fill. To your health, Giacomo.

Among the nobility present that evening, all masked for carnival as he was, one young lady seemed out of place: she was Ancilla Adeodat, a mulatto girl whom a Venetian colonel had brought back from the colonies. She was possessed of a rare beauty, with her red rose in her long dark mane of hair, her russet complexion, white lace flounces and intricately layered gown. Pietro remembered that he had beguiled her once before, as indeed he had Signora Contarini and her charming daughter, whose club this was. But that was before he had met Anna. Ancilla, too, recognised him, in spite of his mask. Doubtless the flower in his buttonhole had betrayed him to the beautiful mulatto for, as he drifted into the music room, she approached him, staring at him intently. She touched the flower pinned to his lapel: 'Can it be that the Black Orchid is a free man?'

She smiled. Standing on tiptoe, she leaned towards his ear and whispered: 'Pietro Viravolta ... *it is you!* What say you to a visit to the islands ... you always loved the exotic?'

He smiled in turn: 'There are some voyages a man never forgets.'

In a trice, they found themselves in one of the upstairs rooms. Landretto stood by the door, listening to the smack of kisses and the rustle of garments hastily discarded. He tried stealing a glance through the keyhole, but to no avail. The key was in the lock. Hoarse breaths, sighs, war waged between the sheets ...

Still Landretto waited ... then at length, he too sighed, removing his hat. There would be naught for him this evening. The valet drifted off to find his own bed.

But the evening did not end; rather, this was merely the overture to a most curious event. An hour before dawn, Pietro was roused by three sharp raps at his door. At first he thought he had been dreaming, but a scratching at the door frame confirmed that someone was there. He glanced at Ancilla Adeodat, 'gift of God'; she was sleeping, her hair scattered across the pillow and the gentle curve of her naked back. She whimpered momentarily, her full lips quivering, and then her breath fell once more into a natural rhythm. Pietro rose, careful not to wake her. He took a candelabrum and stumbled to the door, opening it to find no one. He looked left and right, but the hall was empty. His bare feet, however, felt something. Looking down, he discovered that a note written in a tiny, spidery hand had been pushed beneath his door. Intrigued, Pietro bent and picked it up, held it beneath the candles and read:

Follow me, Viravolta, in this Dance of Shadows
Two paces forward, six sinister
The corner turned, eight paces right
Stoop and through the keyhole peer
And you shall see how weak is flesh.

Pietro glanced once more to the left and right, but found nothing but shadows and silence. Ancilla slept on. Pietro stood on the threshold for a moment, the candelabrum and the note in hand, as in a stupor. He wiped his brow. His mouth felt dry. *What could this mean?* Who could have left this abstruse message? He reread the note, scratched his head, and listened again. Nothing. Gathering his wits about him, he decrypted the message. He blinked, staring out into the corridor at the blank wall facing him, then he stepped forward. *Two paces forward.*

The floorboards creaked. Pietro carefully closed the door to his room, looked down at his feet, and stood motionless for a moment. He imagined how he might look to someone coming upon him suddenly, half-naked, wearing only his shirt. He would surely be taken for a madman, for some spectre haunting the living, or for a restless somnambulant under the influence of some exotic potion. He frowned, moving slowly as if in a dream, or a nightmare. It was a peculiar sensation; as if some force, some higher power had dominion over him.

Follow me, Viravolta, in this Dance of Shadows.

Here he was, dancing with the night. *Six paces sinister.*

He turned to his left, and slowly paced out the distance,

counting until he reached the number six. To his left was the door to the next room, where Landretto was sleeping. To the right, the corridor forked. A drop of wax fell from the candle onto the bare boards. Pietro's heart hammered in his chest; he was surprised to find himself so apprehensive. He cleared his throat. Events were overtaking him. And yet he had the gnawing feeling that he should heed this call, though he barely understood what it portended. He mopped his brow once more.

The corner turned, eight paces right. Pietro turned the corner and took eight paces. Two doors faced one another across the hallway and, further along, two others. He could distinguish curious sounds. Something akin to a gasp, a breathless wheeze, and then a stifled cry and the sound of a bed creaking under the exertions of a body unconstrained. *Stoop and through the keyhole peer.*

Pietro crouched by the door on his right. There was indeed a keyhole with a commonplace, crudely wrought iron escutcheon. He pressed his eye close. There was no key in the lock. Mechanically, he brought the candlestick closer to his face, wondering if perhaps he was dreaming, the *Dance of Shadows* had led him to this door like some antic treasure map. What then of the treasure? An image flickered in his mind, a scene not unlike this when, as a child, he had watched through the keyhole of his parents' room. Julia, the actress, tumbled by Pascuale the cobbler. Vividly he remembered his astonishment, his repugnance, the obscure feeling of envy tinged with jealousy before the consummation of carnal passion. An intimate celebration, a homily to the cult of the body, an eager, animal epiphany of the senses.

And you shall see …

Pietro stood and rubbed his eyes. His heart was beating faster still, and yet what he had espied was far from pleasurable. Had he been mistaken?

He stooped once more and saw a man pressing down

with all his weight upon a slender body, sweating like a pig, panting like a bull over the *putta*, his face warped into a terrifying rictus as he choked his victim's cries. A grotesque carnival mask, the side-piece broken, jerked rhythmically beneath his chin. He had not taken the trouble to disrobe, merely hitched his black tunic up to reveal his sallow, plump legs which were hairy as a spider's. Pietro followed the several stages of this libidinous metamorphosis. The man gasped more feverishly now, his face flushed a turbulent indigo, a pulsing vein clearly visible at his temple, the mask continued to swing back and forth … Abruptly, after several thrusts of unspeakable brutality, his hand still stifling the cries of his victim, the man froze, tensed, his whole body clenched in the ecstasy of *la petite mort*, and lifted his eyes to heaven. In that moment of supreme rapture, he looked like a duellist run through with a rapier, a soldier felled by a fatal blow upon the battlefield.

'*Santa Madonna*,' he muttered hoarsely. '*Santa Madonna*.'

Father Cosimo Caffelli, confessor at the church of San Giorgio Maggiore, sprayed his seed into his victim, beseeching him for mercy. For it was at this moment that Pietro realised that the victim of this painful assault was not some expensive *putta*, but a young man, an adolescent who could not be more than seventeen.

… how weak is flesh.

Soundlessly, still troubled by what he had witnessed, Pietro turned back to his room. For a moment, he had thought to break down the door, surprise Caffelli in flagrante delicto, watch terror and shame steal over his countenance; he thought to swoop upon the priest, heap him with opprobrium, roar with laughter at his hypocrisy. *Tell me, father, is it thus that you magnify the Lord? I am impressed by your exquisite morality, truly you serve as an exemplar for all of Venice!* But no.

Once more, Pietro felt plunged into some phantasm exacerbated by the deleterious effects of all the *aqua vitae* he had drunk that evening. This nightmare vision had invaded his mind, his soul, leaving a bitter taste. He retired once more to bed, keenly aware of the warm body of Ancilla next to him, and drew the covers over them. The features of this dusky, sensual maid seemed to fuse with the remote, diaphanous, heart-rending image of Anna Santamaria. Tonight, he reflected, he had betrayed her. Perhaps there was no other manner to be free of her, free of this hopeless, doomed passion. And yet ... was the bond between them to be broken thus? *I do not know any longer ... as God is my witness, I do not know.*

For some time black thoughts eddied in his mind. He had left the note scrawled with the *Dance of Shadows* by the candelabrum, its candles guttering now. He seemed to see once more the body of the crucified Marcello, the body of Caffelli thrusting over the youth, the face of Brozzi intent upon his autopsy. He tried to imagine the face of he who had written the *Dance of Shadows*, dreamed of The Striges and the Chimera, ringed about with demons. And he thought again of the name Virgil. Sleep did not come.

CANTO V

THE GLASS OF MINOS

THE PROBLEM OF EVIL

Andreas Vicario, member of the Maggior Consiglio
On Evil and Freedom, Chapter I

I might formulate the problem of Evil thus: if sin exists, we must consider whether it is predetermined, that is to say that it exists antecedent to our actions, or *a posteriori*, correlative only to the exercise of our free will. Does Lucifer exist only in the misdeeds of man, or must we assume that he exists *a priori*, an immanent canker lodged not only within man's nature but existing independently, a free agent in the world, predating the Creation itself? This is the duality posed by Jean de Lugio, the so-called Manichean heresy; to my mind it is crucial to our comprehension of evil for, in choosing, we decide whether or not Man is possessed of an ontological predisposition for evil. Either the Devil is a product of mankind's misuse of the free will conferred upon him; a possibility accepted by God in Genesis when he bestowed upon us this precious, perilous gift; if not, then both Evil and Good exist *in fieri*, co-instigators of a creation in which the part of the Devil is no less than that of God. To my mind, Saint Augustine's defence of free will cannot wholly encompass the totality of Evil. There are many Evils – pestilential sicknesses and its attendant sufferings, for example – which proceed not from our exercise of free will, but from the will of God. Ergo, it must be admitted that God orchestrates our sufferings, and this God, this immanent being who alone can be justified by reason, even as reason is inimical to Him, I call Beelzebub. Sin is within mankind as the mark of Lucifer. Hence, to the question 'Is mankind Evil?', I am forced to conclude that he is, but the compass of Evil is not wholly contained within him, for to the attendant question 'Does Satan truly exist?', I am also compelled to answer, without a shadow of hesitation: yes.

In the upstairs chamber of her *palazzo*, Luciana Saliestri was struggling with this abstruse text. Habitually, she enjoyed her own company; relished those tranquil moments when she could give herself over to pleasures other than those of the flesh. Her husband had spent a lifetime building a magnificent library she continued to enrich. From time to time, Luciana enjoyed selecting a quarto in which she set down her thoughts as marginalia. But presently, she was finding it difficult to concentrate her mind for more than a few minutes. She would set down the book, let it drop to her side as she thought of other things, then return to her reading without conviction. Finally, she set it aside and stared into space. She had been troubled by the sudden appearance of this man who had interrogated her about the death of Marcello, for whom she had had felt a deep affinity. She had said nothing of her friend's sexually ambiguous nature, believing that it was surely of no consequence in this terrible affair. And yet, in her heart, she felt no such certainty. What disturbed her more especially was the theft of her brooch. In vain, she had tried to remember when the brooch might have been purloined. She was doubtful that this agent of the Ten had believed her, and yet she had spoken the truth. She closed her eyes. It was a brooch she had rarely worn except on those rare occasions when – snatching a moment from the exigencies of his work as a Senator – Giovanni called on her.

She saw his face for a moment in her mind's eye. Could it be that Giovanni Campioni was somehow embroiled in this? Dear Giovanni had always been very enamoured of her, and she was fond of him. He carried the cares of the world upon his shoulders. *Politics*, she thought. Unbidden, a phrase from the Apocalypse of John came to her: *And I stood upon the sand of the sea, and saw a beast rise up out of the sea, having seven heads and ten horns, and upon his horns ten crowns, and upon his heads the name of blasphemy*, and she remembered that many interpretations suggested that politics was the sea from which the Antichrist would emerge at the Last Judgement. Giovanni Campioni liked to intimate that his duty was to hunt down the Beast. Luciana smiled. Giovanni rarely spoke to her of what was discussed in the Senate, indeed he was bound by his oath of office to divulge nothing of debates relating to the *Serenissima*. But when his body was coiled about hers she could sense his weariness, and the hope, as boundless as his many disappointments, that he would one day make his voice heard. His faith, his commitment, were endearing. There might have been a time, had not the difference in the ages been so marked, when she could have loved this man.

Luciana smiled sullenly. Love. Had she ever truly known love? She rose, the train of her negligee trailing in her wake, and walked to the hearth. Above the mantel stood a portrait of her husband and several sprigs of incense, the *genius loci* of this house. She, like so many, had married young and in haste. She had feigned love for him and, for a time, had even believed in her own charade. When she was widowed, she had felt no real grief. There had been some mourning for the routine of a life she had known, and yet she could not deny that as she gazed upon the body of her husband she had known a surge of terrible, secret joy. It was shameful, but the shame passed quickly. She gazed now at his portrait: the high forehead, the stern gaze, the haughty smile. How many times had she known her husband to lock himself in his study, poring over endless accounts, oblivious to her desires, her needs; presumptuously assuming his wife to be happy and fulfilled. When she had watched him as he worked, endlessly reckoning his assets and liabilities, she thought of Pantaloon in the plays she had seen, forever counting his pieces of gold. Saliestri's avarice had been stronger than his love of her. In those first weeks of nuptial bliss, Luciana had found herself alone. She had been alone even on her wedding night.

She lit a sprig of incense beneath the portrait. Fine whorls of smoke rose in eddies towards the ceiling. She could not bring herself to kneel before his image; that was more than her pride could bear. But he had left her young, rich and beautiful, desired and adored, and she would not rest until she had squandered her late husband's every ducat. Spend, spend, spend ... every last *zecchino* he had hoarded. For her sole pleasure. It was, in sum, a return upon his investment. And if one day she should find her funds depleted, she had only to find a new protector – a man like Giovanni, who ached to care for her.

Only one problem remained. Love. Was she to be denied true love? A fleeting pout, part anger, part melancholy, distorted her perfect lips. She returned to her divan and to her book.

Venice was swathed in mist; an icy fog draped upon the murky canals, a cold to chill the bone and set the teeth to chatter even as the thickening gloom seemed to suspend time itself. It was impossible to see more than three paces ahead. Pietro walked prudently, his gaze fixed on the cobblestone, his mood in keeping with the melancholy climate. Landretto walked briskly by his side. They had left the *casa* Contarini shortly after daybreak. Pietro stopped suddenly, listening intently to the ripple of the echoes. Were these merely the reverberations of his own footfalls, or had he heard another's tread? He placed a hand on his manservant's shoulder.

'What is it?'

Pietro, scanning the mist, made no answer. Just then, he thought he heard a whistle and, in the corner of his eye, shadows flitted and disappeared into the miasma. A knot of men slipped past him, but perhaps these were ordinary Venetians, early risers going about their lives. But Pietro felt chary, his mind, filled with the troubles of night, as impenetrable as the dense fog of day. Emilio Vindicati had told him that he would keep him advised of his movements, doubtless as much to keep him in check as to come to his aid should he require it. It was possible that Vindicati was having him followed. It was essential that he be on his guard at all times. For a long moment Pietro stood motionless and then, turning to Landretto, said distractedly: 'Nothing, it was nothing,' and continued on his way.

The rising curve of the prow, a red ribbon like a cleft tongue drooping from a straw hat, the voice of the ferryman recounting some hoary yarn ... they had arrived at the quay.

As the boat sliced through the void Pietro could hear only the lapping of the water. The ferryman steered a course through the fog, heading for Murano, navigating entirely by instinct, using all of his considerable skill and experience. Landretto, his teeth chattering from the cold, seemed deep in thought. As they pulled away from the piazza San Marco, he could still pick out the silhouette of the buildings, but all too soon they disappeared, engulfed in the foul-smelling miasma through which the boat now sailed. They passed another skiff plotting a course back to the city. On the prow of the skiff, a hooded figure held aloft a lantern; he and the ferryman exchanged a few words and then the skiff vanished into the mist. Farther out, they passed the sepulchral mass of San Michele before it, too, disappeared. There was some strangeness in the air, as though nature, in some troubled sleep plagued by a thousand magical dreams, was steeling itself for some fresh apocalypse. For what slithered upon the waters and snaked between the beacons which cast long shadows on the murky *laguna*, was a dark and sinister magic. In this dreamlike limbo, it felt as though they had left *Terra Firma* for some indescribable, unsettling new world.

Pietro allowed his thoughts to dwell once more upon the events of the previous night. As yet, he had said nothing of it to Landretto. In truth, he wondered if it had not been some monstrous fruit of his imagination. And yet he knew it was not: the man he had seen had been Caffelli, of that much he was certain. He had kept the note on which was scrawled the *Dance of Shadows*, he would show it to Brozzi, perhaps the Quarantia Criminale could identify the paper or the ink. The images haunted him still. What he had witnessed was surely not the priest's first transgression. Caffelli was foolhardy. Pietro, in his youth, had given up his tonsure and his robes for the pleasures which women had to offer: he had met many in Rome who had done as much. Such a man as he was ill-placed to lecture Caffelli. But to surrender to the pleasures of the flesh was one thing; for the pastor of San Giorgio Maggiore it was sheer lunacy. Moreover, Pietro's intuition that Caffelli and Marcello had had a 'particular friendship' now seemed well founded. Pietro knew too much of human nature not to know that man was, above all, a product of his frustrations, joys, sorrows and sins. But Caffelli's behaviour revealed a serious malaise, and what he had said now came back to Pietro: *Santa Madonna ... Day and night I prayed for some deliverance from this shame. How could it end thus, Lord? Marcello was a boy who deserved to live ... He was ...*

Marcello was haunted by sin – as undoubtedly was

Caffelli. This, surely, was what had brought them together – the one a traitor to his nature, the other to his faith. From their mutual confusion an intense friendship would have developed, for they could truly understand one another's suffering. Aside from whatever political intrigues they might have been caught up in, this shared misery would have favoured shared confidences. Two men with double lives, torn apart, despising the object of their love and loving nonetheless, condemned to hide their secret pleasures which, in the eyes of the world, were an abomination – as they were in their own eyes. A life poisoned and unwholesome ... secrets and confessions. An agent of the Council of Ten and a minister of San Giorgio, two souls confident of their own damnation, tormented both by their duplicity and the intractable urges of their natures, drawn to ideals that were utterly unattainable. Though Pietro was also a disciple of the pleasures of the flesh, the tortures these men had suffered was something he could not fathom. He put a hand to his brow, closing his eyes.

He thought again of the note slipped furtively underneath his door. Who could have written such a note? It had been signed simply Virgil, but he knew no one by that name, save the long-dead author of the *Aeneid*, and so he was no further advanced in his investigation. Perhaps the note had come from *il Diavolo*, the mysterious Chimera of whom Caffelli had spoken, or from one among the sect he had called the Striges. Pietro now feared that he, too, was constantly observed. An agent of the Ten could have slipped the *Dance of Shadows* beneath his door to lead him to a vital clue in the enigma. It seemed hardly likely that the Council of Ten would conduct a investigation parallel to his own. It was more likely that Virgil was in some way enmeshed in the murder of Marcello. Increasingly, Pietro was convinced that the murder had not been the act of a lone criminal; that the manner in which it had been staged still veiled some message, as yet obscure. And if the killer had not worked alone, then he had surely acted under the aegis of some occult organisation. Perhaps the mysterious Firebirds.

He had yet to secure proof, if there were any. In the meantime, there was another thread to unravel: the shards of glass found around the corpse and lodged in the mutilated eye sockets of the dead man had been traced to Murano where, Pietro hoped, he would uncover some new information.

More than an hour had passed before the boatman indicated the misty coast of Murano and began preparations for landing. At last they emerged from the fog.

Since the thirteenth century, when the Maggior Consiglio, fearing a conflagration in the city, had first ordered glassmakers to move their foundries to the island of Murano, the Glassblowers' Guild had become a powerful institution. In the fourteenth century, its wares were famed as far abroad as London, a fame which grew with the Renaissance. The glassblowers of Venice attained a degree of perfection seldom equalled in the history of the decorative arts. The dazzling enamelled colours and gilding of these shimmering creations, adorned with contemporary portraits or scenes from mythology had become the pride of the guild which, alone, was the arbiter of taste throughout the Royal Courts of Europe. Later, the technique of *lattimo* and *aventurine* was developed – transparent pieces shot through with whorls and eddies of milk-glass or spun gold. It had been these incomparable pieces that prompted glassmakers in far-flung countries to create pieces in 'the Venetian style'. The secrets of glassmaking, so jealously guarded by the republic, began to be known, and the publication of Neri's celebrated *Arte Vetraria* in 1612, marked the fruition of an art, a science, which had first bloomed in the Middle Ages. Innumerable scientific uses were found for glass, from the lenses used by astronomers to pipettes, phials and alembics used by physicians and alchemists. Eyeglasses and pince-nez had been developed, first for the use of scholars – like Brozzi, the coroner for the Quarantia Criminale – later for the public at large. Far beyond the traditional uses ascribed to it, Venetian glass was increasingly used in radically different industries. Its translucence was compared to that of rock crystal, and for clarity, weight and robustness it rivalled that of Bohemia. The use of charcoal to fire furnaces had made new innovations possible: it was discovered that lead-oxide, added to molten glass, created *cristallo* – lead crystal of astonishing clarity, purity and sparkle which bore witness to the talents of the glassblowers of the *laguna*. Venice then, as now, was the supreme master of the art, creating plate-glass mirrors, cylindrical panes, vases, statues, goblets, and decanters; objects both practical and decorative that were amongst the finest in the world.

As Pietro and Landretto moved through Spadetti's glassworks, they saw examples of all of these objects. The stifling heat recalled Hades, the commotion a teeming cavern which the great god Vulcan would have been happy to call home. The spectacle of dozens of glassblowers at work in the immense workshops beneath the soaring vaults was dazzling. This chthonic people moved about carrying myriads of incandescent blooms; thousands of brawny demons, some stripped to the waist, others clad in sweat-soaked rags; they wheezed and gasped, weaving amid the sparks to carry some finished piece for painstaking inspection. The verdict would be pronounced, and the piece could proceed to the next stage or melted down again. From everywhere came the clatter of tools, the resonant ringing of glass, the roar of hundreds of furnaces constantly stoked, and the songs and shouts of men. From this forge poured forth the finest jewels of Venetian glass, pearls of limpid water wrenched from the swelter of magma and shadows.

The Glassblowers' Guild, like many societies, had a ruling council, presided over by an officer whose role it was to defend the interests of the profession, apply its statutes, settle internal disputes and rule on the admission of new members listed in the *Giustizia vecchia*, a copy of which was filed with the relevant magistrate. Only masters within the guild could establish a glassworks, and the hierarchy within the profession was strictly regulated. Once admitted, a young man would work as a 'boy', or assistant, for some five years before progressing to the status of 'youth', or 'worker', where he would ply his trade for a dozen years more; then, and only then, when he himself had created a *capolavoro*, a masterpiece worthy of the name, might he become a *maestro* or *capo*.

The Venetian guilds were not entirely autonomous, but owed their fortunes to the Council of Ten, who took a special interest in the Glassblowers' Guild. A century earlier, Jean-Baptiste Colbert, minister to Louis XIV, had despatched secret agents who had succeeded in bribing the glassmakers into giving up the secrets of their trade, thereby allowing the French to establish rival foundries which produced mirrors and glass. Such subterfuge was commonplace, and the punishments meted out for such crimes ranged from being clapped in irons to death. There could be no question of the guilds playing a political role in the affairs of the republic, though each year the doge received representatives from the guilds at the state banquet held in honour of the Ascension and on the feasts of San Marco, San Gui and Saint-Étienne.

A sweaty, broad-shouldered man led Pietro and Landretto through the foundry to Federico Spadetti, one of the most powerful members of the guild. Wearing a rag tied about his head in guise of a cap and a blackened linen shirt, Spadetti was a man of some fifty years with a swarthy complexion, his face smudged with sweat and soot. But for the god's mythic beard, he was Vulcan himself. With pincers and tongs he was fashioning a white-hot piece of glass which danced and undulated on the end of his blowpipe. He flexed his intimidating biceps for a moment before replying to Pietro's salutation. Pietro showed the man his letter of safe conduct from the doge, snatching it away before Spadetti should smudge it with his grimy fingers.

'Federico Spadetti? I should like to ask you a few questions.'

Spadetti sighed, laid down his blowpipe and pincers, and mopped his brow. He stood, hands balled into fists by his side and, plainly incensed to have his work disturbed, demanded to examine the *salvacondotto* once more. He scowled briefly and then, suddenly more biddable, he said: 'Speak on, then. I'm listening.'

With the flourish of a conjuror, Pietro produced a kerchief that held some of the glass splinters found in the Teatro San Luca at the foot of Marcello's crucified body.

'Would it be possible for you to identify the characteristics of this glass?'

Spadetti frowned, rubbing his chin, and leaned towards the kerchief. 'If I may ... ?'

Pietro gave him the kerchief. The *capomaestro* delicately picked up a shard and studied it attentively. He weighed the pieces in the palm of his hand, then compared them to a selection of fragments laid out upon a nearby workbench. He returned to where Pietro waited.

'*Cristallo*, I'd say, to judge from the weight, the polish, the clarity. It certainly looks like lead crystal.'

'We thought that perhaps the glass might have come from your foundry,' said Pietro. 'What say you?'

Spadetti peered again at the fragments. After a moment he said: '*È possibile*, though as you know, I am hardly the only man that makes glass. Without the glassmaker's mark, Messer, I'm not sure I can tell from pieces as small as this.'

'Of course,' said Pietro. 'But surely, Messer Spadetti, you are the foremost manufacturer of *cristallo* in all Murano; it is, as they say, your speciality. Could you tell me from what object the fragments might have come?'

Spadetti examined the glass once more, his nose all but buried in the kerchief. He sniffed loudly and turned away to sneeze. Then he gave a heavy sigh and clicked his tongue: 'Hmm … Not a decorative object, certainly. There's no colour, no filigree, nothing. A drinking goblet, maybe, a vase or a statuette, it could be many things …'

Pietro moved to a workbench where, some way off, a variety of pieces were arrayed. He was ominously silent, then suddenly he seized one of the objects and held it to close to Spadetti's face.

'What of this? Could it perhaps have come from an object such as this?'

He was holding an elegant razor-sharp *stiletto*, the hilt crafted in mother-of-pearl, on which was carved a serpent coiled about a skull.

'I … I don't know …' said Spadetti. 'Could be. What is it exactly that you're looking for, Messer?' He stood defiantly before Pietro.

'Might I take one with me?'

'Be my guest. That'll be two ducats.'

'I see you don't miss a trick, Messer Spadetti, even in your dealings with the Council of Ten.'

'*Especially* in my dealings with the Ten,' murmured the *capomaestro*.

Pietro smiled and took his purse from his belt. He opened it and handed Spadetti two ducats. In exchange, he proffered the crystal dagger.

'Tell me, *amico*, have you heard tell of the Striges?'

'The who?'

Pietro cleared his throat. 'The Striges, known also as the Firebirds?'

With bated breath he awaited a reply from Spadetti, who glowered at Pietro menacingly.

'No.'

'Excellent. On one matter at least you seem confident.'

The Black Orchid moved away. Hands clasped behind

his back, he whistled softly as he wandered idly between the workbenches.

'With all due respect, Messer,' said Spadetti, 'if you have quite finished, I've got work to be getting on with.'

Pietro stopped short before a young man labouring on an object of extraordinary beauty. It was a remarkable object: a dress, but no ordinary dress. Surmounted with a collar woven from threads of glass, the bodice was composed of slivers of crystal, each shot through with a shimmering rainbow of a thousand translucent arabesques about the bosom. The folds of the skirt glistered in a profusion of flounces and opalescent lace, belted at the waist with pearls closed with a starburst clasp. A crystal gown. Pietro let out a low, appreciative whistle.

'Magnificent, *maestro*.'

Spadetti came over, pride welling in his eyes. His voice was gentler, more relaxed now. 'This is the *capolavoro* my son Tazzio is preparing to present to the guild,' he said, gesturing toward the young man who knelt a few feet away, intent on his task. 'It is he who will one day take my place here. But first, he must become a *maestro* in his own right. This is an exceptional piece, a masterpiece. The guild has decreed a contest between the workshops on Murano. The doge himself will present the prize to the victor at the height of carnival, on the feast of the Ascension. With this gown ... we have every chance. You see, Tazzio is in love. Ah yes, the boy has given his heart to a young girl from San Severino, Messer! He feeds upon her beauty, he tells me; it is his inspiration for the gown. What more propitious inspiration could there be than love?'

Spadetti ran his fingers through his son's blond locks and the boy looked up. His cherubic gaze fell for a moment upon Pietro and he smiled, nodding a silent greeting.

'*Congratulazioni*,' said Pietro. 'It is truly a thing of remarkable beauty. But surely you do not leave it here for all to see?'

The glazier smiled. 'Everything we create here is remarkable, Messer. It is fitting that everyone should know our work. The glassworks of Murano are friends; rivals but friends. Let us simply say that this gown is a means of …' He fumbled for words.

'A means of proving he is a master of his art?' said Pietro. 'But do you truly think that a woman could wear the gown?'

Spadetti smiled, half-mocking, half-disdainful. 'That is the question.'

Pietro considered the man for a moment, then turned back to the gown. The contest for the rank of *maestro* was not the prerogative of glassmakers alone. For centuries, each of the guilds had organised such tournaments. The church of San Giovanni, by the Rialto, held an annual tournament where artisans and merchants came to participate: the creations of the former determined by the donations of the latter – it had a certain beautiful symmetry. This gown was a perfect expression of that art. At length, Pietro coughed.

'Federico, would you permit me to examine your order book? You must have a register … records of some sort?'

Spadetti stiffened, hesitating for a moment as he eyed Pietro warily, then he relented.

'Do you know how many orders this workshop fulfils each month, sir? More than three thousand, despatched to cities across Europe. Of course I keep records. And I have a very large register. Come, let us go into my office, we shall be more comfortable there.'

The two men stepped into the small room which set the *capomaestro* apart from the commotion on the floor of the workshop. Pietro had despatched Landretto to show the *stiletto* to Brozzi and to enquire whether the coroner had discovered anything further about the case. The Quarantia Criminale had perhaps uncovered some new information. He sat at Spadetti's grimy desk as the glassmaker rummaged through his paperwork, finally placing a gargantuan tome before him. Pietro studied the volume for several hours while Spadetti returned to his labours. Onto a clean parchment Pietro transcribed details of those who had ordered *stiletti*, together with anything which seemed out of the ordinary – orders for unusual objects or those where a customer attempted to conceal his identity. Two hours later, he had made little headway in his task and was beginning to wonder if it were a futile exercise. He rummaged in the desk where he discovered two further dust-covered volumes from beneath a pile of order forms.

'Well, now …'

He redoubled his efforts, poring over the volumes for a further half-hour. Then suddenly he let out a cry. Clutching the register, he went in search of the *capomaestro* who was once again at his furnace, near to where his son was working on his masterpiece.

'Messer Spadetti. Who is this man, this "Minos"?'

Blinking, Spadetti glanced at the order book. 'Well, I … I don't rightly know. The order came in six months past.'

'In addition to the book you gave me, I discovered two more volumes of orders.'

'There'll be nothing of importance in them.'

Pietro raised an eyebrow. 'I am not so sure. You made the entries in the registers yourself, did you not? And yet the name Minos means nothing to you? Perhaps he made the order in person?'

'That he did not, Messer. Most times orders come through a middleman, besides Tazzio sometimes takes the orders for me. If I had to go round memorising all my customers, I might as well throw myself into the *laguna*.'

'Indeed …' said Pietro doubtfully. 'Look here. According to your entry in the register, the order was for a number of lenses – magnifying glasses to be exact. See for yourself.'

'Magnifying glasses. Could be, could be.'

'Could be?' Pietro's voice was incredulous. '*Twelve thousand ducats* for a few magnifying glasses?'

The men glared at one another.

'With twelve thousand ducats' worth of glass, you could make enough lenses to cover the *laguna* itself, Messer, so I'll not have you tell me that such an order somehow slipped your mind.'

Was it simply irritation at being interrupted at his work, or was Spadetti suddenly very, very anxious?

'Why the devil would any man have need of hundreds, perhaps thousands of magnifying glasses?' demanded Pietro.

Spadetti smiled, somewhat contrite, and removed the rag that served as a cap. 'It was … let's say, a curious order. From time to time, I am commissioned by ambassadors of foreign kings and governments and, now you come to mention it, I wouldn't be surprised if …'

'And this Minos was an emissary sent by a foreign power?'

'Very likely, Messer I remember the man now. A young lickspittle, a clerk or some such. For that kind of order, I don't care to quibble. Long as I hear the ducats clink in my purse and the guild get their share …' He glanced at Pietro, no longer abashed.

'If some foreign king wants to cover his palace in lenses, Messer, that's his business; I couldn't give a fig. And them that work for me make what they're told to make.'

Confounded, Pietro considered the glassmaker for a moment. 'Have you some means of discovering the man's name and address?'

'There'll be an order paper somewhere …' Spadetti paused. 'Suppose you want me to go look for it?'

'Indeed I would, and I'll thank you to do so with better grace, Messer Spadetti. You would be wise to show yourself as being rather more cooperative.'

Spadetti sighed, but he knew only too well that behind

Pietro loomed the shadow of the Council of Ten. He slapped his thighs and got to his feet. 'All right, all right, I'm going!'

He shuffled back to his office, where he quickly located the document. Spadetti seemed sorely troubled as he tendered Pietro a parchment bearing a scrawled, illegible signature. There was no seal or stamp upon the document. A blasphemy escaped Pietro's lips.

'Do you take me for a fool, Messer Spadetti?' Pietro sputtered. 'You have a decidedly lax and curious fashion of keeping rec—'

He had not finished when a labourer suddenly burst into the office.

'Are you the man was sent by the Council of Ten, Messer?'

Pietro looked up and saw a terror-stricken youth of no more than twenty.

'I am he. What is it?'

'I got a message for you from your manservant and a physician at the Quarantia Criminale.'

'Then get a hold of yourself, *giovane*, and give it to me.'

The boy took a moment to compose himself and said: 'A terrible thing has happened.'

While Pietro had been in Spadetti's workshop, dark clouds had gathered over Venice, unleashing a storm of extraordinary ferocity. Furious squalls whipped up monstrous waves on the *laguna* and Pietro was fortunate indeed to return safely. When, at length, he disembarked at San Giorgio Maggiore, a throng of citizens were standing before the church in the torrential downpour. A hundred souls stood petrified, gazing heavenward. They covered their mouths with their hands, made the sign of the cross, and shrieks and screams came from all around as they glanced at one another in horror and revulsion. Pietro cut a path through the milling crowd and, unable to make himself heard above the tempest, he elbowed his way to join Antonio Brozzi and Landretto. He bellowed to Brozzi: 'What is it? What has happened?'

The coroner said nothing, but gestured for Pietro to lift his gaze to the portico that towered above the entrance. Soaked to the skin and buffeted by the driving rain, Pietro had some difficulty focusing at first. Then, suddenly a monstrous peal of thunder broke with the sound of hell itself yawning. The heavens blazed, the clouds rent by lightning bolts.

Pietro turned, dumbfounded, to Landretto, shocked by the abomination he had witnessed, for in the livid glare he had seen a human form, tossed like a weather-vane by the gale. The body was held in place by a thick cord, attached to the apex of the portico, seeming to embrace the chalk-white statue which crowned the tympanum. Above, the thunderous peal of the bells threatened to rupture Pietro's eardrums. The corpse continued to sway back and forth, arms and legs dangling uselessly. The body had clearly been struck by a thunderbolt, for it had been charred beyond recognition and was now no more than a grisly mass of smoking flesh tossed about by the storm. The grotesque figure looked like a spectre sprung from some demonic vision. Tattered garments hung in rags from the body, which merely added to the piteous spectacle. Two men had clambered to the summit of the portico and endeavoured to disentangle the monstrous corpse from its gibbet. Using ropes, they had scaled the interior of the church before venturing out onto the treacherous, rain-slicked roof. They laboured to maintain their balance as they reached out to reclaim the body, while below them, the drone of the crowd grew louder.

'It is Caffelli,' said Landretto. 'Marcello's confessor. They have hanged him … hanged him from the summit of his own church!'

When, at last, the ropes about the priest had been

loosened, the body was lowered on long ropes to the piazza. The officers of the Quarantia Criminale struggled to keep the mob in check in order that Brozzi, Pietro and Landretto might make their way into the church. The double doors opened before them and they stepped into San Giorgio. The church was in darkness, and the men darted about with a taper. They lit the candles on the altar in the *Cappella dei Morti*, where they laid out the body. Brozzi, his sodden medical bag by his feet, began the autopsy. Standing over the altar and cadaver, the coroner looked like a *Pietà*, as if he were giving the priest the last rites. As he surveyed the scene, Pietro feared he was losing his wits, for looming behind Brozzi was the immense canvas depicting Christ being taken down from the cross. Suddenly overwhelmed, Pietro brought his hand to his mouth to stifle a blasphemy. *The Deposition* ...

Beads of water still dripped from the brim of his hat as he stepped out of the shadows and mounted the steps to the altar.

'I shall see whether it is possible to salvage anything,' said Brozzi. 'The body has clearly been struck by lightning.' He turned his attention to the upper body, gently probing with tweezers as a strip of flesh fell away. 'Some two-thirds of the body and all of the hair have been charred and burned. The hair on the upper body seems to be ... Pietro, if your manservant has no other task, he might take notes for me – there are some sheets of vellum and a quill in my case. It will save time, and I shall need them for my report. The lad can write, I take it?'

Landretto glanced enquiringly at his master. Pietro said nothing, but nodded almost imperceptibly. Landretto approached the altar, rummaged in the coroner's medical bag and withdrew parchment and plume. He started diligently noting the physician's comments. For his part, Pietro had only half an eye on the proceedings, still drawn to the painting of *The Deposition*. In the foreground, the Virgin,

Mary Magdalene, and Joseph of Arimathea are collecting the blood of Christ and in the background are the Roman centurions, thunderbolts rending the heavens with the wrath of the Almighty. Above the fresco was the tabernacle. Pietro stepped forward. Decidedly, the murderer had a taste for biblical metaphor. The connection between the '*Deposition*' of Marcello, lowered from his own cross, and that of Caffelli from the portico of San Giorgio was no coincidence.

'Father Caffelli was bound with cords,' said Brozzi. 'Ligature marks are still visible around the throat, the torso, the wrists, knees and feet. Wait ... here is something ... There is a small bruise at the nape of the neck and slight fracturing at the base of the cranium, which indicates that he was knocked unconscious before the body was hoisted onto the portico. It is difficult to imagine that such an abomination could have been carried out by one man. It is likely that Caffelli regained consciousness up there, swinging in the winds.'

Surely the Chimera could not command the natural elements, could not know that a thunderbolt would strike the church and thereby kill the priest? Unless he truly was *il Diavolo*, a fiend incarnate, with the power to call down a thunderstorm upon the city. Pietro could not put the idea of some occult magic from his mind.

'There is something else ...' said Brozzi.

He removed his pince-nez and wiped the lenses, fighting the urge to retch. Removing a tattered scrap of fabric, he discovered charred flesh about a fresh, gaping wound. 'He was castrated.'

Brozzi took a deep breath and settled the pince-nez on the bridge of his nose. 'Had lightning not struck him, he would have quickly bled to death. Clearly he was not stripped of his clothes, but was still wearing his alb, though little of the garment remains.'

Pietro lightly touched the painting of *The Deposition*, at which he had been gazing. It was, he now realised, a painting and not a fresco, as he had first imagined. Suddenly, he noticed a slight difference between the colour of the whitewashed wall and the spot where the painting *should have* been. There could be no doubt that the painting had recently been moved. The frame seemed to hang at a curious angle, the painting not quite level. Pietro ran a finger along the border then, stretching his arms wide, he gripped the frame and, bracing himself, attempted to unhook the canvas. Landretto, seeing his master lurch for an instant, dropped his quill and, to Brozzi's astonishment, ran to help. Pietro and his manservant lifted down the immense canvas and placed it some distance away. Then they looked back at the space where the painting had hung: there was a great jagged crack in the plaster.

Brozzi continued to mutter to himself, but Pietro could not hear him. *Miseria.*

He stepped back slowly. When he drew level with the physician, Brozzi, perturbed by the sudden, deathly silence, removed his pince-nez and turned to look at the wall.

La bufera infernal, che mai non resta,
mena li spiriti con la sua rapina;
voltando e percotendo li molesta.

The hurricane of Hell in perpetual motion,
Sweeping the ravaged spirits as it rends;
Twists and torments them.

And, a little farther down: *Vexilla regis prodeunt inferni.*

A new inscription, not cut into living flesh as it had been with Marcello, but inscribed upon on the wall.

'Written in blood,' whispered Pietro. Aghast, he turned to Brozzi.

The coroner of Quarantia Criminale let his hand fall upon the mutilated corpse. The banner of the King of Hell is raised.

CANTO VI
THE HURRICANE OF HELL

THE PROBLEM OF EVIL

Andreas Vicario, member of the Maggior Consiglio
On Sin and the Divine Retribution:
Evil and Power, Chapter IV

The entire edifice of Judeo-Christian faith is founded upon a single concept: the awareness of sin, and – owing to the nature of original sin – the transmission of such awareness to succeeding generations as the cornerstone of civilisation. Faced with such a concept, heretical groups may adopt only one of two positions: they may reject it outright and thereby devastate the underpinning of morality, or they may declare it to be incomplete, inconsistent with the source texts, and appeal to the rigorism of *Extra Ecclesiam nulla salus*. In either case, sin is triumphant, for it is a rejection of the Divine that conditions the exercise of spiritual power, without which Lucifer reigns. Where terror breeds, power multiplies: from this stems the paradox that Evil is the supreme instrument by which religion governs; this is why empires are imposed only by force; it is why the Problem of Evil is not merely personal but political; it is a further sign of Satan's triumph in the world.

'The murderer or murderers worked quickly,' Pietro

concluded. 'Quickly, but, it must be admitted, with considerable skilfulness.'

Alarmed, the doge appeared to lose his customary composure. Pietro, Emilio Vindicati and Antonio Brozzi were sitting before him in the sala del collegio. Outside, the storm raged and inside the chandeliers had been lit against the darkness. From time to time, Brozzi gazed up at the frescoes on the ceiling. It was evident that he would have preferred to be elsewhere. So much anxiety was injurious to his heart.

'It cannot be, it cannot be …' Francesco Loredan repeated, shaking his head. He pounded his fist on the armrest of his throne. 'We may have succeeded in suppressing news of the murder of Marcello Torretone from the populace, but this time, all of Venice knows what has happened! The affair cannot but be brought before the Maggior Consiglio, Emilio. Prepare yourself, for you and several members of the Quarantia Criminale will be called upon to give an account of the investigation. We must once more plot a course through turbulent waters if we are to preserve state secrets from public scrutiny. The Council of Ten and the Quarantia Criminale must allay suspicion if Pietro's clandestine investigation is to have any prospect of success. I do not like the look of this, Emilio, I do not like it at all. You have put me in a most unpleasant position. The men of the Great Council are not fools; if they suspect they are being circumvented, they will be merciless. What have we learned so far?'

'The note signed Virgil – the *Dance of Shadows* – has led nowhere,' said Pietro. 'At first, I confess I thought Virgil to be some accomplice of Emilio, but he assures me he knows nothing of the letter. We know, however, that the note and the discomfiting scene I witnessed at the *casa* Contarini is connected to the murders both of Marcello and of Father Caffelli. If, as I believe, Marcello and Caffelli were lovers, it is likely that both posed a very real threat to the man or men we seek. But what I find most disturbing is the fact that someone is already aware that I have been charged with this mission! Indeed, on my trip to Murano I believe that I may have been followed. And Father Caffelli told me that, "The enemy is everywhere.' Information about this investigation has been leaked, either by one among us – forgive me, but I must consider every hypothesis – or perhaps by Caffelli. That, or one of the players at the Teatro San Luca suspected something and spoke of it. Or it may have been Luciana Saliestri, whose brooch was found in the theatre.'

'The pastor of San Giorgio,' murmured the doge. '*Dio Onnipotente!* What a terrible thing for his parishioners ...'

'If this goes on, then our investigation cannot long remain secret,' said Pietro. 'I agree with you, *Serenissimus*: whoever is behind this wishes to flush us out, to thrust this scandal into the public eye and thereby embarrass us. The murderer has cleverly plotted, leading us into a trap which reeks of political conspiracy. The spectacular, theatrical nature of the murders tends to support Emilio's intuition that we are dealing with a cunning and skilful man; a man intimately aware of private peccadilloes of his victims. It could be a man from one of our patrician families – or indeed a foreign agent, *Serenissimus*, who has contracted vile men to carry out these despicable deeds. It is not unheard of.'

'But who is this man?' demanded the doge uneasily. 'A Venetian nobleman, a foreign spy, the ambassador of a powerful enemy? Could it be this Minos, who, right under our nose, from what you discovered in Spadetti's register, can order a vast shipment of lenses for we know not what purpose? It makes no sense ... and what would be the motive of such a man?'

'I fear I do not know,' said Pietro. 'To shake the republic, to bring our institutions to their knees? True, neither Marcello nor Caffelli were obvious political targets; but

Marcello was working for the Ten and as his confessor, Caffelli knew too much, that much is clear.'

The doge half-nodded. He wiped his brow and adjusted his *corno ducale* and then rose. He walked towards the great windows, staring at the intricate constellations formed on the glass by the driving rain, and beyond them lay the grey-black abyss of the *laguna*. As he turned back, a thunderbolt ripped across the sky.

'Beneath these elegant facades all is rottenness and sin and putrefaction! What, then, is hidden in the souls of men, Lord? No … No, this is not enough – we need to move quickly.'

Emilio Vindicati raised his hand. 'Let us think logically, *Serenissimus*, we must not allow ourselves to be swayed by the bizarre convolutions of these murders, nor credit our adversary with more cunning than he has. I have despatched agents to comb the ledgers of Spadetti and the Glassmakers' Guild. As we speak, the order has been given to interrogate every glassblower in the city – beginning with Spadetti, who claims to know no more than he has said. We have threatened him, but he remains silent as the grave. We have no proof that he is in any way involved in these crimes. He does not deny that he received and fulfilled the order, but claims he can remember no more, and that a clerk failed to note the details or the transaction in the ledger – this he regrets. His amnesia is, however, fortuitous. The problem remains that, in the absence of any information as to the identity of this Minos who ordered the lenses, I cannot detain Spadetti indefinitely … and I am surprised the Council of Ten did not act more quickly in verifying the *capomaestro*'s documentation: this was an oversight that I cannot comprehend. If we are to release Spadetti, let us have him followed, try to get him to talk, though I cannot tell whether there is much to be gained. We need to focus on discovering something more about the Firebirds and the verses both on Marcello's torso and behind the painting in San Giorgio Maggiore.'

'Yes.' said Pietro. 'What most intrigues me is Luciana Saliestri's brooch and her liaison with Senator Giovanni Campioni. This seems to me the only physical evidence. I need to speak with Campioni, but to do so entails taking into our confidence one of the most senior politicians whose connections to the Maggior Consiglio are well known. In this, I shall have need of you, *Serenissimus*, or perhaps Emilio, to prepare the ground for me. And we must agree upon a strategy. Campioni is our chief suspect, though I confess I think he is a little too obvious.'

'I agree,' said Brozzi. 'It almost seems as though we are being deliberately led to him. The golden brooch found by the body of Marcello in the Teatro San Luca may well have been left there by design. It may simply be another trick. But if all evidence leads to Senator Campioni, then Pietro must attempt to discover what the senator knows.'

There was a silence, broken only by the hammering of the rain on the windows. Francesco Loredan took a deep breath and said: 'Very well. Let us see what the senator can tell us.'

The *Broglio*, as the *piazzetta* garden at the foot of the *Palazzo Ducale* was known, was among the most curious of places. It was here, every morning, that patricians gathered to discuss public affairs. Indeed, the *Broglio* fulfilled a political function, for it was here that the *prima vestizione della toga* took place – an initiation whereby a nobleman recently come of age and called to serve on the Great Council 'first donned the robes'. But the *Broglio* was also the place where schemes were planned and conspiracies hatched. This was not without irony, given that here in the *Broglio*, engraved upon plaques which ran the length of the arcade itself, was a list of the crimes committed by traitors to the republic, and the punishments meted out to them. And it was here that Pietro had arranged to meet with *Sua Eccellenza* Giovanni Campioni. The sky was still overcast, but the weather more clement; from time to time a ray of sunshine burst through the clouds, illuminating their path through the garden. The flowerbeds exuded that sweet perfume of the calm after the storm.

'So,' said the senator, 'you are the Black Orchid! I have heard much concerning you ... your escapades have long been the talk of the Maggior Consiglio and, indeed, the Senate. Many have wondered – indeed, many wonder still – whose side you are on. Is Senator Ottavio aware that you have been released?'

'I do not know ... but I do not believe so, and it is perhaps better thus.'

Pietro allowed a silence to settle for a moment. '... but we have a more pressing matter to discuss, I think.'

'Indeed ...'

Campioni heaved a sigh. 'Marcello Torretone, Father Caffelli ... You tell me that the Council of Ten believe these two incidents are connected?'

A man of some sixty years, Giovanni Campioni was dressed in the black ermine-trimmed robe of the noble members of the senate, buckled at the waist by a belt of silver plate and, upon his head, the black skullcap, the *baretta*. Head down, frowning, he leaned upon his cane as he walked by Pietro's side. After some moments, Pietro stopped and turned to him.

'Have you seen Luciana Saliestri of late?'

Surprised, Campioni stopped short. He stood beside a verdant flowerbed whose vivid colours contrasted sharply with the austere robes and the sombre expression of the patrician. 'I have ... that is to say ...'

'Forgive my question, *Eccellenza*, but as you shall discover, the matter is intimately linked to my investigation. I wonder, did you perchance give Signora Saliestri a gift some time ago, a gold brooch set with pearls bearing the initials L. S. on a design of crossed swords and a single rose?'

Campioni was completely taken aback. 'I did indeed –

you have described it most accurately. Nonetheless, I would like to know by what right you …'

'And when did you last see Luciana Saliestri wearing that brooch?'

'A fortnight since, perhaps, but …'

'Two weeks ago … and you have not seen the jewel since?'

'No. Now I demand that you tell me what connection there might be between my gift and the murky deeds of which you spoke earlier.'

'The brooch, *Eccellenza*, was discovered in the Teatro San Luca, at the foot of the body of Marcello Torretone. Though Luciana said nothing of the matter to you, she claims that the brooch was stolen from her some days earlier, though she cannot say by whom.'

Campioni lifted his head and scowled; the hand which held the pommel of his cane trembled. 'And this is why the Council of Ten insisted that I speak with you?'

'Indeed, *Eccellenza*. Tell me, were you aware that Luciana Saliestri was also Marcello's lover?'

Campioni nodded, clearly finding it increasingly difficult to retain his sang-froid. 'How could I fail to know of it when all of Venice knew? Luciana has many men in her life …'

Something in the senator's tone, though it was barely a whisper, told Pietro all he needed to know. Campioni was in love with Luciana Saliestri, and the very idea that the courtesan should take other men to her bed was clearly a torment for him. Campioni's face crumpled into a mask of pain which he did his best to conceal.

'It is true. I love her,' confessed Campioni, as though he had somehow guessed Pietro's thoughts. 'For ten years now, I have loved her. It is ridiculous, what say you? That a man of my stature should tremble at the mere thought of holding in his arms a courtesan, a young harlot well known beneath the arcades of the *Procuratie*? I know it only too well. But this woman is my opium, my spice, I cannot cure myself of her company. She is my shame, and yet I shudder at the very thought that some day I shall lose her. She is one of those women who can bewitch a man, cause him to suffer the bitter torments, and yet ensnare him more surely than Diana the huntress. She is a praying mantis, worshipped but deadly. Dear Lord ... But this, I take it, is something you have already discovered for yourself?'

The image of Anna Santamaria, the Black Widow, flashed before Pietro's eyes. He did not reply directly. 'Have no fear, *Eccellenza*,' he said, walking on a little, 'I find your candour refreshing in these duplicitous times.'

They fell silent again for a moment, and then Campioni spoke: 'As to the brooch, if it was stolen from Luciana, I am in no way blameworthy. Surely you do not believe that I am in some way entangled in these sordid crimes?'

Pietro smiled. 'Far be it from me to accuse you of such a thing, *Eccellenza*.'

Campioni seemed reassured; his breathing was calmer now. But Pietro had simply sidestepped the senator's more probing questions. He rummaged in his pocket and withdrew two scraps of parchment which he proffered to Campioni.

'These inscriptions were discovered at the crimes; the first was carved into the torso of Marcello Torretone, the second was found in the church of San Giorgio Maggiore. Do they mean anything to you?'

Campioni took the parchments and read:

I was new to this condition when I beheld
A Mighty One who descended here arrayed
With a crown of victory

The hurricane of Hell in perpetual motion
Sweeping the ravaged spirits as it rends,
Twists and torments them.

Vexilla regis prodeunt inferni.

'Well,' said the senator, clearly struggling to decide what the words evocated. 'To speak truly, I believe I have read these words before. But where?'

He wiped his brow and turned to Pietro. 'What is the significance of these epigrams? They seem almost like a poem.'

'With no context, even when taken together, they do not seem to signify anything ... The context is all, and that is what I am determined to discover.'

Pietro took a deep breath and, throwing caution to the wind, said: '*Eccellenza*, I would like you to tell me all you know about the Chimera, and about those who call themselves the Striges – the Firebirds.'

Campioni's fingers trembled as he clutched the parchments. He glanced about them. Pietro knew at once that his words had hit home. With bated breath, he waited for the senator to speak. Campioni had reacted at a mere mention of the Firebirds, just as Caffelli had done when Pietro informed him of the crucifixion of Marcello Torretone. The same sickly pallor overcame the senator, the blood drained from his face and he began to perspire. He brought his hand to his chest, grasping with his other hand for Pietro, as though the scraps of parchment, still clutched between his fingers, had been impregnated with poison. His eyes gleamed with terror and he leaned towards Pietro and whispered: 'Then you know of them?'

'Tell me what you know!' demanded Pietro.

Trembling, Campioni hesitated. He glanced about them again to ensure they were not overheard.

'I ... I see shadows, I constantly fear that I am followed. I tell myself they are but creatures of my imagination. But in truth, I am afraid.'

Pietro persisted. 'Two foul murders have been committed, *Eccellenza*, and we can have no reason to suppose that there will not be others. It is imperative that you tell me all you know. Who are the Firebirds?'

The two men stared at one another for a long moment, and then Campioni placed his arm about Pietro's shoulder and led him farther off. When at last he spoke, his voice was troubled and uncertain.

'I speak of a cult, *amico*, a secret organisation led by a man known only as the Chimera, or *il Diavolo* – no man knows his true identity. I speak of a satanic cult whose head is here in Venice and whose limbs stretch far onto Terra Firma ... It is said that their power and influence extend beyond the republic, beyond Italy itself. These, then, are the Firebirds. But there is worse, much worse ...'

'What do you mean?'

'Some of their number have infiltrated our institutions, have inveigled positions in the judiciary, the Holy Office, all the way to the Senate and the Maggior Consiglio!'

Pietro had to think quickly. 'But to what end? What is their goal?'

Giovanni looked at him again. 'Their goal? Come, *amico*, that much is surely evident! Noblemen are fleeing the city for the country or abroad, our naval fleet is forced to retreat, the city teems with gambling and debauchery; Venice is in decline! The Black Orchid – you yourself – are but a product of the times! All the splendours of the republic are not enough to hide the gangrenous canker which eats away at it. *Power is their goal!* They seek to establish a *dittatura* – or, if you prefer, an autocratic government. Do you know on what the glory of Venice is founded? On our mastery of the seas. Who commands Venice, commands the Adriatic, the Mediterranean, and the trade routes to the Orient. Is that not enough for you? Truly, you are naïve if you believe that is not enough for all the world ... But if all are agreed that the golden age of Venice is no more, none can agree on how it might be restored. These murders you speak of are but the trees for which you cannot see the wood! I plead with the Senate to be more generous with the citizenry, to allow them to participate fully in our institutions, but to no avail. Do you realise what is being talked of in France, in England? The crowned heads of these countries live in fear; it is said that their philosophers propagate dangerous ideas among the people. Yet we must have faith in our power to reform our institutions, for they are in sore need of reform! Many among the members of the Maggior Consiglio are of like mind, but we know only too well what such democratic ideas cost Doge Falier. And in speaking my mind I have whipped up much ill-will, and now voices are being raised, demanding harsh and repressive measures to bring order to the city. There is a mood of intransigence abroad. The Firebirds are an accursed sect who seek to heap disgrace upon the government and I fear that I am in their sights. As, no doubt, are you. The only thing which stays their hand is the knowledge that should their plotting be too blatant, it might well rebound on them. The war we wage is more insidious: it is a war of shadows, a power struggle waged by courtesy and precedence. I have tried many times to forewarn the doge, but he seems ill-disposed to listen. There are several statutes currently under discussion which challenge every means by which we might prevent this serpent's egg from hatching. My attempts to thwart the Firebirds are frustrated at every turn – not directly, you understand, but insidiously, calculatedly in such a manner that I can never tell from whence the fatal blow has come. Do you know why that brooch was stolen from my beloved Luciana and left in the Teatro San Luca for you to discover? To incriminate me, evidently. They want rid of me, me and the partisans to my cause. I cannot even sue for protection, for who could say there would not be a double agent among my protectors? Trust no one, *amico*, no one is above suspicion.'

Giovanni Campioni had not paused for breath as he spoke, but here he broke off, hung his head, and allowed his shoulders to droop.

'Enough of this, I have perhaps said too much already.'

Pietro still had a thousand questions he longed to pose. He would have persisted, but the senator raised a cautionary hand.

'No. I have said enough. Two lives are at stake here; mine and yours. Leave me now, I beg of you. I must reflect on how best to protect myself and those dear to me. If I should come upon information I believe may be useful to you, I shall convey it to you at once. Where are you lodging?'

'In the apartments of the *casa* Contarini.'

'Very well … but any information I impart is for you alone; you must speak of it to no one, excepting the doge himself, *capisci*? You must tell no one else, not even those among the Council of Ten.'

'I give you my solemn vow.'

Campioni strode away, his countenance grim, waving his hands as if to dismiss Pietro, though Pietro remained where he had stood in the centre of the *Broglio*. *A dictatorship in Venice. A conspiracy of satanists!*

The Black Orchid allowed his fingers to trail along the curve of Ancilla Adeodat's generous buttocks as she lay laughing, reading aloud from a play, playing each of the characters in turn. Indeed, she was an actress of considerable talent. From time to time, she would turn to Pietro and smile, but his thoughts were elsewhere. He caressed the dark flowing hair of the young woman who he had once more inveigled away from her husband, a captain of the Arsenal, who was presently far at sea somewhere. The beautiful Ancilla had something of the soul of a poet. Of her native Cyprus she retained memories of the scent of gardens in bloom, of olive oil and ochre, and the spices of the Orient; her mother, a native of Nubia, had been sold as a slave to her father, an Italian nobleman born in Verona. Ancilla, too, had been bought and sold her whole life until the unconditional love of her brave captain had rescued her. He was forgiving of her indiscretions while he was away at sea; anything which made his beautiful wife happy, made him happy also. He asked only that she be home in Verona when he returned. Pietro could not but pay tribute to the officer's noble selflessness.

Ancilla's merry voice echoed in the room.

FULGENCE: Listen to me and speak as I do bid you. Signor Leonard is about to make a most advantageous marriage.
BERNARDIN: I am well pleased.
FULGENCE: But unless he has the means to pay his debts, he may miss out on this profitable venture.
BERNARDIN: How so? Such a man as he need only stamp his foot and money doth appear from every side …

Ancilla turned to Pietro, mocking him:

PIETRO: I pay you no heed, sweet light of my life.
ANCILLA: Why such a sullen glare, Pietro? *Oh, Pietro!*

Tearing himself from his meditations, Pietro smiled and apologised. 'Forgive me, Ancilla. It is simply that I have a curious matter on my mind.'

Ancilla rolled over, winding a sheet about her as she sat cross-legged on the bed, her hand on her knees. Pietro admired her shapely legs, the russet areolae of her breasts and her dark hair cascading about her shoulders. She took a piece of fruit from the small table and bit into it with gusto before asking, with her mouth still full: 'Can't you tell me what it is? Perhaps I can be of some help? Mmmm … this is delicious.'

'No, my love. Such matters are better kept to myself.'

'What is it that you do with the Council of Ten? You know that people have begun to gossip about you?'

'I expected as much. And what exactly do they s—'

A sudden knock interrupted him. Pietro rose, threw on some clothes and opened the door. There stood a small child dressed in rags, smiling radiantly up at him. The boy was picking his nose, his angelic face was filthy, and he was missing several teeth, but his laughing, insolent smile more than made amends.

'Who let you up here?'

The boy's smile broadened. 'Viravolta de Lansalt?'

'Himself.'

The boy handed Pietro a parchment which had been folded and sealed. 'I got a message for you.'

Surprised, Pietro snatched the letter. He was about to close the door, but the child did not move. Pietro understood, went and found his purse and handed the urchin a few small coins and watched the boy scamper down the stairs. Intrigued, Pietro broke the seal and ripped open the letter. On the bed, Ancilla sat up.

Well, well, things are moving swiftly, thought Pietro as he read:

The birds are flocking and tomorrow will be gathered in the aviary: should you wish to see this magnificent spectacle, you must go to Terra Firma, to the Villa Mora in Mestre. The place itself is a ruin, but by the light of an open fire, you will find it a cordial place to exchange confidences. A note of caution: as at carnival, fancy dress is customary.

G.C.

G.C. – Giovanni Campioni. And by birds he clearly intended the Firebirds, mused Pietro.

'Bad news?' asked Ancilla.

'Quite the contrary, my dove.'

Pietro sank into an armchair, crossing his legs, lost in thought. Ancilla heaved a short, impatient sigh as she toyed with her hair.

'Very well. Since you refuse to tell me your little secret ...'

She fell back onto the bed and returned to her reading.

Pietro bent down to study a low table by his armchair. The table was covered with a delicately embroidered cloth, and on it stood a bronze statue: Cerberus, the three-headed dog, guardian of the gates of hell. Pietro gazed at the creature's savage mouths, its impressive musculature and the forked spiral of its tail. He could almost hear the beast growl and see its fiery breath.

There are thoughts that find a path as singular as it is unexpected, bursting into the mind with sudden clarity: such sudden moments of inspiration are rare indeed. But as he laid the letter down beside the statuette, Pietro knew one such moment of grace. The doubts which had been whirling in his mind crystallised suddenly into a revelation. Suddenly his questions took shape and form, unravelling to reveal a truth he had long searched for. The twin inscriptions – the one carved into Marcello's torso, and the other in San Giorgio Maggiore: *I was new to this condition when I beheld a Mighty One who descended here arrayed with a crown of victory*. Emilio's words as they first stepped outside the doge's palace: *Mark my words, you are about to step into the antechamber of hell*. The signature appended to the *Dance of Shadows* – Virgil. The name of the mysterious customer who had ordered lenses from Murano, Minos. *The banner of the King of Hell is raised*. And now this statue, this three-headed beast; a figurine to which, in other circumstances, he would have paid no heed.

In other circumstances, perhaps, but not in *these* ... His face lit up and his hand flew to his brow. Ancilla leapt from the bed and came towards him, staring in astonishment at his contorted face.

'You look as though you've seen the Devil.'

THE THIRD CIRCLE

CANTO VII

CERBERUS

Pietro headed directly for the *piazzetta* a few short steps from the *Broglio* where he had met with Campioni. From here, one might gaze out at the sweeping panorama of the *laguna*, taking in San Giorgio Maggiore and the Giudecca. The doge's palace was flanked on one side by the *piazzetta*, and on the other by the *Libreria* Marciana. Built by Sansovino some two centuries earlier, it numbered more than 500,000 volumes and was among the finest libraries in all Europe. Pietro had directed his enquiries to Ugo Pippin, one of the librarians, who had advised him on the type of book he sought. Naturally, the *Libreria* had the volume in which Pietro had an especial interest, but Pippin had recommended that he consult the Vicario collection, a private, 'specialised' library located in Cannaregio. Retracing his steps, Pietro stopped for a moment by the Campanile. There, beneath the powerful, majestic winged lion, the symbol of the glories of the *Serenissima*, which seemed to tower over the whole city, Pietro donned the cloak proffered by the waiting Landretto. But as they made their way along the Mercerie, Pietro stopped, suddenly paralysed with fear. He had come face to face with an apparition.

She stopped short at the far end of the street. Pietro could feel his heart thumping in his chest. Anna Santamaria's face was ashen. Her gloved hand tightened about her parasol. She did not move a muscle. She stood no more than twenty metres from him; passers-by moved between them, jostled them, but they stood, frozen, as though unable to move. The meeting was so unexpected that this fleeting moment seemed to last an eternity. Pietro gazed upon her, and felt himself sink into that sweet enchantment. She was swathed in a white sheath dress, the sleeves adorned with flounces of sheer, translucent silk, and a simple belt of ultramarine. Pietro had immediately recognised her inimitable silhouette, her face with her dark doe eyes, long lashes which seemed to be misted with dew from the *laguna*, her wig with its intricately coiffed braids and curls, the marbled whiteness of her throat about which hung a sapphire pendant and, tucked into her bodice, an azure kerchief which accentuated the beauty of her breasts. Her lips parted in a gasp of emotion, lips which she caressed with her trembling fingers and, her eyes shining, she gazed upon him. God, how beautiful she was! The Black Widow, a most unjust and inappropriate soubriquet for, if this were danger, then it was delectable and the torments it provoked exquisite. At that moment Pietro would have given his all for her to truly be a widow, free of Senator Ottavio, her husband. Where was Ottavio, Pietro wondered. Close at hand, no doubt, lurking in the shadows, ready to forbid her her true love. But she was in Venice, not on Terra Firma. Clearly she had not been sent away to some fearsome nunnery, dispatched to some far-flung relative or cloistered in some dreary villa, for *today*, at this moment, she was here! Did Ottavio believe that Pietro still languished in prison, and so allowed his wife to walk abroad?

Anna Santamaria. The lovers gazed at each other, bewildered, unable to take a first step toward the other. Memories of banishment, of prison, came flooding back and, with them, the fear that a simple glance might reawaken in them that which all the world condemned. And yet, as they stood there at that moment, their eyes spoke of a certainty that could not lie.

They looked at one another for a long moment, and then Anna Santamaria took out her fan and lowered her gaze. Her cheeks were flushed. She turned away. Pietro understood. Two of her maidservants caught her up. Happily, they did not notice the Black Orchid. Pietro took cover in the doorway of a nearby merchant as Anna and her ladies-in-waiting rounded the corner.

Pietro could sense that she wanted to accord him one last glance, could feel it in the tremor in her shoulders, in the way she turned her head, and then, as suddenly as she had appeared, she was gone.

Pietro stood for a long moment rooted to the spot. She is here. In Venice.

Pietro felt the urge to rush forward, to run after her, but to do so would be madness. Not simply because of the barely veiled threats made by the doge and by Emilio Vindicati, but because to do so would be to put her life in danger. What, then could he do, now that she was here, now that she was so near, and yet so far? Perhaps Ottavio had brought her to the city for a day or two? Nervously cracking his fingers, Pietro tried to decide what he might do. It made no matter, the simple knowledge that she was near, that all was well with her, was reprieve enough.

Pietro smiled though his throat was tight with emotion. He took a moment to compose himself. There is a time for every purpose under the heaven.

And as he walked briskly towards Cannaregio, he thought: *She is here. She is here ... and she knows that I am a free man.*

Half an hour later, having recovered somewhat from his shock, Pietro presented his *salvacondotto* to gain admittance to the Vicario private collection. He endeavoured to focus; he had to concentrate his energies on his investigation.

According to the owner, a nobleman with the Maggior Consiglio, a man of great disdain and condescension, the Vicario Collection was a trifling thing of some 40,000 manuscripts ranged over two floors. It was a perfect relic of the golden age, the flowering of intellectual and artistic endeavour which Venice had known some decades earlier, when the arts had flourished, in part inspired by the flowering of humanism at the University of Padua and la scuola di Rialto, where philosophy and Aristotelian logic were taught. Printing houses, like the Aldine Press founded by Aldus Manutius, had made Venice the most important printing centre in all of Europe. Historians and chroniclers rubbed shoulders at the Aldine Press, they edited and published the octavos, spoke Latin and Greek, corresponded with the great humanist philosophers of Europe and published some of the most important works in Europe. But as Ugo Pippin had intimated, the Vicario Collection was somewhat particular.

The place itself was fascinating. It had lofty ceilings and bookcases of dark polished wood with ladders strategically placed to access books whose leather spines, chestnut, emerald or scarlet, embossed with gold, wound like great serpents along the walls. Each floor of the annexe to the Palazzo Vicario comprised four separate rooms containing the most precious volumes in the collection, ordinarily reserved for members of the great family and their intimate friends. In the centre of each room was an escritoire where one might read or study at leisure. In the farthest room a window overlooked the canals of Cannaregio. A thin shaft of sunlight from a rose window in the ceiling created a diagonal pattern on the wooden floor.

The Libreria Vicario owed its reputation to the rather particular nature of the treasures contained therein: Andreas Vicario had assembled every possible volume dealing with esoteric philosophy and the occult sciences, whether in Italian, Latin, Greek or any of a dozen European languages: obscure Transylvanian treatises, horrific tales from the Middle Ages and the Renaissance, anthologies of immoral tales, satanic breviaries and works on astrology, numerology and cartomancy – divinatory arts in which Pietro had, at one time, dabbled. In short, every manuscript in the Vicario collection smacked of heresy.

Pietro had requested that he be left alone with the library, and was now idly browsing the bookshelves. He took down a manuscript at random, unfastened the hasp of the purple leather wallet and removed an ancient manuscript on yellowing vellum. *Trasgressioni*, by Tazzio di Broggio, a former Count of Parma of whom Pietro had never heard. Curious, he opened the manuscript and leafed through it rapidly.

> She crouched over him and, continuing to stimulate his member, she released the tension building in her bowels. A smile of relief played upon her lips as she relieved herself, defecating into his mouth as Dafronvielle was sodomised by Messer M***. Then it was the turn of …

'I see …' Pietro murmured to himself. He ran his slender fingers over his lips, a momentary flash of sunlight glinting on one of his rings. He had been warned, but nonetheless the library appeared to contain some unexpected reading matter. Pietro resolved to begin his research in earnest. On every shelf of lustrous wood he discovered some new and hideous oddity. He felt as though he had been thrust into an Aladdin's cave furnished by some evil genie. Here were words which seemed graven into the flesh as if by daggers, fantasies which catalogued the dark side of human passion; goading the imagination to the very brink of nausea. More than once he had to restrain the urge to retch as he perused these scabrous tales. There were four shelves of works dedicated entirely to the subject of Beelzebub. Pietro took down an illustrated manuscript entitled: *Carmelite Studies on Satan*. The introduction to the book had been scrawled with marginalia in red ink. Over the opening sentence, 'Does Satan exist? To the Christian, there can be no doubt', a feverish hand had scribbled a thunderous NO!!, and a second hand had written YES!! Clearly the existence of the Prince of Darkness was still hotly disputed. Pietro ran his fingers along the shelf of manuscripts:

Van Hosten: *Rituals of Exorcism*, Amsterdam, 1339
Augustine of Hippo: *The Enarrations, or Expositions, on the Psalms*, Stuttgart, 1346
Cornelius Stanwick: *Laughter in the Monasteries*, London, 1371
Anasthasius Raziel: *The Forces of Evil and the Diabolical Kingdoms*, Prague, 1336
Dante Alighieri: *The Divine Comedy – Inferno* – copy – Florence 1383, republished 1555

Pietro stopped. This was what he had been seeking. He seized the manuscript. Vicario's copy was a voluminous work of 3,500 numbered vellum sheets, bound in leather and protected by a velvet slipcase. The Florentine scribe who had copied the manuscript had done so in the Gothic style, illustrating the poem with divers episodes from the narrator's travels through the three realms of the dead. The first of these, depicting the gates of hell, had a singular effect on Pietro. It was a curious image, drawing on an improbable alchemy of medieval iconography and the Kabbalah to produce something which seemed to have existed since the dawn of time. Moreover, the gates themselves seemed somehow familiar – though he had braved no gate such as this except perhaps in nightmare. But perhaps it was precisely some vestige of dream and memory, some insensible emotion which made it seem as though he might decrypt the strange symbols which suddenly presented themselves to his gaze. Lurking behind the shadowy portal some radiant flora seemed to have rooted itself in the earth like a towering, funeral cypress from which, knotted and entwined, gnarled branches spread forth as if to burst from the confines of the parchment and clutch the heart. As he surveyed the image, Pietro truly felt as though a hand might surge from the book and seize him, dragging him into the abyss. He might disappear, leaving only a cloud of shimmering dust, the book would close of its own accord, falling to the floor among the millions of pages in this curious library. Perhaps these gates had been waiting for none other than Pietro, they might hold his soul prisoner for all time among the thousand symbols and condemn him to an eternity of torment. He could see himself behind the pier-glass howling, lost in the limbo between worlds. But his terror was swept away in a smile as he read these words, Dante's masterful evocation of the torments of the damned.

At the summit of the portal, where the gates came together in a lancet arch, he could make out a face, the grinning features – half-goat, half-human – of the Prince of Darkness himself with his horns and his forked tongue. His cloak appeared to be the gates themselves, which he parted to reveal the folds of his own flesh and the damned souls within: a mass of skulls, dead shadows, weeping faces, hands seeking purchase to clamber from the quicksand which held them trapped: their tangled limbs shot through with arrows representing their eternal torment. And among the damned, were hordes of winged demons, whirling about the souls of the dead, thwarting their escape. At the base of the gates, the final touch to this catalogue of woe, one could discern the body of Lucifer, the intimation of his cloven hooves disappearing into the darkness, standing astride the abyss. Above the gates was carved the inscription: *Lasciate ogne speranza, voi ch'intrate*.

Pietro immediately recognised the phrase which marked the entrance to the doleful city.

Abandon every hope, who enter here.

Pietro slowly clambered down the ladder. Taking the manuscript, he moved towards the escritoire, placing the volume on green baize next to a paperweight in the form of a ram. He read the preface, doubtless penned by the Florentine scribe who had made the copy:

The Divine Comedy: poem by Dante Alighieri, composed between the years 1307 and 1321. Lost in the 'dark forest' of sinfulness, the poet is led by wisdom (personified by the poet Virgil) through the three realms of the dead. The poet must first truly acquaint himself with the horrors of Evil and witness the sufferings of the souls who inhabit each of the Nine Circles of Hell. Only then may he ascend to Purgatory, where he may expiate his sins. It is from here that, led by Faith and Love, embodied by Saint Bernard and by the poet's paramour Beatrice, Dante ascends through the Nine Heavens of the Ptolemaic cosmology, to the Crystalline Sphere from whence he may glimpse the Empyrean, and know the light of God. Dante gave his work the title *La Commedia*, for he thought it a journey of hope rather than a litany of despair and human iniquity. Later commentators amended the title to La *Divina* Commedia. The compelling structure of the poem draws strength from the mystical value of the number three. It is composed of a hundred couplets, a prologue followed by three parts, each of thirty-three cantos, written in *terza rima*. The cantos abound in rich metaphors and significations: metaphysical, political and social, shifting easily between the classification of infernal punishments, the cosmology of the Heavens, and pointed criticisms of contemporary matters of politics in Florence and Italy; here, biblical personages rub shoulders with those of mythology, historical figures and persons contemporaneous to the author.

> A moral fresco, at once allegorical and lyrical, mystical and dramatic, Dante's work will remain an incomparable masterpiece.

Pietro nodded. How had he failed to realise? Why had he not thought of it sooner? Virgil. Clearly the allusion intended not only the author of the *Aeneid*, but Dante's guide on his descent into Hades.

Pietro picked up the manuscript once more and began reading from the first canto of the *Inferno*. Virgil first meets Dante while the poet is lost upon the paths of sin, and leads him through the Nine Circles of Hell so that Dante may witness the catalogue of human iniquity and the punishments meted out to sinners by the Almighty. The *Inferno*, Virgil explains in Canto XI, is divided into nine circles; three circles for each of what Aristotle names those 'three dispositions that strike at Heaven's will / incontinence and malice and mad bestiality'. Pietro settled back in the chair, running his fingernails along the velvet armrest. Aside from Aristotle's *Ethics*, Dante had drawn his catalogue of inexpiable sins from a myriad sources – from the canons of Roman law to the prophets of the Orient. Indeed, the poet's vision of Hell was based in part upon the ancient Islamic text, *The Book of Muhammad's Ladder*, in which the archangel Gabriel leads the prophet through the three realms of the dead.

As he read on, following Dante as he crossed the River Acheron and descended, circle by ghastly circle, into the very bowels of Gehenna, Pietro learned of the teeming hordes of liars, informers, forgers and adulterers suffering the torments of Hades. Here, catalogued among the ever-descending spiralling circles, depicted with ferocious artistry by Dante, was a catalogue of every cardinal sin:

FIRST CIRCLE

Limbo – The Virtuous unbaptised, whose only chastisement shall be to be for ever deprived of seeing the face of God.

SECOND CIRCLE

The Lustful, who shall be carried away by the Hurricane of Hell.

THIRD CIRCLE

The Gluttonous, here Cerberus stands guard as the gluttons are forced to lie in the mud lashed for ever by rain and hail.

FOURTH CIRCLE

The Avaricious and the Prodigal, who shall be made to push a great weight one group against the other for all eternity.

FIFTH CIRCLE

The Wrathful and the Sullen. In the fetid waters of the Styx, the wrathful shall be made to fight one another on the surface, while the sullen lie beneath the waters.

SIXTH CIRCLE

Heretics, who shall be trapped for ever in fiery tombs.

SEVENTH CIRCLE

The Violent.

The violent against others are plunged into a river of boiling blood. The violent against themselves are transformed into gnarled trees, torn at by Harpies, speaking only when their branches are broken. The violent against God (blasphemers), the violent against Nature (sodomites), and the violent against Art (usurers), are condemned to spend eternity in a desert of flaming sand as fire rains upon them from the heavens.

EIGHTH CIRCLE

The Fraudulent

Panderers and seducers shall be whipped by demons.

Flatterers are steeped in a river of excrement. Those guilty of Simony together with Sorcerers, False Prophets, Hypocrites shall be transformed into serpents. Fraudulent advisers are encased in solitary flames. Sowers of Discord are hacked by a demon wielding a sword. Alchemists, Counterfeiters and Perjurers are visited with mange and leprosy.

NINTH CIRCLE

The Treacherous

Entombed in the icy wasteland of the Ninth Circle are traitors to parents and to kindred, to party and country, to guests, to benefactors and to all authority human and divine. Here, too, is Lucifer, whose three faces devour the most grievous traitors.

Pietro brought his hand to his brow. He thought of Marcello, an actor crucified upon a stage, framed by the red curtains of the Teatro San Luca; of his confessor, Father Caffelli at San Giorgio Maggiore, hanged from the pediment in the midst of a tempest. He took a deep breath. His intuition had been correct. At last, he could begin to discern some dark design behind these grisly deeds. But before he could pierce the heart of this mystery came the thought that he was being manipulated and, with this dawning realisation, came a dark dread. *Il Diavolo* had led him to this place, like some sovereign hand playing with a marionette. The Black Orchid bridled to think that he was being manipulated. But he could not delude himself: discovering that the *Inferno* was at the heart of this enigma owed nothing to his own intellect, but to a clue left for him by a killer of keen intellect. Pietro was being invited to take part in a shadowy game, to solve a puzzle which would draw him into some monstrous netherworld. It did not augur well. Pietro feverishly scanned the verses, reading as if his life depended upon it. Marcello crucified:

'Now we descend into the sightless zone,'
The poet began, dead pale now, 'I will go
ahead, you second.'

Led by Virgil, the poet descends into Limbo, the First Circle of Hell, where Dante pleads with a soul in torment to know whether any soul has ever ascended from Limbo to join the blessed. The next verse shocked Pietro to the core:

I was new to this condition when I beheld
A Mighty One who descended here arrayed
With a crown of victory ...

There could be no longer any doubt – these were the very words that had been cut into the mutilated torso of Marcello Torretone. Brozzi had been convinced the words came from the Bible; Giovanni Campioni recognised the verse, but could not remember its source. Pietro now had proof that the words had not come from any biblical source, but from one of the masterpieces of humanist literature, from Dante's *Inferno*. It puzzled him that he had not thought of it before.

In the First Circle, Dante encounters the antic Poets Homer, Horace and Ovid; here too he meets with emperors and philosophers: Socrates, Plato, Democritus, Anaxagoras and Thales, with Seneca, Euclid and Ptolemy. Illustrious men of art and science whose only sin was that they died unbaptised. It had been here that Christ had descended, from the moment of his death upon the cross until his glorious resurrection, sojourning briefly with the damned. The damned had called him 'the Mighty One', for his name could not be spoken in Hell. Arrayed with a crown of victory, he had come to set free Abel, Moses, Abraham and David, and to lead Israel into paradise.

Christ in hell. Pietro sat back in his chair, pensively stroking his chin. The grisly tableau he had seen at the Teatro San Luca suddenly made sense. It had been carefully staged by the murderer to evoke the First Circle of Dante's *Inferno*. The details that had puzzled him suddenly slotted into place. Like the souls in limbo, Marcello had been a great artist – but one who had renounced his faith for something pagan, for he had been an informer and a spy … and troubled by his desire for other men. Suddenly, Father Caffelli's words came back to him *Marcello was lost. He had renounced his baptism. I was struggling to lead him back to the path.* He had been crucified in the theatre where he had known his greatest success. On the very stage where he had played out his life, Marcello, the most talented of Goldoni's actors had played one last role. Marcello had been tormented and desolate, consumed with sin and by the enigma of his own nature. Marcello, whose eyes had been plucked out in penance for his sins. Condemned forever to look for God, yet never see him …

Pietro shook his head. As he read on, Pietro discovered that Caffelli's death too was eerily described in Canto V of the *Inferno*. Men and women, driven by their base urges as Cosimo Caffelli was, are tormented by the eternal buffeting of the Hurricane of Hell. This was the punishment reserved for Tristan, for Semiramis, for Dido, Lancelot and Cleopatra … and for the priest of San Giorgio Maggiore, his body twisting in the wind beneath the livid heavens. This was the chastisement meted out to The Lustful in the Second Circle of Hell.

Suddenly, Caffelli's words came back to him once more: '*Il Diavolo!* Have you heard talk of him? The Great Council and the Senate know of him, they tremble at the mere mention of his name. Surely the doge spoke to you of him?

The Devil is come to Venice!' Suddenly the words that had tumbled from the terrified Caffelli came flooding back. *Il Diavolo* had staged his second murder; the storm and the lashing winds a deliberate reference to Dante. Then, like a black gondola moving over dark waters, the words of the *Dance of Shadows* returned to Pietro:

Follow me, Viravolta
And you shall see
... how weak is flesh.

As he expected, Pietro had no difficulty discovering the strange epigram he had found in San Giorgio Maggiore behind the painting of *The Deposition*. It had been lifted directly from an eloquent passage in the *Inferno*.

Now I am where the noise of lamentation
Comes at me in blasts of sorrow. I am where
All Light is mute, with a bellowing like the ocean
Turbulent in a storm of warring winds,
The hurricane of Hell in perpetual motion
Sweeping the ravaged spirits as it rends,
Twists and torments them. Driven as if to land,
They reach the ruin: groaning, tears, laments,
And cursing the power of Heaven. I learned
They suffer here who sinned in carnal things –
Their reason mastered by desire, suborned.

Pietro closed the book with a dull sound. The descent into hell. The hurricane. Just as he had suspected, the Chimera was not motivated by chance, but fed upon such wickedness as filled this library. The verses scratched on Marcello's bloodless corpse and scrawled in blood upon the chapel wall of San Giorgio were but the distillation of his studies, pervaded with the stench of death, vacillating between damnation and redemption, martyrdom and resurrection. As to

Minos, arbitrator of sins, judge of souls, he too appears in Canto V, at the threshold to the Second Circle. It is he who discerns for every soul its proper place in hell. Wrapping his tail around him, '*With as many turns/As levels down that shade will have to dwell.*' A wailing crowd of souls press about him – *Oh, Minos, sorrow's hospice* – and to each according to his sins, Minos the dreadful, with a raucous growl, assigns a place in hell. Proof, if proof were needed, that the mysterious customer who had ordered glass from Murano was caught up in the affair. And if Minos was caught up in the conspiracy now taking shape, then it were wise to interrogate Spadetti again. But the irony of the situation did not escape Pietro. In offering him the key to the mystery, *il Diavolo* was daring him to forestall the crimes to come. The Chimera, Pietro was now convinced, was throwing down the gauntlet to everyone – but especially to him.

There are Nine Circles in Dante's *Inferno*.

Pietro cursed. It is a game. A conundrum. He metes out death as Minos metes out punishment to those in hell to expiate their sins. He wants to guide me … as Virgil guided Dante from one Circle to the next until his masterpiece is complete!

And in the Ninth Circle of Hell, as the poet and his guide approach Lucifer himself, Virgil introduces the King of Hell with a Latin phrase which parodies a hymn by Venantius Fortunatus, composed for the Vespers of Good Friday. A line that reads: *Vexilla Regis prodeunt inferni*. The banner of the King of Hell is raised.

The Black Orchid returned to Landretto who was waiting outside the Vicario and together they took the gondola back to San Marco.

'Is all well, master?'

'Believe me when I tell you, Landretto, we are adrift upon a sea of madness. And what is worse, we are dealing with an aesthete.'

'We have been summoned by the doge. He is waiting at the palace.'

Pietro sat down, taking care that the full sleeves of his shirt did not brush the damp sides of the gondola. He smoothed his jacket, and adjusted his hat. 'Well, I'll wager he shall be surprised by what I have to tell him.'

THE FORCES OF EVIL

and the Kingdom of Hell

Anasthasius Raziel

A discourse on the revolt of the angels.

Preface to the edition of 1436

> When they revolted against their Creator, the rebel angels rallied to the banner of Lucifer and demanded to be allowed to wield divine power. They raised an army of nine legions and established a Diabolical Kingdom and dispersed to the four corners of the heavens to prepare themselves for the last battle. To each was allotted a rank, a title and a weapon, upon each was bestowed a particular mission in prelude to the final revolt. When all was in readiness, Lucifer surveyed the winged hordes with satisfaction. One last time, he called upon the Almighty to share his power and, receiving no answer, declared war upon the Godhead. And lo, from end to end, the universe did flare with the conflagration of a thousand stars – for the Time was at hand.

'*The Divine Comedy*? But what has Alighieri's poem to do with the matter?' Francesco Loredan adjusted the folds of his ermine robe, toying with the ducal sceptre.

'It is the key to the mystery, *Serenissimus*,' replied Pietro. 'It is the link which unites these murders. Let us simply say that they are inspired by episodes in Dante's epic. The murderer seeks to mock us.'

Emilio Vindicati leaned forward. 'It is a most important

discovery, your Serene Highness, even if it seems clear that the discovery owes nothing to chance. Pietro's reasoning is sufficient unto itself – it is clear that we are dealing with a man, or faction, of diabolical cunning. If the Chimera is truly set upon executing this plan, the worst is to be feared, for plainly he takes a grisly pleasure in acting out this deadly charade. Nine Circles – nine murders?'

'Are you saying that seven crimes remain to be committed?' The doge's words died in his throat.

Pietro frowned. 'I fear as much.'

Francesco Loredan wiped his brow. 'It is beyond belief.'

They fell silent for a moment, and then Emilio said: 'What we most feared has clearly come to pass. But we have hope yet. If what Giovanni Campioni tells us is true, if indeed we are dealing with a band of conspirators, then I wager that the Council of Ten can quash the threat, as they quashed the conspiracy led by Bedmar when, with foreign assistance, he plotted the sack of Venice itself. We cannot know whether this Minos, with whom Spadetti had been dealing, is the emissary of some foreign power intent on our destruction. Such intrigues have occurred before, *Serenissimus*, at a time when the Most Serene Republic was more powerful still than it is today. Campioni does not ignore the possibility. Nor should we forget that Dante's *Commedia* contains within it a virulent condemnation of several high-ranking political figures in the Florence of his own time.'

'In Florence, perhaps – but this is Venice!'

'The principle is no different. Those who perpetrate these crimes seek to denounce some alleged criminality within the government of Venice. I tell you: these crimes are staged as much to ridicule the power of the Republic, as to dispose of those who stand in their way.'

'But what then? Are you suggesting that this be the work of some foreign power? This is a nonsense!' said Loredan. 'We have our tensions with neighbouring powers, but

Venice was ever thus! We are no longer torn between allegiance to two Empires – as once we were – while struggling to govern our own! In truth, our affairs with foreign powers have been peaceable of late – as indeed it must remain. The newly appointed Ambassador of France arrives next week – it is vital that when I receive him, there is no hint of this upheaval. It is imperative that this matter be resolved within the week. It is unthinkable that Venice should remain mired in terror. Tell me, Emilio. Who among our enemies could sow discord in the republic with such skill? The Turks, the Austrians, the English? Come, I do not credit it even for an instant!'

'The key to solving the mystery lies with the Firebirds,' said Pietro. 'We must determine who holds sway over them. As I have told you, Senator Campioni has sent a message informing me that tonight in Mestre, on Terra Firma, the sect is to assemble. I shall be there.'

Silence fell once more upon the company.

'It might be a trap,' Vindicati said at length.

'If so, then you shall truly know the nature of your enemy, Emilio. If the worst should befall me, you have lost only a prisoner of the republic. I am still a prisoner, am I not?'

Emilio turned to the doge. 'Should we express our gratitude to Viravolta de Lansalt, *Serenissimus*? Certainly we must acknowledge that he lacks neither zeal nor ardour for the task. In other circumstances, such zeal would seem suspect.'

'I stake my honour upon it, *Serenissimus*,' said Pietro. 'I have no more love of ignominy that your Serene Highness. These murders consume my every thought. I am convinced that Giovanni Campioni has information he has not yet confided. If I am walking into a trap, it is one that he alone could have set. Thus he would have been unmasked. Unless, perchance, he is the victim of some loathsome act of blackmail. But for now, we have learned nothing of the enemy ranged against us. I believe Campioni to be sincere, something which cannot be said for the others I have questioned. We can but endeavour to discover more about him, and to continue our interrogation of Spadetti. He may, as he vouchsafes, be innocent, but I rather believe that he has been compelled to hold his tongue.'

'This is all very well,' said Francesco Loredan after a moment's silence, 'but time is short. The emissary of the King of France will arrive any day, and next week, at the feast of the Ascension, the carnival begins again. We cannot allow the festivities and merriment of the city to be blighted by some new tragedy.'

Emilio turned to Pietro. 'I shall delegate a band of men to accompany you to Terra Firma. The time has come to let the Firebirds know that we have discovered their conspiracy – it might dissuade them from further action.'

Pietro shook his head. 'No, Messer. It is too great a risk. We do not know how many are ranged against us, nor who they are. To strike blindly would be foolish – it might simply precipitate their plans. A reconnaissance is vital to any concerted action. If I can ferret out the identity of the assassins, then we shall have the upper hand, especially since they will believe that they have not been unmasked. Moreover, I have faith in no agent but mine own self. I shall need a pair of horses and an escort to the outskirts of Mestre. Nothing more.'

'This is madness,' said the doge.

'Great wits are sure to madness near allied …' said Pietro smiling.

As they left the sala del collegio, Emilio tugged Pietro's sleeve and led him to another room in the palace. Since the Senate convened only on Saturdays, the hall was empty. Here it was that the thorniest issues of Venetian diplomacy were resolved; here that Giovanni Campioni, and perhaps some among the Firebirds, sat in conclave. Now, only Emilio and Pietro stood in this richly decorated hall whose sheer scale accentuated the sense of impending danger. Above them, the graceful arabesques of gilded mouldings framed many frescoes, and in the centre was Tintoretto's masterpiece, *Venice, Queen of the Sea*. Emilio placed a hand on Pietro's shoulder, his face grave.

'You risk your life tonight.'

'If I do not, we risk much more than that. Venice risks her freedom.'

'I must tell you something. The doge has spoken of the new ambassador from France who arrives next week: I have been asked to receive him with all due solemnity. As matters stand, as you can imagine, I shall have to be careful that he learns nothing of what is afoot in Venice and further, to be wary lest anything befall him.'

'We shall know more tomorrow, you have my word on it. Though we are still fumbling in darkness we have made much headway.'

'Your horses and the escort which will accompany you will be posted two hours hence before the palace gates. Prepare yourself.'

Pietro opened his cloak, placed his right hand on the hilt of his sword, his left on one of the flintlocks at his belt. 'I assure you, *Eccellenza*, I am ever prepared.' Pietro smiled. 'Tonight, the Black Orchid will do a little birdwatching.'

CANTO VIII

The Nine Circles

> The birds are flocking and tomorrow will be gathered in the aviary: should you wish to see this magnificent spectacle, you must go to Terra Firma, to the villa Mora in Mestre. The place itself is a ruin, but by the light of an open fire, you will find it a cordial place to exchange confidences. A note of caution: as at carnival, fancy dress is customary. G.C.

'You are the Black Orchid?'

'I am.'

'Come then, night draws in.'

As arranged, an escort went with Pietro and Landretto to Terra Firma. When they arrived at the outskirts of Mestre, the escort withdrew to a safe distance where they had arranged to wait until Pietro returned. If he did not return before daybreak, they were under orders to advise the doge and Emilio Vindicati.

Since the founding of the city, Venetians had come to Terra Firma to escape the urban sprawl of the city. Country houses had sprung up and it was not unusual for families to acquire vast tracts of land and sell their home on the *laguna* to build a new life here. Others were content to have a villa where they might seek refuge for idle weekends, or bring their children, their horses, and their friends to make merry. Here, the nobility enjoyed hunting, organised banquets, tended their gardens or simply took promenades in the countryside. To own a villa on Terra Firma had become a veritable obsession. Pietro and Vindicati had wondered about the Villa Mora mentioned by Senator Campioni in his note: it would have proved most useful to know who owned the property, but once more they met with an impasse. For the Villa Mora, it transpired, was not the country retreat of some mysterious member of the Maggior Consiglio, but a ruin, vacant for decades.

At dusk, Pietro and his manservant rode to a spot from where they could observe the desolate house, which lay on the outskirts of Mestre, where the small town met the low hills. It was unseasonably chill, indeed, since the storm over San Giorgio Maggiore, the weather had been very unsettled. Pietro alighted from his horse and Landretto did likewise. From where they were stationed, they could see the tumbledown villa across the wilderness of bramble and thistle. The villa was enclosed by a low wall of cracked bricks which had also crumbled. Night was drawing in, and thick fog began to unfurl across the landscape. Doubtless carried by the wind from out on the *laguna* – if it had not surged from the bowels of the earth itself – its tattered gossamer snaked into the ruined villa, weaving between misshapen columns. Pietro shivered. It was hardly surprising that the Firebirds should choose such a place for their clandestine meeting: with its tumbledown walls, unkempt gardens, and crumbling archway, it was a bleak and sinister vision. The distant baying of a pack of hounds heightened the mournful atmosphere. Yew trees and cypresses loomed about the perimeter like gravestones and, indeed, some twenty metres from the villa lay a cemetery – a forest of wooden crosses outlined against the dark sky, a myriad tiny spires against the darkness imploring clemency of the night which was fast falling.

'We were better off at the *casa* Contarini,' muttered Landretto.

Pietro stamped his heel, flattening a clod of earth. He

checked his sword and the twin pistols he wore about his belt before drawing his cape about him. Sheltered behind a tree, he peered out from between the dense foliage, staring intently at the villa.

'Unless the moon should come to our aid, we shall soon be able to see nothing. When darkness comes I shall creep closer to the house. You lead the horses off to a safe distance, but not too far, Landretto. Should we need to leave in haste, we shall be glad of them. You see the hill down there? That shall be our rendezvous. If dawn should break and I am not returned, you know what to do.'

'I know.'

They waited. The whole world seemed to teem with phantoms. In the mist it was easy to imagine one could see the mournful souls rising from their sepulchres to wander the earth, the clanking of their chains seemed to echo in the whistling wind. A pale crescent moon appeared from time to time. At about ten o'clock, Pietro and Landretto went their separate ways. The manservant, leading the horses to the post by the hill, Pietro creeping stealthily, ever on the alert, towards the wall which ringed the villa. His eyes seemed to shine in the darkness. His thoughts were consumed by everything that had happened. He thought of Dante and of the engravings he had seen, of the damned entombed for ever into the murky depths of hell, the howling of the tormented souls, of Marcello Torretone and of Father Caffelli, bound to one another by their secret. And then he saw the face of Luciana Saliestri, the beautiful courtesan, and that of Senator Campioni, who had quaked at the very mention of the Chimera. Lastly, he had a vision of Anna Santamaria, as he had seen her on the Mercerie, tugging still at his heart, and felt once more the helplessness this glimpse of her had awakened in his heart and, for a moment, he was unsure how best to proceed. There he remained, kneeling beneath the yew trees in contemplation.

Two hours later, still deep in thought, the drone of the

wind still whipping his ears, nothing had happened. It had grown colder. The hounds were still, the birds asleep. Caught by a sudden wave of drowsiness, Pietro stretched and sat down behind the low wall. He was beginning to believe he was the victim of a rather bad joke. Would he wait fruitlessly here till daybreak? As he was bitterly considering this eventuality, he heard something. He raised himself onto his knees and peered over the wall. Footsteps. He could hear footsteps on the soft ground. A torch flared. Pietro suddenly felt adrenalin course through him.

The flame danced a few scant metres from where he knelt, moving between the bushes along one of the paths in the wild, unkempt garden. It seemed to move of its own volition. After a moment, it came to a halt. The flame licked at the darkness, and suddenly Pietro could make out a hooded figure who seemed to be gazing in the other direction. The mysterious stranger walked on, then stopped again, nodded his head, and another torch blazed into life.

Pietro watched as the twin shadows approached the broken archway of the ruined villa, standing by the overgrown fountain which had once marked the entrance to the place. Then, suddenly, the torches descended by gradual degrees towards the ground and, all of a sudden, they seemed guttered out. Pietro wondered if he had not imagined them. He sat back again. Was it possible, he wondered, that the archway concealed some hidden doorway which led into the bowels of the earth? He had to make sure. He did not have long to wait for barely five minutes later, another torch appeared and the scene played out again. The new arrival walked for a moment, stopped and was joined by a companion before both vanished among the ruins. Thus did the Firebirds arrive, two by two, at regular intervals before proceeding to the place where they were to assemble. *Well then* … thought Pietro. *Our turn to move!*

He waited for a moment and then, with a bound, vaulted the low wall and quickly slipped between the trees to the place where he had first seen the torch appear. When he heard the gravel of the path beneath his feet, he stopped and waited. In the distance, he could distinguish a shadow making its way towards him. It was a hooded figure robed in a monk's cowl, belted at the waist with a white cord. As it drew close, the shadow halted and, in an uncertain whisper, murmured: 'Because the lion roars so loud …'

Pietro blinked, his hand moving instinctively to the hilt of his sword, ready to draw it from its scabbard if the other man were quick. He might sound the alert.

'Because the lion roars so loud … ?' the Firebird nervously said again.

A codeword. It had to be a codeword.

The shadowy figure lit his torch the better to see his interlocutor. As he did so, Pietro's gloved fist caught him square in the face. There was a strangled cry as he was knocked cold. Pietro listened: nothing. In an instant he had dragged the man into the undergrowth and stripped him of his monk's robe. He lashed him securely to a pillar using the cord from his own cape and gagged him with a kerchief, then used his cape to cover the inert body. The face of the man he had thus despatched was unknown to him. Pietro slipped on the monk's attire and returned to the path, struggling to conceal his sword beneath the robe. He drew the cowl over his head, picked up the torch from where it had fallen, then walked down the pathway.

A second torch flared as he was approaching the archway. Pietro cleared his throat, his mouth dry. 'Because the lion roars so loud …' he murmured.

'… he knows no fear of death,' the other man replied.

Together, Pietro and the other 'disciple' walked toward the archway. Pietro was unsurprised to discover, hidden between the ruined archway and columns, a narrow stone stairwell leading down. He followed close behind his acolyte, trying to keep his breathing even. Now, he was truly on his own. The stairwell spiralled downwards, finally opening onto a hall lined with burning torches. Pietro suppressed an exclamation. The vast hall had clearly once been the family vault for, in an alcove, he espied a dusty statue, a supine figure carved in marble, hands clasped in prayer, with a sword by its side. Here and there were other tombs, and cobwebs wreathed the damp catacombs. Six pillars held aloft the vaulted ceiling and a rusted gate of iron barred the passage to a stairwell – long since walled up – which had probably once led to some secret entrance in the garden or, perhaps, to the cemetery adjoining the villa Mora. Those who had preceded Pietro and his stooge were already here. The assembled company nodded to one another in silent salutation before taking their seats on the wooden benches that lined the hall left to right, like church pews. Pietro made certain to sit at the far end of the bench and, bringing his hands into an attitude of prayer, he waited. An altar had been erected at the far end of the room and beside it, a lectern, upon which a book lay open. Drapes of purple velvet framed the altar and, sketched in chalk upon the ground, was a pentagram and various symbols incomprehensible to Viravolta. But what most drew his eye were the paintings which hung left and right. *The Inscription above the Gate*, depicting two men standing on the threshold of the underworld, reminded him of the engraving of the gates of hell he had seen in Vicario's library. In *The Simoniac Pope*, a figure plunges into a cauldron of flames as jagged rocks tumbled all about. Looking closely, Pietro noticed that the artist had given the man the face of Francesco Loredan – the doge himself exposed to public obloquy! Closer still, *Charon* led the souls of the damned across the River Acheron while a storm raged about them. *The Striges and the Demon Hordes* – depicting the Firebirds themselves – stood upon a precipice, grouped about the poet Virgil, flapping their bat wings. There were nine paintings in all. This, surely, is hell itself, thought Pietro.

Little by little, the room filled as other dark-clad figures arrived. Soon, some fifty souls were gathered. They were now arriving more frequently, in groups of three and four. There was no sound but the murmur of voices and the rustle of fabric. As they entered, each group hung up their torches, adding to the glow which bathed the room. Pietro, nervous, was careful not to move. He did not dare imagine what might befall him should he be discovered. Slowly the hum of activity abated and the Firebirds, now ranged by rank and order, turned and, for a long moment, they contemplated the bare altar in hushed silence. Pietro wondered whether they were praying, or perhaps waiting for someone else.

His silent question was swiftly answered when the Supreme Shadow appeared, robed like all the others except for the golden pendant which hung about his neck, upon which Pietro could make out a pentagram of pearls and an inverted cross. *Il Diavolo* – the Chimera – moved soundlessly between the pews and, like an ebbing wave, from the farthest pew to the nearest, the acolytes fell to their knees. After a moment's hesitation Pietro, too, knelt. Since he had been among the first to arrive, he was seated near the altar; if he were forced to flee, he would have to brave more than half the congregation before he reached the stairwell. The thought was not a comforting one but, as he reminded himself, he could not have done otherwise without attracting suspicion. He steeled himself, hearing the collective sigh of the disciples in the presence of their master. If, in other circumstances, Pietro would have found this occult ceremony ridiculous, now it had taken on the quality of a nightmare. Though he was not an impressionable soul, he felt a shudder run through him as the Supreme Shadow passed close to him. He was trapped – he could do no more than remain inconspicuous and play his part in this bizarre ritual. He suddenly realised that he had been a fool to reject Emilio Vindicati's offer to despatch a company of men – a secret militia of the Council of Ten might have stormed this mausoleum and captured these madmen in one fell swoop. But then again, those gathered here amounted to a small army, and might easily have annihilated such a company.

The Chimera invited his disciples to sit. From nowhere, his assistant produced a live cockerel. A rapier glinted in the torchlight as the Supreme Shadow whipped the blade through the air, cutting the bird's throat as he held it above the chalk circle. The wretched fowl uttered a strangled cackle and blood sprayed in long arcs across the pentagram and the altar as the high priest filled a chalice with the warm blood which he brought to his lips. Like Carnival, Campioni had described this sinister and esoteric masquerade. Could it really be that these cowls hid some of the most high-ranking figures in the republic? Could this merely be some deadly game which the decadent noblemen of Venice, inured to evil and to the vilest depravity, played to alleviate their boredom? Surely this travesty cannot be in earnest, thought Pietro. And yet he could not blot from his mind the abject terror he had seen on the faces of Father Caffelli and Senator Campioni.

Suddenly, a voice – *his* deep stentorian voice – broke the silence. The master of ceremonies was standing by the lectern now, poring over the book:

> I am in the Third Circle, a realm of cold and heavy rain
> A dark, accursed torrent eternally poured
> With changeless measure and nature. Enormous hail
> And tainted water mixed with snow are showered
> Steadily through the shadowy air of Hell;
> The soil they drench gives off a putrid odour.
> Three-headed Cerberus, monstrous and cruel,

Barks doglike at the souls immersed here, louder
For his triple throat. His eyes are red, his beard
Grease-black, he has the belly of a meat-feeder
And talons on his hands: he claws the horde
Of spirits, he flays and quarters them in the rain.
The wretches, howling like dogs where they are
    mired …

Il Diavolo continued to read for some minutes more then, turning, went to the altar where he raised his hands:

'As once the poet foresaw the strife of the city of Florence, I say unto you that that same strife is come to Venice, and that you shall be chief among those to sow discord. I say unto you that Francesco Loredan, purported doge, deserves to die, that he too will be devoured. Remember what this great republic once was, only then shall you see what it has become: a place of sin and corruption. Soon, we shall bring it low, only to raise it up to what it was in that golden age. Venice shall once more be Queen of the Seas. And with our fresh powers, we will subjugate lesser nations – as once our Empire subdued its colonies – from end to end of the known world. The city on the *laguna* shall once more be inundated with the wealth and riches worthy of its name; we shall save the destitute, buttress our armies. Our sovereignty shall be strengthened with the wisdom of the ages, and the valour of our soldiers. And you, my Striges! You shall be Harpies and Furies; you shall terrorise the city until that time where, over the vestiges of the old world is built the new, the world of which we dream so ardently.'

'*Ave Satani*,' shouted the disciples with one voice.

A laugh rose unbidden to Pietro's lips, but he masked it with a sharp cough. One of the disciples turned to glare at him. The Supreme Shadow, too, turned its keen eyes upon him for a moment. Pietro froze: but he could make out nothing beneath the cowl, nothing but a black void where the face of his enemy should be. Before he had recovered his wits, a curious procession had begun. One after another, each of the disciples of Satan rose and went to kneel before the altar, in the centre of the pentagram, where they swore an oath of fealty.

'I dub you Semyazza, of the Seraphim of the Abyss,' intoned the Shadow, drawing an inverted cross in ashes upon the brow of the disciple. 'I name you Salikotal of the Cherubim of the Abyss, and the legion of Python-Luzbel. You shall be Anatnah, of the Thrones, led by Belial.'

Pietro had no choice but to follow the throng. Before him, disciples continued to kneel. His tongue flickered over his lips as he wondered whether he would be able to distinguish the face of the Shadow beneath his cowl. This was his one chance, but if he attempted to look, he might himself be discovered. He closed his fist, his hand in the glove damp with sweat. The sword which hung from his belt encumbered him, and he worried that when he knelt, the blade beneath his robes might be revealed. He carefully unfastened the cord knotted around his waist.

'Alcanor of the Dominations of the Abyss, you shall be led by Satan; Amiel and Raner, of the order of Powers, you shall serve Asmodeus. Amalin, you shall follow Abaddon, the destroyer, who leads the Virtues of the Abyss ...'

Pietro barely heard the words of the Shadow, his attention fixed upon the ground as slowly he drew nearer to the altar.

'Sbarionath, of the order of Principalities and Golem of the Archangels shall follow Astaroth ...'

This cannot be. This is some farce, some guile ...

At length, Pietro arrived before the high priest of the sect. He hid his left hand by his side, gripping his sword through the robe. He made an awkward movement as he fell to his knees, and the powerful voice of the Shadow wavered for an instant. Happily, the scabbard made no sound. Pietro found himself kneeling in the centre of the pentagram, gazing at the kabbalistic symbols, then he looked up … The two were face to face, hidden only by their cowls. Pietro could not make out the face of *il Diavolo* any more than the Shadow could discern his. As the Shadow's hand moved to his forehead, Pietro wondered if he would notice that it was damp, and indeed the Master's hand seemed to linger longer than was necessary. Pietro struggled to retain his composure, though he could feel himself begin to sweat and suddenly he feared that the Shadow could sense this, could *smell* his fear, for he seemed to sniff as a wild beast sniffs the air before it falls upon its prey. Kneeling before this giant, Pietro could sense something bestial, and the voice, when it came, seemed suddenly inhuman.

Finally, the Devil's thumb drew the inverted cross in ash upon his brow. 'You shall be Elaphon, of the order of the Angels of the Abyss, and Lucifer your master …'

Pietro rose slowly, wary that the least movement should betray him. He turned on his heel and, taking advantage of the confusion, did not return to where he had been sitting, but headed towards the back of the room near the stone stairwell. As he drew closer to the steps, he felt a surge of relief. The ceremony was not yet over, but it was futile to linger here; it had been madness to venture alone into this nest of vipers. He had to slip away and inform Vindicati of what he had witnessed, though he wondered whether anyone would believe this lunatic tale. Behind him, the Shadow had regained his place at the altar, and raised his hands in supplication: 'And now, my Angels, my Demons, my Firebirds! Go, scatter yourselves abroad through the streets of Venice, but be ever vigilant to the call! But before you go …' Pietro was but a few steps from the stairwell.

'Before we go our several ways, pray join me in a salute. For we have among us one whose presence ennobles this, our ceremony. He is, I have no doubt, the finest swordsman in all of Venice. Gentlemen, the Black Orchid!'

Pietro turned, suddenly rooted to the spot. It was too late now to turn back, to take a seat among the pews. For an instant, he stood stock-still, listening as a clamour rose among the assembled company. The hooded forms looked about them for some sign, some explanation. The Shadow laughed, a long booming laugh which echoed hideously from the vaults of the crypt. Slowly, Pietro turned and saw that the Chimera now pointed a gnarled finger towards him. The hooded faces turned as one to gaze upon the place their Master indicated.

'Behold, my friends, an impostor! *Seize him!*'

Beneath his cowl, Pietro smiled uncertainly. *I knew things would turn ugly.*

For a moment, nothing happened, and then, as one man, the horsemen of the Apocalypse hurled themselves at him.

Instinctively Pietro snatched the flintlocks from beneath his robes. As he did so, his hood fell back, revealing his face. It was time to discover if demons, too, were mortal. Two shots rang out with a sulphurous stench of gunpowder and two of his assailants crumpled with a gurgling whimper, just as they were about to lay hands upon him. The clamour became a roar, demons came at him from every side. Pietro spun on his heel and hurled himself into the stairwell, taking the steps four at a time. He ripped off his robes, throwing them down onto the heads of his pursuers. Outside, two of the Firebirds were standing watch. Taking them by surprise, Pietro pushed past, knocking them to the ground. Without a moment's hesitation Pietro ran, heading east across the garden, vaulting the low wall, the Firebirds still hot on his heels.

Pietro streaked across the meadow, heading for the low hill where he was to meet Landretto. His manservant lay half-asleep beneath a yew tree, his cloak wrapped about his shoulders.

'Landretto!' roared Pietro. 'Landretto, for pity's sake! Fly!'

The terrified lad bolted from beneath the covers and leapt onto his mount. Pietro reached the brow of the hill, a horde, a veritable army of demons brandishing weapons and torches howling behind him like a pack of wolves. Landretto could scarce believe his eyes – for an instant it seemed to him as though the graves had yawned, and the dead returned to life to hunt his master down with curses and enchantments. The valet grasped the reins of Pietro's mount, while his own horse pawed the ground and whinnied. In a final burst, Pietro ran and leapt into the saddle, whipping the poor animal until it reared and broke into a gallop. Master and servant fled, the horses' hooves gouging a salvo of divots from the soft earth.

Their flight brought them quickly to the place where the escort afforded by Emilio Vindicati waited at the outskirts of Mestre. Pietro ordered Emilio's men to follow them without delay, for they had not sufficient numbers to meet the demon horde head-on, and so the company rode hell for leather towards Venice.

Pietro had not found himself in such a situation since his tenure as a warrant-officer of the republic, stationed in Corfu, when he had had to flee the wrath of peasant hordes from the mountains wielding pistols and pitchforks. He would gladly have banished the events he had witnessed tonight from his mind and yet, as his horse galloped toward the *Serenissima*, he could not shake the memory of *il Diavolo*, of his monstrous presence and his voice, which seemed to bellow from the depths of hell.

Vexilla regis prodeunt inferni. The demons of the King of Hell were abroad in Venice.

CANTO IX

THE GLUTTONOUS

Pietro let the manuscript fall back upon the desk with a dull thud, then, moistening his finger, he thumbed through the book to find the passage which had interested him:

> The terms *devil* and *demon* were not introduced to the Bible until some three centuries after Jesus Christ, and were first used by those who worked upon the great translation known as the *Septuagint*. The history of its composition comes to us from a letter by Aristeas, an Egyptian, to his brother Philocrates relating how his librarian, Demetrius of Phalarum, urged the King of Egypt, Ptolemy II Philadephus, to commission a translation of the Pentateuch. Thus the king wrote to his high priest, Eleazar, who chose six men from each of the tribes of Israel, seventy-two men, who were sent out of Jerusalem and into Egypt and there they were met by the king, who wept with joy. For seven days the king did question these men on matters of philosophy and, satisfied with their wisdom, thence did send them to the Isle of Pharos where, locked away from everything, they completed their task in seventy-two days. Legend has it that each was shut up in a different cell and yet, when all of their translations were assembled, they read as the labour of one man, for their hands had been guided by the Lord himself. It was these men who rendered

the Hebrew *shedim* – signifying *lords* or *idols* – by the Greek *daimon*.

Thenceforth, the *daimon*, the great divisive force, which Cyprian called the sprite *which misleads and deceives, and with tricks which darken the truth, leads away a credulous and foolish rabble*, Socrates, became the lifeblood of theology and magick. The authors of the Apocrypha make much of these spirits, favouring them with the names of ancient patriarchs: Henoch, Abraham, Solomon, Moses – the better to be understood. Several among their wisest men sought to set down the hierarchy of the demon hordes. In the year of our Lord 1050, Michel Psellus first divided them into a hierarchical system of six orders contingent on the region of hell in which they dwelt. Others have devised vast demonic kingdoms, offering titles and appellation to seventy-two princes and to 7,450,926 demons, grouped into legions numbering 666 – the number of the Beast as related in the Revelations of Saint John the Divine.

The eyes of the doge widened as he stared at the book. Pietro turned the manuscript so that His Serene Highness might read more easily.

'These are the names I heard *il Diavolo* speak – clearly he has drawn his inspiration not only from the *Divine Comedy*, but has also been inspired by dipping into *The Forces of Evil*, a late Medieval treatise on demonology by a scholar named Raziel. Its hypothesis – that the Nine Legions of the Angels of the Abyss would usher in the apocalypse and the Last Judgement of mankind – was widely credited. See here ...'

The doge leaned over the escritoire to study the book. Here, in complicated engravings, were names in gothic script, together with formulae inscribed in impenetrable tongues.

'The Seraphim, the Cherubim, and the Thrones of the

Abyss make up the First Sphere,' Pietro explained, 'then come Dominations, Virtues, and Powers, and lastly, in the Third Sphere, Principalities, Archangels and Angels. Each legion is governed by a different entity – an avatar of the Devil himself – Beelzebub, Luzbel, Belial, Satan, Asmodeus, Abaddon, Moloch, Astaroth and Lucifer. Their legions will defy the Heavenly Host on the Day of Judgement.'

Pietro snapped the book closed. The doge started at the sound and Pietro looked up to see that Francesco Loredan was ashen.

'Those we are dealing with are lunatics and chief among them, one who believes himself to be the Devil incarnate, one who takes delight in playing this parlous game. I believe he represents a palpable threat, perhaps the most redoubtable the city has ever faced. He goes by many names but the Chimera gives an accurate sense of his mordant wit. He is most partial to arcane symbols, which he uses to embellish his ruses, luring us into his elaborate charades. The most important of these seems clear: he intends that Venice should pass through the Nine Circles of Hell, there to be subjugated by his Nine Legions who, alone, can lead it through Purgatory and to a new golden age. To do this, he would first have to remove you, *Serenissimus*; you are already in their sights. The Striges must assassinate you if they are to seize power, and so bring about the Apocalypse. What I witnessed was some demonic baptism – the naming of the legions with which Satan will mount his *coup d'état*. But there is something else ...'

Pietro took a few paces, then stopped. 'He knew that I was there.'

Francesco Loredan looked at him in horror. Pietro returned, and sat himself at the desk.

'How much time do we have?' asked the doge.

'We have arrived at the Third Circle, *Serenissimus*.'

Slowly, the doge looked up – there was something implacable, unflinching about his gaze now; his eyes seemed to spit fire.

'Names, Viravolta! *I need their names!*'

Pietro glanced at Vindicati, but Emilio said nothing.

'Instruct the Council of Ten and the Quarantia Criminale that, by my command, they are to allow you free access to all their men and means in pursuance of this matter,' said Loredan, 'but *find* these men!'

The doge rose from his seat in a rustle of purple silk. 'We are at war!'

Emilio Vindicati was commanded to recruit seventy-two men in whom he might place absolute trust. In one of the secret chambers of *i Piombi*, such as ordinarily were used to interrogate common criminals, each candidate was interviewed by Pietro. Finding himself once more within the bounds of the prison, Pietro resolved to visit Giacomo. Arriving at the entrance to the cells, he was met by Lorenzo Basadonna who raised his lantern and smiled, revealing his decaying teeth.

'Back so soon?'

Basadonna refused to allow Pietro entry to the cells, boorishly clanking the keys which hung from the belt below his considerable paunch.

'May I at least speak to Casanova?'

'As you like,' Basadonna laughed coarsely.

Pietro shouted through the grille. 'Giacomo! Giacomo, it is I, Pietro!'

After a moment, Casanova answered his friend's greeting and the two were permitted to converse for some moments, with Basadonna ever in attendance, anxious to flaunt his meagre authority. Magnanimously, he ushered Pietro a little closer to the cell, but Pietro could see only Giacomo's eyes staring through the spyhole of his cell door. From time to time, their conversation was interrupted by a howl or an entreaty from some neighbouring cell, but they had time enough for Pietro to reassure himself that his friend was in good health. Naturally, he said nothing of his own concerns. Pietro considered asking Vindicati whether Casanova might not be brought into their ranks, but he knew that as chief of the Quarantia Criminale, Emilio would never countenance such an arrangement.

'And what of women?' asked Giacomo. 'How fare the women of our fair Venice, Pietro?'

'They pine for you, Giacomo!' Pietro laughed.

'Remember me to them! Tell me … have you seen your fair Anna Santamaria?'

Pietro hesitated, staring down at the dust on his shoes. 'Well, I … Yes … that is to say no … I …'

'Pietro, *amico!*' said Giacomo in an implacable tone. 'Do me this small service. Find her, and take her far from this city and never look back!'

Pietro smiled again. 'I shall think on it, Giacomo. I shall think on it. What of you? How will you hold up?'

Casanova's voice was firm and clear when he spoke: 'I shall stand firm.'

Pietro and Emilio continued to recruit the agents they would require if they were to contend with the demon hordes. If dark forces were massing, Venice would need its own. Each new recruit swore an oath before Emilio Vindicati, pledging his life, his chattels, and his family as security of his loyalty to the republic. The Council of Ten were informed of the nature of the oath. Treachery was punishable by summary execution. If the man guilty of such treason were unknown, then the Ten would rain down thunderbolts, striking down agents at random, the better to strike fear into those who escaped with their lives. In three days a secret army had been assembled and deployed throughout the *sestieri* of the city. Noblemen, merchants, artisans, actors and harlots were stationed about the city from the Piazza San Marco to the Rialto, from the Procuratie to the Mercerie, Cannaregio to Santa Croce, the Giudecca to Burano, each charged with the same mission: to gather by wile, by guile and by charm, any information that they could. More than ever, the exemptions afforded the Council of Ten in matters of law allowed them to take unprecedented measures. They acted as they deemed fit, and gave no quarter. Ten armed men were delegated to watch over the doge day and night and, should they sound the alarm, fifty more were poised to come to their aid. The least panic would force the army to close ranks. If the Shadow had Dominions, Principalities and Archangels at his disposal, the republic had its Heavenly Host: the legions of Raphael, Michael, Gabriel, Hesediel and Metatron. A search was made of the crypt of the villa Mora, but nothing was discovered – no altar, no lectern, nor the copy of the *Inferno*. There were no paintings on the walls, no sign whatever that anyone had ever been there. Indeed, the staircase among the ruins, which lead down to the crypt, had been walled up.

Three days later, in the late afternoon, Pietro found himself with Landretto on the Rialto Bridge. Life in Venice had, meanwhile, continued apace as if nothing had happened. Pietro and his manservant had reached the Rialto by way of the warren of streets paved with marble quarried in Istria, roughly chiselled to offer some traction. With a span of ninety feet, the Rialto Bridge bestrode the Grand Canal. After the weeks of rain and storm, the sun had come once more to Venice and the market was buzzing with life. A constant stream of barges unloaded fresh vegetables and meats, fruits, fresh fish and cut flowers – anything one might want could be found here. The air was thick with the cries of spice merchants in shirt-sleeves, jewellers offering finery for ladies to admire, and merchants selling wine, oil, leather, garments, ropes and baskets. Here too, were clerks who had fled the offices of magistrates, insurers and notaries. And still more people came – the three narrow streets leading onto the resplendent bridge constantly teemed with idlers, officers, and tradesmen. Venice was alive! And beneath the bridge the gondoliers passed, singing *Viva Venezia Possente sui mari. Cinta de glorie, speranze ed amor …*

'You know, Landretto,' said a weary Pietro as he rubbed his temples, 'I am beginning to miss my quiet little prison cell.'

'Do not talk such rot. You are a man of action, not a man to languish in some dark dungeon. Now at least you are free.'

'Indeed I am – free to take to my heels to escape howling wolves.' He turned to his manservant and smiled.

'Perhaps Giacomo is right. Perhaps should I find Anna. We could pack our bags this evening, Landretto, take three good horses and disappear to find adventure elsewhere …'

A fleeting vision passed before his eyes. In it, he saw himself with Anna Santamaria somewhere in Venice, then in Tuscany, then elsewhere – France, perhaps.

'But I am implicated in this affair now, Emilio was right. Given what I know, I could be portrayed as an enemy of the republic, even though it would be the height of absurdity.'

Pietro turned and leaned over the bridge, gazing out to the Grand Canal. The great villas which bordered the canal gleamed in the sunset, all pink and orange. Venice seemed infinitely soft and joyous, a softness that stirred Pietro's heart. He would have liked nothing more than to give himself up to quiet contemplation, the city to be once more what it had been, *la Serenissima*.

'Do you know what will be the ruin of mankind, Landretto?'

'No, but I'll wager you are about to tell me.'

'Look around you at the villas, the *palazzi*, the *laguna* – feel the hum of life, listen to the laughter and the songs. Hardship will not be the death of man.'

'No?'

'No,' said Pietro, 'for poverty does not breed envy.' He stretched his arms wide, his face grave: 'No, the ruin of mankind is wealth.'

For a long time, Pietro and his manservant remained thus, leaning over the bridge, gazing at life as it whirled about them. Then, suddenly, Pietro's hand gripped Landretto's shoulder. As the last rays of the setting sun, gleamed upon the water, she reappeared.

She stood a little way off, smiling in the soft, honeyed light, the evening pale yellow with a trace of orange, which glittered on the facade of the villas and in the waters of the canal. Anna Santamaria was smiling. She had stopped barely a few steps from him, standing on the quay beneath the bridge among the stalls of the merchants. Once more, Pietro felt himself bewitched; he gazed at the blondeness of her hair, her graceful poise, her slender fingers. She walked before him with a natural grace, and a searing wave of passion coursed through the Black Orchid. Anna Santamaria seemed to have materialised from some distant paradise, to which she would soon return. But for now, she was here, unbidden, unexpected. She had not yet seen Pietro, lost as he was in the throng.

Then, suddenly, Pietro frowned, for beside his beloved goddess he saw Senator Ottavio. Anna took the senator's arm. Ottavio. Ottavio with his hooked nose, his fat pock-marked jowls, his double chin, his sweaty face framed by two ridiculous tufts of white hair. Ottavio the stern, the arrogant, the fatuous: the man who had once been the Black Orchid's protector. He walked with an imperious gait, dressed in black from head to foot with vulgar medallions of glistening gold hung about his neck, on his head a *beretta*, like that of his colleague, Senator Campioni. Pietro gazed at him and he did not like what he saw.

Would she flee from him again? Would you let her go? No – the moment was perfect. Casanova's words. Anna appearing suddenly before him. It was destiny. That, at least, is what I hope.

Pietro turned to Landretto, who was surprised by the fire in his master's gaze.

'Master, no.'

Pietro hesitated a moment, then ripped the orchid from his buttonhole and pressed it into Landretto's hand.

'Just as I feared,' Landretto shook his head.

'Do as you see fit, only make sure she receives this flower, and bring me news of where she lodges tonight.'

The two men stared at each other for a long moment then, with a sigh, Landretto took the orchid.

'Very well,' He turned on his heel.

'Landretto?'

His manservant turned. Pietro smiled. 'Thank you.'

Landretto adjusted his hat. *At your service*, he thought, *but what of me? When shall it be my turn?*

That very evening, somewhere in Venice, by the light of a single flickering candle, a lady named Anna Santamaria sat intoxicated by the scent of the Black Orchid pressed against her cheek. She thought now of the thousand nights she had longed for this moment. Now, once again, she could begin to hope. The waning moon seemed to set in her eyes, which brimmed with tears of joy.

Night had fallen. Federico Spadetti, *capomaestro* of the Murano Guild of Glaziers was alone in his vast deserted atelier. That is, he believed himself to be alone, although he knew that the Council of Ten had him under surveillance. More than once he had almost spent a spell in *i Piombi*, and his fate was as yet far from clear. But Federico Spadetti had his feet firmly planted on the ground. He was an enterprising and daring man, something of which the guild, who had championed him, were acutely aware. Even his rivals among the glaziers of Murano would have admitted as much. Certainly there was rivalry between the workshops and ateliers, but if professional enmity was an accepted fact, the intervention of the republic was not.

The situation in which Federico found himself was unenviable. Ordinarily, he liked to linger in the empty workshop when the roar and clank of man and machine were gone, when Vulcan's forge fell silent and the furnaces guttered out. Now there was not a glazier nor an apprentice moving about. No clamour of voices, no din of hot metal hissing and clattering. He had always enjoyed the convivial darkness of his workshop at night, when a man could see barely ten paces before him. Spadetti stood, motionless, gazing into the shadows, gathering strength and succour from the quiet. His gaze fell upon the crystal dress, the robe which Tazzio had fashioned for love; the bands of glass and belt of pearls. Even in the darkness it seemed to glimmer. Federico smiled; his son had finished his masterpiece that day. In a few short weeks, it would once again be carnival. If truth be told, Venice was constantly caught up in the madness of carnival which, nowadays, lasted six months of the year – but it was in the weeks that followed the feast of the Ascension that it was truly at its height. Federico took a deep breath. Everything, he hoped, would go off as he had imagined it. He and Tazzio would present the crystal robe to the doge and such mastery would surely triumph in the contest held by the guild. Francesco Loredan would stare in wonder at the creation, would congratulate father and son, would absolve Federico, and they would be crowned with garlands of laurels. Then, Tazzio would go in search of the beautiful Severina. When he thought of the life which awaited them, Spadetti envied his son. Severina loved him with all her heart; she would swathe herself in tulle to protect her satin skin so that she might wear this miraculous robe of crystal. She would burn with the fire of a thousand stars, with all the fire of youth. She and Tazzio would be married and

Spadetti would give his blessing to their union. He would watch over them. He would remind them of his own wife, so soon departed, and two thousand members of the Glassblowers' Guild would sing their praises.

Federico wiped his mouth with a grimy hand. *Yes … all will be well.* At the thought, he felt foolish tears brimming. Federico Spadetti, proud citizen of the Most Serene Republic, the son and grandson of Murano glassmakers, stood in the darkened workshop and felt his heart surge. Already this night Tazzio had gone to serenade Severina beneath her balcony, hoping to climb to the *altana* to steal a kiss. *How lucky you are, my son! And how happy it makes me to see you happy!* His own youth had long since faded; what would become of him now?

A veil of darkness fell about his eyes. He had stood firm when the Council of Ten and the Quarantia Criminale had interrogated him. After all, for what did he have to reproach himself? *You know very well, Federico.* An error of professional judgement. A mistake. He had done it for the money, for the good of the workshop, for Tazzio, so that the boy might have his crystal robe. It was a lapse which, at the time, had not seemed important. He had sold no secrets to foreign powers, nor trafficked in contraband. He had simply done what any glassmaker would do: he had fashioned lenses. And, if his client had elected to remain anonymous, then that was his prerogative. Why then, did he feel this guilt? Perhaps because the man who called himself Minos had insisted that his name not figure in the general ledger; he had persuaded Spadetti to falsify the order form. Perhaps because, from the beginning, he had had an inkling, a vague but nagging feeling, that what was being purchased was his silence. But the prospect of twelve thousand ducats had allayed his doubts. Twelve thousand ducats. It seemed to him unjust that those who worked hardest should be accused of treachery.

No, thought Federico Spadetti, clenching his fists. *It shall not come to that*. He was a strong man still. He would fight. And, if he were compelled, then he would name the man who had called himself Minos. He had made a solemn pact with the man, it was true, but there had been no mention of the Council of Ten prying into the affair. What precisely did they hope to discover? Moreover, it had been eminently clear that Minos, too, had something on his conscience, doubtless something much more criminal. That much was crystal clear. Federico would hold his tongue no longer – if he did not speak now, he might yet fall into disgrace with the government, his goods and chattels might be seized and he might be sentenced to imprisonment or even death. The Council of Ten could prove nothing, of that he was certain. Thus far, they had been courteous. They had made no attempt to intimidate him, but such a stratagem would not last, and Federico knew all too well of what methods they were capable. So *tomorrow* – tomorrow he would extricate himself from his viper's nest. If, in doing so, he admitted to his foolish offence and his weakness for the sound of ducats, then so be it. He would endeavour to explain to Tazzio how this had come about. His son would surely understand. He would surely realise that what Spadetti had done, he had done for Tazzio and Severina.

Something is afoot. Federico looked around, sensing he was no longer alone. Someone was watching him out of the nameless dark. And then one of the furnaces roared into life.

'Who's there?'

Federico glanced for a moment towards the shadows and saw the silhouette of a man, though he could not see the face. Perhaps it was Viravolta, the man from the Council of Ten. Or perhaps …

'It is I,' came a dark voice.

Federico could not stifle a cry of astonishment. He recovered himself quickly. He had already considered this eventuality. He steeled himself so as not to tremble.

'Who?' he asked the darkness in a resolute voice.

For a moment, he heard nothing but the regular rise and fall of the man's breath.

'Minos.'

Spadetti was unruffled. He stood stock-still, but his eyes flickered towards a hot poker that rested against the bench. Farther off, he saw the furnace, vermillion sparks eddying behind the metal grate.

'Minos. Ah, Minos, what brings you here?'

'You have had a visit recently. An agent acting for the Ten and for the Quarantia Criminale. Or perhaps I am mistaken?'

'No. There was a man,' said Federico.

'And did you know that this man who came to rifle through your ledgers was the Black Orchid, one of the most feared agents in the service of the republic?'

Spadetti peered into the blackness. The man was alone. Their voices rang in the cavernous space.

'And did you know that a warrant has been issued for you to be brought for questioning before the Tenebræ ... ?

Minos paused momentarily, and heaved a sigh. Unhurried, he took a wooden chair and sat beside the tank in which the molten glass was cooled.

'What did you tell them, Federico?'

'Nothing, I told them nothing.'

'And yet they discovered ... my modest order, did they not?'

'They didn't need me to tell them to find that. The Ten would have found it sooner or later. This one had a bit more gumption than the rest, is all.'

'Indeed.'

The man crossed his legs. Federico said nothing for a moment, then began again. 'They have no idea what the lenses were for, any more than I do, Messer. What were they for?'

'That, I fear, is no concern of yours, Federico. I seem to

recall that I told you to dispose of all evidence of my order.'

'They were about to question my apprentices, and they would hardly forget an order such as yours. If I'd done what you asked, I could have been in trouble. I can't miraculously make some order vanish. My accounts are reviewed by the Guild. I didn't breach the terms of our agreement: I fixed it so that they can't trace the order back to you, just like you wanted. And they can't … at least for now.'

Minos laughed. He did not cajole or threaten, though the malice in the staccato laugh was obvious, and for the first time Spadetti felt a gnawing dread course through him.

'That, Federico, is your story. For my part, I believe that, being a consummate businessman, you hedged your bets. But, you see, Messer Spadetti, the Devil has no time for the irresolute.'

'Listen, all this talk of the Devil and Lucifer, it doesn't frighten me.'

'Indeed not? Then you are wrong not to fear them, Messer Spadetti, very wrong.'

The man leaned towards him, his voice now a low growl.

'The name Minos was found in your ledger, was it not?'

'What of it? Minos means nothing.'

'Do you truly believe that the name of he who judges the souls in hell *means nothing*, Spadetti? Why did you not decline our order if you were incapable of respecting our agreement in every detail? I shall tell you why. Because, my friend, you were greedy. And greed is a terrible flaw; it is one of the Seven Deadly Sins. You thought to lay up for yourself treasures on earth … for what? So that your son might finish his masterwork – that crystal gown – in time? Was it for him, Spadetti?' Spadetti moved as if to protect the precious jewel.

'Oh, do not worry – I do not intend to destroy so

masterful a work, Federico. You are no different from your forebears, who sold the secrets of Murano glass to the French and, with them, the honour of *La Serenissima*. Men such as you are always ready to sell the secrets of the republic as long as you see the glint of gold at the end of the road. You are no different from the corrupt, pox-ridden businessmen of the city, willing to sell themselves to foreign powers. But it is not gold awaiting at the end of the road, Spadetti. Not gold.'

Minos rose to his feet. Spadetti froze suddenly, glancing once more to where the poker lay against the workbench.

'As I told you, I do not intend to destroy the crystal gown.' For the first time, Spadetti caught a glimpse of a smile, a flash of eyes. 'Oh no, I intend to destroy *you*.'

Federico lunged towards the bench to seize the poker. He never made it that far, for the other man also lunged and, with all his force, drove a blade into Spadetti's belly, twisting it in his entrails, turning and turning the handle as Spadetti, his eyes rolling back in his head, a stream of blood trickling from his lips, slowly slumped against him. Only then did Minos withdraw the blade, holding it before Federico Spadetti's eyes.

'Look, Spadetti, is it not ironic that it is your own *stiletto*, its mother-of-pearl hilt adorned with a serpent and a death's head, that has sent you to the realm of the Shades? Is it not poetic justice that the sinner should die by the work of his errant hands? You are the representative of the Third Circle, Spadetti. You do not know what this means, but it is no matter. You need know only this: it will be the last title anyone bestows upon you.'

Federico spluttered once more, his breath misted with blood, and crumpled to the floor.

'What waits at the end of the road, Spadetti, is hell itself.' And Minos turned toward the furnace and gazed into the glowing embers.

*

An hour later, his task accomplished, Minos smiled with satisfaction.

'Decidedly, you have worn me out, Messer Spadetti.'

Andreas Vicario, member of the Maggior Consiglio, famed for his *Libreria*, the infamous, satanic library, turned once more to contemplate his work. Then he departed, his footfalls ringing in the vast empty hallways of the glass-works. The crystal stiletto, smeared with dark blood, fell with a clink to the ground.

THE FOURTH CIRCLE

CANTO X

ARSENAL AND OLD LACE

The tumult in Federico Spadetti's glassworks was no different than on any other day, with the exception that today it had been joined by thirty agents of the Council of Ten and the Quarantia Criminale who had come to interrogate each of the glassblowers and apprentices – everyone, indeed, employed by the atelier, together with several other members of the Guild of Glaziers. This sense of orderly investigation did little to allay the helplessness felt by Emilio Vindicati and of the doge himself at the thought that a new blow had been struck against the republic. Emilio fulminated, the four sentrics assigned to watch Spadetti's every movement had been bound and gagged, rendered helpless before they could sound the alarm. Now even the Minor Consiglio – Francesco Loredan's Privy Council – were aware of what was afoot. The institutions of the city were reeling. Pietro stood with Brozzi in the office where he had so recently scoured Federico's ledgers, and where Spadetti himself had met with Minos the night before. Pale and mute, Tazzio, with haunted eyes, unthinkingly wiped spatters of blood from the ruff of his crystal gown. Antonio Brozzi, coroner with the Quarantia Criminale, had arrived an hour earlier carrying his black medical case and his ornate, faintly ludicrous cane. Now he stood stroking his beard.

'Forgive me for troubling you once more,' said Pietro.

'Do not concern yourself.' Brozzi's smile was almost a

scowl. 'It has become something of a routine, Viravolta, has it not?'

And, with a sigh, he crouched and began the delicate task of unravelling this fresh enigma.

The corpse of Federico Spadetti had been dismembered and the pieces placed in the furnace. Shards of glass – similar to those found at the Teatro San Luca at the feet of Marcello Torretone's cross – lay scattered on the floor. Federico Spadetti had been *blown* – fired in a crucible at the end of a pair of tongs – exactly like the glassware he had once fashioned. As a result, much of the flesh had come away from the bones, which had been twisted into grisly and terrifying arabesques. The corpse had been fashioned into some new, unspeakable work of art. Only his wedding ring, which had miraculously dropped to the ground, had made it possible for Tazzio to identify his father. The first of the apprentices to arrive at the workshop had discovered Tazzio, alone, amidst this carnage. Upon his return from his gallant serenade beneath the balcony of his beloved Severina, Tazzio, worried that Federico had not returned home, had spent much of the night scouring his father's regular haunts before, at last, coming to the glassworks to check whether he was still there. Since that time, he had not uttered a word except those his companions heard him speak when they had first discovered him kneeling before the crystal gown. 'My father ... they have murdered my father ... Murdered him ...'

'I had begun to worry,' said Brozzi, 'It has been a whole week since I have had word of you and these fantastical murders, Pietro.'

What little remained of Federico Spadetti's flesh had been placed in a crucible where it had been mixed with sand, limestone and potash and placed beneath a spigot, where it had been stirred into a thick, pestilential mud. Upon the crucible were chalked the words:

Noi passavam su per l'ombre che adona
La greve pioggia e ponavam le piante
Sovra lor vanità che par persona

We two had come
Over the shades subdued by the heavy rain
Treading upon their emptiness, which seem
Like real bodies

'The punishment meted out to those in the Third Circle,' murmured Pietro. 'Obviously …'

'The Gluttonous,' said Brozzi, raising an eyebrow.

'Forced to lie in mud and lashed forever by icy rain and hail.' Pietro considered the blackish sludge in the vat. 'The Chimera's sense of humour has not deserted him.'

'What can I hope to learn from this?' asked Brozzi, dipping a spatula into the mire of blood and clay which once had been Federico Spadetti.

Pietro turned to look at Tazzio. The crystal gown was pristine now, yet still the lad went on cleaning. Pietro took a stool and went to sit by the boy while, all about them, the agents of the Quarantia Criminale went on with their investigation. Pietro was moved by the young man's grief. The murderer's allusion to Spadetti's greed had doubtless escaped Tazzio, who was ignorant of the details of this crime. But the horrid spectacle of his father reduced to a shapeless mass of clay, like Adam before the creation, would haunt the boy for ever. For his part, Pietro was shocked and enraged; though he had had his suspicions about Spadetti, it had not occurred to him that the Chimera might dispose of him so quickly, and with such heartless savagery. Livid now, he felt compelled to act.

'Tell me, lad,' said Pietro gently. 'Do you remember me?'

Tazzio stared vacantly before him, saying nothing.

'Believe me when I say … I shall do everything within

my power to find the man who has done this. I too have lost someone close to me so I know how great is your suffering, and I know, too, how futile are words at such a time.'

Pietro hesitated for a moment, and then gently placed a hand on the young man's shoulder.

'I know my questions could not come at a more terrible time, *amico,* but I need your help. If I am to find this … Minos. For this is his work, is it not? Have you heard your father speak the name?'

Tazzio did not reply, but stared unblinking at the crystal gown which he continued to burnish. Pietro made another vain attempt, but did not persist, going instead to join the agents of the Quarantia in interrogating the other apprentices. Late in the afternoon, he was compelled to accept the fact that only three people had heard talk of Minos – though most had worked on the lenses he had ordered, none among these three was able to identify the man.

Pietro returned and sat on the stool near Tazzio, endeavouring to collect his thoughts, to run through the sequence of events in his own mind. First there had been Marcello, and the brooch belonging to Luciana Saliestri, which in turn had led him to Giovanni Campioni.

In a low voice, Pietro began to talk to himself. 'Marcello Torretone is an agent with the Council of Ten. Let us imagine that Father Caffelli stumbled on the existence of the Firebirds and confided this fact to Marcello, who discovered something of their conspiracy but did not have time to make his suspicions known to the Ten before he was murdered in the Teatro San Luca. Meanwhile, one among the Firebirds has visited Luciana Saliestri – doubtless in her professional capacity as a courtesan – and there stolen the brooch which he leaves at the theatre in the hope of incriminating her. Unless, perhaps, she herself is among their number and gave the brooch willingly. Two birds, one stone. In this way, suspicion would be cast on Campioni, and he and the liberals he represents would be marginalised.'

Pietro ran his fingers through his powdered wig, tapping the ground in his elegant silver-buckled moccasins, as if keeping time.

'So far it is a plausible account of events. But if true, then Luciana Saliestri is the key to the enigma. I must visit her again; it is possible that she has kept some piece of information from me. Yes, my sweet, you shall tell me everything, or I shall know why. Very well, it follows that Father Caffelli is so terrified that he dare not confide what he knows. But how were the Firebirds led to him? Did Marcello mention the priest's name under duress? The insentient Caffelli is strung from the pediment of San Giorgio Maggiore, and so the Firebirds are content. But the shards of glass found in the Teatro San Luca have led me to Murano, to Federico Spadetti, and to the mysterious Minos. Then Spadetti, too, is murdered and we are left with nothing – for we know nothing of this Minos, nor his lenses. Thousands of glass lenses. *Santa Maria, ma per che cosa?*'

Pietro sighed, rubbing his eyes. 'I know only this; the investigation is being manipulated. Virgil would lead me to Dante and the forces of Satan and Campioni would have me believe this is the work of the Firebirds. And if *il Diavolo* sensed that I was present at the villa Mora – unless he was informed *prior* to my arrival – why spare me when, at any moment, he could have had me seized? Can it be that I have some role to play in this affair? No. No, I think this, all of this, is merely a trap. A grand illusion.'

He shook his head.

Suddenly, he heard a voice beside him say: 'Minos went to the Arsenal.'

Pietro's hand hung, frozen in the air. He turned to Tazzio. 'Say that again?'

'Minos went to the Arsenal.'

Pietro leaned towards the lad. 'You know him? You know who he is?'

'No, I know only that he went to the Arsenal. I heard my father talking to one of his men six months since.'

'What man? Who was he?'

'That I do not know.' Tazzio continued to polish the crystal gown, his own face gazing back at him in a thousand shifting reflections. 'Minos went to the Arsenal,' he said again.

L'arsenale was an extraordinary fortress set in the *sestiere* of Castello which alone accounted for a considerable part of the city of Venice. Here, for several centuries, the military and political dramas of the republic had been played out. The Arsenal employed more than two thousand artificers, shipbuilders, fitters, sailmakers and ropemakers – it was a world unto itself, ringed about with towers and sentries standing guard over the dry docks, the workshops, the shipyards and the foundries. This was the yard which had built the five galleys and eight galleons which patrolled the Adriatic, and the schooners that plied between Venice, Zante and Corfu; the frigates and armoured ships carrying forty, fifty, or even eighty cannons, which controlled the Mediterranean from Gibraltar to Constantinople.

The moment Pietro learned from Tazzio that Minos had been to the Arsenal – though in what circumstances and to what purpose he had yet to determine – he sent word to Emilio Vindicati informing him that some months previously Spadetti's son, Tazzio, had overheard a conversation between his father and a man who had claimed to work for Minos. Although the lad had heard only snatches of the conversation, it was enough to know that Minos had had some dealings with the Arsenal, and might have secretly placed a private order with them. Pietro told Vindicati that he would head immediately to the Arsenal, taking with him a company of twenty agents, and asking that the Council of Ten despatch a further troop.

*

At the Arsenal, the arrival of the Black Orchid flanked by the henchmen of the Tenebræ was like a thunderbolt. With Pietro at the head of the party they marched through the gates, indicating with a nod or a wave for those about them to disperse; their footsteps echoing through the shipyards and the workshops. The agents dispersed, some to the workshops, others to secure the dry docks. It was clear from the tumult that something of great moment had occurred. As Pietro was interrogating one of the foundry workers, one of his assistants brought him the Arsenal ledgers. As before, the Firebirds had acted in secrecy, under the very noses of the Ten and the Quarantia. The entry in the register indicated that Minos had ordered the construction of two frigates, but there was more, and the more he learned, the more Pietro felt his blood freeze. The information gleaned at the Arsenal was cross-referenced with that of the military authorities of the city. Fifteen people were questioned, none of whom knew the true identity of Minos since the man clearly operated through a series of dubious intermediaries. Pietro left the registers and wandered for a moment through the shipyards, the foundries turning out cannonballs, the warehouses filled with kegs of gunpowder, before hurrying to meet Emilio. Though he could barely credit it himself, what he had to relate was only too true.

'The Black Orchid!'

Pietro's arrival was discreetly announced. He found Emilio in the sala del collegio. Francesco Loredan was not with him – the doge was meeting with the members of his Privy Council. But Emilio was not alone. Beside him stood a man of about thirty with slender features, the long slim fingers of a pianist and skin so pale it seemed like marble – his ghostly air accentuated by a wispy, well-groomed beard. He wore a capacious white shirt and a jacket whose cut and colour Pietro – with a consummate knowledge of matters sartorial – judged to be of French fabrication. Emilio, with a broad smile, was welcoming his guest effusively. In a mixture of French and Italian, he flattered the man's 'prodigious talent', bowing deeply and professing himself 'privileged to welcome such genius to the court of the *Serenissima*'. Pietro shortly learned who might be worthy of such sycophancy.

'Ah, Messer, may I present Pietro Luigi Viravolta de Lansalt, one of the ... special councillors to the court,' said Emilio, a little obsequiously.

'Pietro, this is the celebrated artist Maître Eugène-André Dampierre, lately arrived at court with His Excellency the Ambassador of France. Maître Dampierre will be exhibiting a number of his most excellent paintings of sacred subjects in the narthex of the Basilica di San Marco.'

Maître Dampierre bowed with great dignity, a bow which Pietro returned in kind.

'Might I speak with you for a moment, Emilio?' Pietro asked. 'I realise the moment is ill-chosen, but it is a matter of some urgency.'

Vindicati's smile stiffened and he turned to Dampierre: 'Will you excuse me a moment, Monsieur? The affairs of the city leave us little respite. I shall return in a moment.'

'Of course.' Dampierre bowed again.

Vindicati led Pietro into one of the adjoining rooms. 'The new ambassador has come from France. He is, even now, in conclave with the doge and the Privy Council. He formally took up his post yesterday; his predecessor has already returned to Paris. Hence his wellbeing, that of Dampierre and the doge himself, must be my chief concern – and safeguarding them from harm will be no meagre task, since they must know nothing of what has happened. The official receptions present little difficulty. But they will join his Serene Highness at the public events – at the feast of the Ascension – something which promises to be more troubling, the more so since we have scant time to prepare. The last straw, however, is that His Excellency would fain sample the humble pleasures of our city – and to do so incognito, if possible. He has already arranged to attend Andreas Vicario's masked ball in Cannaregio tomorrow evening. Have you any idea of the trouble this may cause?'

'I fear your troubles are far from over, Emilio,' said Pietro, his expression sombre. 'In the course of my visit to the Arsenal, I have come upon new and disturbing information.'

Emilio shot Pietro a worried glance. 'What do you mean?'

'It is now clear that this conspiracy has been long in the planning. I know not how, but Minos has circumvented the authorities and, with private monies – unless the Firebirds have somehow misappropriated public funds – ordered the construction of two frigates about which we knew nothing. In itself, it seems an act of extraordinary audaciousness, but there is still more disquieting news. Six months ago the Arsenal launched the *Santa Maria* and the *Gioia De Corfù*, two formidable galleys built to ply the waters of the Mediterranean. Then, two days ago, the galleys disappeared somewhere upon the waters of the Adriatic. Neither the Arsenal nor any of our military powers has knowledge of their whereabouts.'

There was a silence.

'You ... you cannot mean ...' stammered Emilio.

Pietro took him by the arm. 'The *Santa Maria* and the *Gioia De Corfù* are each equipped with ninety cannons, Emilio. God knows what they may do when they return to port.'

Emilio Vindicati brought his hands to his brow. 'This is madness. Do you truly believe that Minos is arming galleys against us?'

'Since my visit to the villa Mora, I am prepared to believe almost anything. Minos, Virgil, the Chimera – I do not know if these three be one man, but one thing I know: Father Caffelli spoke the truth when he said the Firebirds are everywhere – they have infiltrated the very highest ranks of the Government. Believe me, we are dealing with something infinitely more heinous than we imagined.'

Emilio reeled under the blow. In the distance the two men heard the doors of the doge's Privy Council open to formally receive the French ambassador. A faint murmur and the sound of voices raised in greeting reached them. Emilio leaned against Viravolta, attempting in vain to compose himself.

'Meanwhile, I am expected to bow and scrape to all of Europe! *Porca miseria!* Pietro, I must attend to the ambassador's retinue – in my absence I give you free reign – *carta bianca* – to conduct the investigation as you see fit. I would also like you to attend Vicario's *ballo in maschera* tomorrow evening. In the meantime, God speed in your hunt of the Firebirds; I must attend his Serene Highness and our honoured guests.'

Pietro nodded, and the two men returned to the sala de collegio where Vindicati immediately left him and, arms spread wide, went to greet the French ambassador – a man of some fifty years with a furrowed brow and unruly white locks which peeked from beneath his hat.

Left to himself, Pietro gazed up at Veronese's *Battle of Lepanto*. The war, he mused, is far from won.

Luciana Saliestri stood up from the red chaise longue where Pietro had spoken to her on his first visit. When he had arrived some minutes earlier, she had parried his questions, ingenuously suggesting that they might play a game of dominoes. She laid the pieces out between two coffee cups on a low, handsomely carved table. Pietro watched as she deployed all her charms. She winked at him flirtatiously and traced her full, sensuous lips distractedly with her finger. She leaned towards him, her lace-trimmed gown cut low to reveal her shoulders and her delicate clavicle; a gold pendant in the form of a dolphin hung just above the soft intimation of her perfectly formed breasts whose regular rise and fall he could distinguish beneath the delicate fabric. She wore a gossamer shawl about her shoulders. By the time she had laid out the dominoes, Luciana Saliestri had decided that she did not wish to play after all. *Come, I have another game we can play*! It was at that moment that she rose from the red chaise longue and, with a single movement, unhooked her gown, which pooled at her feet. The silk slipped down her body, revealing her undergarments and her milk-white breasts and delicate nipples, covered only by the gossamer shawl wrapped about her. Luciana was a fragile flower opening its petals to his gaze. It was hardly surprising that Senator Campioni had fallen in love with her. She placed one of her long legs on the low table, sweeping away the dominoes. Pietro contemplated the curve of her shapely thigh, but he had no time for such distractions now. Before, he might easily have succumbed to her proposal, might have charmed information from her by means less disagreeable than a pistol, a sword or a dagger. But many things had changed since his first meeting with Luciana Saliestri. Landretto had returned to his master the evening before. It had been raining and Landretto's eyes were shining, his hair dishevelled as he informed his master: 'Anna Santamaria is at their villa in Santa Croce, where she is jealously guarded by her husband. She knows that you have eyes only for her: I gave her your flower.'

Yes, Anna Santamaria was now within his grasp. Pietro had only to make a sign. And, in spite of Vindicati's proscription, he felt ready to do whatever was necessary to see her once more.

Luciana's voice, at once tantalising and mocking, whispered to him: 'What do you think of my shoes, Pietro?'

Pietro did not answer.

'I hope you know that I wore my prettiest dress for you. In Venice, they say I worry too much about my clothes, but I am not some wench who plies the cloisters beneath the

Procuratie, my lord. I do not stuff foam into my bustier, nor pad my undergarments to enhance my form. I have no need of periwigs, nor do I crimp or tease my hair. Does it please you? Wait, I shall let it down.'

And with a practised hand, she did; her russet locks fell upon her shoulders when suddenly, as if by chance, the gossamer shawl, too, fell away. She brought her hands up to cover her breasts coyly, and then took them away. Her breasts were inches from Pietro's face.

'Powder, rouge and *panniers* I leave to those women who have need of artifice in order to be beautiful. I require only that my gowns be beautiful, something for which I give thanks every day to my dear husband, may God rest his soul. As you know, the poor man had an obsession beyond all reason for trade and money. He was something of a miser. I, on the contrary, have a taste for other forms of trade, for things I cannot refuse myself. What need have I of money if it cannot make me more desirable? Consequently, as soon as the ducats come to fill my coffers, I fritter them away. I have a talent for making *zecchini* disappear. In this, at least, I am a veritable magician ... and with the bounty left me by my husband – a sainted man, if truth be told – it is a trick I intend to go on performing.'

She threw back her head, placing her hands on Pietro's shoulders, undulating her hips, pretending to rub herself against him where he sat.

'Would you care to check?'

'Check what?' asked Pietro

'That I have not padded my undergarments.'

As she spoke, she slipped the remaining garment from her and turned, affording Pietro a glimpse of her hips and the most sensuous, most beautiful derrière he had ever seen.

'You see? Just as Nature intended.'

The courtesan, having finished her dance of the veils, turned toward him again. They gazed at one another in silence. With some surprise, Pietro noticed that there was a sadness in the young woman's eyes. For a fraction of a second she seemed completely vulnerable, completely sincere, and then she tilted her head to one side and smiled coyly. A fleeting shaft of sunlight pierced the clouds over the Grand Canal, illuminating the room with the gentle warmth of evening.

'Come, Pietro Viravolta, take off your cape and your frockcoat, and tell me your deepest desires …'

Pietro slowly stood. He hesitated for a moment, then stooped to pick up the young woman's gown. 'I fear not, Madame.'

Disbelief flickered for a moment over the face of Luciana Saliestri.

'You have charms enough to tempt a dozen popes and, know that in other circumstances, I would not have wavered for an instant. But time presses and I have another game we can play. I pray you, do not take my rebuff as an offence, for none is intended.'

Luciana, more distant now, looked puzzled, uncertain whether to play the outraged courtesan or the wounded girl. At that moment, there was something profoundly feminine about her. Suddenly her guile, her affectation had slipped away, leaving her human and vulnerable. Pietro could not help but wonder how Luciana would have reacted had he withdrawn his reservations and thrown himself at her feet. Pietro was not easily taken in by a woman's simpering airs; indeed long experience often made it possible for him to intuit much about a woman's personality, even how she would make love. Luciana Saliestri, he speculated, would make love with fierce passion, a sort of fervent ecstatic intensity akin to a thirst for revenge. At the height of her ecstasy, he would have clung to her like a drowning man. Already her eyes were wild. Something told Pietro that, despite her fervent protestations, Luciana Saliestri would have done anything to find true love. Accustomed to the baroque excesses of pleasure, she could hide her aching need behind a moué of boredom; constantly running away from her true self. It was something Pietro understood only too well. As he watched the emotion play over the young woman's face, the Black Orchid glimpsed her fragile humanity and felt moved. He had come to interrogate a courtesan; now he felt himself softening toward her, and yet, he realised, he would be wise to be cautious. If Anna Santamaria were a Black Widow, then Luciana Saliestri was a tarantula. One could never be quite sure of her ... You too have your dark places, Luciana, you too are lost to this world.

At length, in a neutral, somewhat aloof tone, she said, 'I see ... Doubtless you have eyes only for *her* ...'

He recognised the note of bitterness in her voice.

'... this Anna Santamaria.'

Now it was Pietro's turn to be disconcerted. 'I beg your pardon?'

Luciana looked up at him with a forced smile.

'What? Surely you realise that I, too, would wish to know with whom I was dealing? Pietro Luigi Viravolta, the Black Orchid, recently incarcerated in *i Piombi* ... A spy in the service of the republic jailed for trampling the pride of Senator Ottavio underfoot ...'

Pietro ran his tongue over his lips.

'Perhaps you thought me merely a foolish, shameless libertine? But as you can see I, like you, have kept my cards close to my chest.'

'How did you come by this information?'

Luciana looked down at her coffee cup.

'Tell me, Messer Black Orchid, what reason have I to help you?'

There was a silence.

'For Marcello Torretone. For Giovanni Campioni who, at this very moment, is in a most perilous situation. Come, Luciana, there are many reasons! Believe me, the Council of Ten and the doge himself will be indebted to you. I pray you, if you know something, tell me now.'

She hesitated a moment and then, with a long sigh, she said, 'There was another senator who called on me from time to time. Someone, Viravolta ... who bears you no great love.' She stared into Pietro's eyes. 'Senator Ottavio.'

Pietro frowned. Suddenly, pieces of the puzzle began to slot into place: the purloined brooch, the Firebirds, Giovanni Campioni's fears. To say nothing of the fact that it had been Ottavio who had Pietro incarcerated in *i Piombi*.

'Ottavio ... My former mentor. Well, well.'

He turned to the courtesan. 'Why did you not tell me of this sooner?'

Luciana shrugged. 'Come, Messer Viravolta. I know where my interest lies.'

Pietro said nothing. She had scored a palpable hit. A curious idea occurred to him.

'You know, Luciana, you would make an excellent agent. I shall suggest as much to the Council of Ten if you wish it.'

She smiled. 'The Tenebræ and I do not play by the same rules.'

'And yet, it would greatly please me to play the recruiting sergeant for a change. And I have already devised a *nom de guerre* for you ...'

He looked down at the playing pieces scattered on the table and delicately picked one up. Double six.

'Luciana, I have a proposal I would make to you.'

Her smile broadened.

'Would you do me the honour of being my "Domino"?'

The Duke von Maarken, who had left the Gothic crenellations of his Austrian chateau two days earlier, stepped from a gondola at Cannaregio, a shadowy figure shrouded in a dark cloak. Glancing up, he saw the moon disappear behind a bank of cloud. Guided by a pair of torchbearers, he made his way to a *palazzo* where, in a hoarse whisper, he gave the agreed codeword. The great double doors groaned as they swung open and the Duke stepped inside. Some minutes later, he was ensconced by the hearth of the great hall, a glass of wine in hand. Facing him sat the Chimera.

'The time is ripe,' said von Maarken, 'Venice has been defenceless since the Treaty of Požarevac. Tell me, what news?'

'The plan – *my* plan – is nearing fruition.'

'Indeed, indeed. I allowed you to devise a plan after your somewhat baroque design, my friend, but I begin to doubt whether such fantastical theatrics are effective. What do we gain by staging the murders in such a fashion? Are Venetians credulous enough to believe in such elaborate parlour games? A satanic sect? No sensible individual would fear such a painted devil.'

The Chimera gave a brusque laugh. 'Do not believe it! We are in Venice now. My parlour games have excited a general panic. The doge and his men are helpless. It is these illusions, these distractions which have baited our trap. The Council of Ten do not know what they are dealing with. They cannot understand the logic of our plan, precisely because we do not wish them to. True, I have fashioned it as a diversion for myself; I delight in watching them fall into each snare I fashion along the way. They are so entangled in this web that they will not realise until we strike the final blow. When that comes, you will be grateful to Dante Alighieri and to the imagination of your humble servant.'

'You have an extraordinary imagination, that I concede. You should have been a playwright. Incidentally, how was … how fared your little drama in Mestre?'

Il Diavolo laughed again. 'Have you heard anything of Carlo Gozzi or the Accademia dei Granelleschi?'

'Nothing whatever.'

'We call them the Inept. They are a sort of society composed of several important literary figures, cultivated

Venetians all, who would purge the city of all foreign influence and promote the "purity of the tongue". Each year, they meet to elect a leader – a *gogo archiniais* to minister to their flock. It was from them I took my inspiration for the Firebirds. My flock, too, come from the noblest Venetian stock and each has played his role to perfection. And, be assured, when the time comes, we shall be able to count upon their loyalty.'

'We shall see,' said von Maarken. His eyes flared as he gazed into the blazing hearth. 'We shall see, and very soon ... In a few short hours Venice will fall. And at that moment, Austria and the House of Habsburg will have the Queen of the Seas, the sublime jewel of the Mediterranean, on a silver platter. And you ... you shall be amply rewarded for your pains. The empress will see to that.' Eckhart von Maarken clicked his tongue and drained his glass.

The night was already well advanced by the time Pietro arrived beneath the balcony of Senator Ottavio's villa in Santa Croce, wearing a mask, a hat and *tabarro* of black felt, his cloak wrapped about him. By his side, the golden hilt of his sword glinted. At his lapel, a black orchid.

He narrowed his eyes as if to gauge the distance to the third floor balcony and hesitated a moment before giving a low whistle, as he had done so often in the past. He whistled again. On the third floor, nothing stirred. Perhaps Anna Santamaria was already asleep. And yet a lamp still glowed. Should the senator make a sudden appearance, the Black Orchid could easily slip into the shadowy doorway. He whistled a third time, glanced to left and right. He had to act. Come, Anna!

He was about to scale the wall when he heard a movement. He glanced up and, framed by the window, glimpsed Anna silhouetted against the light as she stepped onto the balcony. He could not make out her face, but seeing her bring her hand to her heart, he knew that she had guessed his identity. She stifled a cry and then turned abruptly and went indoors.

Pietro took a deep breath and groped for a foothold. He was possessed of considerable agility and, in a moment, had reached the balcony on the first floor, then the second, clinging to the rough surfaces of the wall. Darkness was his ally. He stopped and held his breath as a messenger passed, singing loudly, followed by a group of *Signori della Notte*. Had he been discovered hanging thus like a spider from the wall, it would have proved awkward. Pietro panicked as he felt his boots slip from the narrow ledge. His cloak draped about him, he clung on, pressing himself into the wall as if he would merge with the very stone. Finally, the men disappeared. Pietro glanced up in search of a handhold and, with a rustle of his cape, vaulted casually onto the balcony, landing with the sureness like a cat. Before him, the gossamer drapes wavered in the light breeze. He edged forward, intensely aware that his heart was beating wildly. Behind the curtains, he could make out a reclining form. He parted the drapes.

There she was, lying upon a canopy bed, gazing at him with her great dark eyes, wearing an expression which fluttered between joy and trepidation, like a doe at bay. She wore a bedgown of burgundy satin and lace and her blond hair was pinned up with a silver brooch. For a long time they remained thus – he, hardly daring to cross the threshold from balcony to room; she, silent and supine upon the bed. When at length, she rose, she hastened to him and threw her arms about him and the kiss she bestowed upon him wiped away the memory of his long months of incarceration, and the torments which had haunted him since his release. To be once more in the arms of the woman he loved, to feel the warmth of her body, feel the softness of her breasts pressed against him, smell her bewitching scent – it was magical. He wondered now how he had restrained himself from abandoning his investigation and spending every moment since his release finding her once more. Suddenly, all danger seemed to dissipate. And yet, he had always known he would find her again, and what a moment before had seemed miraculous, now seemed fated. He loved her – of that he was certain. When, eventually, she reluctantly broke their embrace, it was to gaze into his eyes.

'Dearest one, you are mad! Mad to come and find me here!'

Over her shoulder, Pietro espied the crushed petals of a black orchid beneath her pillow. Her forehead pressed against his shoulder, she murmured: 'Landretto told you I was here, did he not?'

'Anna, I could not bear to lose you … A minute has not passed when I did not think of you. While I was imprisoned, I thought perhaps I should be forced to forget you.'

'And so you should have, my dearest one, so you should!'

Pietro would have given much to savour the fruit fate had dropped into his lap. Anna Santamaria was here, in his arms, stifling tears of mingled joy and fear. He would have liked to sweep her into his arms, lie beside her, forget all the world in the deep heart of the night, or perhaps make off with her, take her far from this place, make real the dream which had seen him through his darkest moments … But as he knew all too well, he was in enemy territory.

He took her by the shoulders. 'Anna, we have little time.'

She gazed at him, helpless, both of them trembling.

'Where is Ottavio?'

'He is not at home,' said Anna, 'else I should never have dared allowed you in. But he may return at any moment … It is madness to have come to see me here! On that day when I saw you at the Mercerie, I thought I should die! And yet some part of me knew …'

The Black Orchid glanced about the room. 'Tell me, Anna … where is his writing desk?'

Anna's fingers tightened about Pietro's arms. 'What?'

'Show me to his study, I beg you. Quickly, I shall explain all.'

She hesitated a moment, then led him to the door. 'We cannot. My ladies-in-waiting are nearby; they may wake at any moment ...'

'I shall not make a sound. Take me to Ottavio's study, I beg you.'

This she did. Anna seized a candlestick by whose light they crossed the shadowy boudoir, and then Anna put her ear to a door and listened for a moment.

'It is here.' Slowly, she turned the door handle.

As Pietro stepped into the study and lit another taper, Anna crossed the room and posted herself at the far door, watching for any movement.

'Hurry!' she whispered, her voice panicked.

Two birds with one stone, thought Pietro. The opportunity was too tempting.

Ottavio's study was furnished with deep bookshelves of burnished wood and an astrolabe which surely had never been used. On the facing wall hung a dozen maps of Venice, evidence of the historic expansion of the city across the centuries. Ottavio was clearly a collector of historic maps. Proud portraits of Ottavio's ancestors, haughty and condescending, stared down through the gloom, their stern gaze seeming to stand guard over the rich furnishings of cedar and mahogany; a commode with carved gold escutcheons, a dresser in dark walnut, an ornate escritoire, the open drawers bulging with correspondence, and a larger desk some ten feet in length, whose lock Pietro stopped to pick. He rummaged beneath his hat in the secret pocket of the powdered wig he had worn for the occasion. The carnival mask he wore made the task more difficult, so he removed it. Using a pin held between his teeth, and another between his long fingers, he began to tinker with the lock mechanism while Anna, standing by the door, began to lose her nerve.

'What are you looking for? Hurry, I pray you, hurry!'

Pietro too felt a dull dread overcome him. He struggled with the lock, stifling a cry of victory when at last it snapped open. He opened the drawer. There were various documents of little interest, a paper-knife … and then his fingers stumbled on a rolled parchment tied with a purple ribbon. Pietro set down the candlestick and spread out the parchment on the leather blotter of the desk.

It seemed to be a *plan* of some sort. The parchment was covered with strange markings, mathematical symbols and arrows; there were schemas of the facades of villas, angles carefully calculated and diagrams of conic sections; it looked for all the world like the work of some demented architect. Vague sketches of buildings sat next to detailed mechanical drawings scribbled over with abstruse mathematical formulae. Pietro examined the drawing closely: two words leapt out at him: and written in the margin, as though the pencil had barely grazed the parchment, the name Minos.

He almost cried out, but bit his tongue when he saw Anna start. He could hear noises below. Anna looked at him, aghast.

'Ottavio has returned!' The candle stick in her hand trembled.

Pietro had a few scant seconds in which to think. He rolled the parchment quickly, placed it back in the drawer and wrestled to secure the lock. Anna, quaking now, shot him an imploring glance.

'Pietro, *please!*'

Pietro's brow was damp with sweat.

'I've almost got it …' he muttered, a pin still clenched between his teeth.

There came a footfall on the stairs. 'Anna?' a deep voice rang out – a voice Pietro knew only too well.

'Anna, are you not abed?'

Anna's eyes filled with dread, the candlestick now shaking so violently, it seemed as though she might drop it.

'I've almost got it ...'

'Pietro!'

'Anna?'

There was a soft click. Pietro stood up, pushed the chair back against the desk and blew out his taper. Anna lifted the skirts of her nightgown and together – almost running – she and Pietro hastened back to her boudoir, closing the door just as Ottavio opened that of the adjoining room. He stood on the threshold a moment, a sly look on his face. He brought a hand to his double chin. Then he entered. In Anna's boudoir, Pietro rushed onto the balcony but, before he vaulted the low wall, he turned to Anna and embraced her with all his might, pressing her lips hard with his.

'We shall see each other again, I swear it. I love you.'

'I love you,' she whispered.

Ottavio opened the door just as Pietro's cape fluttered across the balcony and vanished into the nameless dark.

'Are you well, my angel?' asked Ottavio guardedly.

On the balcony, Anna turned. The pale moon emerged from behind its shroud, like an eye piercing the night. The drapes fluttered on the breeze and Anna Santamaria's face broke into a glorious smile.

CANTO XI
A MASKED BALL

THE PROBLEM OF EVIL

Andreas Vicario, member of the Maggior Consiglio
On Lying and the Art of Politicks, Chapter XIV

In the political domain, evil is principally manifested in the propensity to lie, which is not only a commonplace, but a part of the very fabric of practising politicks: many believe mendacity to be necessary either to protect or to subjugate the common horde such that they pose no threat to power. For this reason, all political regimes amount to a fool's errand in which promises of bounty and munificence are made to the populace, only for those elected to use all their considerable skill and talent to renege on those very promises. The antithesis of the aristocratic oligarchy is the utopian defence that lying is in the public interest. I hereby declare that Athenian democracy is dead, and in its place we are guided merely by human egoism. Is Satan not the Prince of Lies? That is why he feels so at ease in the corridors of power.

Landretto was waiting for Pietro by the gondola which was to take them to Andreas Vicario's *ballo in maschera*. In other circumstances, the prospect of a masked ball at Vicario's villa in Cannaregio would have afforded Pietro and his manservant the opportunity to win hearts or at least to carouse as they had been wont to do. But the knowledge that they were to be joined by Emilio Vindicati, the Ambassador of France, and a detachment of costumed agents of the Quarantia Criminale rather dampened their ardour. It was customary for foreign diplomats to ask – with a show of modesty – to be introduced to the more iniquitous pleasures and beauties of Venice. The city had always encouraged such things, and the image of the Queen of the Seas as a marriage of exotic pleasure and dissipation had long been one of the cornerstones of the republic's reputation. Naturally, propriety forbade the doge himself from participating in such revelries.

Pietro had spent his day sifting through the information accumulated by the Council of Ten and the Quarantia Criminale, though they advanced his investigation not one whit. His vexation was magnified by the disagreeable feeling that he was going in circles. Now, to cap it all, he was compelled to attend this banquet in costume. He donned a *mezza maschera* of black and gold, a hat bedecked with white feathers and an extravagant redingote which made him look like Harlequin, or like one of the exotic birds he had seen on his travels through Constantinople and the Ottoman Empire. As a precaution, he wore his sword and his pistols and a *stiletto* concealed in his boot. As always, Landretto would remain aboard the gondola and await his return; it promised to be a long night.

With a dull thud, the boat struck the steps which led up to the villa. The lapping of the waves subsided and Pietro disembarked. To left and right, other *gondoli* arrived. Periwigged men and women in masks and outlandish costumes came ashore; gentlemen offering their ladies an arm with which to steady themselves as they disembarked, before heading indoors. Liveried servants held torches aloft to guide the guests. The entrance, festooned with garlands, was flanked by two lions which Vicario had placed there for the occasion. Pietro gazed up at the sumptuous *palazzo* –

truly a palace – its elegant balconies, pillars and cornices of Gothic, Moorish and Byzantine design somehow coming together to create a facade of beauty and harmony unparalleled in Venice. A little farther off, Pietro could just make out the pillars of the esoteric *libreria* where he had consulted Dante's *Inferno*, together with divers baleful works.

He nodded to Landretto and stepped inside the building and into a different world. Inside the portico stood a grand fountain and the vestibule had been adorned to resemble the atrium of an antic Roman villa. Here, a host of lackeys verified the identity of each guest, took their capes and coats and received the gifts intended for the master of the house. Andreas Vicario himself, in a costume of silver and black, wore a mask in the form of a sunburst, which he removed to greet his guests, parrying their flatteries and inviting them to lose themselves in a world of his imagining. Close at hand stood Emilio Vindicati, dressed in a matching jacket and pantaloons of reddish-brown, a lion mask, and wings which seemed to sprout from his back. Vindicati was carefully studying the guests as they arrived. Seeing Emilio, Pietro hesitated a moment, acutely aware that, despite his mentor's proscription, he had tracked down Anna Santamaria. Emilio had placed his trust in Pietro, his instructions had been clear and the Black Orchid's freedom depended on observing them to the letter. And yet, he had to tell his mentor of the parchment he had discovered in the senator's study. Ottavio was embroiled in this affair, that much seemed certain. Pietro vacillated a moment longer. He had to talk to Vindicati as soon as possible. What matter if, in passing, he had to confess some minor betrayal – his transgression was trivial compared to what was at stake. But this was not the moment. *Tomorrow. I shall talk to him tomorrow.* The Black Orchid took a deep breath and approached Vindicati. Each had been apprised of the costume the other would be wearing. They looked each other up and down, stifling the urge to laugh at their ridiculous apparel. But they had more pressing matters to attend to. Emilio introduced his protégé to Andreas Vicario, who smiled and nodded, then drew him aside.

'The ambassador has already arrived, Pietro. You cannot fail to notice him for he is dressed as a peacock, a costume well suited to his character, believe me. His friend, the artist, is wearing a white toga and a crown of laurels – the French are not without a certain sense of humility, don't you find? It is one of their most charming traits. The doge is safely under armed guard at the palace. I have brought a detachment of ten men who, like you, are to remain anonymous. Simply mingle with the guests and keep your wits about you.'

'Very well,' said Pietro.

The hallway opened onto an immense *loggia* with ornate picture windows adorned with garlands which ran the length of the ground floor to a second entrance, surmounted by a portcullis, which led to the courtyard and thence to the street. Above the room, a vaulted ceiling was lit by a thousand candles. A stairwell led to the apartments above. Two vast fireplaces framed the room to east and west. Great tapestries, precious furnishings and paintings by the great Venetian masters adorned the cavernous space which had been cleared for the festivities. Upon a row of refectory tables the most sumptuous delicacies were presented: quail and woodcock, partridge, capons, haunches of roast veal, a dizzying array of *legumes*, sole and eel, octopus and crab; cheeses, baskets overflowing with fruits and a veritable cornucopia of sweetmeats and cake, to be washed down with the finest French and Italian wines. The servants busied themselves with cutlery of gold and silver, plates of finest porcelain, and crystal goblets. Painted wooden statues of slaves carrying baskets of spices flanked the buffet as if standing guard. Vermillion drapes and marbled wainscoting surrounded chaises longues and divans laid out in circles to afford guests a place for tranquil conversation, while the centre of the room was reserved for dancers – few in number so early in the evening. At the far end of the room, in front of the *cortile*, was an orchestra – the musicians, too, were in costume. Some forty people had already arrived and moved about the room conversing gaily. More than a hundred more guests were still expected.

Pietro wandered among characters of the *commedia dell'arte*: Columbine and Pulcinella, Pantaloon, Truffaldino, Brighella, Scapin and a dozen other plumed figures; the men hidden behind white masks with beaked noses and the women concealing extravagantly painted faces behind finely wrought Venetian fans. It was a sea of greatcoats and gowns, blouses and tricornes, gleaming silks and satins, daring décolleté, flowing gowns and beauty spots artfully placed upon downy cheeks or the curve of a bosom. Pietro quickly caught sight of the ambassador who was wearing a little black hat surmounted by a ruff; he was dressed entirely in blue and a voluminous cloak trailed behind him, painted to resemble a peacock's tail. Already he was surrounded by a veritable rainbow of courtesans whom Vicario, without revealing the identity of his noble guest, had assembled. Not far off, the painter in his toga was heading towards the tables there to find some sustenance to accompany his glass of Amarone. The agents of the Quarantia were doubtless scattered throughout the room. As a flood of new guests arrived, the orchestra began to play softly in the background. Wine was flowing like water. The *loggia* was the largest of the rooms on the ground floor; to left and right doors opened onto other salons just as imposing in their finery: deep divans, convivial armchairs and dressers laden with priceless ornaments. Two balconies made it possible for those who wished to take the air to view the splendours of the canals by the light of the waxing moon. Pietro knew that beyond these salons,

Andreas Vicario had appointed boudoirs and alcoves in which his guests, drunk on wine and ardour, would wander at the end of the evening in search of other pleasures.

Pietro smiled as he recognised Luciana Saliestri, ravishingly costumed, wearing a *moretta* – a half-mask – of sensuous, stylised beauty and swathed in a robe of incandescent splendour. Her earrings glistened and she had piled her hair into a chignon. As he approached her, she recognised him.

'Good evening, Domino. I am enchanted to see that you decided to attend.'

'I could hardly decline Messer Vicario's generous invitation, *amico*. And I would be grateful if you would refrain from calling me "Domino"; I don't recall accepting your proposition. I am fiercely independent and the idea of working for the Tenebræ is anathema to me.'

The Black Orchid smiled more broadly still. 'Come now, you are perfect. I have no desire to impinge on your independence, Domino, I ask only that you keep your eyes open – you may learn something which will help our cause. After all, there are many people here, and wine loosens people's tongues ...'

He saw a gleam in her eyes behind the mask. 'Of course, I shall do what I can. Of late, I have become a veritable saint in the service of the republic. And who knows, perhaps you will reconsider *my* proposition?'

Pietro did not reply. Luciana laughed, and turned on her heel. '*Ci vediamo*, my angel.'

He watched her as she walked away. Though she looked radiant, still he could not help feeling that beneath her finery was a sadness she dared not confess. An image of sweet Ancilla Adeodat flitted through his mind. Where was she, he wondered, at this very moment? Did she pine for him, or for her sailor, or had she moved on to other bodies, other pleasures? Pleasures which henceforth he would renounce for the sake of Anna Santamaria. When he thought again of their hurried meeting, Pietro felt his heart race. It had been everything he could have wished for: the sense of passion, of danger, the thrill of being alive. Truly he had better things to do than to amble among these anonymous *aristocratici*.

When the last of the guests had arrived, Andreas Vicario welcomed them with a few words, bade them eat and drink, and the ball began. Couples swirled about the floor in graceful minuets to the sparkling strains of the orchestra. There was much laughter, much flirtation, and some whispered gossip while others serenaded. Luciana quickly found herself besieged by suitors; the ambassador held court in the small area reserved for him, laughing as others teased him for his poor Italian. Maître Dampierre studied a Veronese drawing and sketched the statues of the slaves. Vicario's *loggia* was transformed into a garden of earthly delights. As the night wore on, conversations became animated and joy was unconfined. The dancing continued into the early hours as, elsewhere, little by little, couples and groups made their way to the secret rooms and alcoves. Pietro stayed close to Monsieur de Villedieu.

'You, *Signora*,' the ambassador said, kissing the hand of a mysterious dark-haired woman, 'you have charms enough to cause the greatest beauties of Europe to pale. And, believe me, I know whereof I speak ... As to you,' he turned to a blonde temptress with a devastating smile, 'you are her twin, her equal in splendour and in loveliness; you are twin stars, contradictory facets of a harmonious whole and, together, I prize you above the treasures of this earth. Imagine, therefore, my dilemma, *Signore*, how can I choose between fire and water? Perhaps I may be permitted to taste of both?' He bowed, leaving them in a paroxysm of falsetto laughter. Before him, two courtesans bowed and simpered.

Night had paled into the early hours of morning and still the revelry continued. The ambassador surveyed the *loggia* for a moment, judging the time ripe to steal behind the purple drapes into the secret alcoves, there to find some easy conquest. The very thought of it so delighted him that he postponed the moment, the better to savour the anticipation.

Vicario had one last trick up his sleeve. Releasing two nets cunningly concealed with the ceiling, he unleashed a rain of red and white rose petals upon the merry throng and the dancing and feasting began once more. Rice and confetti were handed round and tossed into the air. Some slipped on spilled wine and valets stooped to aid the injured parties.

Well, thought Pietro, I have learned nothing advantageous to my cause.

Two hours before daybreak, the ambassador was still preening and strutting like the peacock he resembled. The guests had begun to disband, the dancers had dwindled until there were none, the weary orchestra bowed their violins without conviction. The tide ebbed as swiftly as it had risen. Small groups of two or three conversed in low voices by the drapes, but the hall was almost empty now, the salons were deserted, and gradually the honoured guests bade their host farewell while others sought refuge in the alcoves. Andreas Vicario had prepared rooms in the apartments upstairs for those who wished their tryst to last the night. Eventually, the ambassador, taking with him the two Venetian beauties, disappeared behind the drapes. Pietro, who had recognised a number of the agents of the Quarantia Criminale, nodded to them and they discreetly shadowed the ambassador. As he did so, he noticed Emilio Vindicati, who had not left his post in the vestibule.

Pietro made his way through the salons; he could hear whispered words and moans. Looking up, he saw a woman lying upon a deep rug of Persian silk, one leg hitched up on the shoulder of a masked stranger. Her cheeks were flushed and she smiled as she ran her hands along the back of the man as he pleasured her. Pietro shrugged. Further off, a man stood, his face half-pressed into the drapes as a courtesan knelt before him.

The ambassador had repaired to a room prepared for him upstairs. Pietro climbed the steps and saw the Frenchman disappear arm in arm with his Venetian beauties; the door clicked shut behind them. Heaving a weary sigh, Pietro posted himself in the doorway. *Here I am once more listening at keyholes*, he thought. A fugitive vision of Father Caffelli in the *casa* Contarini flashed through his mind and he thought again of the *Dance of Shadows*. He sighed once more, taking up his position as sentry. It was a task he did not relish. He stared down at his polished boots. He, the Black Orchid, Pietro Luigi Viravolta de Lansalt, compelled to be a vulgar footman. Such tasks as he often entrusted to Landretto. All of a sudden, he felt a surge of sympathy for his manservant as he realised the cruel drudgery he inflicted upon the lad. He rubbed the back of his neck. It would soon be time to leave. Another agent would relieve him and *basta*.

As he stood guard, he saw again the procession of masks worn by the guests at the *ballo in maschera*. Masks – a game of masks which seemed to parallel everything that had happened these past days.

He heard moaning from within and squirmed nervously. Then he heard fresh groans, but these were not groans of pleasure. He recognised the voice of Luciana Saliestri.

No. She was crying for help. Pietro glanced about, trying to identify the source of her screams. He burst open a nearby door where a woman, still wearing her mask, straddled her lover; he tried another door – but here too he was mistaken. Still another …

He stopped dead. The man turned towards him. He was standing on the balcony overlooking the canal, dressed in the traditional costume of *Bauta*: black tricorn hat, a black veil falling about the shoulders, a death-white mask and long black cape. Seeing Pietro burst into the room, he turned quickly, his cloak fluttering behind him and, with a single bound, leapt from the balcony, scaling the trellis with extraordinary agility to land on the roof below. With a roar, Pietro rushed to the window. Hearing a strangled whimper, he looked down to find Luciana. She hung from the balcony by a thick rope; a net filled with black rocks attached to her feet, from which she could not free herself. She clawed at her throat, gasping in agony. The plaited rope had begun to ravel under the weight. Pietro lunged and grabbed the rope, but too late. There was a sharp crack, the wooden balustrade gave way and the rope slipped through his fingers with a shrill whine, flaying his fingers until they bled. He howled with pain, staring into the darkness as Luciana Saliestri plummeted, her head shattering on the low roof of the boathouse below, then fell into the canal where she sank beneath the dark waters. Two men who had observed in stunned silence – doubtless agents of the Quarantia Criminale drawn by her screams – dived in after her.

Pietro gripped the trellis and climbed down onto the roof, then tore off his mask and threw it aside. It fell into the canal to be carried away by the gentle current.

He teetered for a moment, on the roof of the Vicario boathouse, but steadied himself. He realised he was standing on a wooden terrace upon which generations of Venetian women had bleached their hair in the sun's rays. He leaned against a chimney and caught his breath, glancing about him. In the first glow of dawn he could see the shadowy figure disappear along the lines of roofs through the forest of chimneys from which, at this hour, no smoke drifted. Pietro jumped onto the adjoining roof. The next leap was more dangerous – some ten feet separating the two roofs. The cape of the mysterious assassin – doubtless one of the Striges – fluttered in his wake. Suddenly, the man turned and raised his fist. There was a flash; he had clearly drawn and fired his flintlock. Pietro threw himself down onto the roof, almost slipping and falling into the void. Profiting from the distraction, the phantom scaled the wall of the villa. Picking himself up, Pietro gave chase. He reached the brink and looked down to see the man still clambering to safety.

Pietro opened his coat and snatched the pistols from his belt, taking aim at the fleeing figure.

'Messer!' he shouted. The man stopped his climb and looked up at Pietro. For a moment they stared at one another. Then, scrambling to reach the ground, the phantom lost his footing. His arms flailed as he tried to stop himself, but he slipped and fell with a dull thud into the street below.

Barely pausing to catch his breath, Pietro climbed down after him, careful to take a different route. At length he reached the cobbled street where the man lay. He stooped, seizing the phantom by the ruff of his shirt. Beneath the mask, blood trickled from the corner of his mouth.

'Who are you?' roared Pietro, 'Give me your name!'

The phantom gasped, then his face distorted into a baleful smile, teeth gleaming in the moonlight.

'Ramiel ...' he rasped, 'of ... of the order of Thrones ...'

The smile faded and the man's hand clutched Pietro's shoulder, his body stiffened, and he fell back onto the cobbles gasping a last breath. Pietro stood and wiped his brow, leaving the corpse where it lay.

They were here. And they have murdered Luciana.

CANTO XII

THE AVARICIOUS AND THE PRODIGAL

Fourth Circle: The Avaricious and the Prodigal, who shall be made to push a great weight one group against the other for all eternity.

The corpse of Luciana Saliestri, the widow who had squandered her avaricious husband's fortune was hauled from the dark waters by the Quarantia Criminale. The canal, cut to allow the passage of large boats, was deep and though it was dredged as quickly as possible, it was some time before her body was brought ashore. It made little matter, for she had been dead before she reached the water: the weight of the stones had all but severed her neck, and her head had been shattered when she had fallen against the quay. As he watched her remains being lifted from the depths, water coursing from her long veils, her face livid, lips parted as if to speak, Pietro thought of drowned Ophelia. The rocks which had dragged her down were left in the mud. Black gondolas passed on the waters, silent, funereal barges. Upon the wall of the room in which he had surprised the murderer, Pietro discovered the customary inscription:

Tutti quanti fuor geruci
si de la mente in la vita primaia
che con misura nullo spendio ferci

Every one of the shades here massed

In the first life had a mind so squinty-eyed
That in his spending he heeded no proportion

Luciana. Luciana, whose fortune had been squandered on elegant gowns to flatter her charms, a fortune bequeathed to her by a husband renowned for his great avarice – like Pantaloon in the *commedia dell'arte*. Pietro could still hear her melodious voice as she spoke of her husband: 'May God rest his soul,' she had said. 'As you know, the poor man had an obsession beyond all reason for trade and money. He was something of a miser. I, on the contrary, have a taste for other forms of trade, for things I cannot refuse myself.' She had prized her freedom above all things; she whose youth and beauty had turned the head of Senator Campioni and so many others would soon be in the ground with worms her only company. Giving of her body yet again.

Weary, Pietro sat against the wall some metres from the great entrance to the Villa Vicario. Landretto sat next to him. For his part, Emilio Vindicati was questioning the master of the house, and the agents of the Tenebræ had been despatched to interview each of the guests who had attended the ball. Pietro was convinced that such interrogations would lead them no farther than any of the 'clues' they had yet discovered.

Luciana, the short-lived Domino. *Murdered.* Another death.

Pietro was devastated – remorseful that he had not kept the courtesan from harm, mindful that, in playing the recruiting sergeant, he had doubtless placed her in mortal danger. The very thought that such a thing might have happened – might yet happen – to Anna Santamaria made his blood run cold. The time had come to tell Vindicati what he had discovered in Ottavio's study. Pietro felt a wave of guilt sweep over him. Luciana had not deserved to be so ill-used; her death might have been averted. If Pietro had had greater presence of mind, if he had spoken sooner … He felt the urge to vomit, to weep … As to the ambassador, he had slumbered peacefully in the arms of his beautiful Venetian whores, happy as a pope himself, sated with wine and wenching. He had heard nothing of the commotion which had followed. He had appeared on the steps of the *palazzo*, sleep-eyed and still wearing his peacock feathers, in time to see the body pulled from the dark depths of the canal. He had launched into a flurry of horrified exclamations until Emilio had reassured him and – in a rude blow to diplomatic relations – sent him under armed escort to his official residence in Venice. But Emilio Vindicati would devise some explanation, and the ambassador would allow himself to be persuaded that all had not been as it seemed. The painter, for his part, had disappeared during the night, doubtless returning to his bed.

The Firebirds' infernal machinations had not faltered and, while Pietro had been preoccupied with the safety of Messer de Villedieu, they had struck down Luciana Saliestri. If he understood their plans right, Giovanni Campioni might well be the next in line. Thus far, Pietro and those in the service of the doge had been working at a disadvantage. *Il Diavolo* had led them by the nose. Though they knew the circles and the punishments of the *Inferno*, they could not know whom the Chimera had chosen as his victims. At such a game the Tenebræ and the Quarantia could not but fail. The Black Orchid slipped a hand into his pocket to retrieve his latest find. He had had time to search the 'phantom', Ramiel, of the order of Thrones, and had found nothing except a card, which now danced before his eyes.

It was the fifteenth card of the the Tarot, depicting the demon Baphomet. *The Devil*. It seemed to have been crafted for the occasion. The illustration showed the horned figure of Satan enthroned before a zodiacal orb resembling the diagram used by Raziel in *The Forces of Evil* to describe the Nine legions: three of the divisions were masked by the body of the beast. In his right hand, he held the hanged body of a woman, stones tied about her feet; in his left, a shadowy figure rolled a rock upon a hill. Once more, the Chimera employed metaphors that seemed at once clear and obscure. And once again, his emissaries had come out of the night, striking hard and fast, only to vanish into the darkness before Pietro had time to act. Like a cobra striking. Pietro studied the tarot card again. Beneath a goat's horns, the Devil's eyes shot thunderbolts; the lips contorted into a rictus. It was an image familiar to Pietro, who, upon a time, had been a disciple of cartomancy and astrology. This time, he sensed, the message was directed at him.

He looked up to see Emilio Vindicati approach. 'We have not yet discovered the identity of your "phantom", Pietro. Did you know that Luciana Saliestri's fortune was greater yet than either of us could have imagined? She was greatly indebted to her husband. She squandered almost as diligently as he hoarded – an elegant symmetry which doubtless did not escape *il Diavolo*. Do you believe that the Firebirds feared she might confess something to you?'

Pietro rose to his feet, clearly exhausted.

'Go and rest,' urged Emilio. 'I too could use a few snatched hours of sleep.'

Pietro sighed. 'That I shall … But Emilio … There is something of which I must speak to you.'

Emilio turned quickly, alarmed by Pietro's tone, wondering what fresh calamity might have befallen.

'Luciana did confide something to me. There was a third man who regularly called on her … someone who bears me no great love.'

Emilio's brow furrowed. 'By which you mean … ?'

'Indeed, *amico*, I mean Ottavio. And that is not all. Attend me closely: the Council of Ten must immediately summon him to the palace for questioning and, if possible, despatch agents to search his villa in Santa Croce unannounced. All this must be done and quickly, Emilio, before he gets wind of it!'

'Hold! Hold, Pietro! What is it that you have discovered? Have you …'

Emilio Vindicati's face brightened and almost immediately grew dark again. 'You have seen her. In spite of my proscription you have been to visit her!'

'It was a *clue*, Emilio! I had to go there! She gave me access to Ottavio's study and I discovered something – some arcane plans I could not understand, which made mention of Minos! This is no coincidence, Emilio!'

Vindicati shook his head, unable to believe what he was hearing. His face was ashen. The travails of the night were beginning to take their toll.

'Pietro, are you telling me that you went to the villa of Anna Santamaria? You unlawfully searched Senator Ottavio's private study? You went to … I cannot credit it!'

'Emilio, did you not hear me?'

'And *you*, Pietro, did you not hear me? *Santa Madonna!* You made me an oath!' Emilio glared at Pietro, his fury mounting.

'Ottavio is embroiled in this affair, I am persuaded of it! This is grave, Emilio! We must arrange for the villa to be searched this very morning!'

'And do you imagine that with a snap of my fingers I can have Senator Ottavio's residence turned on its head? What search, Pietro? On what evidence? On the strength of the allegations of the Black Orchid, a common criminal whom I released from *i Piombi* and who has repaid me thus? The Black Orchid who vouchsafed never again to see Anna Santamaria? The same Black Orchid who is the sworn enemy of Ottavio? A skilful story that would make. Who would believe that you did not do this to avenge yourself? Who—'

'I know what I saw, Emilio, I did not imagine this!'

'And what precisely did you *see*? Plans? Excellent! And

the name of Minos? But since Spadetti's death, the name has been the talk of Venice! Where is your proof, Pietro? What you have told me does not amount even to an inkling of a suspicion. And yet you would have me send a detachment of agents to search Ottavio's villa by force?'

'It would serve you well. Emilio ...' Pietro clutched his friend's arm, 'you must trust me. Ottavio is our surest route into this mystery.'

Face haggard, jaw clenched, Emilio studied Pietro for a long moment, then sighed and shook his head. 'I shall endeavour to have him appear for questioning before the Quarantia Criminale, but in private, and you shall have no part in it, do you understand? He must have no inkling that you are behind this, else all this comes to naught. And for my part, I can ill-afford to lose face.'

'Very well. But take care not to let him go! He is one of the Striges, of that I am certain. He may be *il Diavolo* himself!'

'*Il Diavolo* ... Ottavio?' Emilio sighed once more. 'But now, Pietro, I wish to know precisely how you intend to proceed.'

'I intend to pay a visit to an old friend.' Pietro toyed with the tarot card beneath his cape. 'A man named Fregolo,' he drew his collar up against the rain, 'who is adept at cartomancy.'

In his costume of black and silver, his sunburst mask in hand, Andreas Vicario stood in the now deserted *loggia*. The agents of the Quarantia Criminale had advised him to touch nothing until their investigation was completed. Andreas smiled. About him rose petals and rice, garlands and ribbons strewed the floor. The masked ball had been a great success. With consummate talent he had played the victim and the baffled aristocrat; it had not proved difficult, he had a flair for such things. Now, he was alone in his demesne congratulating himself on the success of this new exploit. This time, even the Maggior Consiglio would get to hear of it. Only a few days remained before the feast of the Ascension. Venice would be in turmoil. Everyone had left now: the guests, the Quarantia Criminale. As soon as he received formal notification, Vicario would have his servants restore order to the place. There had, of course, been one minor difficulty: Ramiel had been discovered and was now dead, but there was no evidence to lead the Black Orchid and the Quarantia Criminale to him. They might, of course, already harbour some suspicions; but Andreas did not think so. He had made enquiries concerning Pietro Viravolta, whose reputation preceded him. Vicario understood how the man thought; he would not be content with obvious truths, although the truth of the matter was there at hand – so bright, so incandescent it was like the sun. Minos looked down at his mask and laughed.

Somewhere in the Adriatic, near the Strait of Otranto, at 40°N and 18°E, a young sailor left the deck and made his way down to the captain's cabin. He negotiated the dark stairwell and, having knocked three times, opened the door. The captain, wearing his military jacket with epaulettes and gold buttons, and a powdered wig, was sitting behind his desk upon which were spread maps, a sextant and a compass. The sailor saluted and stood to attention. The captain was daydreaming, weary of the fruitless hours wasted here; he was dreaming of Ancilla, his beloved Ancilla Adeodato at home in Venice and hoping that soon they might be reunited, that he might feast his eyes once more upon her nut-brown skin, her shapely form. As the message brought by the sailor confirmed, it would only be a matter of days now.

'There's a detachment from the *Santa Maria* requesting leave to board, Captain. Three soldiers arrived in a boat a few minutes ago to deliver this. And the frigates have joined us, Sir.'

The captain took the letter, broke the seal, scanned the missive quickly, and then smiled. He glanced up at the sailor, pursed his lips, and then said: 'Very good. No need to keep them waiting. I shall meet them on deck.'

Some moments later, the captain appeared. The wet planking creaked underfoot as a number of deckhands swabbed. The sky overhead was leaden. The captain, a telescope in hand, took a deep breath of the brisk salt air. Aloft, a number of sailors trimmed the sails, perched upon the rigging like gulls. The captain gazed out at the horizon to Corfu where the ships lay at anchor, then headed toward the deputation from the *Santa Maria*. He smoothed his jacket, abstractedly fondling the decorations he had been careful to pin there. His other hand moved to the hilt of the sword which hung by his side.

Discussions with the three men from the *Santa Maria* lasted a half-hour, after which the delegation were lowered again to their skiff and headed back to their galley. The captain watched the skiff move away and then rounded up his crew: 'We rendezvous with von Maarken's warships off the coast of Palagruzza. Raise the mainsail, we sail at once!'

Men scurried to the topmast, others manned the oars and the gunwhale; the vast sails slowly unfurled and the deckhands abandoned their pails to hoist anchor, the rhythmic splash of oars breaking the water could be heard, and the ship moved off. Nearby, the sails of the *Santa Maria* spread out. There was laughter and shouting and song from men who had waited too long for this day to come. The vessel shuddered as the wind whipped up the sails and the prow, adorned with a mermaid, sliced through the waters. Along the deck, men checked the cannons and stacked the cannonballs. The captain returned to his cabin, his sextant and his maps.

Framed majestically against the sun, the *Santa Maria* and the *Gioia De Corfù*, flanked by two frigates, moved out of the narrow cove and onto the high seas. Some time later, near Palagruzza, they were joined by two other galleons and four frigates and the armada set sail for *la Serenissima*.

After a few hours of troubled sleep, haunted by nightmare visions, Pietro was once again awake and heading with his manservant to visit the cabinet of Messer Fregolo on the Piazza San Marco. As an astrologer, Fregolo was regularly consulted by the crowned heads of Europe, a fact which Pietro had used to his advantage more than once. But Fregolo and his 'profession' were closely watched by the state. His consulting room was at the rear of what appeared to be a small boutique selling choice pieces of furniture, though the shop was merely a ruse and, in truth, deceived no one. This made it possible to make light of his work as an astrologer, a practice he mocked in the presence of sceptics, and spoke of with deadly earnest in the presence of the clients. Pietro studied the coat of arms upon the door before stepping inside. As he had expected, Fregolo was sitting at his desk, surrounded by escritoires in polished wood, wardrobes of elegant marquetry, and endless curios. The boutique smelled reassuringly of beeswax and antiquity. In a few well-chosen words Pietro outlined to the cartomancer the reason for his visit, while Landretto wandered among the pieces of furniture, amusing himself by searching for concealed drawers and hidden compartments. As he listened to Pietro, Fregolo frowned, then invited both men to follow him, gesturing to the office behind the boutique. Pietro parted the drapes and found himself in a room which was utterly different from the first. Here, rich blue drapes of blue, scattered with golden stars, covered the walls. The room was dim, but on a small, round table covered by a purple cloth, a number of esoteric artefacts were displayed to great effect, and a crystal ball and pendulum lay in a leather case. Pietro sat and crossed his legs as Fregolo busied himself elsewhere. When he returned, he had been transformed. He had exchanged his *tabarro* and his dark pantaloons for a robe richly embroidered with stars, whose form and ample sleeves recalled an oriental caftan, and upon his head he wore a skullcap. With his grey beard trimmed to an elegant point, his bushy eyebrows and lined face, he looked like a wizard, a doge of the underworld. *And so the scene is set*, thought Pietro, knowing how easily such trinkets would impress the credulous.

'Show me the card.'

Pietro proffered the card that he had found in Ramiel's pocket and the magician studied it intently for a moment.

'The Devil. The card was painted recently. It is the first time I have seen one quite like this – I am not altogether certain that it comes from a complete set, but from what you have told me, that would scarcely be surprising. It may indeed have been crafted with you in mind. The Devil's place within the Tarot is similar to that of the dragon or serpent. Ordinarily, it is the fifteenth card of the *major arcana*, between *Temperance* and *The Tower*. It symbolises the bringing together of the elements for the pursuit of passion, regardless of the cost. It corresponds to the Third House in Astrology. It is the antithesis, not of God, but of *The Empress*, who symbolises dominion over all things through intelligence, or the figure of Venus in Greek mythology.'

'Venus, symbolising Venice,' Pietro whispered to Landretto.

'In general, the Devil symbolises chaos, the forces of evil – those upon which you remarked in the allusion to the Nine Legions. Though the traditional version is somewhat different. Here, as often, the figure is half-naked, but usually he sits upon a ball set in a pedestal of six strata. The Devil is a hermaphrodite, with the blue wings of a bat, a red belt about his navel, and claws upon his hands. His right hand is raised, and with his left, he points to the earth with a sword. Upon his head are crescent moons and the five-pronged antlers of a stag. He is flanked by two demons, one male, the other female, each bearing horns and a tail, or crowned with flames. The hanged man – or rather, hanged woman – depicted on your card weighed down with stones, and the spectral figure who rolls a rock, are fabrications invented specifically for this illustration. But the reference is clear: the rocks symbolise the sin which weighs down the hanged figure, while the other figure, like Sisyphus, rolls the rock ever attempting to be rid of it.'

'Do you have any idea who might have fashioned such a card?'

'Not the least,' answered Fregolo.

Pietro leaned towards the cartomancer. 'Have you heard tell of the Firebirds?'

Would the words have upon Fregolo the effect they had had on Campioni? Certainly, the man seemed preoccupied, but he did not seem panicked as both Father Caffelli and the senator had been at the mention of the name.

He sat back in his chair and stared at Pietro. 'Let us simply say that … it is my business to know of divers occult groups.'

'They say the Devil is come to Venice, Messer Fregolo.'

'It is a conviction I would take most seriously.'

'I believe their methods are political, and indeed that many among our noble senators may be caught up in this madness …'

'Politics,' said Fregolo, 'is merely a privileged playing field upon which good and evil may be played out. If you believe the forces of evil are come to the city, look not only to Man, but to the inspiration which impels him. That inspiration – Lucifer himself – is not a myth, but a reality. Do not doubt that fact: if you do, you have already lost. You must prepare yourself for the unthinkable.'

'Indeed, my friend, indeed. But what do you know of these Firebirds?'

'They are a sect of some form, I believe. A number of my clients have made mention of them. One among them is, I believe, a member of the sect. Without saying as much, he invited me to join their cause. But I have no truck with cabals, nor with black magic. In refusing to join the forces of darkness a man may lose his life, but in joining them he risks losing something infinitely greater. He loses his soul, *amico.*'

Pietro's tongue darted over his lips. 'This client of whom you speak, he who would have had you join the Firebirds … what is his name?'

Fregolo hesitated, his hand suddenly frozen in mid-air.

No, no, my friend, I shall not be denied, thought Pietro, *I shall not leave until you tell me this, if I must drag the answer from you by torture.*

Fregolo leaned closer to Pietro and said in a low voice: 'It was – as you yourself suggested – one among the senators of the republic …'

'Ah.' Pietro too leaned forward, craning to hear what was said.

'Indeed. His name is Giovanni Campioni.'

Taken aback, Pietro turned to his manservant. Landretto grimaced. *So it was the other.*

THE FIFTH CIRCLE

CANTO XIII

CARTOMANCY AND PANOPTICA

'It is a lie, an abominable lie! It is a conspiracy, an attempt to unseat me!'

Senator Campioni sat facing Pietro and the assembled members of the Council of Ten in one of the secret interrogation chambers of *i Piombi*. The chief of the Quarantia Criminale was also present. Campioni's outrage was all too real, and the passion and the rage with which he spoke of conspiracies and plots mounted against him seemed convincing. It was Saturday, and the senator should have been with his peers, for the Senate was in conclave. Instead, His Excellency, robed in ermine and wearing his *beretta*, sat facing his accusers looking devastated. News of the death of Luciana Saliestri had aged him by ten years. Pale and haggard, his eyes darted about him feverishly. From time to time, he broke off, choking back tears, unable to believe he could be a suspect. The question remained as to whether Fregolo was trustworthy, but the Ten and the Criminale could not afford to neglect the slightest detail. They sat in serried ranks behind tables disposed in a semi-circle, like a military tribunal. Ernesto Castiglione, Samuele Sidoni, Niccolo Canova and with them, robed in black and stern of countenance, the members of the Venetian secret police, who looked ready to fall upon the senator and tear him limb from limb if he should make the least mistake. Pietro wondered whether this show of outrage from Campioni was a spirited performance, or whether the man's fury was sincere. At this point, Pietro was no longer certain of anything, and yet there was something comical about the situation. Pietro knew that in the adjoining room, Ottavio was being interrogated in like manner by Emilio Vindicati. Pietro would have given his eye-teeth to be in that room, staring down the husband of Anna Santamaria. He was convinced that it had been Ottavio who had stolen the brooch which had been found at the Teatro San Luca from Luciana Saliestri, and that she had died because of it. He would have conducted the interrogation in a rather different fashion – with none of the reserve and the discretion which Emilio would afford the senator in the name of 'protocol'. Pietro wished to corner Ottavio, to drive him to the brink of madness or despair for, in spite of Fregolo's words, Pietro was convinced that Campioni was not the enemy.

'Think, I pray you,' said Campioni, 'The brooch found at San Luca and now this card, this tarot card which has led you to me – do these things not seem to you a little too convenient? I am innocent! Can you truly imagine that I could mount a secret army to overthrow the government? You have taken leave of your wits!'

'Our enemies have already proved their cunning, *Eccellenza*, and that they are capable of anything. Venice has seen stranger things than these. Our fair city has always incited evil men to envy and conspiracy. You say that the evidence against you is so obviously planted that only a fool would credit it. Who is to say that it has not been planted in a clever double bluff? You would be unwise to gamble on our intelligence – we may yet prove to be fools. Do not tell us how to interpret the evidence when what we want from you are facts. You were in love with Luciana Saliestri, were you not?'

'Oh ...' Campioni brought a hand to his heart, moved by the mention of her name. 'Please do not drag that untainted passion through the mire of these grotesque acts of violence. How could you believe, even for an instant, that I could harm such an angel as she? Her death has torn me apart as surely as a pack of wolves.'

'"Untainted passion",' said Ricardo Michele Pavi, chief of the Quarantia Criminale. 'A curious choice of words when referring to – God rest her soul – a courtesan accustomed to welcoming any man to her bed.'

Pietro coughed.

'… The *delitto passionale* – the crime of passion – as old as love itself,' said Pavi, 'surely you were jealous of her other lovers? After all, there were so many!'

'Yes, I was jealous, jealous and distraught, though it was a tragedy which concerned only myself. But what have my feelings for Luciana to do with a hunt for the Firebirds? Go find your cartomancer and—'

'Do you deny that you consulted Messer Fregolo in the past?' asked Emilio Vindicati.

At this, the senator lowered his eyes. 'I … it is true that I consulted him, once or twice. But on matters which had nothing to do with the political, it was simply …'

Seeing the senator struggle for words, Pietro intervened. 'You are not the first,' he said, in a tone he hoped was reassuring. 'Nor indeed the least: did not Caesar Augustus consult with clairvoyants? Do not worry about the astrologer; if he has lied to us, he will be under lock and key by nightfall. What we need is that you tell us all you know, everything you have held back, on the subject of the Firebirds. Who is this Minos? Who is Virgil? Who is the man who calls himself *il Diavolo*?'

Campioni turned to Pietro. 'Yes. Yes, I shall tell you everything I know. But you must remember. One of you may well be one of them.'

At this, Niccolo Canova, a stout man of advancing years with a razor-sharp mind for all that, sat forward in his chair and spoke. 'I should not, in your position, add to the gravity of your situation by making false accusations against those entrusted with the security of the republic.'

There was a long silence as Campioni stared at his hands.

'They made threats against me, but that is not the worst of it.' Campioni glanced once more at Pietro, as if seeking support. 'They threatened the lives of my family and a number of the noble senators. I cannot bring myself to put their lives in peril. You were in Mestre, at the villa Mora; you have seen what people they are, have you not? I offered you the opportunity to apprehend them, it may have been an opportunity to annihilate them. Now I know that they cannot be stopped.' He fell silent once more.

'Very well! I shall tell you everything, believe me when I tell you this is all I know.'

As one man, the Tenebræ, the Criminale and Pietro himself, leaned forward expectantly.

'I cannot go on, I cannot bear this burden alone. This, then, is what I know: Minos is a member of the Maggior Consiglio, though I have never discovered his identity. I believe that it is he who bribed Fregolo, just as he did the others. As to the Firebirds, not all are of noble birth, far from it. Many are humble *cittadini*, minor public servants, the credulous and the gullible forced to believe in an impossible dream. Ramiel, who murdered my sweet Luciana, was one such. I do not know whether those in charge of the sect have allies abroad, but it seems very likely. They are faceless, which makes them all the more powerful. They are masters in the arts of blackmail, which practice they use to bind you to their cause. At first they manipulate through small gifts and favours, later through bribery and corruption, finally – when persuasion and intimidation fail, through terror. They manipulate events so that a man may find himself in an inextricable position, just as I am now. The *coup d'état* they are planning may come at any moment, and you are right to fear what may befall the feast of the Ascension. No moment could be more propitious, since the doge will appear in public and thus be vulnerable.

The rest is naught but illusion and masquerade, mere rumours of black magic and satanic rites intended to instil fear, and make it easier to intimidate their disciples. One among them … I know that one among them has rented an apartment a stone's throw from the Procuratie, a vast building which overlooks the entire breadth of the *laguna*, though I know not to what purpose …'

'We must have names, *Eccellenza*,' Canova interjected again. 'Give us names.'

'I would … There is someone … someone whom I think to be at the heart of this affair, who …'

'Whom you *think*? We are not interested in speculation, senator, we need names!'

There was a long silence. No one among the assembled company moved. At length, in a whisper, barely audible even in this deathly hush, Campioni said … 'I speak of Senator Ottavio.'

The room abruptly erupted in angry recriminations and cries of disbelief. Canova slumped back in his seat. Pietro's face brightened. When they were calm again, they turned once more to Campioni. He sat, eyes closed, his head in his hands, stroking his temples. When he looked up at his accusers he had composed himself somewhat. Canova leaned towards him and said in a tremulous voice: 'You realise the gravity of this accusation?'

Campioni nodded his assent. 'Go to the Procuratie and see. And heed me well – shortly I shall be in conclave with the Senate and I shall not know whether, at any moment – *at any moment* – the decisions made there, the strategies discussed, the reports made to the noble senators, might not immediately be relayed to the Firebirds, or those in league with them.'

He stared at each of his accusers in turn. 'Messere, on one point we are all agreed: this situation has gone on too long. We must unite. I shall immediately enjoin my supporters in the Senate and the Maggior Consiglio to tell you all they know. They, I know, will pledge their allegiance to you. Fine words, I know, when treason is everywhere – but you must take my word on it. Together we shall face down this threat with every means at our disposal – even if it means that the populace at large will know of it. The doge, I know, has just received the Ambassador of France: it is regrettable, but he too may be menaced. I believe ... I believe all Venice should be warned. I believe, and have ever believed, that we must trust in the good people of this city who have seen off treachery before. Beneath the frivolous costumes and the gaiety of carnival, they too know where their fealty lies.'

This last allusion was not lost upon those present, though to some among them, who feared the populace and remembered Doge Faliero only too well, Campioni's words seemed suspect. Ottavio's name still resonated in the room, and though many were not at first convinced, they were won round. The meeting lasted an hour more and Senator Campioni was freed to join the Senate in conclave, leaving the others to ponder what he had said. They were minded to believe him; after all, Campioni knew the risks of lying to the Council of Ten and the Quarantia. It was, they decided, time to marshal themselves for battle. Fregolo was arrested within the hour and taken for questioning even though, were he to confess, he would not be believed.

Ricardo Pavi, chief of the Quarantia Criminale, turned to Pietro. 'Do you believe he spoke true?'

'I do. I believe that Ottavio is the man we want.'

Pavi, barely thirty years old, hard-faced, but with passion in his eyes, was known to be a reactionary. Those who knew him whispered that, in certain circumstances, he was not above conducting interrogations himself. He dealt with criminal matters with a devotion equalled only by his ferocity. He had a formidable mind, and an instinct which was the envy of many a magistrate, though they deplored his excesses. He had seen his wife murdered before his eyes, since which time he had lost all sense of compassion. The only thing that moved him now was his duty. He was a staunch aesthete and a fervent Catholic and, though he was feared, even his enemies did not doubt his effectiveness.

'Campioni maintains that one of the Firebirds rented an apartment at 10 Calle Frezzaria, near the Procuratie. It can hardly be coincidence that the address is not ten metres from Fregolo's boutique ... And if he spoke the truth, it should not prove difficult to discover the identity of the tenant.'

'I shall go there now,' said Pietro. 'We shall see. But, tell me, Messer,' his face darkened, 'what news of the galleys missing from the Arsenal?'

Pavi, too, looked grave and turned away. 'We have had no further news. The *Santa Maria* and the *Gioia De Corfù* are still somewhere in the Adriatic, unless they have been scuttled. We have tried interrogation, but we can hardly clap every man in the Arsenal in irons.'

He turned back to Pietro. 'But come, make haste, I shall send a detachment of agents to escort you.'

Pietro snatched his hat and rose.

No sooner had he stepped out of the room than he ran into Emilio Vindicati, who had finished his own interrogation in the adjoining cell.

'So?'

Emilio gave him a bitter smile, balling his fists. 'So? So? So he denies everything, of course! I can hardly accuse him with no proof! I was forced to release him, and in the process I have been crowned with ridicule just as I feared.'

'*What*? But has no one told you that in the meanwhile ...'

'I know, I know! But Ottavio simply claims that Campioni is politicking! Don't you understand? Each blames the other and, in doing so, they can do as they please. Here we are, seconds to a pair of duellists. If we go on thus, we could interrogate all the noblemen of Venice to no avail for we have no evidence, Pietro. *Nothing!*'

The Black Orchid frowned and said through gritted teeth, 'Not nothing, no.'

'For pity's sake,' said Emilio as Pietro hastened away, 'What are you planning to do?'

'What you taught me ...' said Pietro. 'I shall improvise.'

The apartment at 10 Calle Frezzaria was part of an *albergo* owned by Lucrezia Lonati, who conceded that a gentleman had indeed negotiated with her to rent the third floor, together with sole use of the *terrazzo* some months before. The man claimed to be a Florentine on business in Venice and gave his name only as Messer Sino. M. Sino, as Pietro immediately recognised, was merely an anagram of Minos. Signora Lonati led Pietro and two of the agents of the Quarantia Criminale to the third floor while the others scoured the register of the *albergo*. The apartments had been left empty for the most part, the *duenna* informed them, though on one occasion she had seen a mysterious man receiving guests who wore carnival masks and tricornes. A number of crates had been stored in the apartments, which she had assumed to be M. Sino's luggage. The men had spent a whole day there, she insisted, but she had not felt it her position to ask questions, given that M. Sinos seemed to be a man of some standing and, moreover, paid cash. Her description of the men who had visited was so anodyne as to be worthless. She had seen her tenant thereafter only on rare occasions, and always accompanied by several mysterious figures.

Signora Lonati said she believed that the apartment was empty, but nevertheless knocked on the door before slipping her key into the lock.

Pietro and the two agents stepped into the luxurious apartment, composed of four rooms of equal size. They rapidly focused on the second room. Meanwhile,

Landretto, weary of waiting on his master, came upstairs with the other agents, and every room was meticulously searched.

The room which had first caught Pietro's eye was lavishly furnished. Three armchairs were arranged about an Oriental carpet; along one wall ran bookshelves containing volumes which, though he examined each in turn, turned out to be of no apparent interest. On the facing wall hung a large, detailed map of Venice and its environs, which Signora Lonati assured him had not been there on the last occasion she had visited, though she admitted that the apartment had not been cleaned for several weeks. A fine patina of dust lay upon the furniture. The adjoining room contained the crates which the mysterious lackeys had brought – all now empty. Beside the great windows which looked out onto the Procuratie and the street below was a globe, and a low table on which Pietro discovered several curious tools. Next to these were several tiny coffins some two inches in length, each with a crucifix embossed onto the lid and each carved with a name:

Marcello Torretone
Cosimo Caffelli
Federico Spadetti
Luciana Saliestri

Pietro almost gasped to see the names of the first four victims. Naturally, the murderer had not had the good grace to name his next victim. Near the table, Pietro made another discovery.

'At least we have discovered what was contained in the crates,' he said to Landretto, stooping to examine his find more closely. 'Interesting … most interesting.'

Landretto crossed the room and stared at the telescopes, each mounted on a tripod and seemingly pointed at the window frame. The lad crouched, and peeked through the eyepiece, and was puzzled to see nothing but a patch of yellow wall.

'Can't see a thing!' he said, wiping the lens and placing his eye to it once more. Pietro joined him, but each of the instruments was pointed at random at an area of wall or a scrap of dull grey sky.

Pietro stood and thought for a moment, then turned to Signora Lonati and the agents searching the room.

'Help me with these,' said Pietro to the men of the Quarantia Criminale. 'We're going up to the *terrazzo*.'

Giovanni Campioni had been correct when he said that the building had one of the finest views in Venice. It was amongst the tallest building in a city which, for the most part, contained houses of only two floors. From here, it was possible to see the Campanile, the Clock Tower and the *laguna*, all the way to San Giorgio Maggiore and the Giudecca; one could look at the *sestieri* of Venice laid out as if on a map: from San Marco to Cannaregio and Santa Croce. Pietro had the men place the telescopes at regular intervals around the terrace and, before long, his worst fears had been confirmed. His face grew pale. *Almighty God … I am unaccustomed to invoking your name, but I do so now …*

'What is it?' asked Landretto.

'It is as I feared. What is the chief component in a telescope, Landretto?'

The lad scratched his chin and looked doubtful, slipping a hand into his waistcoat. 'A telescope … I'm not rightly sure as I know …'

'I shall tell you,' said Pietro, looking up from the eyepiece. 'A telescope is made of a series of glass lenses and a number of mirrors.'

He spread his arms wide. 'And Venice is covered with *twenty thousand ducats' worth of glass*.'

*

In a matter of hours Pietro's suspicions were confirmed. Already they had discovered more than fifteen apartments rented in similar circumstances – men calling themselves Semyazza, Asmodeus, Abaddon – the names of the fallen angels of the Legions of Hell. Each had been rented in one of the tallest building in the city, each with a private *terrazzo* overlooking the city, and in each they discovered several telescopes.

Some offered views into the private *palazzi* of some of the great patrician families of Venice, others afforded a glimpse into humble *casini*, the garden of the *Broglio*, and from one it was possible to see into the doge's apartments. Minos had created a complex network of mirrors and lenses on chimney stacks and roofs so that he could peer into even the most inaccessible places. It was so intelligently imagined, and the necessary calculations so dizzyingly convoluted, that it made the city a vast hall of mirrors – a veritable panopticon where, from any point, one might see any other. *Panoptica*. Pietro remembered seeing the word on the plans he had discovered in Ottavio's study. He remembered, too, the elaborate plans, the wild drawing of facades, of buildings and monuments, the mathematical equations, the arrows, and the compass roses. This had been the result of those plans: an eye – an all-seeing eye – which scrutinised every alleyway in Venice.

The apartments were requisitioned, their landlords mercilessly interrogated by agents of the Quarantia despatched to every *sestiere*. A rumour spread through the streets; at first barely a whisper but, as it travelled, the news grew more shocking; fantasy and nightmare mingled with truth. And as the rumour spread down the Mercerie, scurried like flame along a trail of gunpowder through the arcades beneath the Procuratie and from the Rialto to Terra Firma, it said only this, that a shadow had fallen over the city, a vast, nameless shadow from whom no man, no woman, no child was safe.

The faltering peace of the city of the doges was shattered. Even in the quiet of their beds noblemen and paupers trembled with fear.

'What greater surveillance could there be than this, Landretto? Where the subject can never know he is being watched. Clearly Ottavio could not have conceived of such a thing alone.'

Landretto turned to his master, his voice wavering. 'Do you still doubt that the Devil himself is come to Venice?'

CANTO XIV
THE WRATHFUL

The hall of the Maggior Consiglio was by far the most vast of all those in the doge's palace: almost two thousand souls now sat there in conclave. The doge sat, flanked by the members of his Privy Council, the Council of Ten, and the chief of the Quarantia Criminale, who was accompanied by the coroner, Antonio Brozzi. Behind them was spread Tintoretto's celebrated *Paradise*, painted in 1590, one of the largest canvases in the world, in which were contained a myriad of historical personages and symbols of the glory of the city. Palma il Giovane, together with Jacopo Bassano, had painted thirty-four of the great ceiling panels, but the last, the glorious central panel, was Veronese's *Apotheosis of Venice*. It was at this that Pietro now gazed, half-amused by the grim irony of the title. As he had arrived at the Piazza San Marco, he had passed a throng of people queuing to be admitted to the basilica. Among them he recognised Maître Eugène-André Dampierre, strutting proudly among the banners announcing his exhibition. A series of his religious works had been hung, as planned, in the narthex of San Marco. The doge, once more compelled to act as though no turmoil swept through the city, was scheduled to inaugurate the exhibition in the presence of the French Ambassador later that day. Here, in the hall of the Maggior Consiglio, however, the mood was not one of celebration. Ordinarily, the Maggior Consiglio convened on Sundays and on high holy days, and the sessions closed at five o'clock when Francesco Loredan concluded, and the magistracies were closed. Any debate which had not been concluded was adjourned until the following session. In the case of more grave or pressing matters, the *correzione*, as the Grand Council was sometimes known, was called upon to sit on a daily basis. Though it was Tuesday, an extraordinary session had been called, and all the noblemen of Venice, stiffly formal in powdered wigs and ceremonial robes of red and black, were in attendance.

Before so many painted faces, Emilio Vindicati gave an account of the matter at hand, and of the investigation led by the Council of Ten. It was a difficult speech for, 'given the delicate nature of the investigation', as he put it, some of what was known to the Tenebræ had to be passed over in silence. This was a matter which Pietro had hotly disputed, but Emilio was adamant: 'There can be no question of formally accusing Senator Ottavio before the Maggior Consiglio, Pietro! Mention his name and I vouchsafe that they will disembowel you where you stand. To accuse him publicly would put an end to your efforts.'

'What, is Ottavio to be untouchable?' cried Pietro. 'What of the panopticon – an invention worthy of da Vinci himself?'

'I understand, Pietro, and I am glad that we have finally found something of substance. But we must yet be subtle. Ottavio could not have devised such an invention alone, and Signora Lonati has been unable to identify any other. I shall speak to the doge and arrange for a search of Ottavio's villa. Must I remind you, Pietro, that I still lack something essential: proof. Without evidence linking Ottavio directly to this conspiracy I am powerless. Nor should you forget that we have the advantage: though he may sense danger, Ottavio does not know how close we are. Come, humour me! Would you not destroy all we have achieved for a fit of pique?'

And Pietro understood his mentor, though he cursed

himself that he had not purloined the plans for the panopticon when he had the opportunity. Though, when he remembered why he had not done so, his resolve faltered and he could not regret his decision. To have placed Anna Santamaria in peril of her life was more than he could do. And the danger troubled Pietro. Anna had somehow to be removed from Ottavio's ambit and afforded sanctuary. The cruelty of the Striges knew no bounds, as the Black Orchid had seen, and if anything should befall Anna Santamaria, Pietro would never forgive himself. He would plead his case with Vindicati, wrest from his mentor a guarantee that she would be protected ... If not, then he would act alone, regardless of the risks.

In the meantime, as sunlight filtered into the hall of the Maggior Consiglio on this bright May morning, the lurid nightmare continued. Some among the noble senators grew pale at Emilio's words, others exclaimed, or shook their heads in silent disbelief. Among those present, Giovanni Campioni sat among the most prestigious members of the Senate, who had been invited to join the deliberations of the Maggior Consiglio. Ottavio, too, was in attendance, which made the situation that much more delicate. A meeting of the Senate was scheduled to take place later that day. The Collegio, which sat each morning, had despatched the *comandadori* at daybreak to advise the senators of the extraordinary meeting. The senators were accustomed to extraordinary conclave, and indeed often sat at night, but the curious manner in which they were convoked did not escape their notice. In camera the palace notaries and solicitors, robed in *ormesino* trimmed with precious furs, whispered, argued and paced the room anxiously. All of Venice was present; every institution of the republic represented; all the power of the *Serenissima* had been marshalled.

Along the walls of the great hall were the portraits of the procession of doges – a long line of stern faces interrupted by a black veil which shrouded the space where once had hung the portrait of Baiamonte Tiepolo, who had attempted to reopen the Pandora's box of democracy just as the Great Council had turned its face against it. Memories of the traitorous Doge Marino Faliero still lingered here, as did those of Gianbattista Bragadin, Chief of the Quarantia – falsely accused of selling State secrets to the Spanish crown and condemned to death. Campioni, pallid and drawn, sat beneath the shrouded portrait, constantly mopping his fevered brow. Neither he, nor the doge, nor anyone present could now prevent this conspiracy from becoming a matter of public record. It might, in some sense, be to the good, for in this way the highest institutions of the republic might be purged before the gangrene spread. A resolution was made to inform the principal authorities of the State of the incidents which had occurred since the death of Marcello Torretone. The populace of Venice vaguely sensed that some threat hovered over the city, but the imminent feast of the Ascension, the revelries of carnival and the firm, reassuring hand of government might allay their fears. Though rumours of increasing horror and grotesquery spread from one *sestiere* to another, the government of the *Serenissima* continued to attempt to calm the citizenry.

Pietro stared fixedly at Ottavio, who returned his stare, his face grim. If he had not already known that his archenemy was free, he knew it now; and facing one another across the floor of the Maggior Consiglio gave both men some inkling of the battle yet to come. Ottavio wore a crucifix about his throat which gave him the air of a bishop. From time to time, he tugged at the collar, his double chin trembling. He screwed his eyes up against the light, and it seemed as if, at any moment, he might explode. The two men stared each other down, and then each turned his gaze on a third man: Giovanni Campioni, who had suddenly joined the debate. A perfect triangle. Pietro thought again of what Emilio had said: *Don't you understand? Each blames the other and, in doing so, they can do as they please. Here we are, seconds to a pair of duellists*. At that moment, Pietro was prepared to believe almost anything – perhaps Ottavio and Campioni had contrived this conspiracy together the better to sow confusion among the Quarantia Criminale and the Council of Ten. Though the Black Orchid did not quite credit this theory, still he could not ignore it. The wordless glances exchanged across the floor of the hall spoke eloquently – those assembled here were not merely instruments of government, but individuals weighing up what was to come. Already lines were beginning to be drawn.

And yet, for all their private passions, everyone present was aware of the solemnity of the occasion; each of the nobles of the Maggior Consiglio remembered the oath he had sworn; an oath that, with each passing moment, it seemed likely he might break: 'I swear upon the holy gospels that I shall uphold the honour and the glory of Venice … When the Maggior Consiglio is in conclave, I shall not stand upon the stairway, nor in the doorway, nor in the palace courtyard nor anywhere in this city and importune votes in my favour nor to the disfavour of others. Nor shall I, by bulletin or pamphlet, petition or cause to be petitioned, by words, acts or deeds, votes favouring any cause; and if another solicits my vote I shall denounce him. Of the arguments presented to me, I shall choose that which seems to me most reasonable, in all earnestness. I shall utter no words of insult, nor perform any dishonest act or gesture, nor shall I rise in my seat with the intention of speaking ill of whomsoever … If I should hear one among us blaspheme against God or the holy Virgin, then I shall denounce him to the *Signori della Notte*.'

And so, two thousand men on whom depended the safety and honour of the Most Serene Republic of Venice, listened attentively to every word spoken in debate.

*

Emilio Vindicati began by explaining the events surrounding the murder of Marcello Torretone, and when he mentioned that a brooch belonging to Luciana Saliestri had been found at the scene, all hell broke loose. There was a smug hypocrisy to these protestations. Most of those present already knew that the courtesan had been involved with Senator Campioni – such affairs were always common knowledge – yet Campioni was devastated to discover quite how widely known were the details of his passions among his enemies and his friends. He hunkered in his seat as if about to leap upon his foes, or perhaps merely to make himself inconspicuous while one half of the chamber vilified his reputation and the other defended him tooth and nail. In a few short seconds he heard the best and the worst of things proclaimed about himself, and he felt unwell. At this point, Francesco Loredan intervened and recounted the details of the murders of Cosimo Caffelli, Federico Spadetti, and the fair Luciana Saliestri. Antonio Brozzi, the coroner with the Quarantia Criminale, was called upon to speak. When he had finished, an architect passed a reconstruction of the vast panopticon around the shocked and worried senators. Matters came to a head when it was announced that, following an investigation at the Arsenal, it had been determined that two armed frigates had been constructed for an anonymous client and that, furthermore, two galleys attached to the navy had disappeared somewhere in the Adriatic.

It is too much for any man to stomach, thought Pietro. It was clear the republic was in the throes of a crisis of great magnitude. Though much of what had been discovered was not disclosed to the Senate, the chaos which ensued was such as Pietro had never witnessed. As reasoned debate was drowned out by a cacophony of angry voices, Pietro stared up at the ceiling, attempting to collect his thoughts. How many of the noble senators here present, he wondered, had taken part in the arcane ritual he had witnessed at the villa Mora? How many were members of the Firebirds? In his hand he clutched a sheet of vellum:

First Circle: Marcello Torretone – PAGANISM
Second Circle: Cosimo Caffelli – LUSTFULNESS
Third Circle: Federico Spadetti – GLUTTONY
Fourth Circle: Luciana Saliestri – PRODIGALITY

Marcello Torretone, who had renounced his baptism, who had searched in vain for God, had been crucified. Cosimo Caffelli had been hanged from the pediment of San Giorgio Maggiore and there exposed to the hurricane of hell for sins of the flesh. Federico Spadetti who, in his hunger for money, had unwittingly helped to fashion the panopticon for the forces of evil, had been reduced to a formless, bloody sludge. Luciana Saliestri, a libertine squandering the fortune which her avaricious husband had spent fifty years amassing, had been weighted down with stones and hurled into the dark waters of the canal. The Legions of Hell, with Dante to guide them, had cunningly orchestrated these tableaux like works of art, an artist's eye in the service of a madman's hand. It was a work of terrible beauty. Pietro had already taken pains to discover what imminent punishments awaited those in the lower circles. The fifth circle was reserved for the Wrathful, whose blind, impulsive fury caused them to lose all reason. Spies had been posted throughout the *Serenissima*. Setting down his quill, Pietro looked up again. Emilio quelled the commotion, raising his hands for silence: 'I propose that the floor be given to Pietro Viravolta de Lansalt. Many of you already know his other identity, so it is fruitless to hide the fact that he is also the man known as the Black Orchid. Ask him what questions you will.'

Vindicati stepped aside and gestured to Pietro to take his place between the tribune, where the doge sat enthroned, and the ranks of the senators. Far from quieting, mention of Pietro's *nom de guerre* brought new uproar from the benches. Some rose and heatedly protested. Ottavio was quick to join these voices of dissent, though careful to preserve a vestige of dignity. What business had Viravolta de Lansalt, a man who was a disgrace to the Most Serene Republic, in this noble chamber? How could this scoundrel, this criminal, have any bearing on the fate of the *Serenissima*? Other senators, curious now, and troubled, asked their colleagues to take their seats and listen. All those present were shocked by what they had learned and – as he had feared – many blamed Francesco Loredan; some overtly accused him of some part in the conspiracy. How was it possible that the Maggior Consiglio had not been informed of these murders, of this conspiracy which the Council of Ten had uncovered? Some fifty senators moved to walk out in protest, and only a call to order persuaded them – provisionally – to remain. There were calls for the session to be postponed, while others called for an extraordinary session to continue the debate until matters had been resolved. Pietro, head held high, rose from his seat and moved between the benches and took the floor. He raised his hands and, slowly, the commotion died away. The doge, unnerved by events, struggled to reassert his authority.

'Pietro Viravolta,' Loredan said, turning to where the Black Orchid stood facing the assembly, 'pray, share with us your thoughts on the dangers facing the republic, since *you* have been charged with leading the investigation.'

Pandemonium broke out once more. How was it possible that such a mission had been entrusted to a man who was perhaps more dangerous than those he was charged to investigate? On this point, the Council of Ten and the Minor Consiglio intervened and, while they did not go so far as to congratulate Pietro on his handling of the investigation, they nonetheless explained his appointment. Standing before a chamber which seemed likely to explode at any moment, Pietro stood, impassive, and waited for the uproar to subside. But the doge's words of introduction had not been lost on him. To present him as *responsible* for the investigation was also to suggest that he was accountable for any failings by the authorities, thus making him a scapegoat – an all too easy task, since he was already the black sheep of the *Serenissima*. Pietro glanced at Emilio Vindicati, wondering if perhaps this was not why he had been recruited in the first instance.

Pietro waited until the chamber was silent, then placed his hands behind his back. Looking down, he cleared his throat and began: 'Your Serene Highness, Your Excellencies, Messere, I understand that what you have learned has taxed your imaginations and your moral sense … You may think it madness that the Council of Ten should entrust this mission to such as I; that all noblemen should have been advised of the dangers sooner, even if doing so might mean panicking the citizenry and alerting an enemy whom, I might remind you, we have yet to identify. But what is important now is not to quarrel about what should have been, but to decide how we shall face the real and tangible threat to the city.'

Pietro looked up now. 'Our chief task is to ensure the safety of the doge and of the institutions of the republic. *Serenissimus*, from what I saw and heard in Mestre, there can be no doubt that they plan to make an attempt on your life. For some time now, I have come to believe that the other murders are a smokescreen, an illusion intended to distract us from their true plan. If this is so, then we have much to fear on the feast of the Ascension.'

A murmur ran through the chamber.

'I believe all public ceremonies should be cancelled.'

Pietro had barely uttered the words when the uproar began again. 'The Ascension! The feast of the Queen of the Seas! Carnival will be at its height! It's unthinkable!'

'Viravolta, the feast of the Ascension is Venice itself –

the populace will be abroad and the nobility of Europe will be in attendance! Have you forgotten that the French ambassador is to take part in the proceedings? It is vital that he know nothing of this affair.'

'The worst thing to do would be capitulate! Venice yields to no one and to nothing!'

Pietro stepped forward, glancing to left and right. 'Precisely. Everyone will be in attendance, everyone will be vulnerable to attack, the doge most of all. What should we do if there is a concerted attack, if our enemy should strike when thousands of people are gathered, all in costume, all anonymous? How can we guarantee the safety of the citizens of Venice in the midst of chaos and commotion? Our every move, our every gesture has been spied upon, our every plan betrayed! The Arsenal must be on the alert, the city must be sealed, all entrances by land and sea monitored. We must hunt down the *Santa Maria* and the *Gioia De Corfù*. Some conspiracy is afoot, something of such magnitude that it demands the most stringent measures. Messere, remember one thing: Minos is among us, he sits in this chamber on one of these benches!'

At this Senator Ottavio jumped to his feet, robes rustling, belly drooping over the guard rail and demanded the right to speak. In a tone of withering irony he began: 'Who are you, Viravolta, that you should lecture us on justice? This loathsome prank has gone on long enough. It is time that the proper authorities take charge. As for this … this man, he should be hurled back whence he came. You have trifled with the republic and played upon the fears of the credulous long enough! Go back where you belong: *i Piombi!*'

'*I Piombi! I Piombi!*' a general cry went up.

As the commotion began again, Pietro remained unperturbed. Andreas Vicario was also present, his hands clasped as if in prayer before his lips, his eyes gleaming like a fox hunting its prey. His face impassive, he watched the proceedings with interest.

'Come now, let us consider a moment.' Ottavio spat out the words, glancing about him as though to call his peers as witness. 'Are we to allow a felon, a miscreant from our own prison to dictate how we should act? Surely I dream?'

Pietro clenched his teeth, feeling his hackles rise. *There can be no question of formally accusing Senator Ottavio before the* Maggior Consiglio, *Pietro! Mention his name and I vouchsafe that they will disembowel you where you stand. To accuse him publicly would put an end to your efforts.*

'This madness must cease!' roared Ottavio, 'and the Black Orchid consigned to the pit where he belongs!'

Pietro's lip quivered, but by superhuman effort he succeeded in mastering his fury. Then the doge rose. All eyes were upon the *bacheta*, the imperial sceptre. He raised his hand.

'I believe ...' His voice was drowned out by cries and catcalls. Slowly the senators fell silent once more.

'I believe that it is indeed impossible to cancel the ceremonies in celebration of the Feast of the Ascension. As to alerting the Arsenal and the armies, that shall be done. Security at every entry point to the city shall be reinforced and it shall fall to the Council of Ten and the Quarantia Criminale to ensure the protection of the citizens of Venice, of myself, and of those foreign dignitaries who are guests of the republic. The task is immense, I grant you, but we have no choice. In the meantime, Pietro Viravolta ...'

Francesco Loredan paused, he seemed to waver for a moment and then, in a low voice, he said: 'I believe it is time that you were relieved of your duties in this matter. I shall entrust you provisionally to the good offices of Emilio Vindicati. Your case will be decided at a later date.'

Shocked, Pietro bit his lip and was silent. He glanced at Emilio.

'The Feast of the Ascension will proceed as planned,' concluded Francesco Loredan.

*

Pietro found himself alone. He had returned to the *casa* Contarini under escort. He was now under surveillance until the official judgement, which would doubtless have him thrown back in a cell. With some bitterness, he informed Landretto of what had happened and asked him to contact Emilio Vindicati, who had felt obliged to say nothing to him in the Senate chamber. Though Pietro knew that Emilio himself was in a most delicate situation, still he could not reconcile himself to his fate. *Flee*. He would flee while there was still time, while he still had his liberty. But if he did so, it would all have been for naught – the Chimera would have won. If he remained then he would surely be imprisoned again. Though Pietro had known from the outset this might happen, now his cell in *i Piombi* seemed so close he could almost smell it. He could not renounce his freedom now. What, then? He could hardly take up arms against the Firebirds and the forces of the republic. The Chimera had played a long game, thought Pietro, in which he had been but a pawn among so many others. There was no solution, he was trapped. If I do not act, the game is lost – but how to act? How? Pietro suddenly felt alone. He was completely isolated, he could no longer call upon his friends for support; he was once more an outcast, vilified and condemned by all. It had all been for nothing. 'The Sword of Damocles hangs above your head,' Francesco Loredan had said at their first meeting. 'At the first sign of treachery, the lions of Venice will fall upon you and tear you to pieces. And far from preventing them, I will urge them on with all my considerable power.' He had been as good as his word. And yet Pietro had not betrayed him. He was guilty of no dishonour. Faced with the excoriation of the Senate, Francesco Loredan had simply decided to sacrifice him publicly, to use him as a necessary means to restoring order. Pietro realised he had been naïve to believe that matters might have ended otherwise. Pietro understood precisely why the doge had been compelled to act as he did; in such circumstances the cardinal rule of politics was to rid oneself of troublemakers. As for gratitude ... Pietro wondered if he had ever truly believed that Venice might show him gratitude.

Three hours later, Landretto returned, with a note bearing the seal of Emilio Vindicati.

'Things have grown complicated, *amico*,' said Pietro. 'Mine is a conditional freedom – they may come for me tomorrow or the next day; I can already see my prison cell. I cannot go back, Landretto. Purchase a pair of horses, lad, and ready them. If the worst comes, we shall flee and profit from what freedom we may.' He broke the seal of Vindicati's letter:

Pietro,

As you will have guessed, it is impossible for us to meet except under armed escort. I have not yet received orders to return you to prison, the doge, despite appearances, is at a loss. Know then that I shall not abandon you, my friend. Affairs may have soured, but I know how much you have done in our behalf. Let us meet at midnight at the Basilica di San Marco; I shall arrange everything. Pray do not flee, nothing would serve you more ill. For the moment, your name must be forgotten. When tempers have cooled, I shall plead your case again. Tonight we must devise our strategy, especially inasmuch as Ottavio is concerned. All hope is not lost. I have seen Senator Campioni and, though I mistrust him still, he assures me that he has enjoined his supporters to support our cause, and to support yours, Pietro, when the time comes. Coraggio, amico. *I have something to tell you. Through Campioni, I have come by new information.*

E. V.

The Black Orchid looked up, puzzled. He went to the door and opened it. Three armed men stood guard outside. Four more, he knew, had been posted outside the building. Pietro turned to his manservant.

'Listen to me, Landretto. I must go out – I am to meet with Emilio Vindicati. It may be for the last time. I shall try to convince him to take Anna Santamaria to safety. That is now my chief concern. If perchance things should not go as I expect, I shall find her myself and we shall leave together. Arrange a horse for her, and make ready. Landretto, my friend, I trust you to distract the sentries in the hallway. I shall take the window and make my way along the roofs – I shall be back before daybreak …'

He sighed: 'I hope …'

CANTO XV
THE STYX

THE PROBLEM OF EVIL

Andreas Vicario, member of the Maggior Consiglio
On The Roots of Evil, Chapter XVII

> It would be wrong to assume that Evil is necessarily always the fruit of evil intent; the greatest evil often claims justification from the most noble cause. The name given this cause is Utopia, and countless bodies strew the path of this most noble intention. Evil will exist until the extinction of mankind itself: it is the aberrant expression of the Dream which each man carries within him, and the means by which he seeks to realise this dream. This brings me to ask myself this most vertiginous question: Evil is, as I aver, a part of man and of his shattered dreams, or something which surpasses man, some external force whose ultimate incarnation we may call Lucifer, though may he too be a dream – the Dream of God? The nightmare of the Almighty whose creation, even as it sprang from nothingness, forsook immaculate perfection which thereafter was lost for ever in the turbulent river of History.

Landretto's diversion, of feigning drunkenness and perpetrating a breach of the peace, was enough to distract the guards while Pietro slipped though the window and over the roofs. He had grown accustomed to such acrobatics and it proved easy to evade the barrack-room fool caught up in the rumours of conspiracy. As arranged, Pietro arrived at the Basilica di San Marco just before midnight. Here were preserved the remains of the Evangelist, stolen from Alexandria by Venetian sailors, who it was said, packed the saint's remains in pickled pork to evade the scrutiny of Muslim guards. The basilica had been built to house the holy relic and since that time, the history of the *Serenissima* had been inextricably entwined with that of the Evangelist. In the eleventh century, the basilica was rebuilt in the form of the Greek cross, modelled after the Church of the Holy Apostles in Constantinople. Five great porticoes faced the piazza, each surmounted by dazzling scenes in Oriental mosaic, the basilica itself boasting five great domes lined with lead. Byzantine, Islamic and Gothic styles fused here with harmony and lightness. From the balcony the doge officiated at those ceremonies held on the Piazza San Marco below, watched over by the bronze horses plundered by Venetians during the conquest of Constantinople at the close of the fourth crusade. As he approached the entrance, Pietro noticed four scenes which caused him to shudder: here again was the *Deposition from the Cross* and, next to it, *Christ's Descent into Hell*, together with two others depicting *The Resurrection* and *The Ascension*.

When he had read Emilio's missive, Pietro had been intrigued; now he felt troubled. *I have something to tell you. Through Campioni, I have come by new information*. For Pietro, what mattered was to resolve his own situation and that of Anna Santamaria, but if the *capo* of the Council of Ten had summoned him to a secret meeting, so late, and against all protocol, it had to be a matter of great seriousness. What, Pietro could not help but wonder, did Emilio know? Perhaps he had succeeded in identifying Minos, or even *il Diavolo*. Perhaps he had discovered something which tied Ottavio to the conspiracy. Pietro feared the worst, felt that his hours, his days, were numbered. Come what might, he vowed, he would not return to *i Piombi*.

The piazza was almost deserted at this hour. The basilica itself should have been locked, but Pietro had only to knock three times and one of the doors opened, as if by magic, before him. He stepped inside, his eyes adjusting slowly to the gloom.

Marble and glistening gold mosaic glowed faintly in the shadows. The paintings of Maître Dampierre, the protégé of the French ambassador, had been hung on either side of the narthex. The opening of the exhibition had clearly gone off without incident; hundreds of visitors had since filed through the nave to marvel at these works. But as Pietro stepped into the nave, he could not shake a gnawing feeling of unease. He stood motionless for a moment, arms by his side, alert, his senses heightened. At the far end of the basilica, above the high altar, he could see the faint glimmer of the *Pala d'Oro* – the glorious altarpiece of cloisonné enamels and chased gold depicting the life of Christ, wrought by the finest goldsmiths in Byzantium. His eyes, now accustomed to the light, took in the breath-taking mosaics of gold and silver and jewelled colour which made the central nave an illustrated Bible. Though the chapel was plunged into an inky darkness, still, out of the corner of his eye, Pietro noticed two figures and tensed, immediately on his guard. He now realised what had alerted his suspicions earlier – it was a heavy, unmistakable smell, a stench to which he had lately grown all too familiar. Suddenly it was blindingly clear. *It was a trap*.

He stepped closer to the paintings of Maître Dampierre which hung about the nave and, as he did so, Dante's verse ran through his mind, the verses he had read and reread in the hope that he might uncover some clue, some sign as to what *il Diavolo* might do next.

The dismal watercourse
Descends the greyish slopes until its torrent
Discharges into the marsh whose name is Styx.
Gazing intently, I saw there people warrened
Within that bog, all naked and muddy – with looks
Of fury, striking each other: with a hand
But also with their heads, chests, feet, and backs
Teeth tearing piecemeal. My kindly master explained:
These are the souls whom anger overcame,
My son …

The Fifth Circle – that of the Wrathful, compelled to feed on mud in the black river, the River of Blood. Pietro crept closer to the nearest of the Frenchman's paintings. *Most excellent paintings*, Emilio had said, *of sacred subjects …* Pietro reached out with tremulous fingers to touch the surface of the canvas and, in a trice, bore out what he had most feared. He stepped back quickly, his fingers and palm slick with a red, viscous liquor. *Blood*.

He retreated farther, to the centre of the basilica, surveying from this central point the horror and the pity which ringed him all about – each of the paintings was spattered with blood, deformed, distorted, a vile tracery of symbols and, here and there, gobbets of flesh stuck to the canvas! *The Styx* – a line of paintings forming a river of blood. He drew his pistol from his belt and placed his right hand on his sword-hilt as he paced this bloody river. He walked towards the high altar, towards the two figures he had glimpsed, and as they swam into focus, he saw the terrible majesty of *il Diavolo*'s new 'masterpiece'.

A man, all but naked, had been lashed before the altar. Hooks had been driven into the tatters of his clothes – or into the flesh itself – four hooks fixed firmly to his shoulders and his feet were attached by ropes to the capitals of the nave so that he was splayed between the pillars. The man's head had fallen to his chest and from his mouth a blackish mud seemed to trickle, as though he were a human fountainhead. All of a sudden, Pietro realised the man was still alive; the eyes rolled back, the head rolled briefly to left and right, a hoarse whisper came, pleading for succour. Then, just as suddenly, with a harsh, broken gasp, the man breathed his last – a long, hoarse sigh, an agonised cry which hovered in the silence of the basilica ... And then nothing. It was then that Pietro recognised the face of this man who had been so vilely slaughtered and, for a moment, he stood frozen, unable to believe his eyes.

'Emilio ...' The word came as a murmur.

There could be no doubt that it was he: Emilio Vindicati, standard bearer of the Council of Ten. Pietro felt a pang of grief. And then a voice cleaved the silence of the cathedral like the roar of thunder; it seemed to come from everywhere at once, booming between the pillars and the statues, reverberating from the vaults to left and right: 'Thus must they perish, Viravolta, the souls whom anger overcame. I bid you good evening.'

Pietro peered into the gloom. Behind the tattered, wretched scarecrow Emilio had become, stood a hooded figure, *il Diavolo* himself, just as Pietro had seen him at the villa Mora. He stood, fixed in a solemn, hieratic pose that spoke of fervour, of madness, as if officiating at some religious rite.

'I was anxious that you should see the tableau before I hurl the body of your friend into the *laguna*. Emilio Vindicati will end up in another river still, where he will at last become one with the mud from which he surfaced. It is time that you should see what becomes of those who cross me.'

'Emilio,' cried Pietro, his throat dry.

He understood now. He did not know how, but Emilio had stumbled into the trap before him; perhaps he had received a letter identical to the one Pietro had received at the *casa* Contarini. As to the note he had received; the

Chimera had doubtless compelled Emilio to write it before torturing him – just as he had Marcello Torretone and Cosimo Caffelli. A wave of fury coursed through Viravolta; without a thought he bounded forward, drawing his sword from its scabbard; in a heartbeat he was upon his enemy. He did not hesitate, but drove the blade again and again into *il Diavolo*, howling: 'Die! Die!'

Hearing a dull clatter he withdrew his blade and, bewildered, noticed that the robes had fallen to the floor. A metal helmet rolled at his feet and beside it, a broken lance swaddled in straw. *A puppet, a vulgar marionette!*

Once more he heard the laugh echo all around him. 'You disappoint me, my friend. I expected more of the Black Orchid …'

Pietro did not have time to realise the enormity of his error when the enemy lunged from behind a pillar, darted to the altar, and hurled himself on Pietro. Pietro felt a dull blow to his head. For a second, he stood, dazed, faltering, then his legs gave way and he felt himself engulfed by blackness. He collapsed at the foot of the steps of the high altar, his pistol and his sword slipping from his hands.

The hooded figure advanced on him. 'Ah, Viravolta. You are at my mercy, and well you deserve that I should finish you here. But I shall spare you …'

The Shadow stooped and stroked Pietro's face. 'You are still part of my plan, Pietro, you are my victim, the supreme scapegoat on whom the full weight of justice will fall.'

The Shadow laughed again, thinking of the river, the river of boiling blood in which the damned were drowned.

When Pietro regained consciousness, confusion reigned in the basilica. It was daylight. He felt two soldiers seize him by the arms and pull him to his feet. One threw water in his face, the other slapped him hard. As in a nightmare, he saw the anxious face of Landretto nearby, and farther off,

Antonio Brozzi examining the desecrated canvases of Maître Dampierre.

'Take him to *i Piombi*, he is not to be permitted to leave his cell!'

'But … but what of Emilio?'

Pietro glanced over his shoulder, towards the altar. He saw the remnants of the straw puppet which he had taken for the Shadow; the chair on which Emilio was slumped had disappeared: all that remained were the ropes which had bound him and the blood. In spite of Landretto's protestations, Pietro was strong-armed from the basilica and a voice at his back roared: 'What have you done with Emilio Vindicati? You have murdered him! *Murdered him!*'

Struggling to remain conscious, Pietro was dragged from the church into the crimson and orange dawn of the new day.

Some tattered shreds of clothing, all that remained of Emilio Vindicati, were found some hours later floating in one of the canals. The doge, disconcerted, devastated by this twist of fate, learned of the news as Pietro was led back to *i Piombi*. With a mocking gleam in his eye his erstwhile guard, Lorenzo Basadonna, welcomed him with studied obsequiousness, before breaking into a lecherous grin: 'So nice to have you back … my sweet.'

THE SIXTH CIRCLE

CANTO XVI

THE CITY OF DIS

I Piombi. Once more. This time, perhaps for ever – or until the date was set for his execution. While outside the Chimera roamed abroad unpunished. Pietro felt beaten. Happily, he had not been placed in the dungeons, the *Pozzi*, where the most ill-fated of the damned lived out their days in cells with no daylight, in a mire of filth and saltpetre, starved of air by the *acqua alta* when the tides rose; their only comfort the memories of former lives and their prayers of intercession to the saints they scored onto the walls, carving designs upon the stones as if to make a heaven of their hell. Nor had Pietro yet been tortured though, as he arrived, he had seen another prisoner led away to face the rope torture – forced to kneel, his hands behind his back tied to a rope and lifted by weights. He had surely howled as the infernal machine wrenched his muscles and fractured his bones; he had not been returned to his cell. Pietro, for his part, was still alive and in good health, but something within him was broken. He had held fast for as long as he was able, buoyed up by his assurance, his conviction, that the tide of fate would turn in his favour. That was over. He knew nothing now of what happened outside these walls. It was impossible to know, or even to imagine what the doge might be thinking at this moment, nor Brozzi, nor the chief of the Quarantia Criminale. His gaoler, Basadonna, had told him that Landretto had attempted to visit him. The beautiful Ancilla Adeodat had learned of his incarceration but had not been admitted even beyond the gates of the palace. And, as to Anna Santamaria ... Not knowing where she was, whether she was safe, tormented him. It had all happened so quickly. From the moment he had first suspected Ottavio, he should have abandoned his investigation, taken Anna, and fled. But it was not so simple. The silence was now intolerable.

Pietro paced his cell, cracked his head against the walls, and talked to himself. Balling his fists, he endeavoured to think of some escape, racking his brains for a means to alert the city, the people, when even his friends among the nobility now thought him guilty of treason and of the murder of his friend, Emilio Vindicati. Madness was closing in. While *il Diavolo* put the finishing touches to his plan, thuggery and incomprehension reigned. Pietro was no fool; he knew that already several stories circulated abroad. That he had been a part of the conspiracy, perhaps its chief instigator, that this had been why he agreed to leave his cell to join the Council of Ten. Rumour of every sort would calumniate his name, and he could say nothing in his defence.

'No, No!'

Worse still, he now found it impossible to *think*. He was haunted by the image of Emilio's blood-smeared face, of the crucified Marcello, of Caffelli lashed to the pediment of the church, of the bodies of Luciana and Vindicati sinking in the dark waters of the canals. He was haunted too by the shadowy ritual he had seen at the villa Mora, which part of his mind attempted to comprehend, and the other part rejected out of hand. He felt himself sinking into madness, here, alone, he was as vulnerable as the boy he once had been on the *campo* San Samuele. This city, which he would have had acclaim him a loyal subject, a hero, rejected him like a bastard child. Venice was no longer Venice, it had become the city Dante had well described, the City of Dis.

My kindly master said, 'A city draws near
Whose name is Dis, of solemn citizenry
And mighty garrison' ...
We had progressed
Into the deep-dug moats that circle near
The walls of that bleak city, which seemed cast
Of solid iron ...
Above the gates I saw
More than a thousand of those whom Heaven had spat
Like rain, all raging: 'Who is this, who'd go
Without death through the kingdom of the dead?'

Venice was the three Furies; she was Medusa, the gorgon who had turned him to stone here in his dank cell. Pietro tried to rally himself, but it was futile. Each time he tried, he felt some new fissure open up in his confidence; his composure was cracked like the antic portraits of emperors which once had fascinated him. One thing alone seemed clear, and this one thing was enough to make him weep; he had abandoned his dreams. This adventure which had brought him to the gates of madness had led him upon a path that was not his. For the Black Orchid to have become an agent of the Tenebræ was absurd! And, just as all around him seemed mired in deceit, the memories of those things he had once prized flooded back: pleasure, refinement, the delicate game of seduction, abundance of delights. Women, the angels of the only creed he had ever known, the creed of love, love in its many guises, beautiful, fleeting or eternal, tragic or uncertain, the only truth. A hip, the curve of a breast, bodies pressed together, a kiss pressed into silken hair, onto a hidden face, quivering lips murmuring his name at the moment he made them his. And chief among them his unattainable goddess, Anna Santamaria! What had possessed him, why had he not fled with her the moment he first saw her? What foolish pride had led him to renounce his nature? Pietro crumpled, refusing to yield to the bitter tears which would seal his downfall. His back to the wall of his cell, he slipped to the floor, his face turned to the slot through which, from time to time, he saw Basadonna striding through the corridor, ever quick to screw his coffin a little tighter for his own amusement.

Giacomo Casanova was still imprisoned not far away. Pietro had not the heart to explain to his friend what had happened. He had told Giacomo only that all was lost, and when his friend asked for news of Anna Santamaria, the question filled Pietro with new terror. He had suggested a game of cards, as they had been wont to play between their cells, one of the many games which, with Basadonna's tacit consent, they had whiled away their time in prison together. But all trace of humour had vanished from Casanova's voice, who was beginning to fear that he would never escape from these dire circumstances. His trial was soon, and he waited now for news of his appeal, unable to understand why the courts were so slow. Pietro understood only too well.

You should have fled, said Casanova, *you should have fled as I told you to, for France*.

A leaden silence fell between them.

That first night, his head was filled with ghastly dreams of demons from his past, and the fiends which had brought him back to this cell. He tossed and turned, and clutched his mattress as a drowning man at straws, terrified of falling into some abyss. He felt chilled to the marrow, then suddenly hot with fever, and grew pale as he watched the darkness thicken until he could see nothing. He had no horizon but the bare walls of this cell, no feeling now but that of falling endlessly. He struggled to find some reserve of courage, but despair overwhelmed him. A voice within him told him to hold fast, but still he felt himself fall. By morning, the voice was silent.

A shadow passed along the corridor by torchlight. Pietro could see it through the slot in his cell door, he heard a rattle of keys and thought at first it must be Basadonna bringing a tin bowl of gruel and some new wit. Then the door opened … and he knew he must be dreaming.

A slender, hooded figure stood in the doorway. Nothing but a rustle of the robe had heralded its arrival along the dim, silent corridors lit by torchlight. Two hands, fine as lace, pink as the dawn, moved up to the cowl and drew it back. And the face of Anna Santamaria appeared.

It took some moments for Pietro to grasp what was happening. More than ever, he felt he was in the presence of some angel. For the first time, he felt his eyes sting with tears, lost in gratitude for this miracle which had been vouchsafed him. He almost fell upon his knees at her feet. He rose, feeling weak, and almost toppled backwards. Eventually, he found his footing and took her in his arms.

'It is you.'

'Yes, my love. I heard what had happened.'

'But … but how? Anna, you must leave at once, do you understand? Leave while there is still time! Everything I feared has proved true, Ottavio is caught up in this conspiracy, you are in great danger! I thought I would not be able to warn you …'

'Thank your manservant, Pietro. Once again, you owe him a debt of gratitude. As do I. He came to warn me. Do not fear, Ottavio is not at Santa Croce. I do not know what he is doing, but he rarely comes to the house, and then only for a moment … I mean nothing to him.'

'You mean a great deal more than you believe,' said Pietro.

They remained for a moment in their embrace. Pietro could not believe that he held her in his arms again. He stroked her hair, breathed her perfume, held her tighter still. And yet his heart filled with a vague anxiety.

'Whatever you believe, Anna, you cannot stay in Venice. Leave, go far away, tell Landretto to take you somewhere safe! I should feel easier if I knew …'

'The situation is more complicated than you imagine. We have not much time. If I leave now, it will only make things worse. Ottavio already seems to me quite mad. Pietro, I spoke with someone … someone you know. He is on our side.'

Pietro looked at her warily.

'I did not come alone,' she said. At that moment, the figure of Giovanni Campioni appeared in the doorway.

'Good evening, Viravolta.'

Pietro stared at him, incredulous. Giovanni came into the cell and Anna stood to one side to allow him to speak: 'The doge granted me permission to come and see you. It may perhaps be for the last time. Your manservant told me how much Anna meant to you, so I resolved to bring her with me. I have not forgotten … what you tried to do for Luciana and for me.'

He sighed. Then, with a visible effort, he steeled himself. 'Now, I pray you, listen to me. Things are moving quickly. This visit is a secret. Loredan is in a difficult position, already many in the Senate look upon him suspiciously. I know that you are accused of the murder of Emilio Vindicati, and it must be said that you make a fine scapegoat. None of this will surprise you … I do not think you guilty – at least, not of that. When I came to you, you listened, now I shall do the same. And this young lady has convinced me that you are an honest man. All is confusion, anarchy reigns throughout the city; it is exactly what the Firebirds had planned.'

Pietro tried to collect his thoughts. Giovanni's voice echoed in the cell, inside his head. Lorenzo Basadonna had reappeared and was now standing behind Anna and the senator. Campioni glared at the man, the gaoler bowed deeply and withdrew, limping along the corridor like a worm crawling into its cocoon, thought Pietro. He brought his hands to his head. This visit, he now realised, was his last chance.

'I can do nothing alone, Giovanni,' he said. 'They are mad. I fell into their trap. The Shadow himself was waiting for me in the Basilica di San Marco; it was he who murdered Vindicati. If you had seen him, Giovanni, he was ... he was ... I had received a letter from Emilio at the *casa* Contarini asking that I meet him there. I sensed the trap only when it was too late. But I believe the doge is still in mortal danger, especially now that the Council of Ten is without a leader. I trust Pavi, the head of the Quarantia Criminale, but we have need of greater forces, given what we face. Senator, you must get me out of here!'

Campioni shook his head angrily. 'That, I fear, is not within my power, at least not at the moment. But there is something else you should know.' Campioni took a deep breath and, with a broad gesture, took a roll of vellum tied with a red ribbon from beneath his robe. He opened it.

'I have not been idle these last days. I am still on the trail of Minos, and the noblemen who support me have made their own enquiries. It was one of them who happened upon an astonishing piece of information. Something which truly left me speechless.'

He cleared his throat. 'I hold in my hands a rough draft of a treaty, Pietro.'

'A treaty?'

'A treaty found half-burned in the fireplace of one of the apartments rented to construct the panopticon. The document bears no seal, no signature, but two parties to the agreement are clearly identified. One is the Chimera. And the other ...'

'The other?'

Campioni's face darkened. 'The other is Eckhart von Maarken.' He paused. 'The name means nothing to you?'

'No,' said Pietro.

The senator continued. 'Von Maarken is among the richest and most powerful men in Austria. He is considered a renegade even in the eyes of his own government. He stands accused of misappropriating state funds for his own profit but, in the absence of proof, the Hapsburgs were content to divest him of his power. He is a man whose ambition, whose lust for power, will not allow him to be cast aside. For many years he served in the ministry of foreign affairs, and he knows Venice like his own hand. He was an intimate of Francesco Loredan himself. The Austrian empire has long looked enviously upon the Adriatic, Pietro. Once, as you know, it stretched from the Netherlands to a part of Italy. The empire has just survived a bloody war of succession; the Empress Maria Theresa kept the crown only with the support of England, and it is believed that she is too concerned with Frederick of Prussia and the loss of her Silesian lands to contemplate an invasion of Venice. But it is whispered in Vienna, in Hungary, and in Bohemia, that something is being plotted. Von Maarken is a man of great wealth and powerful resources, and capable of acting as he sees fit. I should not be surprised to learn that he was mounting some conspiracy in order to impress the empress and thus restore himself to her good favour. I would be loath to credit a conspiracy of such magnitude but for one further thing: von Maarken left his castle in Knittelfield some two weeks ago and, since that time, has been here in Venice.'

'Then von Maarken is Minos?'

'Or *il Diavolo* – indeed, perhaps the two are the same man. He has clearly won Ottavio over to his cause but, even with his support, von Maarken could not mount a coup in Venice without considerable support. The treaty speaks of a pooling of naval and terrestrial forces, which means that among the Firebirds there must be a contingent of Austrians, but it also means that many are Venetians. They must be stopped, and stopped before celebrations for the feast of the Ascension, which begin two days from now. We have little time.'

Pietro thought a moment, shaking his head in disbelief.

'The treaty is a providential find … Tell me, is the doge aware of what you have discovered?'

'Not yet, I have no proof to support my theories, and this treaty might well be another illusion to distract us …'

'Did you speak of it to Emilio Vindicati?'

'No!' Giovanni looked at Viravolta, surprised.

'No? Very well. Listen, *Eccellenza*, if indeed von Maarken is in Venice, he must be tracked down. He may lead us to Minos. And if Minos is a Venetian …'

'Indeed he is …' a strange voice spoke suddenly. At first, Pietro thought it was Casanova. The voice had seemed to come from an adjoining cell. It was a voice he recognised. He racked his brain, trying to remember where he had heard it.

'He is …' the voice came again.

'Fregolo …' murmured Pietro. 'The astrologer.'

Fregolo had been imprisoned in *i Piombi* since his meeting with Pietro. He had been beaten and interrogated, but had protested his innocence.

Now, it was Casanova's voice that spoke: 'Listen, I do not understand whereof you speak, but from what you say, a general confusion reigns within.'

Campioni's face flushed with anger, but Pietro motioned him to disregard his friend's interruption.

'Fregolo?' Pietro called out.

'It was you, *you* who denounced me to the Council of Ten!' roared the senator. 'That slander should have cost you your life.'

The face of the astrologer appeared at the slot in his cell door. Had they examined it closely they would have been surprised to see that he was no longer the Fregolo of bright robes and crystal balls. His clothes were tattered rags, his face was haggard and bruised. Emaciated and weak, he was barely able to stand. He fell back against the door of his cell, breathing in ragged gasps. There was a clank of chains. Then a long silence before, once again, he spoke: 'Forgive me, *Eccellenza*. I was threatened, like the others. The Firebirds came to visit me … they told me that if I named you, I should be released. Now I fear that I may die at any moment and I cannot keep silent any longer. I do not expect what I say now to win me a pardon … I only hope it may help you in your endeavours.'

Pietro and Campioni glanced at one another.

'Minos could not keep his anonymity from everyone,' said Fregolo.

'Then you know him? You know his name?' cried Pietro.

'Not I … but I know someone who does. You overlooked a clue in this wretched affair, I think. I speak of the first murder, the one in the Teatro San Luca.'

'Marcello Torretone? What of it?'

'I do not mean Marcello, but his mother, Arcangela Torretone. She is a cripple, and half-mad. She spends her days now in the convent of San Biagio de la Giudecca. It was from one of the holy sisters that I heard that Arcangela Torretone was telling anyone who would listen that she had met the Devil himself. The nuns think it is simply one of her ravings, but you'll grant it is a strange coincidence.'

'And … that's all?' Pietro looked at the senator again, doubtfully, as he called to Fregolo.

'It may be enough,' the astrologer wheezed. 'Believe me … talk to her.'

Pietro took Campioni by the arm. 'Senator, this is what I propose. If we reveal our suppositions, we will not be believed, for everyone has his own suppositions about this case. The Council of Ten is headless without Emilio, so I pray you, go to San Biagio yourself and speak to Arcangela Torretone and we shall see if what she says means anything. Thereafter – and in this, I beg you, trust me – endeavour to secure me a last audience with the doge. If there is news, then it might save my life if you would let me impart it to him; I for my part will do everything I can to support you. I grant, I am not much in favour with the government, but I may prove useful in other ways. I entrust my fate to your hands, *Eccellenza.*'

'The doge shall know that I …'

'He is in the same situation as we, Excellency, and we must make alliances as best we may.'

'But … you do not understand … A man in my position … Already I have …'

'Giovanni, Luciana is dead, the doge is in peril of his life; we cannot stand idly by! You came in search of me, and you were right to do so. You must …'

Pietro fell silent. Giovanni hesitated for a long moment, then looked into Pietro's eyes.

'Very well, I shall go to San Biagio. As to the rest … we shall see.'

He stepped out of the cell, and Anna Santamaria slipped once more into the arms of the Black Orchid.

'We must leave you now,' she said.

'What will you do?' he asked.

'I shall be ready and prudent, and Landretto shall watch over me. But I shall not leave the city without you.'

'Anna …'

Campioni called: 'Gaoler!'

'Anna!'

Her fingers slipped from his. She looked up one last time, then slipped out of his cell. Campioni too, looked at Pietro once again, then turned on his heel.

'Amen!' wheezed Fregolo.

From his cell, Casanova's voice called: 'Could someone explain to me what is going on?'

The door to Pietro's cell clanged shut and, as Campioni strode away, Pietro thought: *Please, Giovanni, a man must sometimes count on others: you are my only hope.*

Then he corrected himself. '*Our* only hope.'

CANTO XVII

ARCANGELA

Dressed in a black cloak and wearing his *beretta*, Giovanni Campioni arrived at dusk on the Giudecca. He stepped from his gondola accompanied by two men. Together they wound their way through the narrow streets to the door of the dark hulking mass of the convent of San Biagio. The place was silent. Giovanni gave his name and asked to be announced to Arcangela Torretone. The Mother Superior, a woman of some sixty years, her face pale and lined, considered Campioni sceptically for a moment from behind the narrow grille in the gate, but seeing his senatorial robes allayed her fears. When she opened the door, he saw that she was accompanied by three nuns. A bell tolled somewhere in the convent, and one of the sisters hurried down the corridor. The Mother Superior asked the soldiers if they would wait there for the senator, then led Campioni into the San Biagio. She led him across the courtyard ringed with cloisters, lit only by the stars overhead, then they went through the refectory and into a maze of corridors.

'You do know, *Eccellenza*, that Arcangela does not have all her wits. She has been with us for a long time now. Her son used to come from time to time to visit, though she didn't always recognise him. She has grown old and fat, and she cannot move about as she might like to. Her sleep is often troubled by nightmares. A sad fate, truly, though we do our best to ease her pains and calm her lunacy. The convent is something of a bedlam, and there are nights when the terrible shrieks would tear your soul apart. She calls out to the Almighty, and we have not the heart to abandon her … though she does not make a life of prayer and contemplation easy.'

'You say her son would come to visit her from time to time. When did he last come here?'

The Mother Superior thought for a moment. 'It was … two days before he died, I believe. Marcello was murdered, was he not? We never knew the circumstances, and I pray you do not tell me now – *Santa Maria!* I'm not sure whether Arcangela even realises he is no longer of this world. But, *Eccellenza* … we here are sorely troubled – what is happening in Venice?'

'Nothing that need trouble you here,' replied Campioni in a tone he hoped was reassuring.

'Do you know what Arcangela says? She says that she has seen the Devil himself. The Devil! It's all she can talk of. She wrings her hands and says her rosaries. I think it began when the man came …'

Campioni glanced quickly at her. 'A man? Has someone *else* visited her? Who was this man? When did he come?'

He placed a hand on the Mother Superior's arm, gripping it harder than he intended. She stared at him fearfully. She stepped back, wresting her arm from his grip. The senator muttered a confused apology and repeated his question: 'Who was this man?'

'I … I do not know, *Eccellenza*. He said he was a cousin … He spent perhaps an hour with her and when he left I found Arcangela in a sort of trance. She was petrified, staring into space. But she does that sometimes … She forgets, she …'

'So he *did* come here, Fregolo was right!'

Campioni hurried on, the Mother Superior trotting alongside.

'What can you mean, *Eccellenza*? What is it? Should I have … ? The woman is mad, you see …'

'When did he come? Was it before or after Marcello's death?'

'After, I think, a few days afterwards.'

Giovanni stopped, rubbed his eyes, and looked at the good sister. 'I think he may have threatened her.'

'Threatened her? But why? Surely no one would harm a poor lunatic soul shut up in a convent?'

'Do not be frightened, simply tend to her needs. Do you think she would recognise the man again? Does she know his name?'

'I couldn't tell you. You must ask her yourself, if she has the wit to answer you today, or remembers anything at all.'

They had arrived at Arcangela Torretone's room. The Mother Superior tapped three times on the door and, without waiting for a reply, ushered Giovanni Campioni into the bare, cold cell. A small, barred window looked out onto the night sky. The cell was paved with flagstones, the only furniture a bed, a stool, a chair and reading desk, and a crucifix. Arcangela was seated at the desk, but she had no book before her. Hands clasped in her lap, her face gaunt and her eyes wild, she seemed absorbed in contemplation of something. Her face was pale and worried. Giovanni could not help but shudder. Surely she could not be so old and yet, sitting here in silence, she seemed ageless. She was wearing her wimple, which cast a shadow on her face. Arcangela did not move, did not turn to see who had entered. The Mother Superior gently placed a hand on her shoulder.

'Arcangela, how are you today? You have a visitor, someone has come to see you … He is a senator.'

No reaction.

'Messer Campioni would like to ask you some questions, Arcangela … about your son.'

Slowly, Arcangela Torretone turned to face Giovanni. From her eyes he could tell that the old nun suffered from senility. He opened his cloak and sat on the stool near her. Arcangela looked away, her back towards him. Giovanni moved the stool and came to sit beside her.

'Very well … I shall leave you,' said the Mother Superior. 'If there is anything else, *Eccellenza*, you have only to ask for me.' She went out, closing the door behind her. Giovanni and Arcangela spent a long time sitting in silence, the senator studying the delicate face of this woman who had once, he could tell, been a ravishing actress. He thought of all those sequestered in convents throughout the republic. Many – indeed most of them – came to religious life from a heartfelt religious devotion, but some, he knew, were cloistered against their wishes at an early age – sometimes as young as ten or twelve years old – on the whim of a parent, or to abide by some family tradition. Many of them would spend forty, fifty, even sixty years in the nunneries like this and the convent of Sant'Anna in Castello. To these were joined the legion of disappointed lovers, broken marriages, and those who had refused to accede to an arranged match; to the indignity of being married off to the highest bidder. There were armies of women whose only choice had been a loveless marriage or a nunnery. The more educated among these women accused the republic of a form of tyranny. Giovanni saw once more an image of Luciana Saliestri. In order to escape a similar destiny, she had had to use all of the formidable weapons with which nature had endowed her. The senator's lip trembled. Luciana, for whose sake he would be damned. Luciana; libertine and rebel but somehow, at heart, so pure and unsullied. Of that he had always been certain. Luciana and her interminable quest for an earthly paradise. Giovanni gave her everything, but he had never truly conquered her. Luciana was always in flight toward some new garden of earthly delights. There was no middle ground for a woman, it seemed, between absolute reclusion and restricted freedom: nuns and courtesans were striving towards the same oblivion.

Arcangela was still lost in her meditation. There could be no doubt that it was only by the Mother Superior's compassion that she was still here rather than confined to the madhouse on San Servolo, a lugubrious chasm into which the wretched of the earth were cast, a hell on earth. What, wondered Campioni, could Arcangela be thinking, here, now, as he watched her? Perhaps she was remembering her own funeral – the day on which, during that mournful ceremony, she had prostrated herself among the candles and the litanies and pledged her life to God; for surely to come to San Biagio had been a death of sorts. Half-mad, half-paralysed, she had taken the veil for her second wedding; her marriage to the Lord who had taken her husband and whom, perhaps, she blamed for the sins of her son. Marcello, surely, had understood her, had seen the incomprehension in his mother's feverish eyes. He would have known pain too, for in entering the convent his mother was marrying a Father who had rejected Marcello, just as his true father had. Giovanni wiped his mouth, thinking of something he had read a year ago. *Faith: between brightness and hellfire*. It had been written by one of the Morandini sisters. In large families, sometimes three or even four daughters might be shut up in a convent – it was hardly surprising, then, if some of them did not meet the ideal. There had been talk of forbidden revelries, nuns dancing in parlours and night-time visits by lovers. The Council of Ten was charged with prosecuting such secret liaisons, and the punishments meted out to those found guilty of breaking the sanctity of the convent were severe. An image of Emilio Vindicati flashed before Senator Campioni's eyes. He leaned towards the woman before him: 'Arcangela, my name is Giovanni Campioni. I would like to talk to you about … about the last time Marcello came to see you.'

The old nun frowned, the shadow of a smile crossed her lips, and she lifted her head. Her neck was long and slender, and Campioni was surprised to discover how elegant she seemed.

'Marcello … how is he?'

Giovanni cleared his throat and shifted slightly on his

stool. He clasped his hands. 'Arcangela, do you remember what you spoke of the last time Marcello came to visit?'

'He's my son, you know … Marcello. I love him dearly, my Marcello. He is in the arms of God, as I am. He was a blessed child. I often pray for him. How is he?'

'He came to see you? Did you talk about … the theatre? About his work at the Teatro San Luca?'

Arcangela stiffened suddenly, as though she had seen or heard something strange. She brought a finger to her lips, 'Shh!', then stared at a fixed point on the wall of her cell. Campioni followed her gaze but there was nothing there, or at least nothing that he could see, though Arcangela could clearly see something.

'Marcello comes to see me now and then,' she said. 'Sometimes in the day, sometimes at night.'

'When did he last come?'

'Yesterday – I think it was yesterday.'

Giovanni's face became a mask of sadness. He wanted to reach out to this woman, to draw her from the world in which she was trapped.

'That's not possible, Arcangela. Are you sure it was yesterday?'

The woman scowled, bringing a fist to her chin, and thought. Suddenly, she seemed like a young girl trying hard to think.

'Not yesterday … No … Tomorrow, maybe. Yes, he will come tomorrow.'

Giovanni suppressed a sigh – he was beginning to feel his visit had been futile. In a soft voice Arcangela was repeating to herself, *Yesterday*? *Tomorrow or maybe the day after tomorrow* … If he were more direct, the senator thought, he might get through to her. His natural compassion balked at the idea, but words were the only weapon he had. Perhaps a shock was what was needed to bring her to her senses.

'Arcangela. Tell me about the other man who came to see you. Tell me about the Devil.'

Her reaction was instantaneous. Her face froze and she snatched up her rosary beads from the desk, her fingers trembling, and began, in hushed tones, to recite a prayer. Her eyes were ablaze with fear.

'I saw him, indeed I saw him, Messer, he came to see me, he came to frighten me … He came by night … Oh, he did not tell me he was the demon, but I knew, I recognised him! The Lord had warned me of his coming, I had seen it in a dream …'

'Who was this man, Arcangela? I must know his name.'

'He came to frighten me … He told me I would die, that he would have me suffer the thousand torments of hell … He said I would be paralysed and that nothing, not even the light of God's grace, could save me. He spoke in a kind voice, but his words were full of the hate and the bitterness of the Prince of Lies, the Impious One, the angel cast down. He told me to be silent, he told me never to speak his name or he would come for me and I would be with him in hell for all eternity. He thought my son … he thought Marcello had spoken to me of him – and it is true that we often talk, my son and I; he confessed his troubles to me as he did to his confessor at San Giorgio Maggiore. Perhaps it is he who has taken my son … Perhaps the Devil has taken Marcello!'

'What is his name, Arcangela?'

For the first time, she looked into Giovanni Campioni's eyes. 'You do not know? Oh, he tried to disguise himself, he took the form of a Venetian nobleman, he assumed a human form. I speak of Andreas Vicario, Messer! He who has the *libreria* in Cannaregio, the Devil's Library. It is he, Vicario!' She repeated the name over and over, and then the words trailed away into a long, terrible, agonised wail.

CANTO XVIII
THE HERETICS

They came for Pietro early the next morning. Woken from a troubled sleep, he was so pleased to see his gaoler Basadonna that he might have blessed the man. Fregolo and Casanova implored him not to forget them to the doge and Pietro promised, if he could, to intercede on their behalf. Everything now depended on his audience with Francesco Loredan. Pietro was met by Campioni outside the sala del collegio, and almost embraced the man when the senator informed him what Arcangela had said. A moment later, they were received by his Serene Highness in the presence of his Privy Council.

'I have had to deploy all my diplomatic wiles to have you granted this last audience,' whispered Giovanni. 'All the skills I learned in a lifetime of service in the royal courts of Europe were barely enough. Be worthy of my trust, Viravolta, for if you fail now … Loredan is not a fool. He knows that it was the Maggior Consiglio who compelled him to imprison you, but he will grant you only a few minutes before you are returned to your cell. No one wants to hear speak of the Black Orchid. The Privy Council are already prepared to cause a scandal – they are ill-disposed towards you and have accorded you this "favour" only because some among them are friends of mine. But friendship counts for little in politics, and in truth they have allowed you to speak because of the present danger – for without Vindicati, without you or me, they have no way of solving this affair, and the feast of the Ascension begins tomorrow.'

'Vicario,' muttered Pietro. 'So it was not by accident that I was led to his library in Cannaregio ... and it was under his room that Luciana Saliestri was murdered. We have our murderer, Giovanni, now he must be made to pay. We shall invite him to another sort of ball. His influence with the Maggior Consiglio has shielded him thus far from our investigation; it must have greatly amused him to play the victim. But the books in his *libreria* give some measure of the man's perversity. Vicario, Ottavio and the mysterious von Maarken ... Take heart, senator! We have seen the face of the enemy – and they are not one, but legion.'

'Indeed. But do not forget one crucial detail, Viravolta. Aside from the rough draft of a treaty written by a madman, we have no other proof than the ravings of a nun. To say nothing of the plans for the panopticon you saw in Ottavio's villa. It will not count for much.'

'Even so, the elements of the puzzle have begun to slot into place. The doge and the Privy Council must be advised.'

They spoke in whispers, for they were now flanked by an armed escort who led them through the doors of the sala del collegio.

'His Serene Highness and the Privy Council await you, Messere.'

Pietro glanced at Giovanni and together they stepped into the chamber.

In the presence of
His Serene Highness, the Prince and Doge of
Venice, Francesco Loredan, and the noble members
of the Minor Consiglio, His Excellency, Giovanni
Ernesto Luigi Campioni, member of the Senate
and Pietro Luigi Viravolta de Lansalt.

It is hereby decided that:

I) In view of new information obtained by Messere Campioni and Viravolta, known as the Black Orchid, the Minor Consiglio instructs that Andreas Vicario be immediately summoned for questioning, all relevant authorities being given the power to ensure compliance with this order on pain of the immediate arrest of Andreas Vicario on charges of murder and high treason.

II) Michele Ricardo Pavi, chief of the Quarantia Criminale, together with the *capo* of the Arsenal, shall be apprised of the alleged involvement of Duke Eckhart von Maarken, and pursue their investigation into the disappearance of the *Santa Maria* and the *Gioia De Corfù* and further, shall be responsible, together with the forces of the city, for ensuring the safety of the doge during the ceremonies celebrating the feast of the Ascension, and thereafter until the menace which looms over the city has been countered.

III) Whereas Pietro Luigi Viravolta de Lansalt appears to have been the victim of a conspiracy to implicate him in the murder of Emilio Vindicati, for which no proof has yet been attested, and that the aforementioned Pietro Luigi Viravolta de Lansalt has brought to the attention information which may prove decisive in thwarting this conspiracy, he is hearby granted a conditional discharge and shall be released to the good offices of Michele Ricardo Pavi. At the request of His Serene Highness, he shall be anonymously posted to the defence of the city for the duration of the feast of the Ascension, after which time he will once again be brought before the courts. Upon the worth of his actions will depend the punishment or mercy which the magistracy will then impose with regard to the charges against him.

iv) His Excellency Giovanni Ernesto Luigi Campioni …

Francesco Loredan rubbed his eyes. He could still see Viravolta's face, still hear his words: *But … what of Ottavio? What is to be done about him?* Loredan sighed. He had taken a great risk in doing what he had done; his eyes rolled heavenward and he prayed to the Blessed Virgin, then turned again to his clerk.

'Vincenzo …'

'*Serenissimus*?'

'The account of these proceedings …'

'Yes, *Serenissimus*?'

'I should be grateful if you would … burn it.'

Vincenzo gave the doge a puzzled look. Francesco Loredan brushed a fleck of dust from his robes. 'For God's sake, Vincenzo … I said burn it!'

But what of Ottavio? What is to be done about him?

The Doge had hesitated. *I shall leave it to you to bring proofs against him. But I pray you* … He had begun to cough. *Do what you must do discreetly!* He remembered Viravolta's eyes as he left the sala del collegio, the stern face belied by the gleam in those eyes. *Leave it to me.*

He had taken his sword.

The doge rose from his throne and walked slowly, one hand on his sceptre, his shoulders stooped; he could see the institutions falling like dominoes and, with them, all semblance of order and of protocol. The world was falling about him. And tomorrow was the *festa della Sensa*.

Senator Ottavio mounted the steps of his villa in Santa Croce. These were troubled times, and he was grave. True, he had succeeded once again in removing the Devil,

Viravolta, from his path. But the discovery of the panopticon had been a serious setback. It had taken more than a year to set up the apparatus. It had been based on the work of a Neapolitan architect and mathematician, long dead now, whose design for a panopticon predated that of Jeremy Bentham by some thirty years. Ottavio was now obsessed with the thought that the device might be traced to him. Never underestimate one's adversary; forty years in politics had taught him that. If the conspiracy were to succeed, it would happen in the days to come; in the meantime it would be prudent for him to devise an alternative plan in case it should fail, though he had not yet decided what such a plan might be. All would soon be clear, however, of that his recent conversations with Minos and *il Diavolo* had left him in no doubt.

As he climbed the stairs to his office, Ottavio felt weary. He had removed his *beretta* and his senatorial robes, though he still wore his medals: one of the Blessed Virgin, the other a locket which contained portraits of his parents. His father had been a senator before him, and his mother had been an intimate of the doge. Two brass keys hung from his belt; he used them to lock Anna Santamaria in the apartments when he was out. When he had first sent her away to a convent, after the Black Orchid was imprisoned, he had had no need to do so. Anna could not leave Marghera without his consent. But now that she was back in Venice, his fears had returned, especially while Viravolta had been at liberty. Thankfully, the session of the Maggior Consiglio had gone in his favour, disgracing his former protégé and returning the traitor to the cells. For several days now, he had found Anna Santamaria to be happier, more serene, almost gay. He had seen her fleeting smiles and her pensive air, so unlike how she had been at Marghera. She was calmer now; he had been wise to let her know who was master. And once she had forgotten Viravolta, she would return to his bed, if only of necessity.

It was impossible to be the servant of two masters, as Senator Ottavio knew only too well. One had to choose. Ideally, choose the winning camp. But all was still to play for.

Ottavio rested on the stairs for a moment, breathless. He was beginning to worry about his health: his heart had been weak now for some time. He tired easily, and sweated much. He pulled a monogrammed kerchief from his sleeve and mopped his brow. Reaching the top of the staircase, he took the keys from his belt and slipped the first into the lock.

To his shock, the doors opened of their own accord. The door led to his study and from there to the boudoir – Anna's boudoir – for she refused to lie with him, her head had been so filled with foolish dreams. More than once, Ottavio had tried to force himself on her, but he knew that while she still pined for the Black Orchid there would always be a shadow between them. It was this shadow he wanted to stamp out, to crush, to annihilate so that nothing of it remained. When the Chimera had charged Ottavio with stealing Luciana Saliestri's brooch – the brooch discarded in the Teatro San Luca to implicate Campioni – he had availed himself of the courtesan's services. More than once. That, at least, had slaked his ardour. But his wife's continued rebuffs had become intolerable. She would bend to his will, whatever the cost.

Intrigued, and suddenly concerned, Ottavio peered into the darkness of the study. Could it be that Anna's smiles of late, her sudden gaiety … Had she seen *him*? As Ottavio pondered this idea – it had occurred to him before, but he had given it little thought, but now it seemed all too possible – he began to perspire. What if the doge had been informed of his role in the conspiracy, what if the Black Orchid knew more than he had said before the Maggior Consiglio? What if …

Ottavio took a taper and lit it, the flame quivered,

casting a flickering light into the study. A figure – *someone* – was sitting at his desk.

'Ottavio, I have been expecting you.'

'*Viravolta*,' Ottavio whispered through clenched teeth.

There was a moment's silence and, in that moment, strange memories passed through the mind of Senator Ottavio. That evening at the Palazzo Mandolini in Santa Trinità, when the senator had first been charmed by the wild lad who had played the violin before launching into a discussion of Aristotle, all the while courting the assembled ladies with his less scholarly charms. That was the evening he had first met Pietro Viravolta, the evening on which the lad, with a word, had saved him from a wager which might have ruined him. He had been fascinated by Viravolta, by his picaresque tales, half-invented, half-autobiographical, of Corfu and Constantinople; his weakness for cartomancy and numerology. But why … why had Ottavio made this lad his protégé, almost adopted him as his own son and heir? Pietro had charmed him, hoodwinked him … He had been enchanted by the young man's company. It was Ottavio who had first spoken to Emilio Vindicati about Pietro, had watched the young man's first exploits as the Black Orchid. In a sense, he and Emilio had *made* him. With their support, Viravolta had become an agent of the Council of Ten whose exploits were the talk of the city; in the taverns and at the tables of the nobility. Until that fateful day when Ottavio had introduced his protégé to … Anna. He had seen the spark in her eyes and in his uncharacteristic awkwardness, a misty-eyed infatuation. He should have flayed them alive.

Pietro, too, was thinking of these things. Sitting in the half-light, his face was hidden in shadow, only his arms, resting on the senator's desk could be seen from the doorway. He had placed his hat on the leather blotter. One of the drawers had been forced. The drawer in which, on his previous visit, he had seen the plans for the panopticon. The plans, of course, were gone.

'I thought you were a guest at *i Piombi*,' said Ottavio weakly, leaning against the dresser near the door.

'You know me. I cannot bear my own company.' Pietro glanced at the fireplace in the corner of the room. He had not noticed it on his previous visit. 'I assume you have burned them?'

Ottavio did not answer. He drummed his fingers on the dresser. 'What have you come for, Viravolta? You know I have only to say the word and you will be back in your cell in a heartbeat! And believe me, I shall do so, until one day I have your head.'

'I doubt you shall have long to wait, Ottavio.' The Black Orchid sighed. 'Come, face facts, or you shall face the gallows. We know that you are engaged in a conspiracy with Andreas Vicario and Duke Eckhart von Maarken. The plan is folly. Venice will never fall to such a man. You were ill advised to aid them in their plans. Why did you do it, Ottavio?'

Ottavio was sweating profusely now, but made a superhuman effort to retain his composure. Now was not the moment to give himself away. His whole body was taut, his muscles tensed, he needed a way out. He gave his spleen full vent: 'Balderdash! You know nothing, Viravolta! You have no ...'

'*Proof?*'

There was a silence, and then Pietro said, 'Perhaps not ... but I have a witness.'

At that, the door to the boudoir opened. Anna Santamaria, her face in darkness, framed by a halo of blonde hair, stood in the doorway wearing a gown of fine black lace. Head held high, she stared at Ottavio. Her hand, limp by her side, clutched a flower. An orchid.

An ugly smile twisted the senator's mouth. 'I see,' he mocked, his voice trembling, 'This is a plot! You have always conspired against me!' His fingers toyed with the gold handle of one of the dresser drawers.

'It is over,' Anna said simply.

All three fell silent, Ottavio shaking with rage, Anna firm as justice itself, and Pietro between them, sitting at the desk.

'It is over,' she said again.

'We shall see about that,' roared Ottavio, flinging open a drawer and feverishly groping inside.

'Is *this* what you are looking for?'

Ottavio turned to Pietro, his face ashen. The Black Orchid twirled the small silver pistol with the senator's coat of arms emblazoned on the handle. For a moment, Ottavio glanced about him wildly, as if searching for a way out, but there was none. He looked back at Pietro, his lower lip quivering, and then he gathered his forces and launched himself at Pietro …

Pietro was surprised when the senator hurled himself across the desk towards him, sweeping aside the hat, the leather blotter and the papers. He did not have the heart to pull the trigger and simply shoot Ottavio, but he gripped the pistol tightly. The struggle that followed was confused and vicious. The senator's eyes glinted, foam flecked his mouth, and his hands clawed wildly at Pietro. Anna stepped back, stifling a scream. Sprawled across the desk, Ottavio tried to wrench the pistol from Pietro's grasp, like a child who has lost his favourite toy. For a moment he thought he had it then, suddenly, there was a flash and a dull pop as the gun went off.

Anna screamed as Pietro collapsed into the chair. With one foot he turned over Ottavio's body. The senator's eyes had rolled back into his head and blood trickled from the corner of his mouth. Pietro caught his breath. He looked at Anna. Her face was drained of colour.

'It was him or me,' he said simply.

Standing outside the Santa Croce villa, Anna, wearing mourning dress, waited to board the gondola which would take her away from this place for ever. She glanced up at the faded colours of the building, the long balcony of intricate rosettes. Beside her stood Pietro and Landretto.

Pietro placed a hand on his manservant's shoulder and stared at the young man – the dark blond hair which fell in ringlets, the nose a little too long, and the permanent insolent smile. Truly, he thought, the day that he had rescued the urchin had been one of the most fortunate in his life.

'I shall never forget what you have done for me, my friend. Never. Without you, I should be languishing still in *i Piombi* and we three should not be here now.'

Landretto smiled, doffed his hat and bowed deeply. 'At your service, Messer Viravolta.'

'Now, you have only one mission. Keep watch over Anna. Find somewhere safe and do not move from there until all this is done. I shall join you as soon as I can.'

'It shall be done,' said Landretto.

'Ottavio's death will cause a considerable commotion ... I must go at once and talk to Ricardo Pavi at the Criminale.'

He turned to Anna and they gazed silently at one another. He stroked her hair and placed a gentle kiss on her lips.

The Black Widow. Now she truly was a widow. The widow and the orchid.

'Where are you going?' she asked. 'Where is this Pavi?'

Pietro stroked her cheek. '*La Serenissima* still has need of me,' he said, then, with a rustle of his cape, he turned and was gone.

'Pietro,' she called after him, 'be careful!'

The sun flickered and disappeared over the horizon and the Black Orchid turned the corner and vanished.

Giovanni Campioni did not quite know what was going on; it had all happened so quickly. Immediately after his audience with the doge, he had gone to see the chief of the

Quarantia Criminale, Ricardo Pavi, with Loredan's new orders. The Black Orchid had followed him. In the meantime, a detachment of a dozen soldiers had been sent to Andreas Vicario's villa in Cannaregio; Campioni and Viravolta awaited their return with impatience. Early in the afternoon, Viravolta had left the doge's palace for Santa Croce, to see Anna Santamaria and meet with Ottavio. The Council of Ten – or rather Nine, now that Emilio Vindicati was dead – had been shocked and amazed to learn of these new developments. Even they still looked upon Viravolta with some suspicion; nonetheless they could understand the doge's decision, and the memory of the friendship Emilio had with Viravolta reassured them somewhat. Pavi, too, admired Viravolta and was inclined to defend him. The revelation that Andreas Vicario was somehow caught up in the labyrinthine conspiracy had stunned the Tenebræ and the Quarantia Criminale, who looked forward to what promised to be an interesting interrogation. Campioni's evidence that a treaty had been drafted between Eckhart von Maarken and one of the conspirators, gave some measure of the dangers the republic faced. In the confusion, opinions and alliances shifted like a weathercock in a high breeze. Some began to whisper that perhaps Pietro had been right and the festivities for the *festa della Sensa* should be cancelled; but everything was already prepared and it was too late. Only now that they knew of the link between Vicario and von Maarken did the conspiracy begin to take shape, and the notion that Senator Ottavio was somehow involved had meant that they were forced to resort to unofficial methods. When Giovanni had left Viravolta, he knew that Viravolta intended to visit Santa Croce that afternoon. As he had said – the enemy had a face now; the scattered threats posed by the Firebirds were less worrying, though no less real, now that the head of the Hydra had been identified, though they did not yet know if it were a two-headed or a three-headed monster. It now seemed clear that the ritual Pietro had witnessed at the villa Mora in Mestre had been a charade, its elements lifted from Raziel's *The Forces of Evil*, to cloak a political conspiracy in the guise of some satanic sect. Until they had news of the detachment which had been sent to Cannaregio, the Tenebræ and the Quarantia restricted themselves to questioning the agents they had posted through the city: a motley crowd of hunchbacks, courtesans in lace, blind beggar women, and mendicant friars trooped through the offices of the Procuratie in a dreamlike parade. As the sun set over the *laguna*, news of Cannaregio finally arrived at the doge's palace: the villa was deserted. Andreas Vicario had disappeared. Fled.

As to the Black Orchid, as yet Giovanni had not had word of his friend. Faced with Vicario's disappearance, Pavi cursed himself that the Quarantia Criminale had not acted sooner; even so, Vicario's flight might be considered a confession of sorts. Andreas Vicario ... who would have thought it? True, the man was notorious for his accursed *libreria* – Giovanni now understood something of the secret implications of the collection – but the man was a member of the Maggior Consiglio and had held many senior positions in the service of the republic: he had been chief of the juridical offices in the Rialto, had overseen corporate legislation, had been instrumental in the management of the Arsenal ... As Giovanni pieced together Vicario's career in his mind, things began to fall into place: his fascination with the occult, the obsessive erudition which had led to the publication of his famous tract, *The Problem of Evil*. It became clearer now how he might have intimidated Fregolo, and perhaps Spadetti: he had even had Luciana Saliestri murdered under his own roof. At this thought, Giovanni felt a wave of sadness wash over him and vowed that he would make Vicario pay. He would campaign for a public execution, and if Vicario were found guilty of high treason, the doge and the Council of Ten would be only too happy to accede to his request. If he could, he would murder the man with his bare hands. What haunted him now was how blind he had been; they had all been blind, even Viravolta. If they had acted more quickly, might Luciana have been spared? This thought, more than any other, troubled him. His terrible sadness, the devastating heartache, was no secret to those who knew him, and yet the sorrow was so deep they could not share his grief. It was easy, he knew, for matters to seem self-evident in hindsight, but how, Giovanni wondered, how had Vicario managed to evade detection for so long? Who were the Firebirds, how many disciples had the madman embroiled in this conspiracy? Enough to constitute a Senate or a Quarantia? Giovanni had no answers to these questions, and yet he could think of nothing else. Luciana's face flashed through his mind once more, Luciana smiling, her impudent lips mouthing words delightful and perverse with that sweet wantonness which had so captivated Campioni. *Ah, Giovanni … Do you know what I most love about you? It is the fact that you believe you can save the world itself.* Save the world itself! He had not even succeeded in saving Luciana. Giovanni's knuckles were white with impotent rage; of course he knew there had been other men – she had delighted in taunting him with them – but some pleasures she reserved only for him. He could see her face now, flushed with pleasure. *Giovanni … Giovanni …* In part, of course, it was artifice, but he had felt able to confide in her, to lay his head on her breast and sleep. It was a comfort, a security he had never known. She had teased him once, *Come, senator, it is as if you seek a mother not a wife …* For Luciana he would have betrayed his country; she who feared attachment, yet dreamed of an impossible love, who gave herself without ever giving of herself. For her, he might have committed treason, if she had asked … But Vicario? What reason had he for betrayal?

For the power. Merely for the power. To possess the Jewel of the Adriatic, the vestiges of empire …

Before they had received word of the soldiers at Cannaregio, before Viravolta had set off for Santa Croce, he and Pietro had sat in council with Pavi and the nine, deciding how the *carabinieri* should be posted in order to ensure the safety of the doge for the *festa della Sensa*. The agents of the Council of Ten and the Quarantia Criminale were to redouble their efforts to capture Eckhart von Maarken, who, it was rumoured, was already in the city. *Of that there can be little doubt*, thought Giovanni. *He has gone to ground and waits like a viper in the darkness. But the battle is not won yet, Vicario!*

What then, he wondered, was he doing here in the Dorsoduro cemetery after nightfall, as the winds howled around him? For here he was, a torch held aloft, scanning the shadows for some movement. He felt cold, in spite of his ermine cloak – unless his shivers were that of his mounting fear. He fumbled in the pocket of his coat, withdrew the note, and reread it carefully:

You are in the Sixth Circle
Where lie the souls of the Heretics
'Up on the topmost rim of a deep-cut bank
Formed by a circle of massive, fissured rock,
We stood above a pen more cruel. The stink
Thrown up from the abyss had grown too thick
Its excess drove us to shelter in the space
Behind a great tomb's lid. It bore a plaque
Inscribed: "I hold Pope Anastasias,
Drawn by Photinus from the proper path."'
Come, Senator, at the very stroke of twelve
Come alone and contemplate the tomb
Of she whom you so loved
For though she is laid in earth
Luciana Saliestri has one last gift for you.

Virgil

The note, in all respects, resembled those which Viravolta had received. This Virgil, whom Viravolta thought the third member of the Unholy Trinity, had bid him come here to where Luciana had been laid to rest. The wind whistled as he stood among the fallen gravestones, and caused the torch to waver. The note had been delivered by messenger just as Campioni had been returning to his villa at Ca' d'Oro, though Giovanni had been to slow to question the bearer. To invite him to come here had been callous, but it did not surprise him; cruelty was the trademark of this enemy. *For though she is laid in earth/Luciana Saliestri has one last gift for you.* What could it mean? Naturally, Giovanni suspected a trap – this, after all, was how Viravolta had been lured to the basilica. The senator had been asked to come alone. But, though harrowed by grief, Giovanni was no fool. With the doge's permission, some thirty agents had been discreetly posted around the perimeter of the necropolis, hopefully unnoticed by their adversary. And yet, as he stood here now, he felt himself watched, as if the eyes of Minos – or that of the Devil who had so terrified Arcangela – could pierce the shadows and observe his every movement. The senator wiped his brow. He had come to act as bait while Pavi and his men crouched in the shadows, ready to pounce. Campioni felt reassured by their presence. But the Black Orchid had not yet reappeared; perhaps he was en route, his meeting with Ottavio not having gone well …

Pavi had suggested to Campioni that one of his agents disguise himself and take the senator's place, but Giovanni had refused, fearing their trick might be uncovered too soon and that it might hinder their attempt to catch the Chimera. Now, he felt less sure.

He took a deep breath and walked along the gravel paths. Luciana's grave was a few metres away. Giovanni had not seen her body pulled from the canal, without ceremony or fanfare, for at that moment he was being interrogated by the Ten, attempting to prove his own innocence in the conspiracy. Though he had attended her funeral, he had merely glimpsed the black coffin as it had been lifted onto a gondola to make the brief and tragic journey to its final resting place. Giovanni listened to the whistle of the wind and the crackling gravel beneath his feet; he was sweating copiously and yet he still felt cold. He could see nothing but the flame of his own torch. Holding his breath, he took the path that forked right, walked the last few steps, and stopped before the grave of Luciana Saliestri. He stood for a moment, frozen with grief. Then he stooped to read the inscription. Upon the stone itself there was another note, held in place by a handful of small pebbles. Giovanni snatched it up and in the faint light read:

'Pape Satàn, pape Satàn aleppe!'
You too, Giovanni, have joined the Dance of
  Shadows
A half-turn right, advance six paces
A half-turn left, and twenty paces more
Arriving at a second tomb, your Excellency
Will learn what Luciana has reserved for him.

Virgil

'What is this travesty?' murmured Giovanni, trembling. It took a moment for him to steady himself. Then, glancing about him anxiously, he did as the note directed. His heart was beating fit to burst. After six paces, he found himself at the junction of two pathways and twenty paces took him towards the north-east corner of the cemetery. Here he stopped again, his face now ashen. He looked around.

'But … what is the meaning of …'

Again he looked around and, finding nothing, waved his torch to signal to Pavi's men. At that moment the bolt of a crossbow shrieked through the night air and planted itself in Giovanni's gullet.

The senator's hand flew up and clawed at his throat as blood coursed down his cloak. Pain ripped through him. He tried to speak, to scream, his eyes bulged. His torch had fallen at his feet. *The torch* ... The flame had guided the enemy to his target, allowing him to aim his shot with all the skill of a Venetian marksman. He had been a moving target. This was something unexpected and, though Giovanni now dimly heard cries and commotion, gates being flung open and running footsteps on the gravel, it was too late. He was dying

He faltered for a second or two, though for him it seemed an eternity, then he fell. He fell into the pit that had been dug for him; a dark, deep pit with a gravestone and an inverted cross at its head. On the gravestone was carved the inscription:

HERE LIES GIOVANNI CAMPIONI
Heretic Senator of Venice
1696–1756
Gone to be with she whom he loved.

Campioni fell into the soft earth and, with his last thought, realised the irony, that he should go to an early grave, one dug for him by the Devil himself, that he might once again embrace Luciana in the Kingdom of the Shades. Giovanni Campioni sprawled in the mud like the Simoniac pope Anastasias, the embodiment of heresy; he who had tried to reform the republic, who had dreamed of utopias ... *I hold Pope Anastasias/Drawn by Photinus from the proper path.*

Giovanni Campioni was dead. Ricardo Pavi and his men had been thwarted by the Devil. The Black Orchid arrived too late. They had delivered the senator up to the Shadow to be executed.

THE SEVENTH CIRCLE

CANTO XIX

THE VIOLENT

Ottavio and Campioni were dead. The first at the hands of the Black Orchid, the other cut down by one of the Striges. Both, after a fashion, had been eliminated. It mattered little.

Clearly, Ottavio had not had time to reveal anything – had he confessed, he might have proved a nuisance. Just like Minos, he showed a marked tendency to overstep his limits. Now that problem had been solved.

Somewhere in Venice, *il Diavolo* stood before an oval pier-glass in a finely wrought frame, like Psyche at her boudoir. He smiled, bringing his ringed fingers to his lips. Carnival would begin again tomorrow and he had idly prepared himself a costume – though one he would never think to wear in public, since to impersonate the doge was forbidden. It was not this which stayed his hand – soon the *Serenissima* would have no doge at all. He laughed at his reflection. He had donned this showy garb as a homage to the man whose imminent death he had assured. Farewell Francesco Loredan. He laughed again and, raising his hand, began to softly hum the music played at the investiture of a new doge. Then, bored with his farce, he removed the *corno ducale*. The symbol of the doge's power, what Venetians called the *zogia*, the jewel, was a stiff, horn-like bonnet in the Byzantine style fashioned of brocade and set with precious gems: rubies, emeralds, diamonds and twenty-four teardrop pearls.

That which *il Diavolo* was wearing was a mere copy. He removed it with a grimace and dropped it to the floor where, slowly and with great care, he crushed the paste jewels with his heel.

Francesco Loredan's time had come. When he was dead, Venice would pay him homage one last time, his remains would be taken to the *Piovego*, there to lie in state, watched over by agents of the Quarantia Criminale as the rabble came to pay their respects. Then, the casket would be taken to San Giovanni e Paolo, to the mausoleum where his predecessors were interred. At the head of the funeral procession would be *il Diavolo* himself, the last bastion of the forces of evil, the only man who could be trusted to defend the *Serenissima* and restore it to its rightful place as Queen of the Seas. But now was not the time to think of such fripperies, *il Diavolo* was expected elsewhere. The pawns had been played and the endgame was in sight: the Legions of Hell were massing and would soon deliver the death blow to the old republic.

Under the ornate dome of the great hall of the Villa Morsini in Maghera, Eckhart von Maarken and his ally were putting the final touches to their plan. Their headquarters, they resolved, should move to Terra Firma, on the banks of the Brenta; here their combined forces would meet. Gathered here beneath the baroque dome, the Firebirds prepared for battle. The proud eye of some antic God seemed to stare down at them from the fresco above, seeking out the faint of heart. All around the vast, oval hall long mirrors endlessly reflected the hundreds of robed figures, multiplying the army. Night had fallen, and the flickering light of great chandeliers flooded the hastily constructed dais covered with a blood-red carpet.

Recruiting the Firebirds had been a long and difficult affair. It was a motley army composed of men of disparate, often contradictory views and motives – mercenaries attracted by the lure of money, corrupt functionaries, zealous noblemen weary of the intrigues of government and the destitute. Von Maarken, for his part, had marshalled two entire Austrian battalions now aboard the galleys off the coast of Otranto, officers, foot soldiers and renegades whom the Duke had patiently won over to his cause. Those who had gained little in the Habsburg wars of succession swelled the ranks: Hungarians, Bohemians, and even a number of Prussians for, by a clever sleight of hand, von Maarken had persuaded Frederick of Prussia that it was in his interests to have an ally as Head of State in the *Serenissima*. It was a dangerous ruse since, if the coup were successful, the Duke intended to give the spoils to the Empress Maria Theresa and thereby be returned to favour with the court. Von Maarken was playing a double game – Frederick and Maria Theresa were sworn adversaries – but he was accustomed to such manoeuvres. In this respect, at least, he was already a Venetian.

The idea of mounting an assault had been a singular idea. It was an audacious enterprise even now; some decades earlier it would have been sheer folly. Many would have thought it madness even now, those who still believed in the supremacy of the *Serenissima*. But Eckhart von Maarken had only to scratch the surface to discover what many in Europe already suspected: the Most Serene Republic had become corrupt and decadent, its noblemen were idle, its authorities bored, and its merchants easily persuaded to change their allegiance for a ducat. Venice would not be the first empire to fall, indeed. *Venezia* was already little more than the city itself, and to take a city was simplicity itself. The labyrinthine intricacies of planning such a *coup* did nothing to dissuade him, in fact, they excited him. Through secret societies, freemasonry and curious cults, he had steadily rallied supporters to his secret enterprise. Now he had only to think of a plan of battle. The ideal moment, he decided, would be the *festa della*

Sensa – the feast of the Ascension, when all Venice celebrated the city's 'marriage to the sea'. The festivities offered an ideal time when the *polizia*, mingling with the masked and costumed revellers, would be revellers themselves. The strategic buildings in the city would be undermanned, perhaps deserted. If he could take Venice – Eckhart von Maarken smiled at the thought – then the Adriatic and the Mediterranean were his, and he would be redeemed in the eyes of the Habsburgs; never again would he be treated like a pariah, a heretic among his own people.

What had convinced him that such a plan was not merely imaginable, but feasible, was the arcane nature of the republic's institutions. Von Maarken knew all too well that the art of *la superstizione* was ingrained in the Venetian soul, and he knew how to play on it. He had to admit that *il Diavolo*, the man who styled himself the Chimera had, with consummate skill, sown panic among the authorities and the populace. Each murder had been necessary for its own reasons; nothing had been left to chance. Torretone and his confessor, the priest at San Giorgio, had to die, and though he gave little thought to the fate of Spadetti, his proudest trophy was to know that they had eliminated Emilio Vindicati, *capo* of the Council of Ten! As to Luciana Saliestri, her amorous trysts had given her information which had posed a minor threat to his plans, and now that they were so far advanced, he was not prepared to take any risk whatever. Von Maarken had been impressed by the clear-sighted pragmatism of *il Diavolo*. When they had first met at Cannaregio, the Chimera had already elaborated his plans and recruited many to his cause, and arranged the series of arcane, elaborate murders which paid homage to the finest Italian poet who ever lived. If the murders themselves had been dictated by the imperious necessity of protecting the conspiracy and the identity of those behind it, the Chimera, with his cryptic Dantesque tableaux, had succeeded in misleading the enemy. Even now, Viravolta and Ricardo Pavi were mired in superstitious nonsense. By the same token, the panopticon and the scandal at the Arsenal had proved veritable *tours de force*. The Chimera was an artist. But it was precisely this which worried Eckhart von Maarken. What need had there been for all this theatre? Eventually, it had worked in their disfavour. Too much time and attention had been paid to such trifles. To leave a false trail was one thing; to attract attention was another. But *il Diavolo* was a performer. Even Viravolta had quickly realised that he was not on the trail of a lone madman, as at first he had believed, but of a sect with political aims. He had been quick to perceive the importance of Spadetti, and had discovered the manoeuvres at the Arsenal, and indeed the panopticon itself … And though the investigation had borne little fruit, the Black Orchid had moved too quickly, too sure-footedly for comfort. Now, he could no longer count on the authorities to be half-asleep for carnival, on the contrary, they would be especially vigilant; the Arsenal would be on the alert. This might prove a decisive blow, and it was entirely due to the overweening egoism of his ally. The Chimera was too confident, enjoyed the thrill of the chase too much. Was he unwitting or power hungry? There was something of the latter about his manner, but he had proved able and meticulous in planning the campaign. This was why von Maarken was worried. He could not imagine failure – for to fail in this would mean death – but he could not share the unqualified optimism of *il Diavolo*, who he had come to admire and, increasingly, to fear. Eckhart was no fool – if the republic fell, *il Diavolo* might well have ambitions above his station. Once Francesco Loredan was eliminated, the trappings of power seized, and the institutions vanquished, he might well face another battle. Von Maarken knew that he would be caught up in the internecine struggle and that he too might be vulnerable. It was an eventuality for which he was already preparing himself.

*

Standing on the dais, not far from where Vicario sat, *il Diavolo* was haranguing the crowd: it was fascinating to watch him as he spoke, veering between operatic melodrama and hushed sincerity. From the blood-red velvet dais he was recapitulating the plan of battle. There would be four principal theatres of operation: the first, stationed at the Rialto, would take the offices of the judiciary, a manoeuvre which would have to be swift and decisive, and use a minimum of force. The second detachment would take the Arsenal to prevent ships being moved out as reinforcement when Eckhart von Maarken's galleys, flying the Austrian standard, made their appearance on the *laguna*. Next, the *Bucintoro*, the official vessel which was to carry the doge along the canals. Finally, the Piazza San Marco and the doge's palace, which would be the most delicate part of the offensive. These cardinal points would have to be captured quickly, using the cloak of the general hullabaloo of celebration and festivity. *Il Diavolo* now began to issue specific orders to his legions while in his mind he was already refashioning the institutions of Venice in his own image.

He would, he thought, begin by abolishing the Senate altogether and concentrating all power in a single Consiglio, headquartered with the magistracy and the Quarantia Criminale, whose numbers he would cut substantially, putting an end to the alternation of powers by which the *Serenissima* had long thought to avoid a coup. The Arsenal would be placed under close supervision, and he would take in hand the Council of Ten, to whose number he would add twenty new governmental inquisitors. He would keep a tight rein on the Scuole Grandi and the charitable organisations of the city: supreme power would be vested in a patrician monarch who would rule the state (himself, naturally), and who would ultimately make all decisions relating to matters of political importance. Prison sentences and the use of the death penalty would be increased to deter banditry and prostitution. The flood of foreign immigrants would be stemmed by the introduction of a visa. Most importantly, the erstwhile territories of the republic along the Adriatic and the Mediterranean would be reconquered. Enemies of the state would be pitilessly tracked down. The state coffers would benefit from a law forcing all casinos and gaming houses to submit to a monthly audit. The *Signori della Notte* would be replaced by an armed militia charged with patrolling the *sestieri* of the city. Nor did the list stop there. Venice, under his sovereignty, would know true justice and *il Diavolo* would step into the light and reveal himself in his true colours. There would be no more need of Firebirds, no more Dantesque tableaux: he would be the one power. If there remained obstacles to that power, they would be eliminated, as was Giovanni Campioni and his foolish dreams of utopia. *Il Diavolo* smiled. No one, now, would dare stand in his way.

The Chimera turned towards Eckhart von Maarken for a moment. The duke looked up at him and grimaced in what he hoped was a smile.

In time, I shall deal with you, thought von Maarken.

Behind his mask *il Diavolo* also attempted a smile. *Poor fool*, he thought, *little do you know you are but my pawn.*

The two men clasped hands and raised them aloft in a victory salute before the assembled Firebirds.

When everyone had departed, Andreas Vicario emerged from his hiding place. He cocked his ear: silence. The palace was once again deserted. Smiling, he stroked his lips with a long finger. His teeth flashed in the glow of the candles, like those of some carnivorous fiend crawled out from beneath a stone. With an elegant sweep, Vicario threw back one of the drapes, found the undetectable recess in the wall, and pulled the lever. A large section of the library moved back into place with a dull sound. He had always known that the curious designs of his architect would one day prove useful. He had had to refashion the entire west wing of the villa, first to create the library itself but, more importantly, to furnish Andreas with a discreet exit. He paced the passageways of the library. During the several hours he had been in hiding he had had time to think, yet still he could not fathom how the doge had discovered his involvement in this affair – for it was now clear that his Serene Highness knew something. Perhaps one of the Firebirds had betrayed him, perhaps Fregolo, the astrologer, had said too much; perhaps someone had finally heeded the ravings of Arcangela Torretone cloistered in the convent in San Biagio. It was possible that she had seen through his disguise when he had played at being Lucifer. The Chimera had refused to have Arcangela eliminated, arguing that her gibbering pronouncements would not be heard outside the convent. After the meeting in which Andreas had terrorised the poor wretch to the point of madness, it had been impossible for him to return to San Biagio. The Mother Superior and the good sisters were on their guard. Now, Vicario regretted that he had not finished the task – but one could not crucify everyone in Venice! What was done, was done. But now matters had taken a sombre turn. At the thought, Vicario's smile faded, though the knowledge that the moment of truth would come soon afforded some reassurance. He had only to lie low and furnish himself with the necessary provisions until it was over, and he could step into the light once more. It was important too, that he find a means to contact his companions; but he would have to be extremely vigilant. He peered from behind the heavy drapes down toward the entrance to his villa and the canal beyond: a gang of soldiers stood guard outside the *palazzo*. Vicario bit his lip, then began to pace once more, glancing occasionally at the spines of the thousand upon thousand tomes his family had assembled.

E. de Paganis, *The New Behemoth*, Geneva, 1545
L'Abbé Meurisse, *A History of Witches and Witchcraft*, Loudon, 1642
William Terrence, *In Cathedral's Shadow*, London, 1471

Andreas considered leaving the *Libreria* by the door which led to the other wing. From there he might return to his room and procure the hundreds of ducats he kept hidden inside the *mappa mundi*. He would take his pistols and his official seal. He might even have time enough to find something to eat and drink. Then he could return to the library and, via the secret passage behind the bookshelves, take the staircase which led to a concealed entrance behind the villa where a gondola waited. He might easily make his escape. When the men of the Quarantia Criminale and the Council of Ten had arrived some hours earlier, he had barely had time to slip behind the sliding wall, but now he had ample time to prepare his escape. He would leave, unnoticed, and make his way to Marghera, where he would be safe and s— He stopped. For an instant he thought he had seen a shadow moving in the half-light. He glanced about him nervously. The soldiers could not have seen him, unless there were others stationed in the villa. He stood motionless for some seconds, listening. He heard nothing. He began to pace once more.

Anonymous, *Melchizedek*, Milan, 1602
Anonymous, *The Invocation of the Devil*, Paris, 1642
E. Lope-Tenezàr, *Diabolus in Musica*, Madrid, 1471

If fortune favoured him, Vicario thought, he might be in Marghera by morning. Indeed, his absence might have been missed already – though it was uncertain, since anonymity was scrupulously respected at *il Diavolo*'s meetings. He would take the gondola and hire a mount, get word to his family, then meet with the Chimera and Eckhart von Maarken directly. In fact, he reasoned, it was essential that he do so before dawn, not merely for his personal convenience, but as a matter of life and d—

He stopped again and stiffened. He had heard something, this time he was convinced of it. Something like a low groan, something that could be nothing human. Andreas Vicario glanced about him, cold sweat coursing down his body now. He saw eyes in the darkness. Three pairs of eyes glinting in the half-light like three-headed Cerberus unleashed from the pit of hell. *What can this mean …*

At that moment, Andreas Vicario had an epiphany and he felt his blood freeze with dread, and his limbs grow weak with terror; but he had no time to think further on this sudden revelation. From all sides, out of the darkness, came shadows which fell upon him.

THE PROBLEM OF EVIL

Andreas Vicario, member of the Maggior Consiglio
On the Negation of Evil, Chapter XXI

Perhaps it is fitting that I should discuss why some believe that the term 'Evil' will one day disappear, for since Evil is by definition revolt and treason, it cannot create a stable structure, nor impose its power and its dominion except in matters transitory, by the corruption of individuals. In other words, the treason inherent in Evil would be such that Evil would betray itself, as Judas or Peter betrayed Christ, urging him on toward Calvary and rewarded, one by hanging and the other to the Apostolate. It follows that, Evil being incapable of trusting even in itself, thereby prepares its own sepulchre, its own end: it shall be the cause of its own ruin, thereby heralding that which since the Dawn of Time it has struggled to frustrate: the Triumph of the Almighty.

In other words; trust no one. Andreas Vicario had been right.

The Black Orchid arrived at the scene some hours later. Bloodcurdling cries and screams had been heard from the *libreria* and, rounding the bank of the canal, one of the *Signori della Notte* had discovered he was wading through blood – the blood of the agents of the Quarantia Criminale stationed before the villa in Cannaregio.

The evening had begun badly. Pietro had been shocked by news of the death of Giovanni Campioni. Pavi and the senator had long debated whether they should keep the mysterious appointment at the cemetery of Dorsodura and, in the end, it had been Campioni himself who had insisted, hoping thus to deliver one or more of the Firebirds into the hands of the Criminale. Instead, what had come of the meeting was what Pietro had most feared: a sixth murder, the chastisement of those relegated to the Sixth Circle. Campioni had been consigned to the tomb of a heretic and apostate for the simple crime of imagining that politics might be conducted more civilly. Familiar with the Chimera and his taste for spectacle, Pietro would have realised such a meeting would be madness, but Campioni was still grieving his beloved Luciana and was determined to avenge her death. The bolt of a crossbow fired from the balcony of a villa overlooking the cemetery had put an end to that grief, to that life. *What did Campioni imagine was waiting for him?* fumed Pietro. The senator had only belatedly confided in Pavi about the message he had received and, by then, was already on his way to the cemetery. Pavi had been forced to extemporise – most of his agents were already in Cannaregio guarding Vicario's *palazzo* and, though the chief of the Quarantia assembled as many men as he was able, it had not been enough to ensure a cordon around the Dorsoduro cemetery. In any case, they could not have anticipated a lone shot, nor predicted the direction from where it would come. Campioni's desire for revenge had rebounded on him, his impulsive nature had led him to his death. But in the absence of the Black Orchid, it had been an error for Pavi to follow the senator to Dorsodura when he might have prevented him from keeping the appointment. But Pavi, too, had been curious, and had felt the need to act, besides which he would have had to use force to prevent the senator from going. All these things were clear in hindsight. Campioni had not been prepared to listen to reason and perhaps, thought Pietro, I would have done the same. But this new setback did not help matters, and though it whetted the appetite of the Quarantia and the Council of Ten for vengeance, they knew nothing good would be found in Vicario's *libreria*. They feared the worst.

At least, thought Pietro, Ottavio is out of the game. Immediately upon his return Viravolta had recounted to Pavi what had happened in Santa Croce and Pavi advised the doge who – overwhelmed and disillusioned – refused to give the matter any thought, so consumed was he by the imminent *festa della Sensa*.

Now, here they stood before Vicario's *palazzo*. The *Signore della Notte* raised his lantern level with his mask and studied Pietro's face. Pavi had remained at the offices of the Quarantia but had despatched a group of officers with Pietro. As they rounded the corner of the villa, Pietro noticed a figure bending over a body and, for a moment, thought he recognised the round shoulders and neatly trimmed beard of Antonio Brozzi. And indeed it was the coroner of the Quarantia, who had been dragged from his bed at this unholy hour. A fine drizzle began to fall. Pietro walked back to the *Signore* with the lantern.

'Were they all killed?'

'Apparently. No one has entered or left the villa since we arrived. We've been waiting for you.'

Pietro pushed back his tricorn hat and glanced up at the *libreria*. Heaven itself seemed to be crying, though Pietro could feel only a fervent rage, a longing for revenge. He drew the pistols from his belt and nodded to the soldiers, armed with pistols, pikes and swords, to follow him. Behind them, Landretto arrived. He had come to tell his master that Anna Santamaria was now safely in hiding in the *sestiere* of Castello in the villa of an old school friend. Landretto had intended to return immediately to ensure her safety but now, without asking permission, he joined the agents as they stepped inside the villa.

They moved through thc interior courtyard, past the ornate fountain and stepped into the *loggia*. Pietro posted a number of the men along the *cortile* facing the street. A simple glance was enough to remind Pietro of Andreas Vicario's masked ball. It was here that he had last spoken to Luciana Saliestri. He looked around at the twin fireplaces and the tables, bare now, but still watched by the carved wooden slaves – it took little imagination to remember the lights, the masked couples waltzing beneath the falling rose petals, and the buffet tables groaning under the weight of fine foods. Tonight, the *loggia* was plunged into darkness, stripped of all ornamentation; there were no dancing couples, no orchestra, no artfully placed chaises longues on which elegant women sighed with pleasure. Pietro climbed the stairs and found himself by the same door where he had surprised the masked Firebird who had slaughtered Luciana. The agents who accompanied him threw open the doors to each room as they passed; others dispersed to search the rest of the villa. Pietro wandered to the end of the corridor where he found the door that connected with the *libreria* in the west wing. For a moment he leaned against the door and listened, but there was nothing. He turned the handle. Slowly the door opened.

The library was still aglow with torchlight. The bookshelves lining the room created a scholarly labyrinth. Pietro paused for a moment, then stepped into the maze. He turned the first corner, then another, and another, and at length he arrived at the central aisle. He was still some fifteen metres from the end of the first of the library's immense rooms. From here, he could make out furtive movements, shadows crouched over a shapeless mass, and hear gasps and laboured breathing. Pietro took several steps towards the scene and it grew clearer. It was then that he realised that he had disturbed a grisly feast. Just as he was struggling to come to terms with what he saw, monsters, hulking shadows, howling and slavering, fell upon him out of the darkness.

What the ... Pietro let out a cry and stepped back. His pistol already cocked, he aimed at one of the savage hounds, its maw flecked with foam, which bounded towards him, growling. The blast rang out, a flare of light, and the smell of gunpowder. The bullet hit the dog between the eyes and it stopped dead, whimpered and crashed to the floor. Pietro, meanwhile, turned and aimed the second pistol. Another dog fell, but got to its feet again, limping, wounded, a flash of rage in its great, dark eyes, and moved towards him. Pietro dropped his firearms just as two soldiers burst into the *libreria*. Pietro drew his sword just as one of the pack of hounds leapt towards him as though to rip out his throat. Pietro swung the blade and the beast, its head severed from its body, clattered to the ground. The two soldiers now flanked him on either side and the howling, slavering pack disappeared. The alert sounded, the entire escort converged on the library. Landretto's face appeared in the doorway, frantic to know that his master was safe.

Pietro was walking towards the far end of the library where he discovered the body of Andreas Vicario, his black robes ripped and stained with blood. Here and there, beneath the shreds of flesh, Pietro could see where the jagged teeth of the beasts had chewed through to the bone. Pietro crouched, one hand on his knee, and murmured, 'The Squanderers, torn at by Harpies.'

Landretto came to stand next to him. 'What did you say?'

Pietro looked up. 'The violent, Landretto. The violent against themselves shall be transformed into trees which sigh and lament; the Despoilers who shall be endlessly consumed by Harpies ... share the Seventh Circle of Hell with sodomites and the enemies of God and Art ...'

'You mean ...?'

Pietro glanced down at the body once more. 'This was no random act, it was carefully planned like all the others. Clearly, Vicario was an accomplice who had grown fractious. He was betrayed by his own. Perhaps they knew that we had unmasked him ... but how? How, Landretto? Is there a traitor in our midst? Another informer?'

Pietro and his manservant stared at one another. 'Go back to Anna,' said Pietro, 'and do not leave her side for an instant. I shall see you when all this is over.'

The soldiers approached now. One of them, looking down, pinched his nose with two fingers in a parody of disgust. Andreas Vicario, known as Minos, arbitrator of sins, judge of souls, the right arm of Lucifer himself, was dead, snuffed out by his own people.

CANTO XX
THE MINOTAUR

The Carnival of Venice dated from the tenth century and now took up a full six months of the year: from the first Sunday of October it whirled until the middle of December, then began again, stretching from Twelfth Night to Ash Wednesday; then, at the *festa della Sensa*, the feast of the Ascension, it flowered one last time. All Venice was busy with preparations for the feast. The Council of Ten, who would number nine until another had been elected to replace Emilio Vindicati, were charged with the impossible task of overseeing the festivities, with the help of the Quarantia Criminale and the Arsenal. As every year, supervision of the public ceremonies and parades devolved to the officers of the *Rason Vecchie*, responsible for claims on the public purse. This year, the Quarantia and the magistracy had been called upon to ensure strict security during the festivities. It was ordered that no citizen, even one costumed as a soldier, would be allowed to wear a firearm, nor any weapon: cudgel, truncheon, cane or pikestaff. Only the agents of government, who would also be in costume, were permitted to go armed. But what might they hope to do faced with tens of thousands of revellers, all anonymous? For their part, the Arsenal had several galleys ready to be launched into the *laguna* from the Giudecca, from Murano, Burano and San Michele. Meanwhile, light skiffs would patrol the waters.

On land, as on sea, Venice teemed with activity. This was the supreme festival of the year, the moment of exultation, of fulfilment, of liberation, when a common man might style himself a king or a nobleman might play the rogue. This was a time when the world was turned upon its head and every licence, every excess, was allowed. The gondoliers, in full livery, steered the nobility through the canals of a city decked out in pomp and splendour. On the *piazzetta* a wooden contraption in the form of a cream cake attracted gourmands, and crowds began to form around puppet theatres, rope dancers and actors playing scenes from famous comedies. Mounted on stools, astrologers pointed fingers at the invisible stars and foretold Armageddon. There was laughter and rowdy talk, the cobbled streets were thick with fallen sweetmeats and ices, and everywhere the rabble exulted in the sweetness of life.

The woman known only as the Queen of Hearts stepped from the shadows beneath the colonnades and walked a few steps before taking out her fan. Her long lashes fluttered behind her mask and her carmine lips were pursed into a bow. She dropped her kerchief at her feet as she smoothed a crease in her gown. She stopped to pick up her kerchief and glanced to another agent stationed at the corner of the *piazzetta* to ensure he had understood. The signal meant: *he has arrived*.

And indeed, there he was, in the midst of the throng, he whose mission it was to kill the Doge of Venice. Two horns of pale ivory crowned the bull's head mask, the muzzle artfully twisted into a snarl. He wore a suit of armour of chain-mail and plate, light enough that he might move quickly, yet strong enough to protect him. His blood-red cloak concealed two pistols, which he would need to carry out his task. He was a giant, a fearsome creature whose husky breath roared through his painted muzzle.

The Minotaur. Ready to devour the children of Venice, here, in the labyrinth of the city, he prepared himself to change the course of history. Carnival had begun.

CANTO XXI

LA FESTA DELLA SENSA

The Black Orchid stationed himself not far from the *Fondaco dei Tedeschi*, a warehouse on the Grand Canal, strategically placed between the Piazza San Marco and the Rialto, which had been entirely rebuilt after fire had destroyed the original in 1508. Pietro stood at the doorway to the canal, at the end of one of the arcades in the interior courtyard, talking animatedly to a man wearing a carnival mask and swathed in black. Agents of the Tenebræ and the Quarantia Criminale were patrolling the city in costume in order to appear as inconspicuous as possible. Pietro wore no costume, hoping that he might serve as bait. If the conspirators should see him, they might be tempted to act and thereby reveal themselves. Reinforcements had been deployed whose task it was to defend the Arsenal, the Rialto, the doge's palace, and the *Fondaco*, where he now stood. Here alone there were fifty reserve officers, arms and ammunition. Strongholds such as this had been set up throughout the city. The populace, of course, had no idea that they were sitting on a powder keg: the situation was delicate and explosive. Having spoken for a minute to his colleague, Pietro adjusted his hat, straightened the orchid in his buttonhole and, throwing his cape over his shoulder, he stepped out, heading for the *campo* San Bartolomeo and was immediately swept up in the frenzied excitement of the crowd.

Pietro had spent the previous evening in agitated discussion with Ricardo Pavi – it had been a long and gruelling night, and Pietro had slept for barely an hour. Now, however, it was imperative that he was awake and alert. The Black Orchid strode along the narrow streets watching for the least sign of something suspicious. At that very moment, two thousand other agents were doing exactly as he did. Thus they hoped by sheer force of numbers to keep an eye on the crowds of costumed revellers, stopping and searching anyone they suspected of carrying a concealed weapon. Although the crowd was merry and relaxed, the agents who walked among them were anxious. The Chancery and the Magistracy had been sealed off. All entrances to the doge's palace had been secured, and the courtyard leading to it was filled with armed guards. Pietro stopped for a moment at the Rialto. Around the bridge, soldiers in costume pretended to play cards, to converse, some, dressed in rags for the occasion, pretended to beg, but all of them were intently studying the crowds as they passed. A series of coded signs had been devised so that costumed soldiers, officers in civilian clothes, lieutenants, and various agents might recognise one another without confusion. Pietro approached a young woman standing beneath an arcade. For several hours she had been standing guard, a dagger concealed beneath her cloak. They had a brief conversation and she fluttered her fan at the corner of her mouth to let him know that she had nothing to report. Some minutes later, he encountered another agent. She was wearing a carnival mask and had a beauty spot on her right cheek, her hair, piled high, fell in ringlets about her face; she fluttered her fan above her plunging neckline. At court, she was known as the Queen of Hearts. It was she who had just signalled the arrival of the Minotaur. He barely had time to wonder if her behaviour had been noticed, when he disappeared from sight. He must be found.

Further off, a man in a dark cape and wearing an

eyepatch, slipped between a crowd of gamblers engrossed in playing *La lotteria della venturina*, which involved picking from a sack a token which might bear a number or a symbol: Death, the Devil, the Sun, the Moon, the World, in the hope of winning some savoury treat. Pietro stood by the one-eyed man and watched the game in silence for a moment. Eager hands dipped into the sack and howls of delight and disappointment filled the air.

'Fancy trying your luck, Messer?' asked a voice.

Pietro handed over a coin, taking advantage of the distraction to whisper a few words to his neighbour. He rummaged in the sack and pulled out a token, watching from the corner of his eye as the man with the eyepatch pointed to a corner of the piazza.

It was now that he saw the Minotaur. He was standing barely twenty metres from him, fixed in a solemn pose, seeming almost to mock Pietro from behind his mask. 'Well? Well?' the crowd around Pietro shouted, though the voices seemed to come from far away. He opened his hand and showed them the token. 'Death! Death! No prize for you Messer!' Pietro was no longer paying attention to the game. He stared at the Minotaur, who had not moved from where he stood. Slowly, he gave a slight bow. A group of soldiers appeared around the corner of the Mercerie. The Minotaur glanced towards them, then turned and headed in the opposite direction. Pietro followed a short distance behind.

The beast took a narrow laneway, then another, seeming to head towards the Piazza San Marco. At one point he turned and seemed to see Pietro. He quickened his step, forcing Pietro to do likewise. Soon they emerged behind the doge's palace onto the *piazzale dei Leoni*; here again there were crowds and tumult, for it was here that teams of acrobats from different *sestieri* competed in the *Forze di Ercole*, in which each team made themselves into a human pyramid. Gasps and applause came from the crowd as the pyramids rose into the air. Pietro did not even see them, so intent was he on the Minotaur; it was no accident that he had been drawn to the curious costume of the beast. Nor was it any accident, he thought, that the Minotaur had come to present himself to Viravolta.

> And at the broken chasm's edge we found
> The infamy of Crete, conceived within
> The false cow's shell. When he saw us come his way
> He bit himself in rage like one insane ...
> ... As a bull breaks loose in the deathblow's aftermath,
> And plunges back and forth, but thought unspent
> Cannot go forward, so did the Minotaur act.

Pietro swore under his breath as he elbowed his way through the crowd, fearing that at any moment he might lose sight of the Minotaur. He watched as the beast rounded the corner. Rather than attempt to make his way along the perimeter of the throng, Pietro hurled himself into the crown of the *piazzale*. In doing so, however, he inadvertently collided with a plump man on the bottom tier of one of the human pyramids. The man yelled, struggling to keep his balance, and tottered for a second, two ... The small shudder ran through the pyramid and at the summit, a small boy who had just climbed into place faltered, flailing his arms wildly. He managed to clutch the young man next to him, causing him in turn to sway. The crowd gasped and roared as the human pyramid swayed from side to side like a pendulum, then suddenly crashed to the ground. The people milling around formed a circle, vainly trying to prop up the edifice, or to catch the acrobats as they fell in a tangle of arms and legs. But Pietro's fatal error had not gone unnoticed: one of the crowd tried to bar his way. The Black Orchid roared and fought him off, his fist knocking the man sideways. Pietro struggled free of the man's grip and in the confusion made his escape towards the Piazza San Marco.

He had scarcely reached the square when a small, blond-haired girl stopped him. '*Buon giorno!* We are from the convent school of Santa Trinità!'

Not now!

She held out a small box with a narrow slot, chinking the coins in Pietro's face. A score of other girls – some dressed as the nuns they would one day be, others wearing a simple white blouse, blue skirt and a ribbon in their hair, were posted around the piazza soliciting passers-by for donations.

'Messer! Something for the convent of Santa …'

Pietro distractedly fumbled in his pocket and dropped a coin into the girl's box, scanning the crowd for the Minotaur.

On the Piazza San Marco the atmosphere was frenzied; the multitude had gathered. The doge had appeared from the gallery of the basilica to officially inaugurate the ceremonies for the *Sensa*. Delegations of the craftsmen's guilds marched past carrying banners, statues, and the reliquaries of saints. Of the floats, one was more spectacular than all the others: that of the Guild of Glaziers of Murano. As he was still scanning the crowd for the Minotaur, Pietro caught a glimpse of Tazzio, the son of the murdered Federico Spadetti and, though fleeting, the sight took his breath away. Tazzio was standing on a cart decorated with banners and pennants; beside him sat a radiant girl, her cheeks flushed, her smile luminous, wearing a crystal gown. She looked like a vision from a fairytale and from the applause and the cheers it was clear that Pietro was not alone in thinking so. Could this be Severina, of whom Spadetti had spoken, the girl his son Tazzio loved so dearly? She was sublime in her scintillating gown of crystal with its ruff of spun glass and belt of pearls. Each ribbon of crystal reflected the doge's palace, the *campanile*, and the Winged Lion of Saint Mark: a thousand tiny worlds which told and retold the history of Venice itself. Severina smiled and waved as she passed.

Next to her, Tazzio, his angelic face framed with golden curls, stood like an Adonis in the sunlight, or like a young Apollo driving his fiery chariot across the firmament. His face was grave, unlike his smiling bride's; he was still wearing mourning, a long black cloak over a black jerkin. Beside the chariot, two thousand members of the guild marched in step in a sea of banners and pennants. Bringing a hand to his heart, Tazzio bowed deeply toward His Serene Highness Francesco Loredan. The doge took a flower from a basket offered to him and scattered the blooms over the couple, then held up the gold medal which he would later bestow on Tazzio for the crowd to see. Tazzio's face brightened and smiling, he turned to Severina and placed a kiss on her cheek.

Still searching the crowd, Pietro finally spotted the Minotaur as Tazzio's chariot moved off past the Procuratie and around the wooden amphitheatre built on the piazza for the occasion. The mysterious figure stood motionless on the other side of the procession. Time seemed to stand still as Pietro and the horned beast faced one another across the sea of costumed figures following the procession, each waiting for the moment to act. As the last chariot in the procession passed them, Pietro decided that that moment had come. He felt for his pistols beneath his cloak. But the crowd rushed in to fill the space, following the procession; an impassable wave sweeping Pietro with them towards the Procuratie.

Since daybreak, the masses had been celebrating through the city, and bells pealed from every steeple. After retiring for a short while to the palace, Francesco Loredan, this time seated in the *pozetto*, the great sedan chair, led by the chief of the Arsenal, was carried by many strong men through the waiting crowd. The doge tossed coins stamped with his image into the throng, which fuelled their excitement. Behind him came noblemen, throwing bread, wine and money to the assembled masses.

Pietro caught a fleeting glimpse of Ricardo Pavi, the head of the Quarantia, as he passed with the escort guarding the *pozetto*. Pietro desperately tried to elbow his way through the throng that followed the procession, only to have his attempts frustrated with angry cries of '*Stia calmo*, Messer.' But Pietro could not remain calm. From time to time he stood on tiptoe, trying to catch sight of the Minotaur who had once again disappeared. In the distance the *pozetto*, and with it the doge, turned the corner of the piazza and disappeared also. His Serene Highness Francesco Loredan was on his way to the Arsenal, where he would board the ship of State, the *Bucintoro*, and sail out into the *laguna*. If something should befall him before he reached the Arsenal … Pietro rained abuse on those around him, and finally struggled free. Running against the tide of people, he weaved now between the wooden stalls selling lace, jewels, crystal and paintings, erected in front of the palace. Suddenly he stopped. At his feet, as if by a miracle, lay a mask. The mask of the Minotaur.

Pietro snatched it up and discovered a sealed letter inside. Feverishly, he tore it open.

> You are too late, Viravolta,
> We have arrived at the Seventh Circle,
> 'Keep your eyes below us, for coming near
> Is the river of blood – in which
> Boils everyone whose violence hurt others.'
> For know this, Viravolta: upon a river of blood
> Loredan shall perish
> Through your most grievous fault.
> Which of us shall arrive
> First to prostrate ourselves at his feet?

Filled with panic now, Pietro looked up, trying to make sense of the confusion all about him. A sudden commotion startled him and he looked round. It had come from the amphitheatre constructed for the occasion on the piazza.

A new procession had begun in which the nations Venice numbered among its allies, Hungary, England, Switzerland and Spain, bowed before the people of the city. On the tribune, actors and musicians sounded the trumpets and beat the drums. The bullfights would begin shortly: two hundred bulls, monstrous beasts, breath steaming from their muzzles, would follow one another into the ring in a series of bouts which would last for three full days. The image of the bull – an image of sacrifice – flashed through Pietro's mind. His eyes followed the crowd, scanning the piazza left to right, not knowing what to do. Suddenly there was a loud whistle.

Pietro, standing at the corner of the *piazzetta*, looked up toward the *Campanile*, around which a crowd had gathered to watch the *Salto della Morte* – the Leap of Death – also known as the *Flight of the Turk*, a deadly game in which labourers working at the Arsenal flew along a cable strung between the *Campanile* and the doge's palace while performing the most hair-raising acrobatics. It was not unknown for some unfortunate wretch to be impaled on the facade. This year not one, but five, cables had been stretched between the buildings. As he watched the first figures make their way to the cables, Pietro realised what was happening. He turned towards the *Campanile*, then back toward the doge's palace, shocked by what he seemed to have discovered. *But ... but ...* he muttered under his breath as five men robed in black shot across the cables above his head, careening toward the *palazzo*. The Flight of the Turk.

With a sudden dread, Pietro knew that this was no acrobatic feat by labourers from the Arsenal. Instead, the *Salto della Morte* had afforded an ingenious scheme by which the Firebirds, whizzing overhead, could breach the palace security. The Firebirds.

Here were Orinel of the order of Abaddon; Halan of the order of Astaroth; Maggid of the Principalities, Diralisen of

Dominations, Aziel of Thrones. To the cheers of the waiting crowd, they propelled themselves through the mass in groups of five, to be met by their co-conspirators already on the balconies of the doge's palace. Pietro followed the shadowy figures as they hurtled across the cables. Suddenly, he saw masked and hooded figures appear on the roof of the Basilica di San Marco. Glancing about wildly, he saw other men perched on neighbouring buildings. They fired bolts attached to cables from their crossbows, creating a baleful web along which the Legions of Hell passed to the hoots and cheers of the citizenry who were ignorant of what was afoot. Pietro stared at the palace, then turned to where the doge, in his *pozetto*, had disappeared into the crowd. Fumbling beneath his cloak, Pietro took out a small bronze plate and metal rod and banged out a drumbeat as hard as he could to warn the group of soldiers gathered by the *porta del Frumento*, three of whom seemed to be idly watching the shadowy figures slithering along the cables to the *palazzo ducale*. One of them, hearing the banging, looked up and saw Pietro, and all over the Piazza San Marco other agents took up the signal and the clanking noise of drumming echoed from the Procuratie all the way to the Mercerie. The alarm had been sounded. Pietro hesitated, not knowing whether to lead a brigade of soldiers into the *palazzo*, or rush to try and alert the doge. He decided to trust the soldiers to secure the palace and dashed towards the quays. *If I can only reach him in time!*

He had barely gone a hundred metres when he stopped short.

There, on the *laguna*, the majestic silhouette of the *Bucintoro* hove into view. The doge was seated on deck, surrounded by senators, noblewomen and those members of the crowned heads of Europe dubbed *Kavalier*. The *Negronne*, the official barge of the French Ambassador, followed in its wake. Pierre-François de Villedieu was seated next to the doge himself on the *Bucintoro*. The throne was situated on the deck, beneath a regal canopy of purple and gold emblazoned with the signs and symbols of the princes of Europe. The Lion of Nemea rubbed shoulders with the many-headed Hydra, the god Pan holding aloft the globe, and tapestries and medallions spelled out the virtues of the Most Serene Republic: Truth, Patriotism, Boldness and Generosity, Learning, Vigilance, Honour, Modesty, Piety, Purity, Justice, Strength, Temperance, Humility, Faith, Chastity, and Charity. Next to these were the allegorical figures representing Science and the Arts. Pride of place was reserved for the Winged Lion of Saint Mark and the emblems of the Arsenal and the chief guilds of Venice: forgers, carpenters and shipbuilders, architects all of the conquest of the empire. In the prow were the symbols of Justice and Peace, and those of Terra Firma, the Adige and the Po, symbolising the peaceful sovereignty of Venice and its territories. Around the *Bucintoro* and the *Negronne* came dozens of skiffs and gondolas, *bissone* propelled by teams of rowers, and barges owned by the nobility. Each vessel strove to outdo the others in fantasy and splendour: they were decorated to resemble floating chariots, whales, dolphins and giant clamshells on which were poised scantily clad women posed as Venus Rising. The crowds flocked to the quays and gazed in wonder at the enchanting spectacle of this magnificent procession.

There was a barge styled to look like a floating grotto covered in seaweed and coral, mermaids swam alongside and monsters of the deep blasted jets of water high into the air. Here, too, was Neptune himself, a towering statue of imposing musculature. Slowly, the magical scene began to take shape as each boat, each skiff, took up its appointed place, slipping into line according to a complex choreography which determined where each vessel should be. Thus the gaping crowds witnessed a long procession of elaborate tableaux, each designed around a god or goddess. Venus, of course, came first, and behind her Mars, the god of war, appeared, then Juno, Apollo and Minerva. Pegasus, the winged horse, rearing as if about to take flight from the sea, appeared framed by the sunlight. The *Bucintoro* and its fantastical armada sailed towards the piazza.

THE EIGHTH CIRCLE

CANTO XXII

THE MARRIAGE WITH THE SEA

Pietro struggled to reach the quays, which had been transformed with rafts bearing artificial gardens to resemble an exotic land. There were *casotti* in which wild animals were displayed: a lioness prowled and paced behind her bars; a horned rhinoceros brought from Asia foraged uncertainly for food amid the straw and excrement of his dark cage; a leopard snarled and bared its fangs to curious bystanders; lastly an Arab mounted on a dromedary strode up and down among inquisitive promenaders. Rafts floating by the quays had been transformed into verdant lawns; strange plants and exotic flowers lending their beauty to these magical gardens where small orchestras played airs by Vivaldi as people moved from raft to raft on floating bridges. Pietro bounded onto one of these and raced between the rafts and, finding a gondola, leapt aboard. The vessel listed sharply and the gondolier almost toppled into the water, steadying himself just in time, and greeting his unexpected passenger with a volley of colourful insults.

'Take me out to the *Bucintoro*,' Pietro shouted to the gondolier. 'It is a matter of life and death.'

The gondolier was a man of about forty, red-faced with confusion and anger, and hoping perhaps to rid himself of this impromptu customer. But Pietro, staring out at the fleet, noticed that several of the skiffs and gondolas in the fleet were converging on the *Bucintoro*, causing chaos in the procession as they cut across the paths of naiads and

Neptunes twirling tridents. The gondolier made to speak, but Pietro waved the *salvacondotto* given to him by Ricardo Pavi which bore the ducal seal.

'The doge is in mortal danger. Move, *amico*, and move quickly!'

The gondolier considered the scrap of parchment, then stared at Pietro with a dawning recognition. 'You're lucky, Messer, for you've happened on the swiftest gondolier as works these canals!'

'This will be an excellent opportunity for you to prove that fact.'

The ceremony of the *Sposalizio del Mar*, in which the doge was borne over the waters of the *laguna* on the *festa della Sensa*, was one of the most important rituals in the life of the *Serenissima*, a brief symbolic odyssey that took him to the Lido, to the church of San Niccolo. Here, from the deck of the *Bucintoro*, a ring blessed by the patriarch was tossed into the deep with the solemn words: *Desponsamus te, mare, in signum veri perpetuique dominii*; By this we do marry you, sea, in sign of our perpetual dominion. This ritual of communion, of marriage, celebrated the victory of 1177 when the Emperor Alexander, in order to reward the city for its support against Barbarossa, had come to bow before the pope at the entrance to the Basilica di San Marco. It was then that the Emperor Alexander had bestowed on Venice the dominion of the seas. In retrospect, the event might be seen as prophetic for it was from this moment that the *Serenissima* began to build its reputation. Upon the deck of the *Bucintoro*, Francesco Loredan sat enthroned, conversing with ambassador Pierre-François Villedieu, who had been enjoying the revelries of the city since Andreas Vicario's masked ball. He looked suitably enchanted and amazed by the many wonders on display for the ceremony. The assembly gazed out over the *laguna* at the fleet of colourful vessels, gasping in astonishment and congratulation when some new wonder appeared.

Behind his beatific smile, Loredan was sorely worried. Near him on the ship, Ricardo Pavi, stone-faced and pale, hands clasped before him, attempted to contain his anxiety. From time to time, he glanced anxiously towards the Lido.

At the doge's palace there was a sound of shattered glass from the upper storey as a Firebird, robed and hooded in black, crashed through the ornate windows, rolled on the floor, then scrambled to his feet and drew his pistol. Ten of his co-conspirators had already set off in the direction of the sala del collegio where they were met by the soldiers Pietro had alerted. The first skirmishes had begun, shots ringing out beneath Tintoretto's *Venice, Queen of the Sea*. The gunfire seemed all the louder since firearms had been prohibited for the duration of the festivities: outside, there was applause from those who thought these firecrackers a prelude to the much anticipated fireworks display which always accompanied the *Gran Ballo*. After the first volleys, swords and rapiers were drawn and soldiers began to scale the *Scala d'Oro*. Members of the Firebirds continued to hurtle along cables to the *palazzo* from three separate directions. It had taken some time before the scale of the attack was realised and squads of soldiers were dispatched to disperse the crowd gathered around the *Campanile* so that it could be sealed off. Meanwhile, by the Rialto, Barakiel of the order of Python-Luzbel, Touriel of the order of Belial, together with mercenaries in the pay of Eckhart von Maarken, had begun to overrun the offices of the judiciary, the chancellery and the magistracy, while the crowds lining the streets, ignorant of what was going on within, hampered the forces of law and order.

'Faster, faster!' Pietro called, angry that he had not thought to seize another oar with which to row alongside the gondolier, who was already gasping with the effort.

Pietro stood on the prow of the gondola, one hand on his knee, the other by his side. The *Bucintoro*, magisterial at the centre of the armada, loomed closer; but it was still some distance off and the gondola was now compelled to tack from time to time to avoid the skiffs and barges which made up the procession. A hail of insults followed each new altercation, and Pietro's gondola had almost been capsized at least a dozen times. '*Attenzione!*' Pietro roared as they crashed through the wake of a skiff decked out like a chariot. 'Go left! Go right!' He glanced around and noticed that other gondolas seemed to be heading for the *Bucintoro*, and on some of these he could distinctly make out hooded figures robed in black. Pietro clenched his teeth and roared at Tino, the gondolier, to redouble his efforts, and the man somehow picked up speed, his brow slick with sweat and his muscles straining at the fabric of his shirt. They had reached the Giudecca when Pietro realised that, at such a pace, Tino could not hold out much longer and so, spotting a *bissone* equipped with ten oarsmen nearby, he ordered Tino to approach the craft. He hailed the men and there followed a curious exchange in which Pietro and the captain of the *bissone* had to shout to be heard above the din. Pietro turned back to Tino.

'God's grace go with you, friend! You can turn back now – you have done a great deed, go in peace. These men will take me onward.' The he took the flower from his lapel and tossed it at the astonished gondolier's feet. The Black Orchid.

The gondola scraped the bow of the *bissone* and Pietro clambered aboard as the oarsmen huddled together to make room. They were strong and able lads, but had just come from a race along the Grand Canal. They began to scull, chanting between their gasps for breath, the great oars breaking the water as one, as though this too were a race – which, in a sense, it was.

At San Niccolo, the *Bucintoro* seemed to shudder one last time; a quiver ran through its flanks, and it turned slowly so that the prow of the vessel faced the entrance to the lagoon. Not far off, the *Negronne* also turned and drew up alongside. The solemn moment had come. The doge rose from his throne, inviting the ambassador to join him. The senators, the ladies and the emissaries of the courts of Europe, took up their positions to left and right, forming a guard of honour running the length of the ship. Francesco Loredan, the ambassador by his side, moved slowly between the smiling faces of those privileged to be present. Two pageboys posted on either side of the vessel lifted their trumpets to the skies and in their thunderous salute, Loredan thought he heard the roar of the Lion of Nemea. He marched onward towards the prow of the ship. There was another page, a dark-complected child from some far country, wearing a blue turban fixed with a brilliant diadem, who awaited the doge, bearing the ring on a velvet cushion of red and gold. Next to the boy, the Patriarch of Venice, in full ceremonial robes, stood with a hand on the lad's shoulder. Loredan came and stood by them, appearing before all those assembled, robes fluttering in the breeze, *zogia* glittering on his brow, sceptre in hand, and his signet ring glinting in the sun; he stopped and looked out over the sea. A second trumpet voluntary called all those watching to be silent. Boats glided to a standstill from San Marco to the Giudecca; an entire armada frozen on the waves. Everyone fell silent, gazing expectantly at the *Bucintoro*.

Some fifty metres away, a man stretched out on the floor of an unremarkable skiff. The hooded figure removed a purple cloth which covered the prow and settled back onto a cushion which raised his chest and head somewhat, and made it easier for him to hold a deep breath when the moment came. He leaned on one elbow and slowly slid his finger onto the trigger of the harquebus which had been hidden beneath the purple kerchief; his other hand moving to steady the barrel of the gun. Some called him the Bowman, others the Harquebusier, now he was known as

Gilarion of Meririm of the order of Principalities; it had been he who, in pitch darkness, by the light of a single torch, had hit Giovanni Campioni with a single bolt of a crossbow. From where he now lay, with the doge standing on the prow of the *Bucintoro*, Gilarion could not possibly miss. But he was not alone; before he put his eye once more to the telescopic sight he himself had designed and made, he glanced to starboard where another skiff had just drawn alongside the *Bucintoro*. As the world gazed at the prow of the galley where Francesco Loredan solemnly enacted the *Sposalizio del Mar*, the Minotaur, his blood-red cape trailing in his wake, hoisted himself aboard.

There he is, he is aboard the ship! thought Pietro. It was a magnificent tableau: the *Bucintoro* and the *Negronne* sat becalmed in the middle of the still waters of the *laguna* and, all about them, gondolas and skiffs of all shapes and sizes froze as if in a painting. The doge rose and solemnly took the ring proffered him by the pageboy. He held the ring aloft in a gesture of triumph, surrounded as he was by the citizens of the Most Serene Republic and watched by ambassadors from nations far and wide, and in the still silence his voice rang out, uttering the words of communion and fraternal alliance which, for centuries, had wedded the power and glory of Venice to the Adriatic. Beside him, the pageboy in the blue turban smiled. *Desponsamus te, mare …*

Gilarion was on the point of pulling the trigger when his skiff was jolted, causing him to falter. Surprised, he turned to free his robe, which had caught on the gunwale. He was about to turn again, as the doge stood, a perfect target framed against the azure, when he saw a man throw himself aboard the skiff. Pietro lashed out with his foot. The harquebus was ripped from its tripod, toppled over the edge, and plunged below the surface of the water. In a roar of astonishment, Gilarion scrambled to catch the hackbut before it disappeared, but he was too slow. When he looked up, he saw the Black Orchid.

The struggle was over before it had begun, Pietro simply pitching the hooded figure overboard. He stood for a moment, bowed, catching his breath, then looked up. He gesticulated wildly, almost capsizing the tiny skiff in his attempt to signal to those aboard the *Bucintoro*.

Desponsamus te, mare, in signum veri perpetuique dominii. The doge dropped the ring into the *laguna* where it was swallowed by the waves and, from the Piazza San Marco to the Lido, a deafening roar went up as the crowd erupted in exultation.

Ricardo Pavi paced the deck of the *Bucintoro*, searching amid the clamour and confusion of neighbouring boats for a signal, but in the unfurling of banners, the waving kerchiefs and the carnival masks, he could distinguish nothing. He ran his hand across the back of his neck. For an instant, he thought he saw a familiar figure gesticulating from a small skiff nearby. He stopped pacing and squinted against the sunlight.

Pietro ... It is the Black Orchid! He felt his heart judder to a stop. Viravolta was shouting something.

Too far, Pietro! You're too far!

Pavi tried to interpret Pietro's mimed gestures and gesticulations which might have seemed comic if the day, the circumstances, were not so weighted with menace. Among the dancing, cheering figures, Pietro looked like just another reveller. Pavi knew that Pietro was trying to tell him something, but he could not hear a thing above the thunderous applause.

What? What are you trying to tell me?

Pavi turned back to where Francesco Loredan stood. *Desponsamus te, mare, in signum veri perpetuique dominii.*

The doge now turned back to leave the prow of the

galley. He stroked the cheek of the page who had assisted him and addressed a satisfied smile to Pierre-François Villedieu, the ladies, the noblemen, and his distinguished guests. At that moment, a colossus loomed suddenly in front of him. It was the Minotaur, his hoarse breath steaming through the horned mask, his metal epaulettes glinting and his cape like a cataract of blood.

'Francesco Loredan?' a guttural voice roared, and his name, when he heard it, sounded like a death sentence. The doge stood, paralysed with dread.

Keep your eyes below us, for coming near
Is the river of blood – in which
Boils everyone whose violence hurt others

The Minotaur swept the cape from his shoulders and reached, as if by magic, a pair of gleaming pistols. There were gasps of terror and astonishment. For a brief moment, Francesco Loredan thought he caught the flicker of a smile behind the mask of the Beast and he thought, *This is the end*.

Ricardo Pavi roared, and threw himself at the Minotaur with all his strength. The colossus staggered. Two shots rang out, missing their target, punching black holes in the canopy above the doge's throne. As if suddenly woken from a dream, the guards now leapt upon the hulking beast, six of them wrestling with the Minotaur on the deck as a blur of flailing arms, fists, and daggers fell upon the great beast.

From where he stood on the skiff, Pietro could not tell what was happening. There was some mêlée aboard the *Bucintoro*, he could see figures moving, the glint of halberds, and hear the crack of gunfire. Finally, he saw the doge, in full ceremonial robes, return to the prow of the galley. Pietro's surprise was such that he almost toppled overboard. He sighed with great relief. But it was short-lived. *Desponsamus te, mare, in signum veri perpetuique dominii.*

For then, the *Santa Maria* and the *Gioia De Corfù*, flanked by several Austrian warships, appeared on the horizon like a mirage in the haze. The alarm was sounded, and the ships readied at the Arsenal and at San Giorgio prepared to seal off the *laguna*. The enemy galleys, rigged with three square-sailed masts, each propelled by two hundred oarsmen, and laden with weapons and munitions, drew closer under full sail. Already, it was possible to make out marksmen wielding crossbows and hackbuts ranged along the decks. There were 320 cannons trained on the *Bucintoro* and the *Negronne*.

Though the Arsenal had ample weapons and manpower to face down the galleys and the frigates alongside them, the *laguna* was filled with skiffs and pleasure craft – something which would make manoeuvres difficult. If the enemy were permitted to get within firing range of the city, irreparable damage might be done to the Venetian camp.

The Arsenal's fleet – numbering several legendary galleys called *sottile* – raced into the *laguna* while hordes of light squadrons converged upon the enemy. What no one could yet know was whether they could intercept the enemy fleet before the *Negronne* or the *Bucintoro* were within firing range. Some twenty reserve units under the command of the Captain-General of the Fleet unlimbered their artillery.

Pietro, from his skiff, and Pavi aboard the *Bucintoro*, were thinking the same thought. Both turned in panic as they heard a series of explosions which seemed to come from the direction of the Arsenal. A column of smoke could be seen rising in the distance – clearly, a battle was already raging – but would the Arsenal or the Striges be victorious? Both men held their breath. On the quays of the Piazza San Marco, the crowds, speechless, stared about them, trying to decide whether this was some new spectacle arranged to celebrate *la Sensa* ... or something much more grave.

Then, suddenly, a frigate under full sail sliced through the waters, through the smoke and the flames which had followed the explosion of the powder kegs. Elegant and proud, it sailed to join the squadrons of the republic. In its wake came several others.

'Yes! Yes!' roared Pietro. 'They are on our side!'

There was a silence ... Then came the first boom of cannon fire.

Desponsamus te, mare, in signum veri perpetuique dominii. And a new thunderstorm exploded.

CANTO XXIII

FALSE PROPHETS

Sofia, a young laundress by trade, held her six-year-old son tightly by the hand; both were on the farthest fringes of the crowd, on the docks close to the Arsenal. Her son Ettore was greedily demolishing a pink and white *gelato* which seemed almost as big as his head and seemed likely, at any minute, to fall onto the cobbles. The boy licked his lips, turning the ice-cream to try and catch any drips. His mother, Sofia, smiled coyly at the dashing young gallant who had walked with them a little way, then turned back to her son, a little irritated. She leaned over and sighed. 'Ettore, please be careful! If you hold it like that, the *gelato* is bound to fa—'

There was a sudden, terrible shriek nearby, followed by a thunderous roar. At first Sofia thought it was an earthquake. She fell to the ground, shielding Ettore's body with her own. A few metres away, the whole facade of a villa seemed to tremble. Clouds of dust shrouded everything, and from everywhere came the sound of wheezing and coughing. Sofia opened one eye, and above the haze of smoke and dust, realised she could now see into the villa – the facade had crumbled to nothing and she could see the richly furnished apartments. On the threshold of a second-floor room, which now opened onto a gaping void, stood a dazed, elderly man at a doorway who seemed to be saying something she could not make out. A cannon ball from the *Gioia De Corfù* had devastated the *palazzo*. The laundress looked down at her best dress, now filthy and torn. She checked to make sure Ettore was unhurt. She had grazed herself in the fall, and blood trickled from a small cut on her forehead. Numbed by shock, she stared down at Ettore. Next to him lay his fallen ice-cream.

'*Mamma mia* … Ettore, what did I tell you about that ice-cream?'

Pietro, meanwhile, had safely steered his skiff back to the piazza San Marco. Behind him, in the middle of the *laguna*, the *Bucintoro* and the *Negronne* were laboriously wheeling about, desperate to be out of range of enemy fire. The numberless small boats, which had been frozen in a picturesque tableau, were now scattered about, cutting across one another as they raced for safety. Immediate catastrophe had been avoided and while the battle still raged farther out, Pietro rushed back to the doge's palace. The crowds, still dazed and unsure what had happened, were torn between laughter and fear, between applause and utter panic at the spectacle.

Pietro glanced up at the *Campanile* – the cables which had served for the *Salto della Morte* had since been cut by the men of the Quarantia Criminale. When Pietro reached the gates of the palace he crashed headlong into an agent attempting to secure the building. The agent turned, sweating, on the verge of drawing his sword and running the newcomer through, but recognised Pietro and allowed him to pass.

Inside, the fighting carried on, though the Firebirds posted on the roof of the palace and above the prison had realised that the attempt on Francesco Loredan had failed, and that the warships of the Arsenal had held the Chimera's galleys and frigates at bay. The attempt to take the port by force had failed. News of the rout travelled through the *palazzo* like wildfire. Though the battle had begun on all fronts simultaneously, and with extraordinary speed, still the Striges had been routed. While soldiers outside tried to contain the panicked crowd, inside, Pietro made his way through the courtyard. Some of the Firebirds had surrendered, others, overcome by despair, slipped down the lead roofs and plunged into the palace, their capes fluttering behind them. Around the Scala d'Oro and beneath the statues of Sansovino, men were engaged in hand-to-hand combat, bounding over balustrades, leaping from behind pillars, and jumping from balconies onto the harlequin tiles beneath. From everywhere came the screams and cries of the wounded, the crack of gunfire, and everywhere was pervaded by the smoke and smell of gunpowder.

Pietro considered the bedlam for a moment, and sighed heavily. *Accursed day*. Then, collecting himself, he drew his sword and stepped into the chaos. *The time had come to put an end to this!*

Out on the *laguna*, the battle between the flotillas resembled a Canaletto painting filtered through the mind of Breugel. In the waning day, great white clouds flecked with sunset rolled across the sky, and fire flashed from the cannons adding something apocalyptic to the scene. Galleys, frigates and *sottili* sliced through the waters, tacking, repositioning, and firing broadside. From the deck of the *Bucintoro*, it was possible to see, silhouetted against the sky, figures in the rigging of the decks.

The doge was once more seated on his throne on the poop deck of the galley. By his side, the French ambassador, wide-eyed, contemplated the spectacle, uncertain how to react to everything he had witnessed since his arrival. He turned to Francesco Loredan, seeking reassurance.

'*Serenissimus* … all this …'

The doge, still trying to compose himself as Pavi directed the crew to turn the ship about, smiled beneath his mask.

'This … This is a pageant …'

'Indeed?' said Pierre-François de Villedieu sceptically.

'Oh yes. We re-enact a celebrated battle each year on the feast of the Ascension. It is ...' he cleared his throat, 'It is something of a tradition.'

The ambassador looked at the doge and then back out to the violent spectacle being played out on the *laguna*. Suddenly, a cloud of smoke rose towards the heavens and the *Gioia De Corfù*, with infinite slowness, began to list. The mizzen-mast was shattered, flames rose from the prow and the galley was clearly taking in water on all sides. As it listed more steeply, enemy sailors began to leap from the decks and the rigging and, finally, the galley foundered beneath the waves. Some distance away, seeing the battle was lost, the *Santa Maria* tacked into the wind, sails framed against by the setting sun, and retreated under the hail of cannon-fire. Only a number of small frigates now remained but, seeing the galley retreat, they too began to turn tail. As he watched all this play out, Pierre-François de Villedieu's smile had paled to a terrified grimace; now his smile returned. He looked again at the doge.

'It ... looks so ... so real ...' he said, astonished.

'It does, does it not?' replied the doge.

As the *Gioia De Corfù* finally disappeared beneath the waves, the ambassador gave a little cry of joy and began to applaud.

'Bravo! Bravo! That was marvellous, truly splendid!'

Clearly the Venetians knew how to entertain themselves.

'The enemy is retreating!'

At these words, the soldier ran into the courtyard of the doge's palace, followed by a fresh company of men despatched from the Mercerie. As he stepped into the courtyard he found Pietro Viravolta crouching over the body of a Firebird he had just run through. The hooded figure still writhed on the flagstones. Pietro pulled out his bloodied blade and looked around him.

Of the Firebirds who had hurtled down the cables,

rained down from the rooftops, and leapt from the balconies, barely a handful remained. Pietro picked his way through a courtyard littered with corpses. From nowhere, a man lunged at him and Pietro dodged the blade, parried a second thrust, then dropped to one knee and whipped his own blade round, neatly cutting his adversary's throat. A moment later, he climbed the steps of the Scala d'Oro; other bodies lay spread-eagled on the stairs, some of them mortally wounded and begging for the *coup de grâce*. Reaching the top of the flight of steps, he saw a Firebird, encircled, drop his sword and surrender to several of Pavi's men. To his left, hiding in the shadows, another of them, panicked, tried to rid himself of his cloak hoping that he might disappear unnoticed in the confusion. He looked up and saw the point of Pietro's blade ready to run him through. Pietro smiled. 'Decided to change camps?'

Fortunately, there had been little fighting on the upper floors of the palace, so it proved easy to find the last of the Firebirds who had sought refuge in the sala del collegio. The enemy's attempt to free the prisoners in *i Piombi* had served them ill. The Striges now realised that they had emptied cells which they themselves would now fill.

As Pietro left the *palazzo ducale* with the triumphant men of the Quarantia Criminale, he came face to face with a little girl in a blue skirt. She held out a collection box.

'Messer!' The little girl smiled radiantly.

'Messer! Something for the school of Santa Trinità …'

Pietro smiled back.

By some nameless miracle, the revelries of carnival had continued uninterrupted. As if by magic, the people of Venice lost not one whit of their aplomb. The noise of battle had merely merged with the general gaiety and confusion. Word began to spread that the whole thing was a hoax staged for their benefit, a rumour the authorities were only too happy to confirm. At the Rialto, where the offices of the judiciary had been occupied, the Firebirds, isolated and cornered, were forced to surrender. The honour had fallen to the Queen of Hearts to slip into the room which had been barricaded by von Maarken's men to pick up the gun which had fired the final shot.

The carnival festivities held in honour of *La Sensa* in the year of our Lord 1756, were unparalleled.

Aboard the *Bucintoro*, the ambassador stooped and whispered into the doge's ear: 'It's extraordinary!'

Then, remembering that it is imprudent for a diplomat to be so fulsome in his praise, he added: 'A little theatrical, of course ...'

Francesco Loredan smiled but said nothing. He heaved a long sigh of relief. The *festa della Sensa* was over.

CANTO XXIV
THE WELL OF THE GIANTS

A team of six horses, fervently whipped on by the coachman, pulled Eckhart von Maarken's carriage along the road from Marghera. The renegade duke had taken little time to have his trunks loaded and the coach departed immediately. His face expressionless, he gazed out at the landscape as it flickered past. In a few short hours, his dream had crumbled to nothing. From time to time, von Maarken let his head fall into his hands, struggling to stifle the rage, the terror he could feel creeping within him, for now he was condemned to leave the Most Serene Republic, never to return; the vision of his failure melded with the banishment he had already suffered. He would never be able to reclaim his lands or his chattels, much of which had already been redistributed by the Empress Maria Theresa. The coachman's cries, the crack of the whip, the whinny of the horses, the clouds of dust which swirled about him; all these things seemed to drop into his consciousness as into a bottomless well, as though there were some veil between him and reality. This was a nightmare, a nightmare which had begun when he had first been banished. *All is lost*, he thought, *all is lost*.

He clenched his fists. He had left as he had arrived, in haste, a traitor, a deposed aristocrat, a man with no cause but his own. The doge had won. He was still alive. Ottavio and Vicario were dead. The Firebirds – the Striges conjured from another man's nightmare – had surrendered their weapons. Only he and *il Diavolo* had managed to escape. Now they posed a mortal threat to one another – as indeed they always had, thought von Maarken. One man was to blame to all this: Pietro Viravolta. For some unfathomable reason when he had had the Black Orchid at his mercy, when he might have crushed him, *il Diavolo* had allowed him to live. It had been at that moment, surely, that their fortunes had changed. Eckhart still raged to think of it.

And now? Flee. He would flee to some nameless land. He could no longer return to Austria, for the only thing awaiting him there was a prison cell. He would head for France where he had a number of powerful friends; there perhaps he might find the means of his reinstatement. The mere thought of his exile caused his eyes to well with tears of impotent rage. He had nothing now, he was alone and friendless, but he would rise again. The most important thing now was to take refuge, to hide out somewhere where he might knit together once more the tattered rags of honour and pride. He was Duke von Maarken still, though for all the world he felt like a king in exile.

Perhaps it was a premonition, some vague intuition, that made him lean out of the carriage window at that moment. For a moment he was dazzled by the scene: the horizon was lined with cypresses, and here and there lakes and valleys glimmered in the early sunlight. His gaze swept round to take in the muddy track along which they had come and, in the distance, he thought he could make out a dark pinprick; something so small he hardly noticed it at first. But as it drew nearer, Eckhart von Maarken peered more closely.

A man on horseback was following them, his black cape fluttering and snapping in his wake, riding hell for leather. The sleeves of his white shirt billowed and he spurred his mount harder, faster. Between gritted teeth, Eckhart von Maarken muttered an oath. *It is he!* Pietro Viravolta was gaining on him.

*

As soon as he knew of the existence of the Villa Marghera, where the Firebirds had gathered after their rituals in the sinister crypt in Mestre, Pietro had ridden out to the place with a detachment of men from the Quarantia Criminale. He hoped he might arrive in time to unmask the Chimera and Eckhart von Maarken; though he now thought they were one and the same man. Before nightfall, he had arrived at an imposing mansion, the portico framed by antic columns, the grand facade surmounted by a cupola of crystal through which light flooded, illuminating the great reception rooms and banqueting halls. There were ample signs that the mansion had been used – hooded robes lay abandoned on the floor but the mansion had been deserted … or almost deserted.

A slow-witted man crouched in a corner of the villa. Pietro discovered he was von Maarken's valet, and had helped the duke to load his trunks. The valet too had been about to flee, but hearing the soldiers arrive, had hidden in an armoire beneath the stairs. It had been a simple matter to loosen the man's tongue and, with a bony finger, he indicated the direction von Maarken had taken. Before the man had finished speaking, Pietro was already in the saddle.

Already he had put a considerable distance between himself and his escort from the Quarantia, so Pietro rode on alone, an errant knight in search of the grail, galloping through the rising mists of evening as the sun dipped behind the cypresses. He was now within an arrow's flight of the carriage. He spurred his stallion on, reaching down to draw a pistol from his belt. He aimed at the carriage, but it was not yet within range and he resolved not to waste his bullet. On he rode, his arm held taut, the pistol like an extension of his hand.

Viravolta! The duke drew his head back inside the carriage, wiping his feverish brow. He had not expected this. He tried to steady his trembling hands, to ignore the cold sweat he could feel trickle along his spine, and his gloved fingers gripped his cane. He leaned out the window again and hailed the coachman.

'Faster, *faster*!'

The whip cracked, the bridle snapped, and the team of horses strained every muscle. But still the Black Orchid was behind them and drawing nearer.

'In God's name *faster*!' roared Eckhart von Maarken.

The carriage jolted and jerked along the rutted path. The duke was hurled to left and right; it was all that he could do not to topple from his seat. He clutched the small purple curtain to steady himself, swore again, and put his head out of the window once more.

The man pursuing them was nearer still, his billowing cape like the grotesque wings of a bat; suddenly *he* seemed like a demon in a curious reversal of fortune – the Striges seemed to have turned their coats.

The duke gaped at the demon; it was no longer a man but a myth, a legend who pursued him. The galloping hooves. The dust. The pandemonium.

'Faster!' von Maarken howled at the coachman, his blood thumping in his temples, his face purple with fear and rage.

Pietro drew closer; soon he was close enough that the dust-cloud from the carriage swirled about him as he rode; the noise was deafening – seeming somehow louder than the tumult of the crowds the day before. Pietro spurred his horse on, closing in on the rear left corner of the carriage.

He calculated whether he might jump, a treacherous leap from saddle to axle, which might leaving him sprawling in the dirt. For a moment, he almost succumbed to the temptation, but finally resolved to spur his horse on again until he drew alongside. For a moment they rode side by side, Pietro bent over his horse, his hair whipped by the wind as Eckhart von Maarken stared at him through eyes as wide and glassy as the *cristallo* Federico Spadetti had once conceived for the Guild of Glaziers of Murano.

I have not forgotten you, Federico! You and your boy, Tazzio, and his beloved Severina in her crystal gown. It was at that moment that Pietro aimed his pistol and fired.

'No!' von Maarken roared, his arms flung wide.

The coachman's body jerked, his tricorn hat taken by the wind and thin wisps of red hair whipped in the breeze like the strings of a marionette. His body slumped forward, his waistcoat pierced by a single bullet-hole, and teetered for an instant, as if choosing whether to fall and be crushed beneath the wheels, or crash into the ditch. In the end, the lifeless coachman did not fall but remained slumped in the seat, a dead man clutching the reins of a funeral carriage. It was a hellish sight: the man's hair whipped wildly, foam flecked his mouth; his eyes seemed to glow like torches as the six horses galloped on, guided only by his dead hand.

As he fired the shot, Pietro had wheeled his horse wide of the coach; now he rode back and, as soon as he came alongside, he loosened his feet from the stirrups, crouched on the broad back of his mount and leapt into the void, catching the rope which secured von Maarken's trunks to the roof of the carriage. Knees bent, his boots almost level with the rear axle, Pietro clung to the back of the coach. The duke, hearing something, peered out the window once more and was surprised to see the Black Orchid's horse galloping riderless; von Maarken craned his neck and, from the fluttering of his cloak, realised that Pietro was aboard the coach. *Leave me be!*

Pietro steadied himself, freed one hand, drew his sword and, with a flick, turned it so that the hilt was aligned with the wheels of the carriage. His grip slackened and, for a moment, he thought he might fall but he caught himself in time then, bending as well as he was able, he thrust the hilt of his sword between the wheel-arch and the hub. He abandoned his first attempt as a judder ran through his shoulder, almost making him lose his grip. With a loud roar, he thrust again; there was a cracking sound as splintered wood sprayed everywhere, the wheel spun loose and almost broke free of the axle. Pietro released the rope and jumped down onto the dusty path, falling on his back with a painful jolt. Gasping for breath he swept away his cloak which had fallen over his eyes and turned to look at the carriage.

Twenty metres further down the road, the wheel came free, rolling away into the ditch. The coach seemed to crumple. With a screech of wood it tipped backwards, gouging furrows into the dry path, before toppling completely. The horses, dragged by the dead weight, veered to the right; the trunks which had been tethered to the roof fell one by one. The rope snapped and, in a terrifying cloud of dust, the carriage plunged down the sharp incline.

Pietro got to his feet. No bones broken. He raced to the edge of the incline. It was a curious spectacle. At the foot of the hill, what remained of the carriage had landed in a swamp. The horses had bolted, the body of the coachman had been thrown to one side, and the trunks had disgorged their gold, jewels and silks. As for Eckhart von Maarken, he had been thrown clear of the coach as it plunged into the ravine. Beneath his cloak one of his legs jutted out at a strange angle as he lay there, motionless in the mud, his face smeared with blood, breathing in hoarse, wheezing gasps.

Pietro ran down the short incline and over to where his enemy lay. At first, the duke saw nothing but a silver buckle and a pair of leather boots. He tried to lift his head, and the pain forced him to whimper like a wounded animal.

The way a lizard can dash
Under the dog day's scourge, darting out
Between the hedges so that it seems a flash
Of lightning as it spurts across the road.
So did a fiery little serpent rush
Toward the bellies of the two who stayed;

Peppercorn black and livid, it struck out,
Transfixing one in the place where we are fed
When life begins – then fell before his feet,
Outstretched …

'Do you recognise those lines, von Maarken?' Pietro asked. 'They are from Dante Alighieri – the punishment of those condemned to the Eighth Circle of the Inferno – the hypocrites transformed into serpents. This is the Circle reserved for the souls of the Panderers and the Seducers, the False Prophets, the Sowers of Discord. The tables have been turned, and it is we who now mete out the punishments.'

Pietro stood, not deigning to stoop to help the duke who stretched out a hand towards him.

'It is over, von Maarken,' said Pietro.

The duke twisted his mouth into a bitter smile and a feeble laugh came from his lips. His hand fell back into the mud.

'That … that is what you think … But there … there is still one …'

Pietro's face hardened, and he knelt beside Eckhart von Maarken.

'By which you mean *il Diavolo* …' he said. 'Who is he? Who can he be, if not you?'

Von Maarken's laugh dissolved into a strangled whimper; his cold blue eyes staring defiantly, his white hair streaked with blood, his face a rictus of hatred. His breathing was laboured now.

'He is … he is …'

Pietro crouched lower, straining to hear. The duke smiled. 'He is your worst nightmare.'

A hoarse moan juddered through Eckhart von Maarken's body as he breathed his last, and his soul returned to hell whence, perhaps, it had come.

Pietro stood by the swamp for a long time, by the

broken coach foundering in the Devil's quagmire, the yawning trunks, and the two lifeless bodies sprawled in this desolate landscape. He sighed wearily. Lucifer was still at liberty.

Two thousand noblemen were once more gathered in the chamber of the Maggior Consiglio; the doge, at one end of the hall, sat enthroned beneath Tintoretto's magisterial *Paradise*.

The benches of the chamber were half empty now, for those among the nobility who had offered their support to the Striges, now unmasked, were elsewhere in the palace, submitting to the tender mercies of the Tenebræ. For their crimes, many would be publicly executed; those whom the Criminale had not identified, sat on the benches and applauded those very men against whose doom, only yesterday, they had plotted. What was important now was that the republic be united; that the Maggior Consiglio offer the doge their unconditional support. It was for this reason that the Maggior Consiglio, together with the Senate, had met today in conclave. There were plaudits and rewards for those who had distinguished themselves by their courage and devotion in the terrible tribulations the *Serenissima* had suffered. Ricardo Pavi was absent from the proceedings, since he was busy in *i Piombi* pursuing his investigation, but he had already been acclaimed for his heroism on the *Bucintoro* and on the Piazza San Marco. The Queen of Hearts, who had shown her mettle in the battle for the Rialto, was the darling of the proceedings, and dozens of would-be suitors clamoured about her as she flicked her fan. The *capo* of the Arsenal, bedecked with medals, stood leaning on the golden pommel of his cane next to Francesco Loredan.

Having emerged from her safe haven in Castello, Anna Santamaria, noble and regal, was admired by all present. Though she still wore widow's weeds, everyone knew the dangers she had faced and the terrible role Ottavio had played in the abortive *coup d'état*. She was, in the eyes of the nobility, victim and princess, and all were content to learn of her undimmed love for the Black Orchid – an agent whom so recently these very men had booed and jeered, some even calling for his execution. Anna Santamaria, graceful and dignified, smiled and nodded to those about her, then withdrew to stand next to her lover. Pietro, his manservant Landretto by his side, relished this moment of tranquillity. Francesco Loredan was about to speak; the nobles returned to their benches and little by little the laughter and conversation died away and everyone gazed at those standing by the doge's throne: the Black Orchid with Anna Santamaria, the Queen of Hearts, and the head of the Arsenal.

Francesco Loredan smiled and, wordlessly, gave a signal. Escorted by two halberdiers, the olive-skinned pageboy, wearing his blue turban, came to stand by the doge. Francesco winked at the boy, and gave him the *bacheta* and the sceptre to hold. It was a comical moment, for the child, who needed both hands to hold the velvet cushion, tucked the sceptre under his arm, the golden pommel peeking out over his shoulder, and could not suppress a giggle. Then Francesco Loredan turned to the head of the Arsenal and pinned a new decoration to the countless medals on his chest. The doge warmly shook the man's hand and said a few words which the chamber could not hear, then moved on. The Queen of Hearts and Anna Santamaria curtsied and knelt before His Serene Highness, the Prince of Venice. The doge bade them rise and pinned on each bosom a brooch encrusted with precious stones depicting the Winged Lion of Venice.

Lastly, he turned to Pietro. 'For you, I reasoned, a medal would not be appropriate,' confided Loredan, fumbling beneath his robes and bringing out a flower. Smiling, Pietro Viravolta de Lansalt took the black orchid.

'Now you are once more one of us,' whispered

Francesco Loredan. Then, opening his arms, he gestured to the four to turn towards the assembly.

'Behold the champions of Venice!' intoned the doge as he took the sceptre from the pageboy, and turned to face the assembled chamber. A thunderous roar erupted as two thousand pairs of hands applauded and such shouts of joy and celebration made it seem as if Tintoretto's *Paradise* had come to life.

Anna stood beside the Black Orchid, slipped her arm through his. Next to them was placed Landretto, the Queen of Hearts, and a bevy of her suitors.

'Well then, Messer,' said the Queen of Hearts, suddenly contemplating Pietro with new interest, 'What will you do now there are no more birds to hunt? Will you remain in the service of the republic? Or do you intend to seek new horizons now that your cherished freedom has been restored to you?'

'Well, I have not …'

'Know one thing, *amico mio*,' she continued, not waiting for his reply, 'if ever you should have need of a guide to show you new horizons, I am entirely at your disposal.'

Anna Santamaria's smile faded and she stood on tiptoe and whispered into Pietro's ear: 'Look at her once more and I shall kill you …'

Pietro stifled a laugh as Anna turned to the Queen of Hearts with a glacial smile. The latter gave an insolent laugh but, realising that her cause was futile, she cast an admiring glance at the lad who stood beside the Black Orchid.

'And what of you, young man?'

'Me … of me?' said Landretto, surprised.

'And why not you!' said the Queen of Hearts, clicking her tongue. 'Do you like hunting? The thrill of the chase?'

Landretto broke into a broad smile and doffed his hat, attempting to maintain his composure.

'It is … I am …'

Pietro laughed again. 'Dear Queen of Hearts, in Landretto you would find much more than a manservant: Landretto is a king and a kingdom besides; without him we would not be standing here now. Is that not so, *amico* …'

Pietro stopped as he saw Ricardo Pavi enter the chamber. Something about his grave expression amid these smiling faces attracted his attention. The chief of the Quarantia Criminale, who was widely expected to succeed Emilio Vindicati as head of the Council of Ten, strode into the chamber and headed towards the Black Orchid. He placed a hand on Pietro's shoulder and moved to draw him to one side. Pietro made his apologies to Anna Santamaria and the learned assembly and the two men withdrew. Pavi spoke in an urgent whisper.

'I have just returned from *i Piombi*, my friend. I had become convinced that these interrogations would yield nothing, but this morning we succeeded in loosening the tongue of one of the Striges. After four hours of torture on the rack he confessed everything. He was surely one of the few to know, Pietro …'

Pavi stared into Pietro's eyes. 'I have discovered the true identity of *il Diavolo*.'

Pietro's smile vanished and his expression darkened. The two men faced one another in silence for a long moment, then Pavi leaned and whispered something into Pietro's ear. A name, a single word, which caused Pietro's face to pale. He turned to look at Pavi, but the conviction he saw in the man's eyes left no room for doubt. At last, the many enigmas of this affair slid into place, as the last piece of a puzzle may change all that went before. Pietro brought a trembling hand to his face; the conspiracy was more terrible, more fiendish, than anything the Black Orchid had imagined. And yet now that it was revealed, it seemed self-evident, and he cursed himself.

It was a moment before Pietro recovered from the shock

of these revelations. He gestured to Pavi to wait for him and strode over to Anna.

'What is it?' she asked, her eyes wide with fear.

Pietro clenched his teeth and resettled his tricorn. 'I am afraid I have a mission yet to finish. Wait here for me, I pray, and do not worry on my account, I shall return soon.'

'But ...'

Already Pietro had stooped to kiss the brow of the Black Widow and turned on his heel. The Queen of Hearts, smiling, raised a glass as he passed.

'Do you know where he may be found?' Pietro asked Pavi.

'He too has fled, and with more success than Eckhart von Maarken. According to our informer, he is now at large in Florence.'

'Florence?' Pietro frowned. 'Then perhaps I shall be absent somewhat longer than I first thought.'

Il Diavolo was in *Florence*. Of course. The city where Dante Alighieri had penned his masterpiece.

'Ricardo ...'

Pavi turned and saw the black look on Pietro's face.

'He is mine.'

Chocardiel, of the Cherubim of the Abyss and the order of Python-Luzbel, had been returned, bloody and beaten, to his dank cell in the *pozzi*. In the darkness – for in the wells beneath the palace there was no shaft of light – the man whimpered and moaned. He still wore the robes of the Firebirds, his cloak and hood had been torn, and became sodden as the *acqua alta* rose once more. He shivered as water began to trickle into his cell, leaking from every crack and fissure in the walls. Chocardiel would die here, this he knew; but he knew too that the Chimera was doomed. With a lump of coal, he scratched on the damp walls of his dungeon until his fingers and his nails bled. Chocardiel wrote words of no consequence, words which no one would trouble to read, and he drew crosses and strange figures which sprang from his diseased imagination. Here, in his season in hell, he conjured an imaginary paradise. *The Giants! The Giants!* They were all here now. All the Firebirds who had dreamed of being giants languished here in chains until death came to free them. And with a voice made hoarse with madness, he repeated over and over, 'To see paradise ...

For, as on Monteriggione's wall appear
Towers that crown its circle, here, arrayed
All round the bank encompassing the pit
With half their bulk like towers above it, stood
Horrible giants, whom Jove still rumbles at
With menace when he thunders ...

'Paradise ... paradise, to see paradise ...' The words went on and on until at last they were lost in the silence and Chocardiel was swallowed up by darkness.

THE NINTH CIRCLE

CANTO XXV

THE TRAITORS

A small orchestra was playing on the Piazza San Lorenzo. Passers-by stopped to listen for a time, then went about their affairs. The *piazza* was a charming square which still retained something of the golden age of Florence, of the reign of Cosimo the Elder, a noble patron of the arts. Nearby stood the Basilica di San Lorenzo, the simple, unadorned masterpiece designed by Brunelleschi, which had once been the parish church of the Medici. Here were interred some of the most celebrated members, their sepulchres adorned with Michelangelo's majestic statuary: the tomb of Giuliano de Medici flanked by the statues depicting night and day, two companion figures, dusk and dawn reclined between sleep and wakefulness on the sarcophagus of Lorenzo.

In the second row of the small orchestra, Pietro Viravolta bowed his violin. It had been a real pleasure to take up the instrument once more, and though at first his colleagues had had to compensate for an occasional false note, with practice, he had regained some of his erstwhile virtuosity. Pietro, his face powdered, was wearing a periwig and a white jacket braided with gold thread and billowing sleeves. As he played, he thought of his youth, of the time when, fresh from the army, he had returned to Venice and earned his keep playing his violin for the nobility at elegant soirées in San Samuele.

It was a clement June afternoon and the sky was a

limpid blue. As he continued to play, Pietro watched the comings and goings on the piazza and, in particular, kept close watch on a man with a neat grey beard who circled around the orchestra and then came towards him. He did not wait until the music had stopped, but leaned towards Viravolta and whispered over the music: 'You see that man yonder?'

Some twenty metres away stood a plump dwarf wearing a red waistcoat and beneath it white shirt with a large ruff, baggy pantaloons and dark boots. Pietro nodded.

'Follow him … But be wary. The dwarf will lead you to the man you seek.'

Pietro nodded again, almost imperceptibly, and his eyes blazed. There could be no question of forsaking his mission now. He continued to play, picking out a cascade of *pizzicati*, before joining the orchestra in the long, sonorous *glissando* which brought the concerto to a close.

As he followed the dwarf through the maze of streets of Florence, Pietro thought of the city's most famous son, Dante Alighieri. The poet had been born here, and it was here that he had first set eyes on Beatrice, his *inamorata*, whom he had seen only three times, and to whom he had never addressed a word. It was she who would one day play a central role in his *Divina Commedia*. As he crossed the Piazza del Duomo, Pietro stopped for a moment in the shadow of the cathedral to contemplate the great bronze doors of the baptistry depicting *The Gates of Paradise*. Dante's *Commedia*, Pietro remembered, had not been christened *Divina* until after the death of the author, perhaps in honour of *il Paradiso*, the dazzling vision of God with which it concluded.

If God was in his Heaven, Pietro Viravolta was still on the trail of the Devil, the man who called himself *il Diavolo*, inspired by the Prince of Lies in Dante's epic. Nor did Pietro yet know how the battle between good and evil might end. There was no way to know whether this

Commedia, like Dante's, would end with a vision of paradise and the blazing glory of God. Venice had only just emerged from its inferno, perhaps to *purgatorio*, but Pietro would never know paradise, by the side of Anna Santamaria, until he had first descended to the Ninth Circle of hell.

The dwarf turned left out of the piazza, Pietro shadowing him close behind. They were walking more quickly now, circling down towards the Arno, and their footfalls rang out against the ancient stone, sounding in Pietro's mind like funeral bells tolling for those whose sins had led him to this place.

The First Circle: Marcello Torretone: PAGANISM
The Second Circle: Cosimo Caffelli: LUST
The Third Circle: Federico Spadetti: GREED
The Fourth Circle: Luciana Saliestri: PRODIGALITY
The Fifth Circle: Emilio Vindicati: WRATH
The Sixth Circle: Giovanni Campioni: HERESY
The Seventh Circle: Andreas Vicario: VIOLENCE
The Eight Circle: the failed attempt on Francesco Loredan/Eckhart von Maarken: FALSE PROPHETS AND SOWERS OF DISCORD
The Ninth Circle: ... TREASON

If Dante's epic had circumscribed the evils and the sins of Florence under the Medici, such evils had continued unabated after his death. Florence remained a city where treason and perfidy sat side by side with the greatest artists of the age – from Donatello and Fra Angelico to da Vinci and Michelangelo. The intricate corruption of the city had flourished for centuries, and it was here that the Chimera had sought refuge.

Pietro remained in the shadows as he continued his curious tour of the city. Near the Palazzo Vecchio, by the vast chessboard on which, as was the custom, two noblemen were engaged in a game of chess using Florentine citizens as their chess pieces, the dwarf stopped and began an animated discussion with a tall, gangling cleric. Pietro crept around the life-size chessboard, past the Rook and the Bishop. Then, suddenly, the dwarf broke off his conversation and hurried on. Pietro dashed across the chessboard, almost knocking over a young man dressed as a pawn as he did so, and followed the dwarf into the open-air gallery known as the *loggia*, saluting Benvenuto Cellini's statue of Perseus as they passed. Pietro lost sight of the dwarf for a moment, then saw him striding west along the banks of the Arno. It seemed as if the man he was following had been ordered to take this strange, circuitous route; he stopped again, this time to speak to a goldsmith on the Ponte Vecchio. After half an hour had passed, Pietro began to wonder if this was not some farce, until finally they arrived at the church of Santa Maria Novella bathed in the halo of the blood-red sun as it grazed the distant horizon.

Pietro stood for a moment, watching from a safe distance as the dwarf pushed open the great double doors and stepped into the darkness of this basilica which was as sumptuous and elegant as the Duomo itself. Pietro stood on the piazza before the church, opened his cloak and let his hand slip to the hilt of his sword. He took a long, deep breath, then strode towards the portico. The great double doors screeched as Pietro pushed them open. He stepped into the darkness and stood, motionless, waiting for his eyes to adjust. At the far end of the basilica stood the dwarf, who was whispering something to a dark-robed figure. The other man replied, and the dwarf, turning towards Pietro for an instant, nodded before abruptly disappearing into the shadows.

Il Diavolo now stood alone, motionless, framed by the gleam of the high altar. The Black Orchid stepped out of the darkness and into the dim glow of the nave; his hand never leaving the hilt of his sword. For a long time the two men stood in silence, contemplating one another across a space that seemed narrow and yet infinite. At length, Pietro spoke, his voice echoing among the vaults and columns of the basilica.

'Why?'

Pietro could not measure the silence that followed for, to him, it seemed never-ending. When he could bear it no longer, he reiterated his question: 'Why, Emilio, why?'

CANTO XXVI

LUCIFER

I once was as you are, you shall be as I am. These words were inscribed above the skeletal figure which dominated Masaccio's *Trinity*. The masterpiece which had first illustrated the idea of perspective hung in a side chapel of the basilica. Had Emilio Vindicati stood next to it, the illusion of perspective would have been the greater, for it was easy to imagine *il Diavolo* crouching over the grinning image of Vanity; easy to imagine that the Chimera was a figure ripped from the darkest shadows of this sacred image.

'Why, Emilio?' Pietro posed the question a third time as he walked between the pillars of the transept.

Emilio Vindicati smiled and said:

Vexilla Regis prodeunt Inferni
Towards us; therefore look in front of thee,
My Master said, 'if thou discernest him.'

Pietro took another step towards this Devil he had so long sought, and it was he now who spoke:

'Behold the place
Where thou with fortitude must arm thyself.'
How frozen I became and powerless then,
Ask it not, Reader, for I write it not,
Because all language would be insufficient.

Pietro took another step.

I did not die, and I alive remained not;
Think for thyself now, hast thou aught of wit,
What I became, being of both deprived.

The Emperor of the kingdom dolorous
From his mid-breast forth issued from the ice …

Pietro stopped.

Vindicati stood upon the steps of the high altar, Pietro a few metres from him.

'Lucifer,' said Vindicati with a smile, spreading his arms wide like a master of ceremonies. 'Welcome to the Church of Santa Maria of the Vinyards. Did you know that? La Novella was built upon the spot where the oratory of Santa Maria della Vigna was once built. I was raised in Venice, Pietro, but it was here in Florence that I was born, and the sons and daughters of Florence have been my inspiration: Dante, and the Medici … No doubt you had forgotten. I am pleased to see you managed to follow Feodor without difficulty. Now, here we are, in a basilica, just as we were when we last met. In the house of God, you have come face to face with Lucifer. It is a fitting irony, do you not think?'

Pietro heard the creak of doors behind him and turned. Feodor the dwarf had closed the great doors of Santa Maria Novella and now slid a large beam into place to secure it.

Pietro turned back to Vindicati. 'I believed in you, Emilio. That night in San Marco, I …'

'Ah, Pietro, it has been a magnificent escapade. From the day I had you released from *i Piombi*, I knew you would be blind, utterly blind until the moment you believed you watched me die. One of the Striges played the role of Lucifer that night, while I played out my death throes before your eyes. But my body, you remember, was never found. I watched as you dashed hither, and you, always vigilant, never resting for a moment. I was forced to admire your talent. You were – you *are* – the better man. I knew it. I had always known it, and this knowledge makes defeat less bitter somehow. You were my greatest triumph, and my greatest mistake. And I was your guide, I was the twin faces of a single coin – in hell I was your Virgil, in Venice, your Devil. Did you never think that Virgil leading Dante through the twists and turns of his own soul is merely one among the many faces of Lucifer, the innate evil in his conscience? Does not Virgil save the poet by showing him the sins of the world?'

'But that night, Emilio, that night in the Basilica di San Marco … Why did you not kill me?'

'A witness, Pietro, I needed a witness to my own death. What better irony than to choose *you*. My plan was proceeding masterfully. And now, Pietro Viravolta de Lansalt, whom I first dubbed the Black Orchid, we come to the end of our journey. To the last circle. No doubt you have already guessed the ending. The Ninth Circle *was you*. Who better than you to serve my plan? The Black Orchid was already a legend. You epitomised them all, you alone were the quintessence of the cardinal vices on which I based my little charade: atheist, libertine, adulterer, glutton, charlatan, boor, liar, the list is endless. Imagine how sweet it felt for me to overthrow a debauched Venice using as my tool, the very personification of that debauchery. Yes, Pietro, *you*! I chose you to lead the investigation, ably supported by the Council of Ten and the Quarantia Criminale. I had only to observe your progress, which I did with the blessing of the doge and of the Maggior Consiglio. Marcello was but a means to an end – so were they all – Caffelli and Campioni, Luciana Saliestri, the astrologer Fregolo … all pawns just as you were. It was a simple matter to ensure your every move was watched. I had three captains at the Arsenal ready to do my bidding. Vicario controlled the guilds. We held all the cards.'

Pietro shook his head. He could see the flicker of madness in Vindicati's eyes.

'And you thought you could overthrow Francesco Loredan ...'

Vindicati gave a sardonic smile. 'Pietro, I beg you ... open your eyes! For you, whom the republic clapped in irons and would have executed, this is some jest. You saw what happened at carnival – this is what we have become: costumed puppets manipulated by a puppet government! And I was a king among these marionettes, I was chief of the Council of Ten, the Tenebræ, the best and the worst of all of them. But consider for a moment how the world perceives Venice: it is an artificial city which at any moment may be engulfed by corruption, dissembling, treachery – the stock in trade of the *Broglio*. With unbridled nepotism we have destroyed the equality that is the right of every nobleman; we people the Senate and the Maggior Consiglio with our idiot sons – what wonder then, if Venice is no longer great?'

'Emilio, how have you come to believe this?'

'I would have thought that you, Pietro, were opposed to bribery and partiality, I thought that you were dedicated to concord and the majesty of Venice. For my part, I have performed the vilest deeds in the service of the republic, I have spent my life rubbing shoulders with venal politicians, spies, and strangers who would leech our lifeblood, with guildsmen who would sell our secrets to our sworn enemies, with scoundrels and prostitutes. Do you know what it is like to eternally wade through the black swamp of the human heart? To drown each day in a mire of murderers, informants, wickedness and mediocrity until you could vomit up your own soul? With brutality and repression we strove to keep this wickedness in check, just as the empires of old, which had long since died of the disease. We had to take action.'

'Take action? By plotting a grisly litany of murders?'

'That was but a drop in the ocean! The key lay in the institutions, Pietro, this was something your friend Giovanni Campioni understood; unfortunately, he chose the opposing camp. Look to our institutions. Look at the absurd ceremonies we have devised to elect those who govern us, those spiteful mediocrities whose only talents are pettiness and backstabbing. Venice was poised upon a powder keg and governed by incompetents playing with fire. Venice has no government; it is tossed about by events, its policies changing with the season. Not one of our esteemed magistrates is capable of imposing order, not one of our respected patricians could stanch the tide of corruption, of preventing Venice from sinking beneath a rising tide of licentiousness, inaction and indifference. Surely Campioni himself told you that it was impossible for the voice of reform to be heard? Vested interests have bought and sold the city; my only objective was to cut out the gangrene or hasten the inevitable death of the old order so that Venice might have another chance. Upon my word, Pietro, what I did, I did for the good of the republic. The Ottoman Empire sleeps, but it is there and one day will pounce. The King of Spain is allied with the pope and longs to have our wings clipped. We are ringed about by enemies; we had to find new allies.'

'Allies? Allies like Eckhart von Maarken? It is a poor jest! We forge no alliances by signing a meaningless treaty with a powerless duke who has been exiled from his own country.'

Emilio laughed contemptuously. 'Von Maarken and his lust for power served my interests; but even he was but a pawn in my game! He stepped into the trap I had prepared for him; I used his madness to my own ends and, finally, I used it to damn him. You killed him, Pietro, but in doing so, you were only fulfilling the plan I had for him. To imagine that I would deliver dominion over the seas to an alien power; he had to be a madman, a visionary caught up in a delirium of glory. But for a time I had need of him, and of his men, and his considerable wealth.'

'You are deluded,' said Pietro. '*You* are the man you struggled so hard to defeat: a visionary, a dangerous madman.'

Emilio Vindicati smiled again, letting his arms fall by his side. His smile faded. 'I am sorry you think so.'

'And so, I venture, the moment of truth is come?'

'Indeed it is.'

With a shriek of metal Pietro drew his sword.

'Very well,' said Vindicati. 'Let us finish it.'

He loosened the drawstring of the black cape embroidered with silver thread and let it fall from his shoulders to the altar steps. Slowly, he too drew his sword from its scabbard.

Pietro stepped towards Vindicati, unaware that in the half-light Feodor had scaled the pillar nearest the high altar and was now hanging there like a spider some ten feet from the ground. As his enemy passed the pillar, the dwarf hurled himself at Pietro, knocking him to the ground, and the two men tumbled between the pews. Vindicati smiled as he watched. Feodor could fight like a demon. His arm swung back, a dagger glinting in the gloom. Pietro deflected the blow from his face and roared in pain as he felt the blade sink deeply into his arm. The glint of the blade danced again in the darkness above Pietro's head and as the weight of the dwarf crushed him he could feel his hot moist breath on his face. Jolted into action by the pain, Pietro managed to pull his knees against his chest and, with a savage thrust, kicked Feodor across the aisle of the basilica. With the agility of a cat, the dwarf was on his feet in an instant, his eyes glittering as he raised his dagger once again. Pietro fumbled for his sword. His right shoulder ached from the fall and blood coursed from the wound in his arm. Two feet away, beneath the pew, he saw his blade just out of reach.

Furiously, the dwarf hurled himself at Pietro once more. Too late, he realised his error. Pietro raised his arm and Feodor saw the brief flash, heard the crack of gunfire, and fell back upon the cold marble where he writhed and thrashed, clutching himself to stop the blood haemorrhaging from his belly. His body spasmed and rolled towards the altar then, he was still.

Slowly, Pietro got to his feet, his arm still held out before him. His shirt and jacket were tattered. He looked down at Feodor, his ruff now covering his face, his tunic crimson, the lake of blood about him growing ever wider. Pietro allowed his pistol to fall clattering to the floor. Vindicati had not moved.

Pietro retrieved his sword from beneath the wooden pew. Out of breath now, and striving to suppress a grimace of pain, he stepped once more into the transept. His arm throbbed.

'Traitor,' he spat the word at Vindicati. 'You'll stop at nothing, will you?'

Vindicati gave a curt laugh and descended the steps of the high altar. The two men faced each other and took their guard.

'Do you remember, Pietro, when we would cross swords for sport?'

'Times change.'

They faced off, Pietro circumspect and on the alert, Vindicati blasé, and began to circle each other.

'Perhaps I should have enlisted you to the cause, Pietro. There is still time … why not join me?'

'You knew I would never join you, Emilio, that was why you tried to use me. Now, you are nothing. We are here, you and I, alone in this dark cathedral, and the world does not give a damn if we should live or die.'

The clash of metal echoed through Santa Maria Novella. Vindicati had lost none of his skills as a swordsman, skills he had once used to train Pietro when he had first recruited the Black Orchid as an agent of the *Serenissima*. Then they had been mentor and disciple, later they had been equals and friends, now they were simply two men duelling to the death. Along the vaulted arches of the transept, parrying and thrusting, they lunged, attacked and counter-attacked. The blades hissed like serpents in the still air, clashed and parted. With each blow, Pietro felt the pain move up his arm until it exploded in his skull; he knew he could not continue for long. He bounded towards Vindicati and pushed towards the pews. The Chimera staggered, and almost fell between the benches, and Pietro saw his chance to deal the death-blow, but Vindicati caught himself in time. The outcome still uncertain, Vindicati moved between the pews, retreating into the shadows. Suddenly, with a horrid laugh, he spun around and disappeared behind a pillar.

Pietro was sweating profusely now, his breath was ragged and he could hear the thunderous beat of his own heart in his ears. All else was silence; Vindicati had vanished. Pietro stared at the spot where the Chimera had disappeared and slowly, careful not to stumble, made his way along the pews towards it. As he reached the other end of the pew, he peered around the pillar. One of the side chapels was lit by the glow of votive candles, a Giotto altarpiece shimmering in the dancing flames. Pietro took another step. *Where are you? Show yourself!*

Pietro spun around, fearing an attack from behind. No one.

Then, like a ghost, Emilio Vindicati reappeared as suddenly as he had vanished. He roared and slashed, but Pietro dodged the blade and, wheeling round, lashed out towards Vindicati's right arm, hoping to put his enemy on an equal footing. Vindicati surprised him, ducking to avoid Pietro's thrust. The sword struck the pillar. Pietro felt a savage jolt run through his arm as the blade shattered against the stone. Pietro saw that he was holding nothing but a hilt and a few short inches of steel as Vindicati got to his feet. Pietro leapt towards him, hurling the hilt towards Vindicati's head as he rose. His aim was good: dazed, Vindicati stumbled backwards, tripping over the steps of the altar, then he fell and dropped his sword.

Pietro felt as though his whole arm was a gaping wound. He watched as his shattered sword skidded across the marble and dashed to snatch up Emilio's. Incensed, Vindicati stepped back onto the altar and, glancing about him, noticed the great candle ensconced upon a tall base of gilded bronze. He kicked at it with his heel, sending the candle flying, and picked up the base, wielding the heavy weapon with both hands. His reach was greater than Pietro's, and his enemy was tired and wounded, but the candelabrum was cumbersome and difficult to manoeuvre. The two men circled the high altar. Each sized up the other, reluctant to strike the first blow. Pietro, his arm trembling, attempted a lunge, but the blade pierced the vacant air. Vindicati swept the great bronze candelabrum, attempting to keep Pietro at bay. So it continued, Pietro and his adversary flailing uselessly. Nearby, flames from the candle Vindicati had overturned began to lick at the purple drapes which framed the altar. There was a sudden flare as fire swept along the fabric, threatening to spread to the apse.

Vindicati reared up, his shoulder back, twisting on his hips, readying himself to strike the death blow and, for a split-second he was defenceless. He swung the bronze candelabrum in an arc. Pietro ducked, and as the candelabrum swung back, he lunged.

It was an extraordinary sight: the Chimera, *il Diavolo*, Emilio Vindicati, former head of the Council of Ten, had been impaled on his own sword. Run through beneath Masaccio's *Trinity*, into which the blade embedded itself.

The Black Orchid's hand still gripped the hilt of the sword embedded in the bowels of his foe. They stood unmoving, their faces only inches apart. Vindicati's breath smelled of copper, of blood. His face grew rigid, assuming the arrogant expression Pietro knew all too well, the glower of authority, of power, the gaze of the man who commanded the Tenebræ. Realising that Lucifer had been routed, his face contorted, paled, and his mouth fell open in a mute daze. There was madness in his eyes again as they rolled back in his head. Blood trickled from the corner of his mouth. He gasped. Still Pietro clung to the sword. Vindicati placed his hands on the shoulders of his old friend, as if seeking support. Perhaps he tried to say something, but no words came. At length, Pietro stepped back. Vindicati's arms fell heavily by his sides. At his feet the bronze candelabrum gleamed in the flickering flames.

For a few short seconds more, Emilio Vindicati clung to life. He hung like a puppet. Beneath the image of Christ crucified, the image he had chosen when he had staged the murder of Marcello Torretone at the Teatro San Luca, was another image, that of Lucifer trampled underfoot by the Trinity. For an instant, Pietro thought again of the illustration he had seen in Vicario's *libreria* at the outset of his investigation, the illustration depicting the gates of hell. It had been a strange image, drawing on medieval iconography and the Kabbalah. The immense gate rising like a stele or some towering, funeral cypress, and the Prince of Darkness, half-goat, half-human, his cloak parted to reveal the folds of his own flesh and the damned souls within: a mass of skulls, dead shadows and weeping faces. The painting upon which Emilio Vindicati was now impaled reminded him of that illustration; something about the manner in which Lucifer brooded over the abyss as the trinity, transfigured almost at the vanishing point, condemned the Prince of Lies for all eternity. Pietro remembered the inscription which he had read in the *Inferno*, the inscription above the gate: *Lasciate ogne speranza, voi ch'intrate*. Abandon every hope, who enter here.

Above the high altar the purple drapes had been consumed by the flames, leaving only a veil of smoke. The flames had not reached the apse; by some miracle the fires of hell had been extinguished, like the Devil himself. With a judder, Emilio Vindicati's lifeless body fell to the marble floor.

The Guide and I into that hidden road
Now entered, to return to the bright world;
And without care of having any rest
We mounted up, he first and I the second,
Till I beheld through a round aperture
Some of the beauteous things that Heaven doth bear
Thence we came forth to rebehold the stars.

With a groan, Pietro let the sword fall from his hand. This time it was truly over. *Il Diavolo* had returned to the inferno whence he had come.

EPILOGUE

CANTO XXVII

TOWARDS PARADISE

OCTOBER 1756

Pietro Viravolta and Anna Santamaria had spent the evening at the opera – a production of *Andromeda* with a libretto by Benedetto Ferrari: a new production of the opera with which the Teatro San Cassiano had been inaugurated in 1637.

The San Cassiano was comprised of five balconies and thirty-one boxes, and Pietro and Anna were seated in one of them, Anna marking time with her fan. Seeing her thus engrossed, eyes wide, before the spectacle, Pietro smiled. They were together at last, and on the threshold of a new life. Below them, Andromeda sang her siren song in a voice that was enchanting; clear, high and pure. The extravagant finale burst with a cascade of arpeggios, then stilled into silence before the roar of applause.

As they left the box Pietro encountered Ricardo Pavi in the company of a charming wench named Philomena, whose eyes would damn a Christian soul.

'*Amico!*' called Pietro, smiling, 'They tell me that you are head of the Council of Ten now …'

Ricardo smiled. 'A considerable responsibility, as I'm sure you know …'

'You can hardly do worse than your predecessor … if I may say so.'

'The time for such devilry is over. Venice is at peace now,

and so it will remain for many years, I hope. The Empress Maria Theresa has had wind of the deeds of her exiled duke and was driven quite mad with rage. But all is now as it was. You know how Venetians are, they have forgotten already … Where were you this evening? I don't believe I saw you during the performance …'

Pietro smiled. 'We were in the gods, of course, in the gods.'

Ricardo bowed and kissed Anna's hand, then excused himself, and he and Philomena went to talk with some aristocratic friends.

Anna looked at Pietro. 'Well, Messer? Shall we go?'

He kissed her. 'Yes. Let us go.'

A few moments later they stood outside and Anna took Pietro's arm before seeing him wince. 'I'm sorry. Is it still painful?'

Pietro simply smiled.

As they came down the theatre steps, they were jostled by the crowd. The man who had manhandled Pietro did not even acknowledge them.

'Messer! I'll thank you to apologise!'

At the sound of Pietro's voice, the man stopped suddenly, then slowly turned. He was dressed entirely in black with a dark tricorn and a scarf which masked his face. Only his eyes were visible. Then suddenly, the man strode over to Pietro and took him by the shoulder in a peremptory fashion and said, in a voice distorted by his scarf, 'Excuse him one moment, princess. You – come with me.'

Pietro astounded, began to protest. 'Hold up, I pray you, I have …'

'Come with me!'

Intrigued, Pietro glanced at Anna, then allowed himself to be led away. They walked some distance from the crowd to the corner of a dimly lit alley. The man turned toward Pietro and laughed. His eyes seemed strangely familiar. Then he whisked away his scarf.

'Giacomo!'

Casanova smiled, but the smile faded quickly. He looked thin and ill from his long incarceration. His brow was feverish.

'I thought you were still imprisoned in *i Piombi*! I asked the Council of Ten to recruit you to their cause, and even the doge spoke of re-examining your case—'

Casanova held up his hand. 'Peace, *amico*, I have not long to talk. I have escaped. I have a horse waiting and I soon intend to be far from here.'

'*Escaped*? But how ...'

'You remember Balbi? He had a cell next to mine. He tunnelled a hole in the ceiling between his cell and mine, and together we made off across the roofs.'

'But no one has ever escaped ...'

' ... from *i Piombi*? I know. I like to create fashion. So, tell me, Pietro, what news of you? I can see that things have worked out well.' Giacomo glanced over his shoulder at Anna. 'I take it Ottavio has left the scene? I have heard so little ...'

'It is a long story,' said Pietro. 'You know how Venice is. But, tell me, Giacomo, where are you headed?'

'I cannot tell you, do not ask me to. And now, I fear I must leave you. By God's grace our paths shall cross again, Pietro Viravolta. I shall not forget you!'

'Nor I you,' said Pietro.

The two men embraced and, with a smile, Casanova tipped his hat and was gone.

Pietro stood for a moment, still dazed. He looked back at Anna Santamaria waiting for him among the crowd. He glanced into the dark alley, hoping to catch sight of a receding figure, then returned to Anna's side.

Pietro, deep in thought, stood on the Piazza San Marco and stared out at the lagoon. Night had come and gone, and a new day had broken. Wisps of fog rose from the waters.

The gondolas, lined up along the quays, rocked gently to the sound of lapping water. Though his heart was not heavy, Pietro felt a sudden wave of nostalgia. Venice had endured so many trials, he thought. It was unquestionably the jewel of the Mediterranean, but it was a fragile jewel, constantly under threat from tides and storms, from earthquakes and invasions and yet, this scrap of earth, perched in the Adriatic, had sustained an empire which had endured for six centuries. It was a bridge between east and west, a lighthouse for the world. How long could it continue thus, a city of illusion, of masks and costumes and carnivals? Pietro loved Venice as he might love a woman, as he might his first lover.

'Pietro!'

He turned. Anna Santamaria was waiting. She waved to him and climbed into the carriage which was to take them far from the Most Serene Republic. The coachman looked at him too. And Landretto, the good and faithful Landretto, barely recovered from a night of revelry. Pietro walked towards them, staring down at the cobbles, counting each step across this piazza he had crossed so often. When he reached Landretto, he tapped the lad on the shoulder and the boy almost fell.

'Well then, my friend ... What of your Queen of Hearts?'

'Oh,' said Landretto. 'A veritable fury, upon my word, I am worn out. You know how it is: the secret life of Venice – at heart I am not unhappy to leave it behind.'

Pietro laughed as Landretto loaded his trunks onto the carriage roof.

'Perhaps you might tell me now where we are headed?' said Landretto.

Pietro opened his arms wide. 'Have you not guessed? To France, Landretto. We are expected at Versailles and, by the good graces of the doge, we shall want for nothing. You remembered my deck of cards?'

'I did. So, France?'

Pietro turned again and looked out over the *laguna*, contemplating the still faint reflections of sky on water. Slowly, he took the flower from his buttonhole and tossed it into the lagoon.

'The Black Orchid is no more,' he said to Landretto. 'But do not fear, other adventures await ...'

He smiled. 'After all, I am a legend now.' He set his tricorn on his head, looked out toward the Lido and bowed reverently, then climbed into the carriage.

Little is now heard of the astonishing events which shook the Most Serene Republic of Venice in the year of our Lord 1756. The extravagant carnival, among the most dazzling of the century, erased all memory of the conspiracy whose name history itself has forgotten. In truth, little remains now of those turbulent events. The file concerning the Black Orchid was sealed and filed upon a dusty shelf in the archives of the Quarantia Criminale. A file which, in time, was itself forgotten. But legends have no need of history to live on, so it matters little.

ACKNOWLEDGEMENTS

Thanks to my editor, Christophe Bataille, to Olivier Nora, to Jacqueliene Risset for her [French] translation of Dante's *Inferno*; to Philippe Braunstein and Robert Delort for *Venice, Historical Portrait Of A City* (Seuil) and Françoise Decroisette for *Venice in the time of Goldoni* (Hachette), not forgetting Casanova for his *Memoirs*, without which my Carnival would not have been possible; lastly, thanks to Philomène Piégay for her patience and support.